HOME GAME

HOME GAME

ENDRE FARKAS

EDITIONS

Cover design by Doowah Design.
Photo of Endre Farkas by dhfoto.

Acknowledgements
I'd like to thank Zsolt Cziganyik, Odette Dubé, János Kenyeres, Katalin Kürtösi, Ronald Lee, Judit Molnár, Eszter Patocs and Éva Zsizsmann for their help with my research, advice and proofreading eyes.

Excerpt from "Light My Fire" by The Doors used with permission from Alfred Publishing LLC.

This book was printed on Ancient Forest Friendly paper.
Printed and bound in Canada by Hignell Book Printing Inc.

We acknowledge the support of the Canada Council for the Arts and the Manitoba Arts Council for our publishing program.

Library and Archives Canada Cataloguing in Publication

Title: Home game / Endre Farkas.

Names: Farkas, Endre, 1948- author.

Identifiers: Canadiana (print) 2019017790X | Canadiana (ebook) 20190177918 | ISBN 9781773240527 (softcover) | ISBN 9781773240534 (HTML)

Classification: LCC PS8561.A72 H59 2019 | DDC C813/.54—dc23

Signature Editions
P.O. Box 206, RPO Corydon, Winnipeg, Manitoba, R3M 3S7
www.signature-editions.com

For Carolyn Marie Souaid,
partner in our adventures in the creative life

1

He was caressing the brownish stain fading into his palm when the officer prodded him. He stood.

"Tamás, come in," the chief said.

The officer prodded him again.

A man in a dark suit was seated at Chief Barna's large wooden desk. Three portraits hung on the wall behind him. Tommy recognized Lenin and Marx but not the third. He hadn't noticed the pictures the last time he was here. A thick black curtain covered the window.

"Where is Broshkoy?" Tommy asked, looking at a pair of glasses on the floor.

"Who?" the chief asked. He turned to see what Tommy was looking at.

"Frog."

"Why did you call him that other name?"

"Because that's his name. It means frog in his language."

"That's no concern of yours. I ask the questions," the man in the dark suit snapped.

Tommy faced him. He didn't look familiar. He wasn't the one who had been following him. Was he an AVO pig? That's what Dezsö-papa called the secret police, the ones, he said, who came in the middle of the night and took you away, never to return, the ones who had stopped the train and ordered them off. Was he one of those that Dezsö-papa had punched in the face?

"Where did you leave your dagger?" the man in the dark suit asked Tommy.

The question came from a million miles away in a language he didn't fully understand.

"I'm sorry." He appealed to Chief Barna for help. "I don't understand what a dagger is."

"It's a small sword."

"Oh. The blacksmiths made one for me and one for Gabi. We sometimes hid them in our pant legs because our parents didn't allow us to have dangerous toys."

"That's not what I asked!" The man slapped the desk.

Tommy was startled. He thought for a moment. "Oh, in the Nylon," he said.

"Don't joke with me," the man snarled.

"That's what we call the People's Diner," Chief Barna said quietly.

"What I want to know from you is, when you decided to betray the motherland, where did you hide the dagger?"

Tommy wasn't used to anybody being so aggressive towards him. What a strange question. He didn't understand. He turned to Chief Barna again.

"When you and your parents left, did you hide your sword?"

"Oh."

"Are you stupid?" the man shouted.

Tommy concentrated, trying hard to remember. "In the well," he said finally. "It's not fair that they got caught. I missed him."

"Who got caught?" the man asked.

Tommy sniffled.

"Don't disgrace your father." Chief Barna spoke firmly. "Be a man!"

He took a deep breath. "Gabi, Dezsö-papa and Emma-mama."

"I'm not interested in your family's traitorous behaviour then," the man in the dark suit said. "I'm interested in your criminal action tonight. I want to know how it started."

Tommy wasn't sure. It happened so fast. It happened a long time ago. Maybe it began when Szeles whacked the cone full of rock candy from his hand. Or maybe when Mrs. Gombás kicked him out of class. Or when they tried to escape. Or maybe it began with a beautiful goal.

2

Like a shooting star, the ball arced across the darkening October sky. Tommy's calf muscles tensed, coiled, sprang and released him. Defying gravity, he rose. Weightless, as if in slow motion, as if watching himself, as if he had all the time in the world, as if free, he rose.

He met it at its zenith, felt the thud of leather against his temple, flicked his head, changed the ball's direction and sent it on its new trajectory into the top left pigeonhole, past the outstretched fingers of the leaping goalie.

His descent was quick. He lay there on his back being mobbed, barely able to breathe as his teammates piled on.

The whistle blew. The Sir George Knights were the 1966 Canadian university soccer champions!

3

Tommy's father stood on the sidelines, beaming as his son and Speedy stepped forward to accept the trophy. They held it up for all to see. The thirty or so people huddled behind the home team bench cheered and clapped. In his father's eyes, Tamás "Puskás" Wolfstein, the captain of the Hungarian national team, was raising the World Cup to the deafening roar of 60,000 in the People's Stadium of Budapest.

"My son, the captain. My son, the champion. My son, my son," his father cried as he embraced him.

"Hey, Mr. Wolfstein. It's great, eh?"

"It is wonderful, Speedy. Congratulations. *Mazel tov*. Let me shake the hand of a champion!"

"Hey, I'm cold," Schmutz yelled as he ran by. "Let's get changed and party."

"Apu…" Tommy's voice trailed off. He could never call his father Dad. It didn't feel right. Same for his mother. She was Anyu. Even after all these years in Canada. "The team is going out to celebrate. We said we would, win or lose. I won't be too late. Okay?"

"Sure, but not too late. And no drinking."

"A beer or two won't hurt."

"Not too much. You are not legal age yet. Be careful. Your mother will be worried. Call her."

"Okay."

His father grabbed him again and kissed him on both cheeks. "*Mazel tov*."

Tommy watched his father cross the field, stop in the centre circle, turn and wave, then continue to his car. His father had a spring in his step. From across the field, under the street lamp, he waved again. Tommy waved back. Then out of nowhere an inexplicable sadness came over him. It felt like he was waving goodbye.

"Come on, Wolfie, hurry," Speedy yelled as he slapped him on the back. "¡Ándale! Ándale! The vino is waiting. It's not going to drink itself."

Shouting and laughing, the boys were throwing their dirty sweat-drenched uniforms at Ben, the team manager, who cursed, laughed and threw them back at the naked Knights.

Coach Hus came into the locker room and yelled at them, "Listen up!" The boys quieted down. "You did it! You were great. I'm proud of you guys. Enjoy." They cheered and snapped towels at each other as they danced toward the showers. Once dried and dressed, Wolfie, Speedy and Schmutz, The Three Mouseketeers, as the other players called them, led the boys out.

4

El Gitano was on the corner of Mont-Royal and St. Denis. It had a large flashing neon bullfighter sign that could be seen from blocks away. Speedy's father had called ahead to tell his brother, the owner, who in turn announced to the full house that they had won.

"Bravo! Bravo!" The whole restaurant, from busboys to customers, erupted in applause when they entered.

Crimson-draped tables filled the dimly lit first floor. Each had a single rose vase and a flickering candle in a wine bottle that gave the room an intimate, romantic feel. Posters of bullfighters and flamenco dancers on the stucco walls added to the ambiance.

Shaking hands with the patrons, the boys, led by Speedy, wound their way to the back and upstairs to the Salón de Felicidad. Wrought iron chandeliers hung from the dark exposed beams and heavy burgundy floor-length curtains covered the large windows. Two long tables in a V faced a small stage with two chairs and two guitars on it. Tonight, the Salón de Felicidad, usually a place for wedding receptions, baptismal and communion celebrations, was the banquet hall of the victorious Knights.

As usual, Tommy sat between Roberto and Olaf. They had met last year when they were the three rookies who made the team. Olaf, nicknamed Schmutz for being obsessively neat, was studying aeronautical engineering and wanted to be a pilot. Roberto, dubbed Speedy because of his speed and family name, Gonzales, was a pure science guy who loved math. Tommy, aka

Wolfie, was in Commerce, because his parents expected him to take over the business someday. Though they came from different countries and cultures and had different mother tongues, they bonded almost instantly over a shared passion for a game that most Canadians didn't know or care about.

Tommy stared at the steaming black pans heaped with what he thought was rice, though he wasn't sure because the mounds weren't white. They had a yellowish hue and were covered with beans, slices of peppers, tomatoes, onions and other vegetables he didn't recognize. "What's that?" Tommy asked.

"Paella," Speedy said. "*Muy bien, amigo.*"

Vegetables were not a big part of Tommy's meals because his father, who said that he had a bellyful of vegetables in his youth, didn't want to eat them.

"It's what I ate when we were poor and what they fed us in the camp. We're not poor or prisoners anymore. I want to eat meat," he declared every time his wife tried to serve him vegetables other than potatoes.

Tommy had never seen a dish like this. On top of the rice were half-opened shells with slimy white things in them. Since he had never eaten seafood, he wasn't sure if they were clams, oysters or mussels. The more familiar shrimps, with their glistening pink tails poking out of the rice, seemed to be burrowing their way into the rice to escape from being eaten.

Speedy was ladling heaps of paella onto Tommy's plate.

"Whoa, slow down, it's too much."

"Never too much," Speedy said and spooned him another helping.

"What's that?" Schmutz asked, pointing to the pitchers of a reddish drink filled with fruit chunks.

"Sangria. It's wine." Speedy filled his glass, stood up and shouted, "Quiet! Everybody pour a glass. Stand up and let's drink to the Sir Internationals! The best team in Canada!"

"To the Sir Internationals! To the best team in Canada!" they shouted.

Tommy didn't expect the drink to be spicy and warm. The only wine he knew the Manischewitz they drank on Passover, a sugary drink that tasted like grape juice. A tingling warmth spread through his mouth. He took another sip, closed his eyes and savoured the pleasant fruity taste.

"Like this, Wolfie," Speedy said when he saw Tommy, knife and fork in hand, staring at the shells. Speedy lifted the shell with his fingers and pierced the slimy meat with his fork. "Like this," he said, putting it in his mouth. He pulled the fork out slowly. "It's an aphrodisiac, a lover's treat."

Tommy didn't know what Speedy was talking about but followed suit. It tasted moist, slippery and a bit salty but there was something about it that he liked. He took a sip of the sangria, which changed the salty taste into a sweet fruity one.

Schmutz stood. "I'm gonna make a toast too," he shouted.

"Schmutz, Schmutz," the players shouted, banging their knives and forks in unison. Though he was over six feet tall and solid as a tank, his constant grin and hearty laugh made him seem like a little kid. But behind his childlike playfulness was the serious and focused centre-half anchor of the team. He was hard as a hammer on opposing forwards. Very few got past him and those who did paid for it later with a "Schmutz Special." The tackles weren't dirty, most of the time. He sometimes crossed the line between fair and foul but only by accident, he would plead to the referee. Off the field, he was a playful kitten.

"I wanna thank Coach Hustle for making us hustle! He's number one."

"Coach Hustle! Coach Hustle! Number One!" they chanted.

The boys called Coach Hus Coach Hustle because that's what he most often yelled at practices and games. He stood up to hoots and applause.

"Okay, okay! I already told you guys that I'm proud of you. Even though soccer players are the laziest athletes in the world who hate to practise and are prima donnas, today you hustled your butts off and it paid off. You played like a team. All for one and one for all. To the Knights! "And…," getting choked up, he paused and then added, "Thank you."

"To the Knights!" they toasted.

"Now let's hear from the other captain," the coach said, lifting his glass in Tommy's direction.

"Wolfie! Wolfie!" the players shouted.

Although Tommy was co-captain, he didn't like being the centre of attention. And though he was the team's leading scorer, and had scored tonight's winning goal, he was happy just being part of the team. The others joked that they voted him co-captain because he was as quiet as Speedy was loud. He stood up, almost spilling his wine.

"Klutz," Schmutz yelled. "Trade him."

Tommy grinned at his teammates. The Sir George Knights, who called themselves the Sir Internationals, were immigrants from all over the world whose parents had left their homelands for their own reasons. Olaf Knudsen, Roberto Gonzales, Archie Bellafonte, Stanislaus Wojick, Luigi Russo, Ivan Sokolov, Kostas Fotopolous, Agostino Valdez, Tito Popovic, Derek Sullivan, and he, Tamás Wolfstein. He recited these foreign names to himself with the same pride he used to roll call the Mighty Magyars. He almost couldn't believe that this goulash of guys had ended up—through accident, luck, skill and chemistry—Canadian university champions.

The only true Canadians, whose families had been here forever, having come at the turn of the century, were Eric and Peter, the subs, Ben, the team manager, and Coach Hus. But on this soccer team, *they* were the foreigners. Coach Hus knew his soccer more as a gym teacher, from the outside, unlike Tommy and the other Knights, who knew it from the inside. "We're from soccer-mad countries. We got it with our mothers' milk," Speedy once told Coach Hustle.

"I don't have much to add to what Speedy and Schmutz and Coach Hus said. But I can say that it's fun to be part of a team that needs translators at team meetings. I'm proud to be part of the Sir Internationals. To the Knights!"

"To the Knights!" they all toasted and clinked glasses.

"Musica! Musica!" Speedy shouted.

"Musica! Musica!" the boys echoed.

And as if their chants had conjuring powers, two musicians in tight black pants, collarless white shirts and black vests appeared, bowed and walked onto the small stage.

The lights dimmed. A tall girl about Tommy's age emerged from the shadows in a figure-hugging black satin dress that flared from the thighs down. She strode to the centre of the stage. Her black, black hair pulled back into a bun glistened under the lights. Statue-still, her presence and dark eyes silenced everyone. Her gaze and stillness seemed to last forever. Then, almost imperceptibly, she raised one arm above her head and joined the other to her hip.

The notes, her fingers and legs moved as one. Tommy followed the crossing of her legs, the uncurling of her fingers, the serpentine winding of her wrists and the slow graceful movement of her arm rising from her hip to form an arch above her head. A sharp, clear sound sprang from her palms as her heel struck the floor like a gunshot, joining the castanets and guitars. And again and again. The incredible precision of her movements mesmerized him. She wove back and forth across the room, picking up speed. The music and the dancer reached a climax with a firm stomp. She stared at the audience fiercely. Tommy was about to applaud but Speedy put a hand over his and shook his head.

The notes, the fingers, the feet began again, and again sped up to a louder stomp. And a third time even faster. Suddenly with a proud toss of her head, flash of her hands and stomp of her feet, she was statue still again. Tommy was breathless. "Bravo! Bravo!" Speedy shouted. Tommy stood and applauded. The rest of the team followed. She gave the audience a slight nod and walked back into the shadows.

"Wow! That was incredible! How did she do that?"

"Practice."

"Who is she?"

"Marianne Gonzales."

Surprised, Tommy looked at Speedy.

"My sister."

5

Tommy stood in front of the mirror struggling with his tie. He always had trouble getting the front end longer than the back one. He tugged at the knot and came up short. He untied it and tried again. It had to be perfect. Ever since he'd seen Marianne at El Gitano, he had been trying to work up the nerve to ask her on a date. Just before the Christmas vacation break, Tommy, Schmutz and Speedy had been hanging out in the Arts student lounge where, Speedy said, the *chicas hermosas* hung out. Speedy was constantly on the lookout for the *chicas* but Tommy had never seen him with one. Not that Speedy wasn't good-looking. He had a chiselled angular face, a solid build, square shoulders, strong arms and a bulky chest. And he was smart. Maybe it was his intensity and his loudness that put girls off.

He wanted to ask Speedy if Marianne would go on a date with him, but couldn't bring himself to do it. He didn't want to be told that she was seeing someone and then be teased about it by Speedy and Schmutz. So, when it came, he jumped at Speedy's invitation. This way he'd get to see her and maybe ask her and not have to go through Speedy and Schmutz's ribbing.

"My mother and sister said I wasn't being a good amigo and they wanted to know what kind of bums I was hanging out with. So, you guys are invited for Fiesta de los tres Reyes Mages."

"Speak English, you immigrant," Schmutz joked.

"It's the Eve of Epiphany supper."

"What's that?" Tommy asked.

"It's after New Year's. We celebrate the Fiesta of the three magi kings, Gaspar, Melchior and Balthazar."

"Hey, we're three, and we're kings of the soccer world, so it's a holiday to celebrate us. Eh?"

"*Sí*. King Schmutz, Wolfie and Speedy."

"It seems like you guys are always having a fiesta," Tommy said.

"*Sí*. Fiestas are great."

Trying to fend off the cold while he waited for the bus, Tommy tapped his feet together and held the scarf around his nose so his breath warmed his face. He hated winter, even after all these years in Canada. They had arrived in Montreal in December 1956, during one of the coldest winters on record. He had never seen such mountains of snow. The snowbanks were higher than the cars. And the people, all bundled up and waddling like penguins, often ended up on their asses. They had snow in Hungary but never this much, and it certainly wasn't this cold. He still hadn't gotten used to it. His ears, nose, fingertips and toes always felt frozen. For him, winter was a time for staying indoors.

At least he didn't have to worry about the chocolates melting. His mother had bought him a box of Pot of Gold to take. "You always take something sweet when you visit the first time," she lectured him as she wrapped it. "This way you wish them a sweet life and show them that you are civilized."

The bus inched along Jean Talon Street. He'd never been to Speedy's house or Speedy to his. Their friendship took place at Sir George and on the soccer pitch. He hadn't even known that Speedy had a sister until that night at El Gitano.

And, he had never been so far east in the city. St. Lawrence Boulevard, more commonly known as The Main, not only divided the city between the English and French but the French- and English-speaking speaking immigrants, and rarely did they cross it.

The bus window was covered in frost. He put his palm against it to melt a peephole. All he could see in the dark were Christmas lights. There seemed to be a lot more on this side of The Main. As he peered out, a snowball slammed against the window. He jerked back. He smiled. In elementary school, his Canadian friends loved to snowball buses and have snowball fights. He didn't, especially after he got hit in the head a few times. He preferred the warm indoors. He loved watching hockey but had no interest in playing it. Hockey and snowball fights required getting bundled up, going outside and freezing. It was not something immigrant kids did. At least not the Jewish ones he knew.

Tommy had never learned to skate. He had tried once. When he was eleven, he got a pair of hand-me-downs from their neighbour Mrs. Kolchyk, whose son Eddie was two years older than Tommy and had outgrown them. Although the Kolchyks were also immigrants, they came after the war and Eddie was born in Montreal. He was also a whizz on ice. Those things made him a Canadian, while Tommy, having arrived in 1956, loving soccer and being a klutz on skates, made him a greener.

Eddie took him to Outremont Park once to teach him to skate. Tommy didn't like wearing skates. They hurt his ankles and even the extra pair of socks didn't keep his toes from tingling a few minutes after he stepped onto the ice.

The rink was full of boys like Eddie with their duck-ass haircuts frozen stiff and their jackets open, flapping like wings. Their effortless gliding skates slicing the ice made them seem like they were flying, while Tommy, gripping the boards, carefully tip-toed behind in the sub-zero winter afternoon. Although he was coordinated and athletic, moving on thin blades on slippery ice did not come naturally to him.

Eddie got bored trying to help him and took off to play pickup with his friends. Tommy tried to glide but he kept slipping, so he settled for tiptoeing.

"Puck!" somebody yelled. He felt a hard thwack against his elbow and his arm went limp. A sharp pain, like when he hit his funny bone, shot through it. He let go of the boards and his feet went flying out from under him. He landed on his ass. He was surprised at how hard ice could be. The puck had cracked his elbow, ended his hockey career and reinforced his determination to avoid outside activities in winter.

"*Bienvenido*. Come on in," Speedy greeted him. Tommy stomped his boots before stepping inside. He handed Speedy the box of chocolates.

"For me? How sweet of you."

"You're too ugly. It's for your mother and Marianne."

"So, give it to them," Speedy said and shoved the box back at him. "Mama, Marianne," he shouted.

Mrs. Gonzales and Marianne emerged from the kitchen. Mrs. Gonzales was a tall woman with dark complexion. He could see where Marianne's looks came from.

"Welcome. Come in. Oh, *gracias*," Mrs. Gonzales said.

Marianne's hair was pulled back in a ponytail. She was wearing a ruffled black chiffon blouse with large red roses printed on it and an apron over her red skirt. The lady of roses, he thought to himself.

"*Sí.* Welcome and *gracias*," she said and gave him a two-cheeked kiss.

It surprised Tommy. "Thank you," he said after an awkward pause.

"You're welcome."

Tommy blushed. Marianne smiled and disappeared back into the kitchen. Mr. Gonzales led him into the living room. Schmutz was already there. "Hey, Wolfie." He raised a glass to him.

Mr. Gonzales brought him a glass. "Vino?" he asked as he poured.

"*Gracias*," Tommy said.

"*¡Salud!* Sit. So how have you been?" Mr. Gonzales asked.

The Gonzales house was similar to his parents' except it was a split-level. It had wall-to-wall carpeting in the living room and a heavy gilt-framed mirror hung on one wall, reflecting a couple of big paintings of a flamenco dancer and another of bull fighting.

The sofa crinkled under him. Like his parents, the Gonzaleses also wrapped their furniture in plastic. He relaxed a bit.

"Very good."

"What are you doing during the vacation?"

"Mainly staying inside. It's too cold to be outside."

"You're crazy," Schmutz said. "It's beautiful out. So much snow. I've been skiing in the Laurentians."

"You Danes are the crazy ones," Speedy said. "Give me the Costa del Sol and the *chicas* in bikinis."

"Me too," Tommy said.

"The sun, or the *chicas*?" Marianne asked as she offered around plates of appetizers.

Tommy was flustered by the question and the food on the plates. "Battered fried baby squid." She extended the plate in her right hand. "Garlic shrimp." She nodded at the other plate. "Which one?" she asked.

"The shrimp, please."

"No, I meant the sun or the *chicas*, or maybe both." She smiled and walked away before he could answer.

The main course was also exotic. And the table conversation was animated and punctuated with loud laughter. The Gonzaleses spoke as if they were in a constant passionate argument with each other. Schmutz got right into the spirit of it. Tommy stayed quiet, content to watch Marianne.

When the dishes were cleared away, Marianne brought out a large ring cake.

"Roscón de Reyes," Mrs. Gonzales said.

It was decorated with glazed fruit pieces like a crown studded with exotic green and red jewels.

"It's to symbolize the three kings who brought gifts for the baby Jesus," Marianne explained as she poured coffee and her mother cut the cake.

Tommy stuck his fork into the cake and hit something rubbery. It was a small figurine wrapped in plastic, about the size of the plastic toys that came in cereal boxes. The figure was wearing a blue robe and a turban. The Gonzaleses applauded and laughed. Tommy and Schmutz looked at them as if they were crazy.

"It's tradition to hide a little king in the cake. Whoever gets it is the king of the banquet," Mr. Gonzales said.

"And will have good luck for the year," Marianne added.

Tommy smiled at her. She nodded.

"So, King Wolfie, what is your command?" Schmutz asked.

"*Sí*. Speak and we will obey." Speedy said and slapped him on the back. Tommy almost went face first into his cake.

"Loco," Marianne said and slapped Speedy upside the head. "That's no way to treat the king."

Tommy frowned. "Hmm." He had to be careful. "I command the two other kings of soccer, Speedy and Schmutz, and the princess of flamenco to come to my *casa* for Passover." He hoped that by making it a funny invitation, he would cover up his nervousness and not feel let down when Marianne said no.

"What's Passover?" Speedy asked.

"What do you pass over?" Schmutz asked.

"It's a celebration of freedom. *Sí*, for me," Marianne said. "But if you guys are kings, then I'm a queen."

6

"**A**nswer the phone!" Tommy's mother yelled from the kitchen. He was the telephone guard. He had been ever since they got their first phone when he was nine because he understood enough English and spoke it well enough and almost without an accent. He was the first line of defence against the New World as well as the bridge to it, and when it was a French caller, he could recognize it and say *non, merci*, and hang up. Because he was an immigrant, he had been exempted from learning French in elementary school. And in high school, Monsieur Charles, his French teacher from France, repeated daily to his mainly immigrant-filled class "*Si vous n'êtes pas capable de parler comme il faut, gardez vos bouches fermées.*" So, he and the other immigrant kids kept their ears and mouths shut. The French he did know he learned on the street. It was nothing like Monsieur Charles's. In this class, he learned that whatever you said, you put *tabernak, hostie, ciboire*, or *calvert* after it. Some even used them at the start of sentences. He knew that they were curse words and that they had something to do with the church but because he wasn't Catholic, he didn't understand or feel their impact. English cursing was simpler, more universal and made more sense. It seemed to have only one curse word, which was used, in all sorts of ways. Fuck, fucker, fucking, fuck you, what the fuck, and the one that usually led to fights, motherfucker. Even the French kids used it along with their French curse words. The Hungarian curses he'd heard from his father, usually aimed in jest at his cronies, and from his aunt, aimed in all seriousness at merchants she felt were trying to cheat her, were a lot more varied and colourful. They usually involved animal genital parts and genealogy.

He picked up the phone in the TV room, where he was sprawled out on the couch.

"Hello?"

"Hi. Tommy? This is Marianne."

"Oh. Hi." He sat up.

"How are you?"

"Uh, good. And you?"

"How's your toy?"

"Huh?"

"Your king?"

"Oh, I have it on my trophy shelf."

"Place for royalty?"

"Yeah."

"Are you busy?"

"No. No. Just watching TV."

"What are you watching?"

"*Hogan's Heroes*. Do you ever watch it?"

"Sometimes."

Desperately, he tried to find something to talk about. "Umm, what do you like to watch?"

"*The Ed Sullivan Show*. Do you?"

"Uh, yeah, sometimes, when he has groups on."

"Which groups do you like?"

He twirled the cord around his finger. Somehow, he managed to wind it too tightly. The tip of his finger was turning purple.

"I like the Beatles. You?" he asked as he tucked the receiver between his ear and shoulder and tried to yank his finger out. It wouldn't budge.

"The Stones."

"Oh."

"Yeah. I like Jagger, the way he moves around. Like a proud Spanish rooster."

"That's funny," he said as he finally unwound the cord. He watched the purple colour change back to flesh on his fingertip.

"Hey, Tommy, I was wondering. My friend Naomi, she knows you, you're in her Poli-Sci class. Anyway, she's having a party next Saturday and asked me if I wanted to come. She said I could invite some of my friends."

"I don't know her."

"Yes, you do. She's got short red hair and is very opinionated. She smokes like a chimney."

"Oh, yeah, the girl who's always arguing with the teacher and the other students in class."

"That's Naomi."

"How do you know her?"

"She works part time at The Jewish, in the lab."

"Oh,"

"Do you want to come?"

"Sure." He tried to sound matter-of-fact but his heart was racing. He hoped she couldn't hear it.

"Are you still there?" she asked.

"Uh, yeah." He didn't know what else to say. "Is Speedy going too?" he finally managed to ask.

"No."

"Oh."

"It's Saturday night. Nine o'clock."

"What time should I pick you up?"

"You don't have to; I'll already be there helping Naomi."

"Okay." There was more silence. "What's the address?"

She laughed. "Oh, right. 1835 Lincoln."

He grabbed the pen next to the phone but couldn't find a piece of paper. He scribbled it on his palm. "Oh. That's right near the campus."

"Yeah. The cross street is St. Marc."

"Got it."

"Apartment 304."

"Okay."

"Well, see you there."

"Thanks for inviting me."

He was about to hang up when Marianne added, "By the way, can you do me a favour?"

"Sure. What?"

"Don't tell Roberto."

"Why not?"

"I'll tell you later."

"Okay."

"Well, see you."

"Bye."

Dumbfounded, Tommy stared at his palm. This had never happened to him, nor to anyone he knew. Girls like her didn't call guys and ask them out. The guys on the team joked that only ugly, desperate girls called guys for dates. And because they were so desperate, they would put out. Marianne certainly wasn't ugly. He was sure guys would be eager to go out with her. But was this a date? He wasn't picking her up. And she said she was inviting him as a friend. Maybe he was just one of many. But why didn't she want Speedy to know?

"I know nothing," Sergeant Schultz said. Tommy glanced at the screen.

"*Tabernak, hostie, ciboire, calvert*," Tommy said and smiled.

7

Tommy arrived early. He blamed his parents, who were fanatical about punctuality. They had drilled it into him so he couldn't be late even if he tried. To kill time, Tommy strolled along Sherbrooke Street. Though this was his usual route to school, he'd never really paid much attention to it. Only now did he notice how broad it was. The large elm, spruce and maple trees, the apartments that looked like castles, the greystone hotels with uniformed doormen and the expensive stores with brass-framed art deco windows and doors gave it an Old World look. The store window displays got his attention. They were completely different than the ones on The Main where his parents did most of their shopping. Those were packed with as much merchandise as could be stuffed in them. Here the windows were almost bare. One or two mannequins, one or two pieces of jewellery. And the art galleries! In his neighbourhood if you wanted a painting to complement your walls, couch or carpet, you went to a furniture store.

He stopped in front of a gallery that had three windows with a large painting in each. One looked like somebody had thrown paint at the canvas. Another consisted of a bunch of brightly coloured circles in the shape of a target. The third, the one that really caught his attention, was almost blank. It was a large grey canvas and halfway down, at a slight angle, a thin strip of masking tape ran across it. How was that art? he wondered. And who would buy such a thing? He'd never seen anything like this in the homes of his parents or his parents' friends. Their walls were decorated with paintings of ladies in turn-of-the-century dresses, nature scenes and still lifes. His parents' most precious painting was of an old Jewish man with his prayer shawl over his head, reading from an unscrolled Torah.

He checked his watch and headed back toward Lincoln. He felt uncomfortable going to a party where he didn't know anyone, not even the host. At least he knew Marianne, he reassured himself. He stood across the street from the building for a few minutes and watched the people entering. The guys all looked like hippies, with long hair, bell-bottomed jeans and army surplus jackets. Some of them had big bushy beards and almost all of them had moustaches. Most of the girls had long flowing hair and wore ponchos over colourful ankle-length skirts.

He removed his tie and stuffed it in his pocket, then took a deep breath and walked up the stairs. No one answered when he knocked, but the people coming up behind him just walked straight in. He followed hesitantly. Everyone was walking around in socks. In a room off the hall, people were throwing their coats and ponchos on a bed, a mattress on the floor. He put his inside-shoes into his mohair duffle coat pocket and laid it on a wooden milk crate that served as a night table.

The apartment was crowded but not loud. Most of the people were sitting on the floor smoking, drinking and quietly talking to each other as strange wailing music played in the background. Smoke snaked through the air. He searched for Marianne and spotted her next to the stereo, swaying. Her black braided hair, bound by a bandana, made her look like an Indian maiden. Her embroidered blouse reminded him of the traditional Hungarian ones he had seen in his mother's fashion magazines. Her floor-length flowered skirt spread around her like a garden. She seemed to have a thing for roses. Her eyes were closed. He watched her attentively from the doorway. She's so beautiful, he thought to himself.

He made his way over to her. Not wanting to interrupt her trance-like state, he stood still in front of her.

"Hi, Tommy," she said, eyes still closed.

"Oh, hi. Uh…How did you know it was me?"

"I sensed your presence." She smiled and opened her eyes. "I smelled Old Spice. You and Roberto, you jocks all use Old Spice. You're probably the only one here wearing it. My friends here," she sniffed the air, "sprinkle themselves with patchouli."

"Patchouli?"

"Yeah, take a whiff." She leaned over so he could sniff her neck.

He took a quick sniff and detected an earthy scent. "It's nice," he said. He felt nervous being so close to her.

"Do you want something to drink? We have wine or beer. Did you bring anything?"

"Was I supposed to? Sorry, I didn't know."

"Yeah, but don't worry about it, there's plenty to go around. Come, I'll introduce you to Naomi." She took his hand and led the way through the dimly lit room. Her hand held his firmly and felt wonderfully warm.

"Hey, Noni, this is Tommy."

Yes, she was definitely the girl with the strong opinions, whom the professor jokingly called Socialist Sally. Naomi was sitting cross-legged on the floor in front of a coffee table, swaying from side to side.

She looked up, took a long deep drag from her cigarette and passed it on. She held the smoke in, smiled and exhaled.

"Hi," Tommy said.

Naomi and Marianne both giggled. "Yeah," Naomi said. "Sit." She patted the floor next to her. Sitting on the floor in his tight pants was uncomfortable. He could feel his balls being squeezed. He tried to adjust them without touching himself. Marianne sat next to him. Someone passed her the cigarette. She took a deep haul and passed it to him.

"No thanks, I don't smoke."

"It's not a cigarette," Naomi said. "It's grass."

He froze, unsure what to do. It was illegal. He could end up in jail. He'd heard stories about people smoking marijuana and having bad reactions. Some, they said, went crazy and others even committed suicide.

"Just inhale and hold it as long as you can," Marianne said, blowing her smoke in his face. He felt a rush of panic. He didn't want to get arrested, go crazy, or commit suicide. His parents would kill him. But he didn't want to look like a chicken in front of Marianne. He took it and sniffed it. It had a smell he couldn't identify. He looked searchingly at Marianne.

"Hey man, don't Bogart that joint," Naomi said.

"Huh?"

"Toke," Marianne said.

"Huh?"

"Take a drag," Naomi said.

"Oh." He inhaled deeply. His lungs felt like they were being seared, like they were going to be ripped from whatever they were attached to. His head felt like it was going to explode. He began to cough. He couldn't stop.

"Here, man, have some wine." Someone across the table offered him his glass. "But just sip it."

"Thanks," he croaked. His cheeks flushed. He couldn't speak.

"Take a smaller toke," Marianne advised him when it came around the second time. He didn't want any more but wanted to make up for the klutzy beginning. It went down more smoothly, though he still couldn't help coughing. He teared up and closed his eyes. When he opened them, Marianne was gone. Was he already going crazy?

"Where is she?" he asked nervously.

"It's cool." Naomi placed her hand gently on his thigh. "She just went to get you a glass of wine."

"Oh," he said, feeling stupid but relieved.

"So how are you feeling?" Naomi asked.

"Aside from the barbecued lungs and a raw, hoarse throat, I don't feel any different. What am I supposed to feel?"

"Yourself," Marianne said, handing him the wine.

"Oh."

"I'm glad you came," she said.

"Me too." He glanced around the room. "Thanks for inviting me. But why didn't you...?" He turned towards her but again she was gone. He searched for her and found her next to the stereo, eyes closed again. She was moving to the music like the snakes that turbaned guys in India charmed with their flutes. Watching her drew him into the music. It wasn't as monotone as it first sounded. In its repetition, it was getting thicker. He wasn't sure what he meant by that, but he felt it. Some sort of drumming accompanied it. It wasn't the rock-n-roll pounding but more of a leathery sound and more complex.

Marianne wove about the room. Her dancing didn't have the harshness and defiance that it had at El Gitano. Here she was not challenging the world but embracing it. Her arms moved like the wings of a bird in graceful flight and her dress swirled as a cloud of flowers. Others joined her, but none were dancing with each other. Rather they swayed in their own world. It was as if the March breeze coming in through the open balcony door was moving them. And though each seemed to be off in their own world, the dancing resembled a gathering.

"Come. Join," Marianne called to him.

He smiled and shook his head. He wasn't a good dancer and he certainly couldn't move to this kind of music. He felt okay just listening and watching her. But Marianne was insistent, her fingers, opening and closing, reeled him in. They had power over him. As he rose, a light-headed dizziness hit him. He stopped, rebalanced himself and tried again, this time more slowly. He felt a rush of air and a sweet smell envelop him. He sniffed, trying to identify it.

"Incense, sandalwood," Marianne said.

"Sandalwood?" He had never heard of such a tree. "Is that what they make sandals out of?" They both giggled.

Marianne smiled. She was undulating. He found himself following her movements, awkwardly, stiffly.

"Relax. Let the music move you, not the other way around."
She ran her palms along his cheeks, down to his neck, along his
shoulders and arms until she reached his hands and caressed his
fingers. "Dance with your soul."

She stroked him again. He felt the stiffness flowing out of
him.

"Dance with your truth."

He didn't understand what she was talking about, but her
voice and strokes *were* drawing the stiffness out of him. He felt
like he did on the soccer pitch when he was playing well. He knew
where to be and when the ball would arrive at his feet or make
contact with his head.

"Dance with its essence."

He smiled and closed his eyes.

"That's it," she said. "You're a natural."

It was around midnight when he left. He didn't want to, but he
had told his parents that he wouldn't be late. The party was still
going strong and he wanted to spend more time with Marianne,
but he had to catch the last bus. He walked back up to Sherbrooke.
Gloveless, with his coat open, he stopped in front of the same
art gallery where he had killed time earlier. Killing time, what a
violent phrase, he thought to himself. How do you kill time, he
wondered. What kind of weapon do you use? Shoe shooters? he
said to himself as he caressed his inside-shoes sticking out of his
coat pockets. The paintings distracted him from his contemplation.
There was something different about them. The abstract one
was pulsating. The big target was spinning and the colours were
bleeding into each other. It made him dizzy. He turned to the grey
one, the almost blank one. It was alive and calming. The greyness
had become the morning mist and the tape was the horizon
inviting him to go beyond it.

He woke with a severe migraine. He hadn't had one in a while,
and figured it was probably from the marijuana. He wasn't sure,

though, because he'd been having migraines since he was eight, shortly after he was shot. But the doctors who examined him said there was no link between the headaches and the cause of the scar across his forehead.

It had been a strange evening and not only because of the marijuana. They had played strange music. Naomi had told him that the hypnotic music was by Ravi Shankar, a guy from India, and the instrument he played was a sitar. They also played Bob Dylan, whom he had heard before but didn't like. The first time he had heard "Everybody Must Get Stoned" on the hippie radio station that played album-length cuts, he found Dylan's voice unmusical. And he couldn't make sense of the words. But at the party, after he smoked, the song struck him as funny and meaningful. He didn't get it all, but it made him think. The marijuana seemed to have that effect on the people there. They listened. They spread themselves about the room, lay on the floor or just sat with their eyes closed. And even when they danced, they were listening. He too had closed his eyes when he danced. Marianne was right; it really did help to feel the music.

Late into the night, jazz replaced the weird rock and whiny music. He wasn't familiar with jazz either. All he knew about it was that it was played by black musicians. He'd never been at a party where jazz was played. Even at Archie's, the music was mainly happy dance music Archie called calypso. The jazz at Naomi's party was really sad or, as Marianne called it, cool and mellow.

And the people at the party talked. Not just idle chitchat about sports or movies but serious conversations, stuff that Naomi was always on about in class, about war and peace, Vietnam, the military–industrial complex, capitalism, Marxism, trips to India, going back to the land and hippie communes. They all knew so much. Even their humour was different, more word play than punch lines to dirty jokes. And no one got sick or fighting drunk. Best of all, Marianne seemed to like him, though she seemed to like everyone. And not only had she kissed him on both cheeks, she hugged him too.

8

Tommy's parents spent every week before the Seder night cleaning the house. No matter how tired she was after a day at their *shmata* factory, his mother went through each room with the same sharp eyes she used at work to look for a crooked seam or a loose thread. Especially the kitchen. She scrubbed the pots, pans and plates thoroughly, and polished the cutlery, even though they were already gleaming. She emptied cabinets, drawers and the fridge of anything leavened: bread, cake and cookies. She wiped the shelves spotless and swept every nook and cranny to make sure that no crumbs, small spills of flour or sugar remained. And knowing his mother's obsession with cleanliness, Tommy was sure that that was unlikely.

His father, with his hound dog Hoover vacuum cleaner, made sure that every last non-existent morsel hiding in the wall-to-wall carpets was tracked down and sucked up. Even on non-Passover days, his parents were obsessive about keeping the house clean, but before Passover they became fanatical. Tommy, of course, had his assignment. He had to gather the potato chip bags, chocolate bar wrappers and crumbs from his jacket pockets and gym bag that had accumulated in spite of his mother's constant dire warnings about cockroaches.

Tommy knew that this compulsion for cleanliness wasn't only a reaction against their Old World-dirt-floor-and-straw-mattress childhood. His parents had told him that before the war the phrase "Dirty Jew" was everywhere. They heard it from the townsfolk, on the radio, in the newspapers and politicians' speeches. And it came even more so from their time in concentration camps. Having been forced to live in conditions where typhus and diphtheria were rampant had made them obsessively vigilant.

They were constantly sweeping, washing and wiping. They, like all their survivor friends, were obsessively clean Jews.

Everything for the Seder meal, including his mother's matzo balls, which his father declared world famous and every year more perfectly round, more perfectly light, more perfectly golden, and the soup in which they floated more roof-of-the-mouth scalding than the previous year, was made from scratch.

"Her chicken paprika, gnocchi, and veal stew are fit for the Messiah when he comes. And what a *meshuganah* he would be if he doesn't. But if for some important reason he doesn't come, we'll do him a mitzvah and eat his portion too. And thank God himself for the extra helping," his father said every year.

His mother, always more serious, also replied in her own usual way as she brought out the piled-high dishes from the kitchen. "It's for all the meals we missed."

Tommy had waited until the last possible moment to tell his parents that he had invited Speedy, Schmutz and Marianne for the Seder so they couldn't say no. He knew there would be enough to eat. His mother always made enough to feed an army. There was always a week's worth of leftovers.

His mother stopped her cleaning. "Why did you want to invite them?" He sensed her tension.

"Because they're my friends. And they've never been over for one of your wonderful meals." He knew he was laying it on thick, but he also knew that the way to his mother's heart was through her cooking.

"Won't they be uncomfortable?"

What she really meant was that *she* would feel uncomfortable. "They've invited me to their houses, so I figured that I should invite them back. And besides, Apu, you're always saying that they're nice boys."

"So, why the sister?"

"She was there when I invited Speedy. I couldn't not invite her."

"So, how come you didn't tell us before?"

"I forgot. It was four months ago."

His mother gave him a skeptical look but said nothing.

His father, who was more sociable than his mother, said, "Of course it's okay."

Tommy hoped it would be okay. Just as he looked at his watch, the doorbell rang. Tommy stiffened. They're punctual, that's a good sign, he said to himself.

He wondered which Marianne would show up, the flamenco dancer or the marijuana hippie?

"Welcome. Welcome to my paradise," his father said as he greeted Schmutz and Speedy with handshakes and Marianne with a two-cheek kiss. Tommy wasn't sure if he should too but since Marianne leaned in, he did. He introduced the boys and Marianne to his mother, who immediately took charge and led them to the dining room where his aunt was already seated. In the Wolfstein world, you came, you sat, you oohed and ahhed the food, you ate, and only then did you chitchat.

Tommy tried not to stare at Marianne. His mother was not so subtly inspecting her: her soft wavy hair, perfectly parted just to the left, that fell just below her shoulders, her single strand of small pearls against her simple elegant black dress that came to the knee, her black shoes with a trim of white at the bottom whose heels almost brought her to Tommy's height. His mother was eyeing the accessories and the workmanship on the dress as much as she was examining Marianne. For her, one revealed the other. Tommy couldn't tell if his mother approved or was worried.

"Boys, you sit together there and you, dear, sit here." His mother led her to the chair next to hers.

"Thank you," Marianne said. She looked across the table at Tommy and smiled.

His father took out two yarmulkes from a drawer and handed them to Schmutz and Speedy. "Please put these on for the ceremony."

His father loved Passover not only because of the meal but because of the ritual, with him seated at the head of the table, the patriarch to whom all listened.

"Beanies," Schmutz said. "There's writing on them."

"It's from my Bar Mitzvah."

"Bar what?" Speedy asked.

"It's a ceremony to celebrate the time when a boy becomes a man," Marianne explained.

Everybody was surprised at her knowledge of the tradition.

"When did you become a man?" Speedy joked.

"At thirteen," Marianne said before Tommy could answer.

"When did you become Jewish?" his aunt asked.

Marianne smiled at his aunt.

"Please stand," Tommy's mother said. She lit the three candles in the silver candelabra, extended her hands over the flames and drew them inwards three times in a circular fashion. She placed her hands over her closed eyes and prayed. This conjuring act, her quiet recitation of the prayer and almost imperceptible swaying, brought a sacred quiet to the table.

"Please sit." His father smiled admiringly at his wife. "Isn't she a beautiful queen of our home?" "This is how we start the Passover." He was teary eyed. He cleared his throat. "Now we wash hands." He rose. "Only the boys come with me, please." He signalled Marianne to stay seated. Tommy felt awkward leading the boys to the toilet.

As they crowded into the small bathroom Schmutz tapped Speedy on the shoulder in an effeminate way. "I hardly know you," he said. Speedy punched him on the arm.

"Like this," his father said and filled a cup and poured twice on his right hand and twice on the left. "Make sure that the water washes the hands all the way to the wrist. Make sure you separate the fingers to let the water in between them. Fill your hands with water and God will fill them with His goodness." Though not very educated, Tommy's father knew the rituals and prayers by heart and could quote venerable rabbis.

"After washing the hands, lift them this high," he said, raising them to his chest. He recited a prayer, dried his hands and led them back to the table.

His aunt was telling Marianne what kind of food she served at her restaurant and complaining about waitresses. Tommy was glad that she wasn't telling her dirty jokes picked up from her customers.

"Now we bless the wine and drink it as we lean to the left."

"Why do you lean to the left?" Speedy asked.

"Tradition," Tommy and his father said simultaneously.

"Maybe it's where the heart is," Marianne said.

Tommy smiled at her.

"Now, do you see that plate?" His father pointed to the Seder plate. "That's a special plate. Each piece of food on it is special. I will tell you."

"We will die of hunger before he's finished," his aunt interrupted. She always said this at every Seder. And of course, as part of this ritual, his father got upset that his sister wouldn't let him savour the spotlight. Maybe it was natural for brothers and sisters to act this way. Being an only child, Tommy didn't know. He looked at Speedy and Marianne and wondered about their relationship.

His father's English explanation was clunky. He sounded like a child learning to speak. It embarrassed Tommy.

"The horseradish that clean your nose and make us cry remind us the time when we are slaves in Egypt. The apples, walnut and cinnamon mixed up in red wine remind us of the glue the slaves use to build their bosses' houses."

"It's not glue. It's mortar," Tommy corrected him.

"Yes, it is what my university son said," his father smiled proudly. "The putting a piece of boiled potato in salty water is for the crying of being slaves."

His father always linked the bondage in Egypt to their concentration camp experiences. Most of Tommy's father's and mother's families were murdered in the death camps. This was the moment of tears and bitterness that made the Passover real for his family. But when his father launched into one of his camp experiences his mother interrupted. "That story is for another time. The soup will get cold."

His father glared at his mother, who stared back, tightlipped.

"The lamb bone," he said pointing to a skinny piece of meat, "remind us of the sacrifice of the sheep in the synagogue."

"Is that a Jewish lamb bone?" Schmutz asked, puzzled.

"No." Tommy laughed. "That's a chicken neck. It's our family's tradition."

"Huh?"

"Now, for sure, we're never going to eat," Tommy's aunt remarked and lifted her head to the ceiling in exasperation.

"Margit," his father snapped.

"I'm just saying."

"Tradition," his father continued, "say lamb bones, but my family in Hungary was very poor. Sheep was only for the rich and a chicken neck was all we could afford, so it became our tradition."

Tommy loved watching and hearing his father exaggerate the sucking of the marrow from the neck. His loud long slurps, which irritated his mother, made Tommy laugh. Her reprimands made him suck louder. This had also become part of their Passover ritual. Tommy hoped tonight would be different. He hoped that his father would skip that part because he didn't want to be embarrassed in front of Marianne. His father's slurping would make them look like peasant immigrants. Yes, Speedy and his family were immigrants too, but they had seemed so worldly by comparison.

"Hurry up. This taking longer than Moses leading the Jews across the desert. *The Ten Commandos* is my favourite film," Margit explained to Marianne.

"We will talk later," his father snapped at Margit. "This is Seder night. The boiled egg, sitting there like a pasha, means life. And the breaking of the matzo, this big flat bread, remind us the Jewish people escape from Egypt."

Usually at this part his father went into his recollections of their perilous escape from Hungary. His father glanced at his mother, who was staring at her prayer book.

"Escape is the story of Passover. It is the story of going to freedom. It is why we are in Canada, very happy. It is why we do the celebration and tell the stories, so we don't forget. It is why the celebration takes a long time because we come a long way."

Maybe because of his friends and partly to frustrate his aunt, Tommy's father made a bigger show of the ritual than usual. His answers to the four questions were elaborate, the pinky-dipping in the wine ten times slower and grander. He sang the prayers instead of just reading them. Marianne, eyes closed, head moving just the slightest, seemed enchanted by the mournful notes.

"Now, we eat," his father said after the last prayer.

"Amen and Thank God," his aunt said and clapped her hands together.

Marianne offered to help bring out the food. Tommy's mother didn't like anyone in her kitchen. "Thank you, dear, but everything is ready," she said.

Marianne insisted on serving. "Sometimes I waitress at my uncle's restaurant."

"I do that at my aunt's," Tommy said, glad that they had something in common.

"Thank you, dear, you are very nice," his mother said as she reluctantly led Marianne into the kitchen. "Men are not for cooking. They're only good for eating," he heard his mother say.

Marianne laughed loudly. "Yes."

Though the meal was a success, the boys asked for seconds and Marianne complimented his mother's cooking and asked about the ingredients, Tommy was tense. He watched his mother watching Marianne.

Marianne had high-class table manners. She sat straight and brought the spoon to her mouth instead of her head to the bowl as his family did. She made no slurping sounds; she cut the veal into bite-size morsels and dabbed her mouth delicately. She even extended her pinky when she held her coffee cup.

At dessert, his mother began the interrogation. "So, you go to school?"

"No, I work at the Jewish General Hospital. That's where I learned a lot about Jewish traditions."

"So, you are a nurse?"

"No, I'm a lab technician. I take blood from people and check it in the laboratory."

Tommy could see that his mother was impressed.

"My sister is a dangerous person with a needle," Speedy joked.

"Do you have a boyfriend? A nice Spanish boy?" his mother continued.

"Anyu," Tommy interrupted, though he too was curious.

"No. I am not in a hurry."

"That's a good idea, you should not be serious yet. You are too young. How old are you?"

"I am older than these babies," Marianne said, glancing at Tommy.

"She's two years older than me," Speedy said.

"She's an old maid," Schmutz said, biting into his second helping of sponge cake.

"This wine tastes like grape juice," Speedy grimaced.

"Jewish sangria," Tommy said.

"No way, José."

"Okay, boys, clear the table," Marianne said when they were done.

"No, dear," Tommy's mother said. "That is for the women."

"No, Hannah," Marianne said firmly. Marianne calling his mother Hannah surprised Tommy more than her contradicting her. "If they can clear the plate of food, then they can clear the table of plates."

Tommy snuck a look at his mother. She was smiling at Marianne, but her eyes weren't.

"Did I mention that my sister is also bossy?"

The boys stood and took the plates and trays into the kitchen.

"Just leave them on the kitchen table. I know how to wash them best," his mother shouted after them.

While his mother washed and Marianne and his aunt dried, Tommy's father and the boys sat in the living room and talked soccer. Tommy strained to listen to what the women were talking about, but between the loud soccer talk and the running water, he couldn't hear anything. At one point there was a sudden burst of laughter. Marianne's was the loudest.

9

"Telephone!" his mother yelled.

Tommy crawled out of bed and went to the kitchen, where his mother was busy making stuffed cabbage.

"Hi, Speedy. What's up?"

"Are you free tomorrow afternoon? Coach Hustle called me and wants to meet with us."

"School's over. What does he want?" Tommy slid down to the floor and sat with his back against the wall.

"I don't know. Except he said it was important and wanted to talk to both of us."

"When?"

"One thirty in his office. Can you make it?"

"I start work tomorrow but I can probably get time off."

"Nice to have your parents as your boss. Eh?"

"Sure," he exaggerated. "I wonder what the big secret is?"

"I don't know."

Tommy turned to the wall and lowered his voice. "Is Marianne there?" He hadn't spoken with her since the Seder a week ago. He had wanted to ask her out but still couldn't bring himself to ask.

"No. She's out. What do you want with her?" Speedy suddenly sounded hard.

"I just want to ask her something."

"What?"

"Something."

"What? "

"None of your business," he said, trying to sound lighthearted while he tried to think of something quick.

"My sister is my business."

"Okay, don't get so uptight. It's not important. I just wanted to ask her something about flamenco dance. My mother was curious. I'll see you at Coach Hustle's office."

Tommy was surprised at Speedy's reaction. And though he'd forgotten to ask Marianne why she didn't want him to tell Speedy about the party, he suspected that it was because of the marijuana. But after hearing his reaction he wasn't sure about that. What he was pretty sure about was that it was good not to say anything to Speedy. He didn't want to cause any trouble for Marianne or piss Speedy off.

Tommy inhaled deeply. "Smells good," he said as he headed back to bed. This was his last lazy Sunday before he began a summer of factory work. He stared at the ceiling and wondered what the coach wanted but his attention drifted to trying to figure out a way to speak to Marianne. Maybe he could ask Naomi to get her to call him. But he didn't have Naomi's number or last name. Maybe he would drop by after the meeting.

Tommy had never been to Coach Hus's office, which was a small windowless room in the basement of the athletic complex. His real office was the dressing room and his classroom was the soccer pitch. When he had anything to say to the team, he said it there. "Sit down," he said, waving Tommy in. Speedy was already there.

Coach Hus's office was neat and bare. Only three pictures hung on the wall behind his desk: one of him in his graduation gown next to his parents, one with his wife and child, and this year's team picture. Tommy glanced at the coach's bookcase and was surprised to see, next to *Teaching Soccer Fundamentals, The Complete Book of Coaching Soccer* and *Sports Illustrated* magazines, books, including *Interpretation of Dreams, Man's Search for*

Meaning, Man and his Symbols, The Prince, Zen and the Art of Archery, All Quiet on the Western Front and *Catch-22*.

"How you guys doing?" the coach asked and leaned back in his chair. He drew on his pipe and let out a puff of smoke. Tommy had never seen him smoke. In fact, he discouraged the boys from smoking. He was always after Ivan, who was a heavy smoker, to quit.

"Good, good," they replied in unison.

"Any plans for the summer?"

"Work," Tommy answered.

"Any luck?"

"I'm gonna work at my uncle's restaurant," Speedy said.

"I'm working at my parents' factory."

"Are you guys planning to play this summer?"

"For sure. I got a call from Spania."

"Hungaria asked me."

"We'll beat the crap outta you guys," Speedy joked and punched Tommy in the arm.

"In your dreams."

Coach Hus emptied his pipe and put it in his tobacco pouch. "Yeah, the league is busy grabbing the boys from the team. I heard Kostas got a call from Hellanica and Lou is going to play for Italia. There's no Danish team, so Schmutz said he'll try out for the Rangers."

"Yeah, Coach, that's what happens when you're Canadian champions," Speedy said. "Now if they would only pay professional salaries."

Coach Hus grew serious. "I know they pay under the table, but don't you guys dare take a cent. If you get caught you won't be allowed to play college ball ever again. And you still have two years eligibility."

"It's not a lot, Coach."

"Don't you dare!" He slammed a palm on the desk.

"Okay, Coach," both replied at once. Tommy was taken aback by how serious he had become.

"You guys are the leaders and have a responsibility to the team. Understand?"

The boys nodded. He leaned back again. "I believe in the purity of the amateur, one who plays for the love of the game. But that's not what I called you boys in here for. I have another reason."

"What's up, Coach?" Tommy asked.

"Well, you know it's Expo this year, Canada's 100th birthday."

"For sure, party time, *chicas* from all over the world," Speedy said.

"I've got a passport," Tommy said. "I'm going to go to Expo as often as I can."

"Well, you're going to need another passport now."

"What do you mean, Coach?"

"As you know, special things are being planned for the year, including sports events. All sorts of teams are coming here, and all sorts of Canadian teams are going to different parts of the world in exchange programs. Our team just got an invitation to play two friendly games against the university champions of Hungary."

"Wow! Really? Are you kidding, Coach? When?"

"Late August, just before school starts. The date hasn't been set."

Speedy slapped him on the back. "Hey, Wolfie, you immigrant, you're gonna go home!"

"Hey, easy," Tommy said.

"Great, eh?"

"Amazing." Much of what he remembered of his few years in Hungary revolved around soccer: he and his father listening to Sunday games, cheering Puskás, the best player in the world; he and his father going to see his town's team play, practising with them, the coach and star player teaching him moves, sneaking out of Jewish school to play. And, his cousin Gabi. He and Gabi and Frog, his best friend, playing every chance they got. Tommy and Gabi had dreamed about playing for Hungary's national team. Gabi was going to be the best goalie in the world and Tommy was going to be the next Puskás.

"Amazing," he repeated under his breath.

"But before the university accepts, they want to be sure that the players are available. And before I start calling the others, I wanted to know about you guys. It would mean practice at least twice a week for the next couple of months."

"For sure, Coach. For sure." Speedy said.

"And you, Tommy?"

"I don't know if I can afford the trip, Coach. I can't ask my parents for the money."

"No problem. The Hungarian government offered a free trip through their airline and will provide accommodations and daily meals and the Alumni will give you a daily allowance for the two weeks."

"Unbelievable," Tommy said.

He left the meeting in a daze. He hadn't really thought about Hungary in years. His parents kept in touch with the relatives back in Békes, Szabad and Debrecen, but for him, these had become alien places with strange names. They were vague memories. The letters his parents got from his mother's sister, Aunt Magda, gave them news of his grandfather and the ones from Emma-mama informed them about the goings-on in his home town of Békes and of Gabi's progress in school. Occasionally, Gabi wrote a few lines and Tommy added a few lines to his parents' letters, but they meant less and less. Time, distance and his inability to read and write Hungarian broke his connection with Hungary and Gabi. The Hungarian he spoke at home he called Hunglish, a goulash of Hungarian and English. And though Tommy thought of Gabi occasionally, he was too busy becoming Canadian to really care. Though he loved to play soccer, his favourite sport to watch was hockey now. He was a fanatic Habs fan. They were fantastic. They won the Stanley Cup almost every year. He could recite every player's name and number. He didn't follow soccer and couldn't name a single current Hungarian national player. Puskás and Grosics were from another time, from a long, long, long time ago. And he, like the team, had left Hungary behind in '56.

The lobby door of Naomi's apartment was solid oak with brass doorknobs. The hall floor was marble. Once a classy place, it was now run-down. The door was dried out, the marble had cracks in it and the brass mailboxes were dangling from the wall. He rang the bell and waited. When no one answered, he felt both disappointed and relieved.

1 0

"Since when have you known him?"

Tommy didn't know how long he had been answering questions. His ankle hurt. He wanted to sit. He was thirsty and wanted to sleep. The man in the black suit was relentless.

"I asked you a question. Are you deaf as well as stupid?"

Tommy took a deep breath. "We were babies together. His mother..."Tommy searched for the words, "gave us milk together."

"Officer Szeles's mother worked for your family?"

"No. Frog's."

"I'm not asking you about that damned Gypsy."

"Oh."

"Well?" He spat the question at him.

Tommy took a deep breath. He wanted to wake up and leave but he wasn't dreaming. "I had heard of Imre Szeles before I met him. He was in grade two for the second time. He was in Gabi's class. Gabi and I were sitting at the dinner table telling our parents about our first day of school. I had had a great day. We started with the ABC, which I knew because Gabi had taught it to me the year before. I recited the alphabet without fault. Mrs. Gombás patted me on the head and praised me in front of the class.

"Gabi told me that his teacher had already whacked Szeles with the ruler. He got caught carving his desk with his knife. Gabi took great pleasure describing the whacking. Szeles had to go to the front of the class, hold out his hand with his fingertips pressed together like this. Gabi took my fingers and showed me what he meant. And then... Gabi raised his ruler in mid-air. It scared me.

Whack! Gabi shouted as he brought it down. I yanked my hand away. Gabi laughed and said if you move your hand you get it twice. 'Szeles,' he said, 'didn't even wince.'"

11

"**Y**ou're not going."

"What?"

"You're not going and that's final!"

"Why not?"

His mother's eyes blazed, her body tensed and the hand holding a kitchen knife trembled like a volcano about to erupt.

"Because I hate them!"

Tommy took a step back.

"Hannah!" his father cried out. She looked at him as if in a trance. "Hannah," he said softly. She sat and put the knife down.

His father, who had been making tea, brought her a cup. She held it between her hands. In silence they watched the steam rise.

"We'll talk about it later," he said.

In his room, pressing down on the scar, Tommy tried to push back the oncoming migraine.

His mother's powerful pills kicked in and he drifted off.

He was eight years old, standing in a clearing with his hands up. His father and mother were on either side of him. It was the middle of the night, but the full moon illuminated them and the soldier, a stout young man with a round face, who was aiming a rifle at them. "Hands up!" he kept repeating. Tommy's father was edging away from him. He didn't want his father to leave him. He wanted to reach out to hold his hand. His father was talking to the soldier and reaching into his pocket. He was offering him a bottle. The soldier stepped closer to take it but tripped and fell. There was a flash and Tommy felt a burning sear across his temple. Then, just before everything went black, he saw an animal leap.

His father's call for supper woke him. His headache had subsided, but he knew it was more masked than gone.

"I agree with your mother," his father said as he slurped his soup. "You know what they've done. You know what they're capable of. We escaped so that you could be free and never have to live among them."

He didn't need to be told why his parents hated them. He'd heard it often enough. The same stories were retold every Passover and every time they got together with their *lanzmen*. Each of their friends had their anti-Semitic neighbour stories, about those who had stood in their doorways watching them being rounded up and taken away. The ghetto stories of starvation, the labour camp stories of humiliation and beatings and the concentration camp stories of death. He himself had experienced the '56 mob-night stories.

"I'm not going to live among them. I'm going to play soccer against them."

"It's not safe yet. They could arrest you," his father said.

"They can't arrest me. I'm a Canadian citizen."

"Yes, they can. Those rotten lice can do anything they want! I don't trust them," his mother hissed.

Tommy tried a different tack. "We don't have to pay a cent. The plane and hotel are paid for."

"No!" his mother snapped.

"Apu, I'd be playing soccer in Hungary. Our final game will be on the Golden Green."

"What? The Golden Green?"

Tommy sensed a crack in his father's resistance. He could see that he was torn between not wanting him to go, being afraid for him, hating them and having him play in the People's Stadium in Budapest. "It would be sweet revenge."

"You're going to play on the same pitch as Puskás?"

Tommy nodded. His father got a faraway look in his eyes. Tommy knew he had him.

He turned to his mother. "I could visit Grandfather, Aunt Magda, Emma-mama, and Gabi," he said softly. His mother was on the verge of tears.

"No!" She slammed her fist on the kitchen table.

"I want to!" Tommy shouted back, surprising himself. He grabbed his jacket and left.

Park Ex, the neighbourhood north of Park Avenue, was a step up from the immigrant ghetto they had lived in when they first arrived in Montreal. There were no cockroaches in the duplexes of these tree-lined streets. At least not in theirs. And the Town of Mount Royal, the ultimate final step on the ladder for hardworking immigrants, was just a four-lane throughway and a chain-link fence away.

He stopped at Pete the Greek's corner store. Pete, a soccer fanatic, had known Tommy since his high school soccer days and always greeted him with a loud Greek hello. *"Tsikanis."*

"Kala." Tommy always answered using one of the few non-curse Greek words Kostas had taught him. Pete had cut out the *Gazette* picture of the team and had it pinned up behind the cash. Since their championship victory Pete gave him a free Pepsi every time he dropped by. Tommy felt awkward but secretly pleased at this star treatment.

"Efcharisto. Adio," Tommy said using up his two other non-curse words as he left and headed down Bloomfield Avenue. At Lester Park, he sat and watched young kids running up and down the mounds, between the trees playing Cowboys and Indians like he used to with his friends when he was in elementary school. He had started as an Indian but became a Cowboy when he found a broken cap gun in a garbage can. Though small, the park had enough green space for pickup soccer games. When they had first moved to Park Ex five years ago, his mother sent him out to meet other kids and he ended up here. A group of boys his age was playing and after watching for a bit he asked if he could play. They made him wait until one left. After he scored three goals, he was always the first one picked.

Tommy had never yelled at his parents. They had never had a fight. Not even when they didn't allow him to do something he really wanted to do. He couldn't imagine himself going against their wishes or answering back. A good Jewish boy didn't do that to his parents, his father told him, when they heard shouting and screaming coming from the neighbours' house. Because they always told him how much they sacrificed for him and what they had gone through, he could never bring himself to hurt them. They were Holocaust survivors. How could he do anything to hurt them? But now he had, and he couldn't take it back. And in a strange way, it made him feel good.

They were still in the kitchen when he returned. He sat down and his mother put a fresh bowl of chicken soup in front of him. "Mmmm, it's good and hot," he said slurping it down.

"Before we set off to the train station to be taken to Auschwitz, my mother, may she rest in peace, asked our neighbour if she would take care of our hope chest. Magda and I were reaching marriageable age and my mother had started to fill it with bolts of cloth and dresses as part of our trousseau. There was a beautiful polka-dotted dress that was to be mine. I loved polka dots." Tommy's mother teared up. "My mother told the neighbour that if we didn't come back, she could have it.

"When we got back, Magda and I went over to get it. The neighbour said the Russians had ransacked the house and taken everything from the chest. A few days later I was walking on the street and saw our neighbour's niece wearing my polka-dot dress. She smiled and said she was glad to see me back. I nodded and walked on. But I wanted to rip it off her! I wanted to gouge out her eyes! That's the kind of people they are. Liars and thieves. It's why I don't want you to go back there."

Tommy's stomach churned. He didn't know what to say. He took another spoonful of soup to give himself time to calm down. "I won't be alone. We're going as a team and the coach will be there."

"I don't like it," his mother muttered.

But he sensed that his mother was weakening. Maybe his father had worked on her. He had a way with her. Though she wore the pants in the family, his father knew how to charm her.

"How do you know you won't get arrested and conscripted into their lousy army?"

"Why would they arrest me? For scoring a goal? And if they conscript me, I'll end up being a colonel and playing for Hungary."

"Don't joke. This is not funny," his mother snapped and disappeared into her sewing room.

12

"Hi."

"She's not here," Naomi said when she opened the door.

"Huh? Oh, I didn't think she would be."

"You came to see me?"

"Sort of."

"Okay. Come in."

"I don't want to bother you."

"But you said you came to see me. Sort of."

He followed her into the living room. Naomi intimidated him. She was so sure of herself. She always spoke with conviction. And, she lived on her own. He didn't know a single guy his age who lived on his own, let alone a girl.

The living room looked bigger than he remembered. The mismatched old couch and armchair with tufts of stuffing sticking through worn armrests looked less exotic than they had the other night but they blended with the rest of the secondhand furniture and improvised décor. His parents would be shocked to see this. For them old and worn were reminders of their old-country poverty.

A bookshelf of plywood and bricks filled with dog-eared books ran along one wall. The top shelf was cluttered with wine bottles, candles stuck in them and melted wax down their sides. The record player, which looked to be the newest and most expensive thing in the place, sat on a beat-up old chest. A voice was singing about seeing clouds from both sides.

Instead of paintings in fancy frames, the walls were decorated with posters. The one on the bathroom door, a simple black-and-white of a skinny old bald man wrapped in a bed sheet with wire-rimmed glasses, caught his attention. Underneath him was written *Be the change you want to see in the world.*

"Gandhi."

"What?"

"Mahatma Gandhi."

"Oh."

"The guy who defeated the British Empire peacefully."

"Yeah, I remember reading about him in high-school history."

"Sit," she said. She disappeared and returned with a joint. She lit it. She took a deep drag before offering it to him.

"No thanks. I have practice."

"What's up?"

"Well, I hoped that Marianne would be here."

"But you said that you didn't think she would be here."

"Yeah. No. Well, I didn't, but I sort of hoped." His fingers began to drum on the armrest.

"I sort of figured." She smiled and toked.

"Yeah, well, when she asked me to come to your party last week, she asked me not to tell her brother Speedy, but she never told me why. After the party I figured it might be because of the marijuana and the kind of people who might be there."

"What do you mean, 'kind of people'?"

"You know, hippies."

"Oh. Those kind," she exhaled.

"Anyway, I wanted to find out why."

"Why don't you call and ask her?"

"I called," he lied, "but Speedy answered and he got suspicious when I asked to speak to her."

"What would he be suspicious about?" Naomi kept pushing him. Tommy wondered why. "Do you want to know if she likes you?"

"Uh, no, I mean, I wanted to know why she didn't want me to tell him, so I'll know."

"Oh. Do you like her?"

"She's nice."

Naomi made him nervous. Girls made him nervous. Though he' occasionally asked girls to go to sock hops in high school, he had never really had a girlfriend. He didn't know how to be comfortable around them. He was always second-guessing how he should act, so he was never really himself. He wished he could be at ease with girls like some of the guys on the team. They could joke with them like they were guys, although the jokes tended to be different. Some of them were even going steady and boasted that they had gotten to second base.

"That's not what I asked you."

"Would you ask her to call me? I mean, I know girls shouldn't call guys but…."

"Why not?"

"I, well, girls aren't supposed to."

"Why not?"

"Well, because guys are supposed to."

"That doesn't answer the why. Is it because nice girls don't?"

"Marianne's nice."

Naomi laughed. "She's coming for supper. Do you want to stay?"

"I can't. I have practice."

"Right. What time do you finish?"

"About eight."

"We're not eating till around then, so why don't you come over after practice? You'll be hungry and she'll be here. We're making spaghetti."

"Okay. Thanks."

"You want a toke?"

"I shouldn't."

13

"Hustle! Hustle, you prima donnas!"

Tommy didn't like warm-ups. He liked to start playing right away. But today, with the late afternoon sun shining on his face and the slight breeze cooling him, he didn't mind. It helped him think. He still hadn't convinced his mother and he hadn't told Coach Hus that he might not be going. He tried to think of arguments to sway his mother but he couldn't. After the laps, the team formed a circle at centre field for some stretching. He thought of going to Hungary without his parents' permission but the consequences would be huge. He couldn't imagine doing it. But he was thinking about it.

With every bend he was reaching down to the other side of the world. With every stretch upward he was a fingertip away from the lazy clouds. During the sprints he felt like he was floating. His body had a mind of its own. Or was it that his mind had a body of its own? It was hard to figure it out.

"Hustle! Hustle!"

The coach's words brought him back to the practice.

"Hustle! Hustle!" His words sounded profound.

"What are you smiling about?" Speedy asked as he bent over to catch his breath after the sprints.

"He's so right."

"Who? About what?"

The coach, about hustling," he said giggling.

"What's so funny?"

"Just the sound of Coach Hustle and hustling."

Speedy looked at him warily. "Yeah?"

"Yeah. You know those Hungarians are probably much better than us. They grew up living and breathing soccer. You remember you once said we were breast-fed on soccer? It's true, but they never let go of the teat. If we're ever going to have a chance to win a game, it will depend on us outhustling them."

He heard a voice inside his head repeat "hustle, hustle." He was riding alongside the Hussars. No, the Hajdus, he corrected himself. He loved his childhood tales of the Hajdus. They were like the Hussars and for their bravery against the Turks were given land which was named after them. Tommy's hometown of Békes was in the province of the Hajdus. The Hajdus weren't as well known as the Hussars, but for Tommy they were as great. Hussars, Hajdus, hustle, the voice kept repeating as he took shots on Derek.

The coach blew his whistle and called them in. "You need to hustle more. Understand? Without it you're just a bunch of immigrants playing pickup." The guys nodded. "Okay, now I've got news for you. The university has agreed to enter the team into the Major Soccer League and the League has agreed to let us in for this season so you can get top competition before we go to Hungary. Therefore, none of you can play for another team."

A few of the guys groaned. "I know some of you wanted to play for your communities, for the pride and some cash, which I forbade. Remember? For this season your community is the Internationals. Got it?"

"Yeah," they answered in their usual ragtag manner.

"I didn't hear you!"

Coach Hustle's intensity surprised him. He certainly yelled at them, mainly, "Hustle, you prima donnas," but not in the rah-rah sense. They had never been a rah-rah bunch like the football or hockey guys, who screamed, hollered and beat their chests before every game. They sounded like they were off to war. Soccer didn't invite the same ferocious approach. Not that they didn't play hard or that the games didn't sometimes get brutal, but soccer had a different ebb and flow that didn't bring out the tribal in them.

Maybe because they were such a diverse bunch from all over. They weren't a tribe. They were international.

"Yeah!" Tommy shouted in a way that surprised him. He started to laugh.

"What's so funny, Wolfie?" The coach stared at him.

Tommy wanted to say "everything," but didn't. "Nothing, Coach."

"Okay, now hustle in."

Usually, he was exhausted after a practice but tonight he felt refreshed. He was also ravenous and looking forward to supper with Marianne and Naomi.

"You were pretty slow out there," Coach Hustle said to him after the others went in. "Are you okay? Are you coming down with something?"

"I was? No, I'm okay. Sorry, Coach."

14

Tommy sat back and patted his stomach. "That was delicious!"

"*Sí*," Marianne said and raised her glass of wine.

"Your spaghetti is different from restaurant spaghetti. I always thought it was supposed to be soft."

"They boil the shit out it and make it limp. I like to make mine al dente and make my own pesto, with lots of garlic."

He didn't want to appear stupid, so he didn't ask Naomi what part of the spaghetti was al dente and what part was pesto. "I've never had green spaghetti. It's really tasty."

"I guessed that after the third helping," Naomi said.

"How was practice?"

"Pretty good. Tough. He drove us hard, but the strange thing was that by the end, I didn't feel as exhausted as I usually do. Coach Hustle thought I was slow, slacking off. He told me that I didn't hustle like I usually did. But I thought I was busting my ass."

"Ah, the strange effects of grass."

"What do you mean?"

"Well, your sense of time and exertion gets altered. You think you're doing something one way but it's really another."

"I didn't think I was."

"You were too stoned to notice."

"You think?"

"Want to see?"

"How?"

"Let's smoke again."

"Can't you get addicted if you smoke too much?"

"Grass is not addictive."

"How do you know?"

"I've been smoking for a year or so and I'm not addicted."

"Are you joking?"

"I like it, but I don't go looking for it. My body doesn't go crazy wanting it."

"But you always seem to have it."

"Yes, but I don't need it all the time. And I don't have withdrawal if I don't have it."

"I want some now," Marianne said and started scratching her arm like a heroin addict. She plopped down cross-legged on the floor in front of the coffee table. In the candlelight, her hair had a halo about it. She fished out a baggie from her army surplus bag that she had recently sewn a peace sign on.

Marianne fished out a green clump and rolled it gently between her thumb and forefinger. She did it the way Tommy's mother examined a piece of cloth for quality. The crushed leaves and seeds dropped onto the album jacket. She pulled two cigarette papers from her pack of Zig Zags and smoothed their creases. Slowly, she slid one along her tongue in a way he found erotic. But then, he found everything about her erotic. He watched her sprinkle the grass onto the paper and roll it into a joint that was thin at the ends and fat in the middle. It resembled a bean. She twirled one end into a tip, turned the tip toward her mouth and almost swallowed the whole joint, before drawing it out. It glistened. Tommy was hypnotized. He was horny.

She passed it over to Naomi, who was sitting on the floor across from her. Naomi leaned in to the candle flame and drew it in. She took a deep drag and held it.

"Come and join us," Marianne waved. Naomi exhaled slowly and passed the joint to Marianne. She closed her eyes. What was she seeing that gave her that angelic smile? he wondered. He wanted to reach over and stroke her hair. She opened her eyes, exhaled and passed it to him. It felt like they were touching for the first time again. He took a deep drag. Instantly he began to cough. His throat and lungs felt seared. He couldn't stop coughing. He tried to talk but couldn't.

"Oh shit. I should have reminded you to take a smaller toke," Marianne said.

He tried to say something but all he could do was hack and try to pass the joint to Naomi. It exploded. Surprised, Tommy dropped the joint into his lap. Naomi grabbed for it, missed it and got his crotch instead. He jumped as if he had been kicked. Cross-legged, he levitated and brushed the joint and Naomi's hand away. The joint flew across the table and landed near Marianne. Marianne and Naomi burst into hysterical laughter. Naomi was on the floor on her back, her feet kicking the air. Marianne was doubled over, convulsing. He was coughing to death.

"What the fuck was that?" he croaked between fits.

"A seed popped," Naomi said as she tried to contain her laughter. She rolled over and, on all fours, crawled toward the kitchen. She came back, still shaking, trying not to spill the glass of water she was holding out to him.

"Sip slowly," she said between snorts.

"Now, you might get high sooner than you think," Marianne said trying not to laugh.

"Coughing creates a head rush."

"So does crotch burn," Naomi said and both she and Marianne erupted into laughter again. He was not only coughing but tearing.

"Breathe slowly," Naomi said after she got hold of herself and relit the joint. She passed it to Marianne, who inhaled, held it for a few seconds, then leaned over and put her lips next to his.

Tommy froze as he felt Marianne's lips. "Open your mouth," Naomi said.

He felt Marianne's lips open and exhale the smoke into his mouth. A warm fluffy cloud entered and filled him.

"Close your eyes and hold it," Marianne said softly. A calmness nested in him, a pleasant lightness. He was floating.

"Now pass it to Noni," she said. He opened his eyes. Naomi was leaning towards him. Her delicate oval face, piercing green eyes and small open mouth were waiting. He pulled his head back for an instant. "Do it," Marianne encouraged him. He moved his head toward her, put his lips next to hers, opened them and breathed into her mouth. He turned toward Marianne, who was smiling at him.

"Like that," she said.

Naomi sighed and exhaled.

"And now," Naomi said, reaching for the LP on the coffee table, "listen to this. I got it today at Phantasmagoria."

"What is it?"

"Just listen."

A drum exploded. He almost jumped. It was followed quickly by a weird piano sound that made him think of a merry-go-round. And then, the voice.

You know that it would be untrue
You know that I would be a liar
If I was to say to you
Girl, we couldn't get much higher
Come on baby light my fire
Come on baby light my fire
Try to set the night on fire

Tommy was swept away by the pulsing of the drums, the swirl of the piano that wasn't a piano and that husky voice that wasn't a voice. A hypnotic haunting, erotic sensation flowed from the singer to and through him. Song, singer and Tommy were one. He was on a journey with the voice. Marianne's lips were on his. He opened his eyes. They weren't there. She was off in her own space. So was Naomi. He watched them sway to the song. The flame joined them. And the song went on forever. The hard drive of the drums, the curlicues of the weird piano. They headed off in two different directions but were somehow in harmony. Tommy felt the same way. The music went on and on and on. Finally, it slowed down to let the singer back onto the ride. They set the night on fire.

"Wow!" Marianne said when it was over. "Who was that?"

"The Doors."

"Who's the guy?"

"Jim Morrison."

"Wow!"

"Yeah!"

"What kind of piano was that?" Tommy asked.

"Harpsichord," Naomi said reading the album jacket.

"It felt like it was an hour long."

"Seven minutes. See?" Naomi said.

"What?" said Tommy.

"Time's not fixed, it floats, it runs, it stretches for miles and miles and miles when you're having fun."

They stared at him as if waiting for an answer.

"Yes?" he said making his answer a question. They all burst out laughing.

They listened to the whole album again. It was close to midnight when he left.

"Are you staying?" Tommy asked.

"Yeah. I told my parents that I would. It's Friday night, so I don't have to work tomorrow."

At the bus stop, he stood humming, thinking that something was different, something was happening, but he didn't know what it was. He saw his reflection in the art gallery window. For a moment he didn't recognize himself. It was a really stoned Tommy Wolfstein, who kissed two girls, sort of, and...the paintings were gone.

"Shit." He remembered that he had forgotten to ask Marianne his question and had forgotten to ask her to call him. He had been too caught up in the smoke, songs and lips. "Cool," he said out loud and smiled.

15

"Hey, Wolfie. Have you seen Marianne lately?" Speedy asked after practice.

"Huh?"

"Have you seen Marianne lately?"

He was glad that he was bent over unlacing his cleats. "No. Why would I? Why? What's up?"

"She keeps going out at night, coming home late and staying at Naomi's a lot."

"So?"

"Wasn't she in one of your classes?"

"Yeah, but I don't hang out with her," he said and walked off to the shower.

Speedy joined him. "My parents are worried. They've never met this Naomi. They don't know what kind of person she is."

"Why don't you ask Marianne?"

"I did and she just says that it's none of my business and that they're friends and like to hang out together."

"So what's the problem?"

"She wasn't like that until she met Naomi."

"Like what?"

"Like going out so much. She's acting different, dressing different and talking about things like women's lib."

"Maybe Naomi's a lesbian," Tommy said as they left the shower. It had once crossed his mind but after his last visit he didn't think so.

"Fuck off. Is Naomi a lezzie?"

"How would I know?"

"They think that she's seeing someone." Speedy's chiselled face with protruding chin reminded him of Dick Tracy. He smiled.

"What the fuck you smiling at?" Speedy asked.

"Nothing. Can't a guy smile? You sound like her father instead of her brother. And isn't Marianne old enough to date who she likes? She works, so can't she do what she wants?"

"It's what a brother does," he said. "Until she gets married she should sleep at home. And until she gets married, parents have a right to know what she's up to."

Tommy didn't want to rile Speedy. He had the typical hot Latin temper. Tommy had seen it on the field whenever someone pissed him off. He was the most carded guy on the team.

"Does she have a boyfriend?" Tommy asked as he began to dress.

"She's not supposed to. So, if you hear anything, let me know."

"Sure, but how would I know anything about her life?"

Speedy clapped his hands together. "Okay, enough of this, let's go to El Gitano for some vino."

"*Sí*," Tommy said a little too quickly.

"We play our first game next week, against Hungaria. What do you think, Wolfie? You think we can beat those guys?" Schmutz asked as Tommy got in the car.

"I don't know. They're tough and they can be rough. Those guys are older and more experienced."

"So, if they're older, we should be able to outhustle them."

"I've seen them play and they're good."

"So what? We're Canadian university champions!" Schmutz slapped the wheel.

"Yeah. We are," said Speedy.

"Yeah." Schmutz echoed and cranked up the radio. "All You Need Is Love" came blasting out at them.

"She only dances on weekends. But not every weekend," Speedy told him when he asked whether there was going to be music and dancing.

They went to the back. The waiter brought their wine in water glasses and put Cokes and Pepsis on the table in case the cops decided to pay a visit. Speedy's uncle didn't want to get caught serving minors.

"*Gracias*, Hayzeus." Speedy slipped him fifty cents.

"Did you just called him Zeus?" Tommy asked.

"No, I called him Hayzeus. It's how you say Jesus in Spanish."

"That's funny."

"Why?"

"Jesus bringing us wine? Don't you get it?"

"It's a common Spanish name."

"Is Jesus a Gypsy?" Schmutz asked.

"No. He's Spanish."

"Aren't you guys Gypsies?" Tommy asked. "I thought I heard Marianne say it to my mother at Passover."

"Yeah."

"I had a friend in Hungary who was a Gypsy. His name was Frog."

"Really?"

"It wasn't his real name, but everybody called him Frog, even his mother."

"Why?"

"I dunno. Maybe because he always had a frog in his pocket."

"That's weird."

"I remember once we were playing pickup soccer against these bullies and the leader got the ball kicked into his nuts and as he lay on the ground holding his crotch, Frog bent over him to see how he was doing and a frog jumped out of his shirt pocket and landed on his face. The bully started slapping his own face to get the frog off of him. It was a riot."

"How come your family left, anyway?"

Tommy took a drink. "It's a long story. The short version is that there was a revolution and in my town, they beat up the Jews and burned down their houses."

"Why did they beat up Jews?"

"Because we killed Christ."

"Huh?"

"That's what Carrot told me."

"You had a talking carrot?" Schmutz joked.

"It was another friend's nickname."

"Your friends sure had weird nicknames."

"Yeah, *Schmutz*." Speedy punched Schmutz and laughed.

"Maybe, when we go back, if I meet him, I'll tell him that Jesus is alive and well and working at El Gitano as a waiter. So they can stop blaming us."

"That'd be really funny," Schmutz said.

"Were your parents in the war?" Speedy asked.

His parents discouraged him from talking about it to outsiders, the goyim. He took another drink.

"Yeah, they were in concentration camps."

"Holy shit! No kidding."

"How did they survive it?"

"That's another long story, maybe a whole novel, but my mother and her sister escaped. And my father was in a camp that the Germans ran away from when they heard that the Americans were coming."

"Shit," Speedy said.

"Hey, did you know that the Danish king wore the Star of David?"

"What's that?" Speedy asked.

"The Star of David is the Jewish cross, except that they were forced to wear it."

"When the Germans invaded Denmark, they made the Jews wear a yellow Star of David. But the king said that Danes were Danes and if one had to wear the star, they all had to. So, he wore one too."

"Wow. That's brave. The Hungarians sure didn't. I'll have to tell my mother that. She's always telling me that you can't trust anybody who isn't a Jew."

"Hey, Speedy, what do you know about your people, Gypsies?"

"Not much, except we're great musicians and the greatest soccer players."

"In your dreams. But you have great dancers," Tommy said.

"And the word *gyp* comes from Gypsy." Schmutz laughed.

Speedy threw him a sharp look and stuck out his Dick Tracy chin. "Fuck off."

16

Tommy extended his hand. Horvath, the Hungaria captain, trapped the tips of his fingers and squeezed.

"Ahhh!" Tommy squealed.

"Welcome to the men's league." Horvath smiled. So did the referee.

He stared at Horvath, shook his fingers and smiled. Speedy was ready and stuck his hand hard into Horvath's. "*Si. Gracias*," he said.

As they lined up for the kickoff, Tommy glanced into the stands. On one side were about 200 Hungaria fans hooting and hollering instructions in Hungarian as to what to do to the college boys, some of them gross but funny. On the other side were the boys' fathers and a few girlfriends, a Babel of tongues shouting their support. He spotted Marianne sitting next to Speedy's father.

"What's your sister doing here?" Tommy asked, smiling.

"She said that she wanted to support her little brother," Speedy said and waved to her.

Hungaria's style was slow and fast. They played a controlled game, passing the ball back to their halfbacks and fullbacks that drew the Internationals upfield, then quickly sending long lead passes to their wingers, who had speed and good control. The Internationals were not used to this kind of play or pace and kept getting trapped. Only Derek's heroic goaltending kept the game scoreless. But his heroics could only last so long. Twenty-three minutes in, Hungaria struck with a centring pass from the left wing that was headed into the top right corner.

By halftime it was 3-0, and the boys were breathless and confused.

"What are you guys doing out there?" Coach Hustle yelled. "You're not playing soccer, you're playing chase. You're like chickens with their heads cut off. What happened to teamwork? Where is your attack formation? Talk to each other. You need to play smart. You guys are supposed to be smart, people who know how to think. Derek can't do all the work. Schmutz and Kostas, you're giving their insides too much freedom. Wolfie, you're not getting free."

Gasping for breath, Tommy nodded. He looked over to Hungaria's bench. They were laughing and drinking beer. Some were even smoking.

"Okay, you prima donnas, I want you to start by playing their game, let the halfs and fullbacks start the plays but instead of long wing passes, take it down the wing in triangles and have the other winger fill the middle. Speedy, keep cutting in to centre and, Tommy, take his inside position."

Hungaria felt that they had the game won. They were content to let the Internationals come up the sides until midfield and then shut them down. Hungaria tried some long passes but didn't really press. The boys had tightened up against the wingers and didn't fall for their footwork. They kept their eyes on the ball. The triangles were working, they were penetrating deeper and deeper into Hungaria's zone. Archie made a cross pass to Tommy on the left where he was all alone. By the time Horvath got to him, Tommy was on their eighteen-yard line. Horvath tried to tackle him, but he switched the ball to his left foot. His father was always telling him that God gave him two feet for a reason, so use both. He lobbed a lead pass to Speedy who had a free path to the net. Speedy made no mistake and tucked it neatly into the left corner.

"Lucky once, kid. Your ankles next time," Horvath said as he passed him back to the centre kickoff circle.

"Goal! Goal! Goal!" he heard his father yell. The other fathers took up the chant and started to clap in unison. Fist in air, Marianne stood, yelling "¡Arriba, arriba!"

Hungaria's fans yelled back. "*Hajrá Magyarok! Hajrá Magyarok! Hajrá Magyarok! Öld meg öket!*"

Hungaria picked up their game. It was as if the goal was an insult that had to be avenged. They stepped on toes, elbowed and pulled jerseys. But the boys gained confidence from the goal. They realized that Hungaria really had only one system and the boys adjusted, anticipated well and cut them off.

Schmutz and Kostas took control of midfield and were spreading the ball to both wings with accuracy. Tommy drifted back into centre and Speedy to his inside forward position. Then Tommy pulled the same kind of switch with Luigi as with Speedy, and when Hungaria's half went after Tommy, anticipating the same play, Schmutz slapped a pass to Archie, who took off with it up the middle. He had space and by the time Hungaria's half closed in on him, just before he was hard tackled, he got off a sharp high pass to Tommy who timed his jump perfectly and headed it just as he felt a sharp jab in his ribs. He landed with a hard thud on his back. The wind rushed out of him. He lay motionless, clenching his teeth, staring up at the evening sky wondering if the stars were real. Worried faces stared down at him. "Are you okay?" Coach Hus asked. Desperately trying to breathe, he tried to answer but couldn't. It seemed to take forever for his breath to come back and when it did, so did the pain in his ribs.

"You should give that goalie a red card," he heard Speedy shout.

"Who is the referee here?"

"Not you, that's for sure."

"You want a card? Here's a card." He waved a yellow one in Speedy's face.

"Shut up." Schmutz grabbed Speedy and pulled him away.

The pain subsided. Slowly Tommy sat up.

"Get him off the field!" the referee ordered.

He was doubled over on the bench. "What happened?"

"The fucking goalie got you with his knee when he came out to try to stop you," Ben said as he applied an ice pack to his side. "But it's a goal, man."

Pain shot through him every time he tried to take a deep breath. He couldn't sit up properly. He tried to turn around to look for Marianne, but the pain was excruciating.

The whistle blew and his father rushed over to him. "Are you okay? Do you want to go to the hospital for an X-ray?"

"No, it doesn't feel cracked."

"That was a dirty play. That horse prick of a goalie should have been kicked out."

He was surprised by his father's anger and language. He rarely heard him swear. Tommy laughed.

"Ahhh," he winced and pressed his side.

The game ended with handshakes and dirty looks. Tommy searched the stands for Marianne but she was gone.

17

"Those dirty rotten lice!" Tommy's mother hissed as she fussed over him. "Are you all right? Have some soup. We should go to the hospital."

"I just got winded. I'm okay. We could have won."

"I told you they're anti-Semites."

"No, they're just dirty players."

"It was your first game at that level," his father consoled him. "They play a rougher game than what you're used to. You guys are younger. You're good, you'll do good."

"Those dirty rotten lice," his mother muttered over and over again as she placed a bowl of chicken soup in front of him. In his mother's world *dirty rotten lice* was the worst thing you could be called. It was the most feared and hated insect in the concentration camps. She lost many friends to typhus even though every evening they would finger comb each other's hair, hunting for lice. She often recalled, when lecturing Tommy on cleanliness, the burning fever, the blinding headache and the dark rash that her friends experienced before dying an excruciating death. Even now, after all these years, he has seen her stop whatever she was doing and pick at her hair and then carefully examine the flakes on her fingertips. He knew that her curse carried painful memories that the nightly long showers and her many soaps and shampoos could never cleanse.

The phone rang. Tommy went to answer but groaned and sat back down.

"I'll get it," his father said. "Hello. Who? Oh. How are you, dear? That's good. I am fine, thank you. That is very nice from you. He is sick but he is okay." There was an old-world politeness in his father's voice when he spoke English, a clunky formality that he didn't have in Hungarian. As if he had to be on his best behaviour. His accent heightened it. "Yes, that is good. Okay, one minute, dear. Good-bye. It's for you."

"Who is it?"

"Marianne."

He was surprised. "I'll take it in the TV room," he said getting up too quickly. He groaned and levered himself off the chair slowly.

"What's so private that you have to kill yourself?" his mother asked.

"So I can lie down," he said rubbing his ribs.

Gingerly he lowered himself onto the couch and lifted the receiver. "I got it," he spoke into the phone.

"Good-bye, dear," his father said. There was a click.

Tommy listened to be sure that there was no breathing on the line. "Hi," he said.

"How are you feeling?"

"Sore but okay."

"Nothing broken?"

"No. Just sore."

"That was a dirty play."

"Yeah, but it's okay."

"No, it's not. I wanted to kick that goalie where the sun don't shine."

He laughed, then winced. "Ow." He gently massaged his ribs.

"No laughing for you."

"I guess not. Ow."

"Would you be up for meeting?"

He wasn't especially, but he didn't want to miss a chance to spend time with her. "Tomorrow?" he asked.

"Are you loco? You sound like you can hardly breathe."

"I'm okay."

"Can you take a deep drag?"

He tried. "Ow." He gasped. "When?"

"Friday."

"Sure. At Naomi's?"

"No. Um…she began awkwardly. "I'm thinking more like a date."

He was taken aback.

"Tommy?"

"Yeah, yeah, for sure. Where?"

"At the Prague."

He groaned as he changed position. "The café on Crescent Street?"

"Yeah, near Ste. Catherine. East side."

"Sure."

"Around eight?"

"Sure."

"Sure?" She laughed and hung up.

"What did she want?" his mother asked. As usual, she was cooking something. The only time she was at rest was when she was reading.

"She wanted to know how I was."

"For that you had to go to another room?" she said.

"That was nice of her," his father said.

"Yes. She's nice."

"Is she your girlfriend?" His mother didn't waste time.

"No. She's Speedy's sister. We're just friends."

"Boys and girls can't be just friends."

"Sure they can," he countered, but was pretty sure his mother was right. He didn't like her being so nosy.

"And, she's not Jewish."

"Why does it matter if she's Jewish or not? We're just friends. I never even asked her out."

"Do you have a girlfriend? We haven't seen anyone."

"No. I'm too busy with work and soccer." He didn't want to talk to his parents about girls. Especially his mother.

"Girls today are terrible. Their clothes are terrible. Their skirts are too short. The miniskirt is terrible. You can see almost everything. And those hippie girls don't wear what they should. Sometimes not even shoes."

Clothes were important to his mother Seeing girls wear old or used clothes as a fashion statement really upset her.

"When I was young," she would start whenever she saw a girl in patched jeans, "we were too poor to have nice dresses. And in the concentration camp we had to wear lice-infested rags. I promised myself that if I survived, I would have nice new clothes. They don't know how good they have it here. And then they dress like that." And running her own business making women's blazers, she felt she had the right to judge style and morals.

His mother loved well-made clothes. She would spend hours in dress shops, checking not only the styles but also stroking the fabrics, feeling the nap of the material, looking at the cut and the match at the seams. Then she would make them herself, taking pride in making them better than the ones she copied. When friends asked where she bought it, she would bask in their incredulity and their oohs and ahhs.

"People judge you by how you look," she often said. She insisted that her husband and Tommy wear nice clothes to work. There they changed into their work clothes and changed back at the end of the day. On weekends when everybody in the neighbourhood wore casual clothes, his father wore a suit and tie, even to sit on the balcony. His mother wore ironed blouses, skirts and a spotless apron when she cooked. She didn't like but tolerated his wearing jeans on the weekend but not during the week. His mother was always nagging him to dress nicely even when he had a game to go to. She even insisted that he polish his cleats before each game. Because he scored a hat trick the first game he played with polished cleats, it had become one of his rituals.

His mother had an opinion about everything. Even things she didn't know much about. It made arguing with her impossible. One of her favourite expression was "I know everything." His father was less opinionated, but not much. Being survivors of the Holocaust gave them a right to be right about everything. And because of this, Tommy always felt guilty arguing with them. So, he didn't. Until recently there hadn't been much to argue about. Now he was hiding more and more, and he didn't feel good about it. But he liked what he was doing. He certainly wasn't going to tell them about smoking grass. Or about liking Marianne. He wasn't even sure if she liked him in the same way, though after the last call, maybe.

"And what is this free love anyway? It's disgusting."

"It's about loving the person you want to love, that's all. Their race or religion shouldn't matter."

"You can say that all you want, but I know it's not true. If you marry a shiksa and you get into a fight the first thing she'll call you is a dirty Jew."

"Who's talking about marriage?"

"Thank God. And you can't be like them. They won't let you. I know."

"How do you know?"

"Before the war, many Jews tried to assimilate in Hungary. Especially the educated ones from Budapest. They said that everybody is a Hungarian. They said it didn't matter if you were a Christian or a Jew, you were still a Hungarian. But those rotten Arrow Cross fascists didn't think so. Those free-love Jews still ended up wearing the yellow star. Many tried to convert. Even my father converted to keep us from being taken away. And they still took us. So, don't tell me about this everybody-is-the-same craziness."

"But this is Canada."

"It's the same everywhere. Believe me. I know."

There is no winning, Tommy thought and went off to watch *Hogan's Heroes*.

"And when are you going to get a haircut? You're starting to look like a girl," his mother called out after him.

Watching the prisoners outwit bumbling Colonel Klink and simple-minded Schultz, he thought about his parents' concentration camp experiences. Their stories were certainly not funny, although his father often recounted them in a humorous way. He once told him that after liberation, he wandered into an officer's bedroom and beheld a wondrous thing, a bed with a mattress and duvet. "I was going to lie in it. But then I saw another prisoner who had the same idea. I yelled out to him that it was mine, that it was mine. He yelled back the same thing at the same time. We both ran—well, shuffled was more like it—toward that goose-feathered heaven. It was a race between two turtles. Then I realized I was looking into a mirror! For two years I had lived without seeing myself. It's a good thing or I would have scared myself to death. I looked like an old man."

His parents had been his age when they were in the camps. He had never thought about that before.

"I see nothing! I hear nothing! I know nothing!" Sergeant Schultz declared and there was laughter.

18

Café Prague was a hole-in-the wall a few steps below street level. Though it was only two blocks from the campus he had never been inside. He had heard that weirdos, artsy-fartsies and shit disturbers like Naomi hung out there. He sat at a table for two about halfway along the wall. A waitress in a black turtleneck sweater, short suede skirt, black tights and knee-high boots came over.

"I'm waiting for someone."

"Godot?"

"Sorry?"

"Cool." She smiled and walked away.

Canvasses of splattered paint hung on the exposed brick walls. A little stage, big enough for a stool and a microphone, was tucked into the far corner. To its right was a cigarette-vending machine and to its left, a bar with a pastry display case. At one of the tables two bearded guys wearing turtlenecks and smoking pipes were contemplating a chessboard. At another, a girl in an army surplus jacket was absorbed in her book. At the far corner table, near the door, a chubby guy with scruffy hair was busy scribbling. Quiet music filled the room. In his chinos, button-down shirt, navy blue jacket and tie, Tommy felt out of place.

Why did Marianne want to meet here? It didn't feel like a date kind of place. She had danced into his life and drawn him into another world. She was someone close and far at the same time. She was like a guy, loud and tough. She was the one who called him, told him where to be and when. But like a girl, she was a mystery who had kissed him with a kiss that was not a kiss.

She was the lightest touch of lips that had sent smoke and shivers through him and got him high. He sailed on Marianne's kiss for days after. It wasn't just the grass. He was sure of that. And he wanted more.

He spotted her coming down the stairs. He couldn't make out her features because of the backlight from the street but he recognized her outline. She wasn't a pretty girl; she was a beautiful woman.

He inhaled deeply and stood up. Her hair cascaded past her shoulders, and flowed over her black vest. His mother would certainly have approved of her pin-striped collarless shirt but not the patched full-length flowered skirt or sandals.

"Hi."

She offered her cheeks. He inhaled her. She made him feel suave and serious. He kissed her once, twice. He would have loved to embrace her.

"How are you?" he asked.

"Fine, you?"

"Okay."

"Still sore?"

"Not much."

"You sure?"

The waitress arrived to take their order. "Hi, Marianne. The usual?"

"Yeah."

"And you?" said the waitress.

"A Pepsi, please."

"We don't serve pop."

"They only serve coffee or tea," Marianne said.

"Coffee, please."

"What kind?"

"With milk and sugar, please."

"But what kind?" the waitress repeated.

"He'll have a cappuccino also," Marianne said.

"Do you want any pastry?"

"We'll share a mille feuille," she said. "And two glasses of water."

"Okay."

Tommy felt stupid.

"A cappuccino is an Italian coffee and has a milky foam on top. The Prague is one of the few places that has a cappuccino machine in Montreal."

"How do you know this stuff?"

"Well, I come here occasionally, and my uncle owns the El Gitano. They serve it there. Another place is a Hungarian café on Stanley Street, the Pam Pam. Have you ever been there?"

"No."

"They also serve espresso and café latte, two other kinds of really good coffee. And they also have the most delicious Dobos."

"Dobos? He corrected her pronunciation. "The 's' is a 'sh' sound," Tommy said, feeling slightly better now that he could contribute to the conversation. "I love Dobos. My mother buys it from a Hungarian bakery on the Main. I love the creaminess and specially the crunchy top part."

"Then you'll love mille feuille. It's a bit like the Dobos but the layers are thinner. It has a thousand leaves."

"Wow! It must be huge."

She laughed. "It doesn't really have a thousand leaves. That's just its name."

"I figured," he said and smiled.

A hiss, like that of the pressing machine in his parents' factory, whistled through the room. Tommy spun. He let out a gasp.

"Hey, that's a good impression," she laughed.

"What are you talking about?"

"Of the espresso machine."

He winced and smiled back.

The waitress brought their coffee and the mille feuille.

Tommy stared at his. He had never seen one like that. The white foam was flecked with dark sprinkles.

"Chocolate," Marianne said.

"Oh…"

"Try it."

He lifted the cup to his lips and sipped. He nose touched the foam. She smiled and dabbed it with a napkin.

"It's strong."

"It's delicious."

He took another sip. This time he kept his nose out of the froth. He watched Marianne take a sophisticated sip.

"Do you like it?"

"Yeah."

"Here, now close your eyes and taste." She held out a piece of the mille feuille on her fork. He closed his eyes and opened his mouth. She slipped in the fork.

"Slow. Don't swallow it all at once. Enjoy it," she said as she pulled out the fork.

He tasted the sweetness of the icing, the crispness of the feuilles and the lushness of the filling. "Umm. You sound like my father," he said when he finished the morsel.

"What do you mean?"

"When I was kid in Hungary, I loved rock candy. They're these diamond-hard pellets. My father taught me to eat only one at a time and not crunch it but move it around and play with it to get it smooth and round so the pellet dissolves. That way its flavour spreads like a river through your entire mouth. He always eats very slowly and most of the time with his eyes closed. He tells me that it makes the flavour even more flavourful, and it lasts longer, which, when you are poor, as he was, is important."

"I'll take that as a compliment. Your father is a wise man."

Tommy, in turn, broke off a bit of the mille feuille with his fork and extended it to her. She leaned in, opened her mouth and took it in. As he watched her he was overcome with a feeling that he could only describe to himself as a flowing lightness and a grin spread over his face. When she opened her eyes and saw it, she laughed.

"What?" he asked, almost in a panic.

She just shook her head and said nothing. They finished the coffee and mille feuille in comfortable silence.

More people were drifting in.

"You want to know why I wanted to meet?"

He was taken aback by her directness. "Yeah."

"Because I like you."

It caught him off guard. Guys were supposed to make the first move. But so far, it had always been her. "I like you too," he said after a moment's hesitation. "Is that why you didn't want me to tell Speedy anything?"

He watched her run her fingertip around the rim of the cup, skim off the froth and lick it. "Oh shit," he thought, "I had to go and say something stupid."

"My family is very strict about boy and girl stuff. Especially about the way girls should be. Especially good Catholic girls. I used to accept it, but now, I can't. I find it really hard to be what they want me to be. Times they are a-changing," she said. "I want to make my own choices. I don't want to get married yet. Maybe never. I like you, but you're Jewish and Speedy, he's such a big brother with macho ideas."

"You're the older one though, aren't you?"

"I am but he acts like the big brother. So, I thought it would be better if we got to know each other before we started to see each other."

He wasn't sure where this was leading. "He already sort of warned me not to be interested. I don't want to cause problems with you and your parents, and I don't want to lose my friendship with Speedy either."

A silence settled between them. "But I like you a lot," he said.

The waitress went from table to table, lighting the candles. She dimmed the lights and stopped the music. She stepped up to the microphone and tapped it a couple of times.

"Tonight, two people are going to read their poetry. We're going to start with Artie Gold. You all know Artie, the Prague poet laureate. Please welcome Artie Gold."

The scruffy guy who had been scribbling in his notebook got up and strode to the stage. People applauded and called out to him as if he were an old friend.

He talked and read fast. His poems had images and references to things and people that Tommy didn't get but the others did. They responded with comments and laughter.

"And this is my last poem."

Sun filters through my window
Casts velvet bats' shadows that
Flutter about my room. I share the unrest.

The sun is doomed with movement
Sunup sundown; ground sky ground
Its orbit is small comfort to my habit.

Whatever we do is best left at home
The truth of our moment is too predictable
Yet I delight in the sun, it's monumental

In the sky with certainty rising, setting
Looking to the greater cycle, there is colour,
A yellow angel pedals about the world.

Marianne applauded loudly. Tommy also applauded but wasn't sure why. Artie Gold's poems weren't like the ones he had studied in his compulsory Intro Poetry course last year.

"That was great, man," the waitress said. Artie gathered his papers and strode back to his table. He sat, took out his notebook and started scribbling again.

"And now for our open mic part, we have Marianne Gonzales."

Tommy turned to her. She gave him a nervous smile. It was the first time he had seen her so unsure of herself. She reached into her peace purse and took out a folded sheet of paper. He watched her walk up to the stage, hesitant, unfold the paper and smooth it out. She stood shyly in the front of the microphone. The paper in her hand was trembling. She looked right at him, took a deep breath and stood tall. Her voice came out steady and clear.

"I have only one poem to read. It's called 'Nobody.'"

Nobody

Nobody, Nothing is
Who or what they seem

You show up at your door
In your dreams
In all sorts of disguises

Lost soul of the night
Sometimes as a trick
Rarely as a treat

You figure because you give
You should get?

Not so easy my friend

Love
Grace
You
are not earned or learned

You are what you are
daily chores spring-cleaned
the voice in the shower singing perfectly of imperfect love
the hunger in your belly feeding your hunger in your belly
the human cry unheard by passersby
You are you standing erect

Staring at the sun
Howling Beware.

Tommy applauded enthusiastically. She was blushing. The music came back on. He smiled at her with admiration. She sat, folded her poem and put it in her bag.

"You sure know how to do a lot of stuff," he said.

She smiled back at him.

"Let's walk," he said.

On their way out, Marianne stopped by the poet's table. "That was amazing," she said.

"We should get together sometime," he said in a way that made Tommy dislike him intensely. "Here's my phone number." He tore off the corner of the page he was writing on.

"That would be great." She beamed as she slipped it into her purse. Tommy reached for her hand.

"See you," she said

"For sure," he said.

"Why did you take his phone number?" Tommy asked.

"Because he gave it to me."

He didn't know what to say.

"Because I'd like to talk to him about poetry." She gave him a hard look that reminded him of Speedy.

How could she say one minute she liked him and then, in front of him, make a date with this other guy? It made no sense.

"Where to?" she asked.

"I don't know. Let's just walk."

"Let's go up to Redpath Park," she said.

They headed up Crescent towards Sherbrooke. It was a clear night. Her hand felt good, perfect in his, but he was angry.

"I like this park," she said. It was a small one. Mount Royal was behind it and downtown Montreal in front of it. Well-dressed elderly people were walking their dogs.

"Here," she said. She sat on a bench under a huge maple. He sat with a heavy sigh.

"What's up?" she asked.

"Still a bit hard to breathe but it's okay."

"You sure?"

"Uh huh."

They sat in silence holding hands.

"That's Sacred Heart." Marianne pointed to the building across the street. "I went there." With its turrets and fieldstone walls, it resembled a castle more than a school.

"Impressive."

"We used to call it Sacred Farts. We were taught by nuns who put the fear of God and men in us. Every Friday we had to go to confession. Even if you didn't have a sin to confess, you had to make something up." She had a sad look on her face.

"I went to Baron Byng. We called it Bing Bang. Ninety-nine percent of the students were Jewish there. I remember our math teacher, Mr. Bierman. We were pretty sure that he was a Nazi. Maybe his punishment was to teach a bunch of smart-aleck Jewish immigrant kids. When he came into class, we stood and as he walked toward the front of the class, we would click our heels. He would turn and yell, 'who did dat?' I remember there was a kid, Hymie Moscovitch. His family had money 'cause he always had a bunch of quarters that he would noisily stack and restack. One day, Bierman had enough. He stormed to the back and scooped up all the quarters. 'Typical,' he said as he pocketed them, walked back to the front and continued to teach. After a few minutes Hymie put up his hand. 'Vat?' Bierman snapped. Hymie stood as if he were going to answer a question and said 'Sir. Can I have a receipt for those quarters?'"

Both of them laughed. They faced each other. Tommy leaned in, closed his eyes and kissed her. Her lips parted slightly and gently kissed him back. He opened his eyes, reached out and stroked her hair. Oh, how he had wanted to do that ever since he saw her. It was thick. His fingers curled in and out, sliding, tumbling, holding on. She closed her eyes and leaned into his shoulder. He could hear her soft breathing.

"Since when have you been writing poetry?" he asked, breathing in her fragrance.

"Since I was a kid, but I'm not a poet. It's just one poem. What did you think?"

"When I was a kid in Hungary, I liked poems. I liked memorizing them. My mother loves poetry. She can still recite some that she learned as a child. But once we got here, I forgot all about it. I was busy trying to learn the language and spent my free time playing soccer. We had to study them in high school, but I never understood them, I never got the meaning. The teacher always had a better, correct interpretation. I'm not very good at understanding them."

"How did it make you feel?"

He wasn't sure what to say. "It was nice."

"But how did it make you feel?"

He wondered if this was a test of some sort. He thought hard. "Honestly? It scared me a little. It made me wonder who you are. And at the end when you said 'Beware,' it sounded like a warning. But I'm not sure what I'm supposed to be beware of."

"Of me. Of you."

"Why?"

"Because we are not who we seem to be. We have masks. Because there are always our many selves like an ocean that's between us."

"What do you mean?"

She just stared into the starry night. She reached out and took his hand. "Come."

"Where?"

"Naomi's."

"It's late, she'll be asleep."

"No. She went to the Townships to visit her parents and left me the key."

19

Tommy was barely in the door when the hall light exploded.

"Where were you all night?" His mother's voice hit him like a slap.

Tommy looked at his watch. "It's only three."

"Only?"

Tommy's father stood behind his mother. "Your mother was worried to death," he said. "We were thinking of calling the police, and then the hospitals. You want her to feel like that? You're the only child we have."

Tommy needed to pee. But they were standing there, looking more scared than angry, arms crossed barring the way.

"There was no telephone? Why didn't you call?"

"It was too late to call."

"It's never too late to call. Where were you?"

"Like I told you, I was out with some of the guys and we went to a movie and then went for a few drinks and drove around."

"What did you do?"

"Nothing."

His parents kept at him. "So, if you didn't do nothing, why didn't you come home?"

"Did you get drunk?"

"No, just a few beers."

"That's how it starts."

"So, you couldn't call?"

"Sorry."

"Your mother couldn't sleep all night."

"Sorry."

"What's happening to you?"

"Nothing, it's Friday night. I'm nineteen."

"It's illegal. You're not twenty-one."

"You want the police to put you in jail?"

"They don't do that." He really didn't want to be here right now having this conversation. He wanted to be alone to savour the night.

"You don't want to get in trouble with the police. Only goyim get in trouble with the police."

"It was late even for Friday night."

"Don't ever do it again. You understand?"

His mother never slept much, whether he came home late or not. For her, late was ten minutes before the time he said he would be home. She didn't like to sleep because she had nightmares. She yelled out names and Hungarian and German phrases. Tommy had often heard her yell out "never again." He always connected that with her Holocaust experience. The nightmares started shortly after their arrival in Montreal. The first time it happened he was frightened awake but before he could get out of bed, she was in his room, turning on the light. She had a wide-eyed, mad look on her face. Each time she had a nightmare, it would end with her standing in the doorway staring at him. His panic lessened over time, but he never got used to it.

His father tried to convince her to see a doctor but she refused. She didn't like doctors. Finally, a friend recommended the Hertzl, a clinic that had Jewish doctors. Tommy went with her to translate. She held his hand tightly the entire time while they sat in the waiting room. When she saw that it was a female doctor, she relaxed her grip. The doctor asked about her dreams, but she said she couldn't remember. Tommy didn't think she was telling the truth. When he had nightmares, he remembered them. They didn't make sense, but he remembered them. Maybe that was why he remembered them. The doctor gave her sleeping pills and her nightmares disappeared under a heavy sleep.

"It is like a boot is stepping on my head," she said. "I don't enjoy the heaviness in the morning but it's better than bad dreams."

Tommy woke with a smile on his face. He stretched, moaned and sighed. He wanted to shout but that would have freaked out his parents. Jumping out of bed, he headed for the shower. As he was about to step in, he stopped. He didn't want to wash Marianne's scent off. He took a deep whiff, exhaled, stepped in, yelped, closed his eyes and turned his face toward the scalding spray.

As they walked in silence from the park to Naomi's, Tommy had felt like he was in a movie. The starry night, the moonlight, the streetlights and the store lights. All the scene needed was music. He'd begun to hum the theme from *A Man and a Woman* that was playing on all the stations. Marianne joined him. Holding hands, they la la la la lahed along Sherbrooke, down Lincoln and up the steps to the apartment.

Before she could turn on the light, he grabbed her and kissed her hard. She kissed him but gently pushed him back. "Slow," she said, caressing his face.

"Sorry."

"It's okay, but slow."

She lit a pair of candles, got a bottle of wine and poured them two glasses. They clinked and sipped like two sophisticated people. He put down his glass, leaned over and inhaled deeply. Her scent was exotic.

"Patchouli," he said.

"Umm, Old Spice," she said, leaning in.

They laughed. She went to the record player and rifled through the LPs. *Chet Baker 'Round Midnight*, she said as she placed the needle on the disc. A mellow trumpet, smoky and smooth, filled the candle-lit room.

"It's like the music at The Prague. What kind is it?" Tommy asked.

"Cool jazz."

She took out a joint from a little marble box on the coffee table and lit it. He toked, just the right amount, and leaned to kiss her. She opened her lips and breathed it in. The music danced with the undulating flame.

His tongue played along her moist open lips, tasting them. She opened them more. Like an explorer in a new world his tongue slowly entered and met hers. He had Frenched before but with other girls it was like pushing and shoving, trying to get into a well-guarded fort. Hers felt welcoming. He was so focused on the pleasure of it that he wasn't conscious of his fingers sliding down her face, along her throat to the front of her blouse. He became aware only when she placed her palm on his. He felt her breasts rise and fall. He felt heat seep through his palm, travel through his body to his crotch, where it became something else.

Only once had he almost gotten to second base. He remembered how clumsy he was trying to undo buttons, almost tearing them off and how resistant the girl had been. He waited to have Marianne push his hand away. When she didn't, he undid a button. Then another. Tonight, his fingers and the buttons were on his side. They slid through the buttonholes as willing accomplices. His fingers traced the edges around her lacy bra. It felt sexy. He felt himself getting hard as his fingers slid over her breasts. Their curves were so erotic. He wanted to squeeze them, but he'd read in *Playboy* that it could hurt, and besides, he loved the feeling of the light touchings they were sharing. She was gently massaging his neck and running her fingers through his hair. They moved like soft breath through leaves. His fingers slipped under her breasts and tried to slip inside her bra. It was tight. She moved closer to him. He reached around to her back and, like he knew what he was doing, tried to unclasp her bra. It wasn't easy. She pushed him away, sat up.

"Sorry," he mumbled like a bumbling fool.

She rose and extended her hand to him. "Let's go to the bedroom."

Marianne smiled, undid the other buttons and slipped out of her blouse. She reached behind her back and unclipped the hooks. He reached over and slid the bra straps over her shoulders and down her arms. Other than in *Playboy*, he had never seen a girl's naked breasts before. Her skin glistened in the candlelight.

He was glad it was dark because he didn't want her to see his hard-on.

She turned her back to him. "Unzip me."

His fingers were trembling. He unhooked the skirt and pulled the zipper. He bent to pull it over her hips and ended up head butting her in the back, sending her flying onto the bed.

"Hey!" she cried out before starting to laugh.

"Sorry. Sorry."

She rolled onto her back and continued laughing. Reaching up, she pulled him on top of her. A twinge made him wince, but he didn't want to cry out and ruin the moment. They kissed. The heat from her body felt like it was pulsating. He rose and fell with her breathing. She rolled over onto him. He gasped.

"You okay?" she asked.

"Oh, yeah," he sighed. He felt horny. He almost forgot about his sore ribs.

She picked up her clothes and walked out of the room. He sat up, wondering what he had done wrong. Was this it? Was she just a tease? He was pissed but a bit relieved at the same time. She was a nice girl and he was lucky to have gotten this far.

She returned with a towel wrapped around her. "How come you're still dressed?" she asked.

It took him aback. He tried to undress quickly but the pain forced him to slow down. He fumbled with his belt and zipper more than with hers. It was as if he had never undressed. Well, he never had with a girl in the room. He glanced over his shoulder. She was slipping the towel under the covers before getting in. He joined her. They looked at each other as if to say what now? He felt her fingernails on his chest. The touch was light and erotic. It felt like almost not touching.

His fingertips touched down on her breasts. He sighed. His palms rested on her nipples. He kissed one then the other. She arched toward him. He suckled. "Wow." Her fingers slipped between his legs. He gasped. His body felt like it was going to explode. He was afraid to move. Then he reached down to touch her. She placed her hand over his.

"I'm a virgin," she said.

He stopped. Breathed deeply. "Me too."

He wasn't sure what he should do next, but his urges and fantasies did. Every nerve ending was firing at a million miles an hour. He straddled her. He was in a hurry but because of his ribs, he had to slow down. He was slipping into her. Marianne dug her nails into his back. She rose to meet him. She let out a loud gasp as he fully dove into her. Something gave. He opened his eyes and saw a tear slip down her cheek. He worried that he had hurt her. He felt an oozing followed by a contraction. They urged him on. She opened her eyes. They were looking through him. She pulled him tight to her and moved as if dancing a slow dance. He was light as a feather, floating. Their breathing synched.

Afterwards, he just wanted to lie there next to her and feel her warmth. Her breath on his skin, soft and even, like the most gentle breeze in the world. He stared into the darkness. Something had changed. He had entered another world. He turned toward her.

"I have to go," he said, though he didn't want to.

She opened her eyes and pulled him close. She kissed him softly. "I know," she said and pulled the cover over her head.

All the way home in the cab, he hummed their song. He didn't want to go home. Not only because it was really late but because he was going from what he had just become, back to being his parents' child. Going home was going backward. Like becoming a virgin again.

He opened his mouth and let the water fill it, spill over, cascade down his chest, torso, crotch…

"Breakfast," his mother shouted from the kitchen.

2 0

"We know you were planning this crime. We know you went to see your Gypsy collaborator earlier. What did you talk about?"

The voice seemed to come from miles away. Tommy was so tired he could barely see. The man's face was just an amorphous blob.

"Weren't you?" the man in the dark suit snapped.

Tommy wanted to sit, but he made himself stand straighter and tried to focus. "Frog called him a liar and a thief."

"Officer Szeles?"

"No, Béla Bartok."

"What?"

"I was sitting with Gabi and Frog under a huge willow just at the edge of Frog's *putri* talking about old times. Gabi had told me that Frog got kicked out of university but didn't know why. I asked Frog, who told me that it was because he had called Béla Bartok and the Hungarian people liars and thieves. I didn't know what he was talking about. I had heard of Bartok but didn't know anything about him. So I asked him what happened.

"He said he had made the accusation in class. He had also said that Liszt said that Hungarian music wasn't worth much without Gypsy music. His professor got really upset, so he kicked him out.

"I told him that I couldn't believe that he got kicked out for arguing with his professor. Our professors encourage debate. One of my friends lives for it.

'Not here,' Frog said. He also said that he put a curse on him. Frog had a mischievous smile on his face, so I wasn't sure if he was kidding. Frog said that the professor had called him ignorant and uncivilized. So, he figured why not. That's why he got called to the Dean's office.

"The Dean told Frog that he was insolent and disruptive and that other professors had also made complaints against him. The Dean also gave him a lecture about why students at university are called listeners. I've never heard students called listeners, so I asked Frog why. He said that the Dean told him that it was because that was all students were capable of at this stage of their academic lives. He said that they should keep their mouths closed, ears open and their ignorant opinions to themselves. He said that they should listen to their betters, that way they might learn something. Then he questioned where Frog got off challenging a professor's authority.

"I told Frog that I thought that professors do know more.

"He said that when he questioned his professors, he wasn't questioning their knowledge but their conclusions.

"Then, he said, the Dean got really angry and wanted to know where he got his information. Frog told him that he was a Gypsy who had heard Gypsy music from the time he was in his mother's womb. He said that Gypsy music greeted his birth and that he was suckled to Gypsy music and fell asleep to Gypsy lullabies.

"I was really amazed that he said all that."

"Frog said that the Dean called it hogwash. And then told him that the Party was disappointed in him.

"I didn't know what party he was talking about.

"Gabi said that it was the Communist Party.

"I didn't understand what the Communist Party had to do with Bartok and Gypsy music.

"Gabi told me that they had everything to do with everything.

"Frog explained that the Party decreed that Gypsies should be let into schools even though they may not be qualified, so they could be civilized and integrated into the socialist fabric of Hungary. The Dean and most Hungarians were not happy about that. They argued that Gypsies would take the place of more qualified Hungarian students. The Dean also told him that the Party was disappointed in how he was repaying them. He said Frog's behaviour reflected badly on those who were trying to help him, that he was biting the hand that wanted to feed him. And that he was also hurting his people by proving that they couldn't be civilized. Therefore, he had no choice but to expel him."

"I'm not interested in this tripe," the man in the suit bellowed. "I'm interested in the planning of the crime!"

"But that's what we talked about; I swear!"

2 1

Tommy and his father were watching his father's favourite show, *The Three Stooges*. You didn't need much English to enjoy the slapping, punching and eye-gouging antics of Larry, Curly and Moe. Tommy waited till it was over.

"I really want to go. This is a chance of a lifetime to play on the Golden Green. And really, nothing can go wrong. I'm going to be with the team and then with family."

"You understand why we don't want you to go, don't you?"

Tommy nodded and readied himself for another no. But he wasn't going to take no for an answer. He was ready to go without their permission.

"Your mother doesn't like it. She's scared for good reasons and I agree with her. But I convinced her that it's important for you to see your family." Tommy couldn't believe his ears. He jumped out of his chair. He hugged and kissed his father.

"But there is a condition," his father said after the embrace. "We want you to check with the Canadian government. First we want them to write a letter that says that you're a Canadian citizen and Hungary can't conscript you into their rotten army."

"Sure, sure," he said though, he didn't really know how to go about it. Tommy's heart felt like it was about to burst.

"Also, I think it's important that you go there as a champion and leave like a man, not like a mouse, like us."

His father held him by the arms and beamed at him with pride. "You show them what they lost."

22

The season was more than half over and the Knights were holding their own. They were in fourth place in a ten-team league. Coach Hus had them playing not just with their feet but with their brains as well.

"Let's play multiple games, long, short, criss-cross, fast, and slow, but most importantly, smart, and as a team," he kept repeating. "You're younger and in better shape. Be smart. And of course…."

"Hustle," they yelled.

Tommy and Speedy were among the top ten scorers in the league. They were having fun. They had chemistry. Speedy's speed kept defenders hanging back, so Tommy had room to manoeuvre. It gave him the chance to use the give and go with him. Tommy's strength was his two feet, his head and his brain. He could shoot with both feet and had a spring in his legs that let him out-jump most of the defenders. He also had a sense of the game and its rhythm and knew how to play head games with the opponents. He appeared vulnerable because he wasn't bulky. He looked easy to push off the ball, until one of them tried. When an opponent leaned on him, he would lower his centre of gravity and then suddenly rise to send him flying. He was also getting used to the rougher game. Watching his opponents, he learned how to bring up the elbows and deliver sharp jabs without getting caught. Defenders and goalies were more reluctant to come charging at him. He had learned that in this league, part of skill was hiding certain skills.

Archie, the oldest on the team and a Poli-Sci major, had analyzed the rough-and-tumble approach to the game at one of their post-game beer sessions. He was, as usual, lecturing. It's why they called him the Professor.

As always, he began with,"Let me put it to you this way... Most of the players in the league are uneducated, working-class immigrants. They work long shitty hours at shitty immigrant jobs and take shitty orders from shitty bosses. Most of them will never get much further ahead. But on the field they're not at the bottom. They don't have to take shit. They can be the ones dishing it out. Even after a hard day of exhausting, menial labour they can't wait to play a game where they get a chance to kick the shit out of someone. And they love to. Even if it's one of their own."

"Feel like going for some vino tonight?" Speedy asked as they jogged off the field after practice. Tommy nodded.

"Can you get the car and pick me up? My father took his."

"Sure." Tommy answered, a little too quickly. "I have to ask, but I'm pretty sure." He wanted to ask if Marianne would be there but didn't want to arouse suspicion.

When he walked in the door his father greeted him with a big smile. "How was practice?"

"Good."

"When is your next game?"

"Next Thursday. We play Hungaria again. Last time this season."

"That's going to be a tough one."

"Yeah, but we're ready."

"Good."

"Supper!" his mother called.

"I have big news," his father said as they sat down. "I wrote to Emma and told her you were going to Hungary."

"That's not news," Tommy said. "That was last month."

"But we got a letter from her today. She was so excited. I bet she peed her pants."

"Sanyi!" his mother scolded.

His father chuckled. "She pees so easily when she laughs or gets excited."

"And of course, you used to tell her jokes on purpose to try to make her laugh."

"She likes to laugh. Anyways, she's counting the days."

"I doubt I'll have much time. We're on a tight schedule."

"There is no way you will not visit the family," his mother proclaimed with a look that brooked no argument. "If you're going to that lice-ridden country, you're going to properly visit family and the cemetery and you're going to say Kaddish. May they rest in peace. I'm not going to be shamed. Who knows if we'll get a chance again."

"We decided to pay for you to stay an extra week, so you can visit with all of them."

"Thanks, that's great. Wow!" He hugged his parents.

"But you know what's the real big news?" his father asked when Tommy sat down again.

"There's more?"

"Yes."

"What?"

"Guess who's the goalie for the Hungarian University championship team?"

"No!"

"Yes!"

"Wow! Really? I can't believe it! Gabi? That's unbelievable."

Supper was spent reminiscing about when Tommy and Gabi were children: Gabi sending Tommy into the chicken coop and getting his clothes covered with chicken shit. Gabi, the older of the two, making Tommy accompany him to the outhouse at night to hold a candle while he did his business; throwing pebbles through the tavern basement window to see who could hit a bottle of wine and, of course, breaking a couple and swashbuckling with swords that the blacksmiths made for them, which they hid from their parents. Tommy had forgotten about the swords.

"Can I borrow the car?"

"Where are you going?"

"Over to Speedy's for a while."

"Okay, but don't stay out too late. You have to wake up early. You work tomorrow."

"Who gets up at six o'clock in the morning?" he joked.

"Working people!"

"Okay. I'll be home by eleven."

"Not at four. And no drinking."

"I know."

He couldn't wait to tell Speedy and the guys. He couldn't wait to see Marianne.

"Ah, Tamásito," Speedy's mom greeted him. She grabbed his face and planted two big kisses on his cheeks. "Nice to see you."

"Sit down. Are you hungry?"

"No, *gracias*, I just had supper."

"Have a coffee."

"No, Mama, we're going out for a few drinks," Speedy said as he came up the stairs.

"Are you going to El Gitano?"

"*Sí.*"

"Hi," she said. He hadn't seen her come out from her room. Marianne was standing by the upstairs railing of the split-level. He thought of Juliet on the balcony. She was wearing the same blouse he had unbuttoned but instead of her dress, she was wearing jeans. He wanted to tell her she looked great, but her eyes stopped him.

"Hey, can you give me a lift to the bus?"

Her mother turned serious. "Where are you going?"

"To Naomi's. She's got some new albums we're going to listen to."

"You have to work tomorrow. Don't be too late. Understand?"

"*Sí*, Mama!"

She slipped in the back seat behind him. Tommy was nervous. The car jerked as he let the clutch out too soon and stalled.

"Amateur." Speedy punched him on the arm. "You smell funny, like her," Speedy said, sniffing Tommy.

"Huh?"

"That's not Old Spice."

"Yeah." He glanced in the rear-view mirror. Marianne was smiling. "Do you want me to give you a lift to Naomi's?"

Her smile disappeared. "No, it's out of the way."

"Nah, it's not."

"How do you know?" Speedy asked.

Tommy panicked but recovered. "Didn't you say she lived near the campus?" He glanced nervously into the rear-view mirror.

"Yeah," she said. He didn't like the look in her eyes.

"I'd like to see where she lives," Speedy said.

"It's okay, guys. Just drop me off at the bus stop." She sounded angry.

"No, we'll take you. Wolfie offered, so it's okay, eh, amigo?"

"Sure," Tommy said quietly.

Marianne slammed the door shut. "See you later," Tommy said but she was already on the other side, entering the building.

"What's her problem? She got a ride," Speedy said. "Now let's go and get Schmutz. So, what's the crazy news you got?"

Tommy switched on the radio. He didn't feel like talking just now. He needed time to think about what just happened. "I want you and Schmutz to hear it at the same time."

They settled into their corner table and Jesus brought them their wine. "No shit! Really?" Schmutz said when Tommy shared the news.

"I was always Puskás and he was Grosics."

"Those guys were so good."

"Yeah, the best in the world. World and Olympic champions. When they defected during the revolution in '56 and Puskás stayed behind in Spain, I was devastated."

"How come your cousin didn't escape?"

"They tried. Twice. Gabi and I are cousins, but we were more like brothers. Right after the war, his parents got arrested trying to escape. He was just a baby, so he stayed with us while his parents were in jail. When they got out, they moved in with us and we lived in the same house until we escaped. We played soccer every chance we got. And my father, who was the manager of the local team, would take us to practices. The coach, I forget his name, trained us. I remember jogging, like a mile behind the players around the track and learning tricks."

"How come they got caught and you guys didn't?"

"It's a long story."

"We've got time," Schmutz said.

"*Sí*. You're not going anywhere else tonight, eh, amigo?"

He picked up an edge in Speedy's voice. He wanted to tell him. He wanted to tell his parents. He wanted to tell everyone. But what was there to tell? That he and Marianne had had sex? No way! That they were going steady? He wasn't sure of that.

"Wolfie?" Schmutz waved his palm in front of Tommy's face. "Hello."

"Oh, no, just hanging out with the Mouseketeers," he joked.

"How come they got caught and you guys didn't?"

"Oh. Well, the train we were on, heading towards the border, was stopped by the secret police. They asked for everybody's identity papers. Those who didn't have the right ones, meaning bribe money, were ordered off. We didn't have the right papers, so we had to get off, but Gabi's father, who didn't want to go to jail again, punched one of the policemen and the whole packed train went crazy. The secret police ganged up on him and dragged him, Gabi and his mother off the train and in the chaos forgot about us."

"Wow! That's heavy shit," Schmutz said, meticulously peeling the label off the wine bottle.

"It's going to be strange playing against your cousin, eh?"

"Yeah. He was good then. He must be amazing now."

"How do you think we'll do?"

"Honestly, I don't know. They're probably more skilled. It's like, imagine if their best came here to play hockey against our best."

"They'd get massacred."

"That doesn't sound good."

"But we've got hustle."

Speedy lifted his glass in a toast. "Here's to hustle," he said. They clinked glasses.

"We'll start by beating Hungaria and then Hungary," Schmutz said.

"Yeah," Tommy said. He tuned out a lot of their bantering trying to figure out what he should do. "I gotta go."

Speedy put his hand on Tommy's shoulder. "It's early."

"My mother freaks out when I'm a minute late. I have to be up at six. You want a lift?"

"No. I'll get one with my uncle."

"And you, Schmutz?"

"I'll go with Speedy. There are a couple more glasses of wine asking for me."

"Okay. See you."

"Adios, amigo."

"You smell funny," Schmutz said as Tommy rose and headed for the door.

He sat in the car, wondering if he should go to Naomi's. He turned the key, revved the engine and peeled out. He got to Naomi's in ten minutes.

He stood in front of the door, unsure if he should ring or not.

"Hi," Naomi said.

Marianne was sitting on the couch, her feet tucked under her. She had a glass of wine in her hands and was listening to the music. Tommy smelled sandalwood and grass.

"Why'd you do that?" Marianne snarled.

"I was trying to be nice."

"You shouldn't be nice. You should learn to listen."

"What do you mean?"

"Didn't I tell you that I wanted to keep this part of my life mine?" Her eyes bored through him.

"Are you ever going to tell them?"

"About us?"

"No. Yeah, I mean wanting to lead your own life."

"No. Not yet…" She put down her glass. "I better get going."

"Do you want a lift?"

Marianne turned towards him as she gathered her things. "Boy, for a smart guy you can be pretty stupid."

2 3

Tommy loved playing under the lights. The field and the players had a glow about them. All attention was focused there. Only the action under the lights mattered. Everything else was insignificant.

Jarry Park was the only field dedicated to soccer that had lights. It was Tommy's Golden Green. The pitch was without bare patches and the grass was evenly trimmed. The corner arcs, penalty and goalie area lines weren't sloppy afterthoughts. The nets were permanent, with curved back supports that gave them a feeling of depth. A goal scored in those had meaning. The park had a P.A. system through which lineups and goals were broadcast. It even had a little press booth at the top of the bleachers where the *Montreal Gazette*, *Montreal Star* reporters and Mr. Papp of *The Hungarian News* sat. In this park, soccer was the most important game.

As he did his pregame stretches on the soft manicured grass of Jarry Park, Tommy searched the stands for his father He was always the first of the fathers to show up. He was usually near the bleachers pacing back and forth. He wasn't there. It wasn't like him to miss a game.

Hungaria scored first. Ivan was late getting to Hungaria's left winger, who had streaked down the side and had a free run to make a beautiful pass to their centre half, who snuck into the penalty area and blasted a shot past Derek into the left, low corner.

Schmutz got that one back with his own blast that nearly tore through the back of the net before the half ended.

Tommy still couldn't see his father on the sideline. He felt uneasy.

"*Hui! Hui! Hui!*" Ivan was cursing himself as he walked off the field.

"It's okay," Schmutz said, patting him on the back.

"Time to shit or get in the pot," Ivan said and slapped himself in the face.

Archie tapped Tommy on the head. "Hey, man, what's up? Three times you missed me with your passes. Is it too dark to see me? Am I too black for you? Next time, I'll smile." He flashed a toothy grin. His teeth were brilliant white, glowing against his rich pink lips and black skin. Tommy laughed.

"Sorry, man. Keep smiling and I'll find you." He wondered where his father was.

"Okay, we're good," Coach Hustle said, clapping his hands. "Just keep up the pace. And remember, vary the game."

The second half started slow, with both sides almost walking the game. Horvath was his shadow and he didn't miss any opportunity to step on Tommy's toes or try to knee him in the thigh. He chattered in Hungarian, trying to distract him. Tommy was getting fed up. He jogged past Speedy and told him to pull a pick next time they crossed.

Lou had the ball. "Now!" Tommy shouted at Speedy. Speedy came charging across and suddenly stopped behind Horvath. Tommy took off. Horvath backed up to follow but Speedy trapped him. Lou laid a perfect lead pass onto Tommy's right foot. He had a clear run but slowed as he heard Horvath cutting across at full gallop.

"I'll break your fucking ankles into pieces," Horvath yelled at him in Hungarian.

Tommy was seven and the school bully and his gang had taken over their pickup game. They played rough and dirty. They shoved, elbowed and deliberately stepped on their feet. Frog had the ball at midfield. Just before getting knocked over, he passed the ball to Carrot, who sent a lead pass to Tommy. He took it on his instep and dribbled over to the right side. The bully kept charging.

"Jew! Jew! Jews eat dirt!" he shouted as he galloped after Tommy.

"You can do it. You can do it," Tommy repeated to himself. He saw the bully's glowing eyes, his wide grin and big teeth. Tommy spread his arms, leaned back and slipped his foot under the ball. He kicked it as hard as he could. The bully rose onto his toes. His eyes widened and a high-pitched yelp escaped from his gaping mouth. He was as stiff as a statue. Then, in one motion, his knees buckled, his hands grasped his groin, and he fell face down onto the ground with a thud. The players gathered around him.

After what seemed like forever, Horvath slowly rolled over onto his back. He lay there, hand at his groin, eyes and mouth wide open, desperately trying to breathe. A loud sob escaped from his mouth. Tommy bent over him.

"I'm so sorry," Tommy said. He reached down to help Horvath up. Horvath offered his hand. Tommy grabbed two of his fingers, squeezed really tight and bent them back a bit. Horvath tried to scream but had no breath. "I'm so sorry," Tommy said again.

Horvath was helped off the field. He was laid down on the sideline on his back while the trainer slowly pumped his legs to get some air into him.

Speedy trotted by. "Hey, amigo. That was a terrible pass." He winked.

"He's gonna have black balls for at least a week," Schmutz said.

Hungaria's dirty game picked up. They wanted Tommy but couldn't goad him into a fight that would get him ejected. The Knights kept them penned in their own zone. Tommy was racing toward a loose ball inside Hungaria's penalty zone, and so was their goalie. With his back blocking the ref's view, Tommy grabbed the goalie's arm and yanked. To maintain his balance the goalie swung out his other arm and grabbed Tommy's jersey and hauled him down. Tommy yelled as he went rolling. The whistle blew and the referee pointed to the penalty spot. The goalie was screaming at the referee, telling him what really happened. The referee flashed a yellow card at the goalie. Tommy got up slowly, holding his ribs. He was bent over. He looked up at the goalie, who was cursing him in Hungarian, and winked.

The players lined up around the eighteen-yard marker. Tommy, who usually took the penalty shots, walked over to Ivan and said. "Hey, hui. Shit or get in the pot."

Ivan grabbed Tommy's face and kissed him on the lips. "My balls in your net," Ivan shouted and blasted it into the corner.

The Knights won.

"What's up?" Coach Hus asked as Tommy ran past him as soon as the handshakes were done.

"Gotta go," said Tommy. He dressed as fast as he could and was out the door. He found a phone booth near the bus stop and called home.

Usually it was his father who answered the phone when Tommy wasn't around but it was his mother. "Where is Apu? He wasn't at the game. Is something wrong?"

"Yes," she answered, her voice shaking. He's at the synagogue. Israel was attacked."

24

The whole family was glued to the television. His mother cursed the world that was abandoning Jews once again. "When are we going to learn that Jews can only depend on Jews?" she said to the TV. But Tommy knew that she was talking to him.

Usually Tommy and his parents went to the synagogue only during the High Holidays. Only the very devout went in the morning. But since the attack, he and his father went every morning before work. It was packed. For his family and other immigrant Jews, the synagogue wasn't only a place of worship, it was a haven. It was where he and his parents had sought refuge in Budapest, before they escaped. It was also where news, business deals, gossip, worries and jokes were shared. Here, among your own kind, you could feel safe.

For survivors, Israel was not just a country but a precious symbol of hope. *Next year in Jerusalem* was how each Passover service ended. Israel was their Phoenix rising from their mothers', fathers', sisters', brothers', uncles', aunts', cousins', grandparents' and friends' ashes. Most of the synagogue members were survivors who were certain that Israel's defeat would not be just the loss of a war but the end of a people.

Tommy's blue velvet tallit and tefillin bag with a golden-threaded Star of David felt alien in his hand. He stroked it before taking out the tefillin. It was soft. His parents had given it to him for his Bar Mitzvah. All Jewish boys got one on the occasion of becoming a man. From that day on, he was supposed to go to synagogue every morning before sunrise and put on the tefillin. He hadn't put them on since his Bar Mitzvah. He took out the two small leather boxes wrapped in their leather straps and laid them on the bench. He had forgotten how to put them on and in what order.

His father's instructions and explanations always came with a story. As a child he used to love those stories. But that was a long time ago and the long, hard hours of work in Canada left his father with little energy for stories. They were now reserved for the big holidays. Tommy felt he was too old and too Canadian for them. But this recent attack brought back the need for stories in his father.

"You have a brain. It is in one world. Your heart is in another. And your hands are in a third. The tefillin brings them together. These," he said, pointing to the two leather boxes, which resembled small square top hats, "have little parchments about God and our Exodus from Egypt in them. They're in there so we remember His miracles and the wonders He performed for us."

His father rolled up his left shirtsleeve. Tommy had seen the numbers many times before; they seemed like a natural part of his father's arm. But today it felt like he was seeing them for the first time.

"You put this one on first." His father demonstrated on his own arm. "It has to have contact with the skin. Make sure you put it on your left arm."

Tommy started to ask why, but his father shushed him. "Don't talk. Just concentrate on connecting your mind, heart and deeds, and binding them to God." In his youth, his father had attended the yeshiva. He had wanted to be a rabbi but the war had come along.

"Good. Now slip your arm through the loop and place the box up on your bicep, right across from your heart. And now we say 'Blessed are You, Lord our God, King of the universe, who has sanctified us with His commandments, and commanded us to put on tefillin.'"

"Now tighten the strap around your arm. Make sure that the knot stays in contact with the box. Wrap two more times over this little brim and seven times around your arm and once around your palm."

Each time his father wrapped the strap around his arm more of the numbers disappeared, but never completely.

"Leave the rest of the strap loose. Next, take the other tefillin and put it on your head. The box goes just above your forehead. Centre it in the middle of your head right between your eyes. The knot of the noose should rest on the back of your neck. Good. Now wrap the remainder of the arm strap three times around your middle finger, like this: once around the base, then once just above the first joint, then one more time around the base. And the rest of the strap you wrap around your palm and tuck in the tail like this."

He went on to explain how putting the tefillin on the arm next to the heart, and on the head over the brain gives the soul, desires and thoughts of the heart to God. "Remember that putting on the tefillin is a mitzvah."

Tommy and his father put on their prayer shawls. Tommy's was a small one that covered only his shoulders. His father's was floor-length. Tommy remembered seeing his father wearing the tallit in that big synagogue in Budapest. He was praying, rocking back and forth, then turned and strode toward him, his tallit billowing like a cape. He looked like a noble knight. That's when Tommy's mother told him that he and his father were Cohens, Jewish warrior-priests.

Even though Tommy was strapped up, had the tallit over his shoulder, was rocking back and forth like all the other men, he still felt like an outsider. He mumbled the words but didn't really know what he was saying. Though he wanted to, he didn't feel connected or like he belonged to the Chosen. Most of his buddies, mainly soccer players, were non-Jews. And, of course, Marianne, his mother often reminded him, was a shiksa. He was glad that none of them could see him like this. They—well, maybe not Marianne—would have ribbed him about his strange get-up.

As they prayed, Tommy wondered how wearing this stuff and praying would help Israel. It certainly hadn't helped during the war. But six days later, little Israel, born the same year as him, and led by a one-eyed David, defeated the Arab Goliath.

25

"What kind of Hungarian are you?"

Tommy was caught off guard by Mr. Papp's question. He had come by the bookstore to pick up his father's newspaper and his mother's magazines. The Story, the only Hungarian bookstore in Montreal, was kitty corner from his aunt's restaurant on Prince Arthur Street near The Main. The one block was called Little Pest by the Hungarian immigrants in the neighbourhood. Many single men who lived and worked in the area frequented his aunt's restaurant and congregated in Mr. Papp's bookstore because they were hungry for home-cooked meals and homesick for news, serious discussions of soccer and politics. They wanted respite from their immigrant world and the comfort of the old familiar one.

Hardcover books filled floor-to-ceiling shelves on two sides. The third shelf, behind the counter, was filled with Hungarian classical, popular and Gypsy music. On either side of the door were neatly organized racks of magazines. And in a corner, next to the heater, were a couple of chairs, a coffee table and a leather armchair where Mr. Papp often held court.

Mr. Papp, a tall slim man with Old World airs, immaculately coiffed hair and a pencil-thin moustache, ruled here. In his starched and pressed indigo-blue lab coat, with a feather duster tucked under an arm, he patrolled and protected his dominion.

You could look but weren't allowed to touch. You told him what you wanted, or he told you what you wanted, and he got it for you.

Mr. Papp was also a proud sponsor of the Hungaria team and was its unofficial scout as well as the soccer and culture reporter for the Montreal Hungarian newspaper. He had been after Tommy to play for Hungaria since he made the university team. He even attended Tommy's games and had written about, as he put it, his exploits. He was the one who got Hungaria's manager to call Tommy for a tryout.

"What do you mean, Mr. Papp?"

"You're Hungarian, aren't you?"

"I was born there, but I grew up here."

"That doesn't matter. You are a Hungarian. What do you know about Hungary? Of its history, art, music, literature?"

Tommy scanned the books and records on the shelves. "Not much. Just what my parents tell me. I don't read Hungarian."

"It's a shame. Hungarian history is important. You should know your motherland's stories."

Tommy never heard his parents refer to Hungary as their motherland. They spoke longingly of family but not of country. Usually, the country was remembered with bitterness and anger. He didn't understand what Mr. Papp was getting at. He'd always thought his formality in speech and dress strange. "I remember reading *The Paul Street Boys* when I was very young and liking it very much."

"Yes. That's a wonderful and important novel. I have a copy of it," Mr. Papp said and walked off to get it.

"I can't read Hungarian anymore," said Tommy. But by that time Mr. Papp was back with the book.

"Here you are."

Tommy didn't want to spend any money on a book he wasn't going to read, though he now felt obliged to buy it. He reached for his wallet.

"It's a gift."

"I can't. Really I can't."

"I insist."

"Thank you," he said, with hesitation.

"It's important to know your country's history, art, music, and literature, especially when you are going back as a representative of its diaspora."

Diaspora? Tommy didn't want to sound stupid so just nodded.

"You know, I wrote about you last month," Mr. Papp said.

After the team had won the championship, Mr. Papp had described Tommy as a fine, finesse player. Tommy's father carried that article in his jacket pocket and showed it to everyone he spoke to. Even if they didn't read Hungarian. But Tommy didn't know about this article. "Thank you."

"This time I wrote about you for the *Hungarian People's Sports Daily*. It's the Hungarian national sports newspaper. I mentioned that you were the captain of the Canadian university championship team that was going to Hungary to play. It will be published in a week or so. I will save a copy for your father. You will probably be the spokesman for the team since you speak Hungarian."

"He'll be thrilled, but you shouldn't have. I don't speak Hungarian very well. I don't think I would be a good spokesman. I was eight when we left."

"Well, no one else on the team speaks the language. I don't think you have a choice. And you are the captain."

"Co-captain."

"No, captain. Roberto doesn't speak Hungarian. That makes you captain. Therefore, from now on, when you come in, and I hope it's more often, we will speak only Hungarian." With that he switched to Hungarian. "And there is another book you should read." He went off and came back with it. "*The Complete Poems of Attila Josef.*"

"I can't take it, Mr. Papp."

"It's my contribution to your Hungarian education," he said, placing it in Tommy's hands. "It's important to know where you came from." He patted his hand.

Tommy went to put the books in his gym bag.

"No. Books do not belong in gym bags," he said and reached under the counter to get a bag with the store's name and Hungary's crest, the one before the hammer and sickle, the one with the cross. Tommy was anxious to leave but Mr. Papp was as anxious to keep talking.

"And you should get a haircut before you go to Hungary. You'll be representing all Hungarians in Canada. You have to look like a proper Hungarian."

Tommy looked at his watch. "I'm sorry, Mr. Papp, but I do have to go. My parents are waiting for me."

"Very well. I look forward to continuing this discussion." He had an earnest look on his face. "By the way, that was a very unfortunate accident that happened to Horvath," he said with a smile.

2 6

Tommy's bedroom walls were decorated with banners, team pictures and plaques. Most of his bookshelf was occupied by trophies: high school Athlete of the Year, basketball, volleyball, Rookie of the Year medals and his precious Canadian University championship miniature trophy. He had devoured books when he was young but wasn't much of a reader now. He read only what was assigned in school. However, since meeting Marianne and Naomi, he felt the return of the desire to read. Naomi had lent him Herman Hesse's *Siddhartha*.

Lying on his bed, flipping through *The Paul Street Boys*, he remembered fondly his mother reading the boys' adventures to him, and once he learned to read, enjoying the book on his own. Nemecsek was his favourite character.

"What are you reading?" his mother asked. She put a load of folded clothes on the dresser. His mother had a habit of just walking into his room without knocking whenever she felt like it. Whenever he objected, she would ask, "What can you be doing that you should close the door and I should knock?" She didn't think children had a right to privacy, even when they were nineteen.

"*The Paul Street Boys*. Mr. Papp gave it to me."

"We still have your copy."

"Huh?"

"Don't you remember? We brought it with us when we escaped. You insisted on it."

"No."

She left and returned with a dog-eared book.

"I remember now. I brought my soccer ball too. Did you keep that too?"

"No. You kicked it into the ocean."

"I what?"

"We were coming to Canada on the ship and you were playing soccer on the deck with some of the sailors. You kicked it and it went overboard."

Tommy laughed. "That I don't remember."

"You cried for days. Did you get this from Mr. Papp also?" she asked picking up the other book.

"Yeah. He said I needed to know more about Hungary."

The sky shuts its blue-blue eyes
The houses too shut their many eyes
Under eiderdown sleep the fields
So, you too, sleep sweetly, my darling young son.

His mother's eyes misted as she recited by heart. When she finished the poem she muttered under breath, "Rotten louse."

"What? Why is Mr. Papp a rotten louse?"

"Oh no, not him." She went silent again.

"What? Who?"

"You don't remember?"

"What?"

"You've forgotten a lot," she said shaking her head. "When you were in grade one in Hungary you were learning this poem. I helped you to memorize it. You were so proud that you knew it perfectly by heart and I was looking forward to hearing you recite it in front of your class and all the parents. But a week before the recital, your teacher, Mrs. Gombás, that rotten louse, called you a dirty little Jew and kicked you out of class. You don't remember?"

"Now I do."

"Good. Don't ever forget. They won't," she said and dropped the book on his bed. "Oh, a girl, a Naomi called and asked you to call her. She left her number. Is she Jewish? Naomi is a Jewish name."

"All is almost forgiven," Naomi said.

"Huh?"

"Why don't you come over tonight? Around eight for green pasta and green grass."

He laughed. "For sure."

As he had driven home after his fight with Marianne, he had replayed what happened. He was new to this. It was their first fight. He didn't think he had done anything wrong. He just screwed up. He had apologized but it didn't help. What could he say? What could he do? It couldn't be undone. He didn't want it to end like this. He didn't want it to end at all. Tommy wanted to talk to somebody, but he couldn't think of who. Certainly not Speedy. Or Schmutz. Guys didn't talk about stuff like this. When the guys on the team had fights with their girlfriends, it was usually about the girls not putting out. Guys usually got together in taverns and over a few beers, cursed them, called them teases and then next day, tried to make nice to get back together.

He'd parked, shut off the engine and sat there staring at the house. He couldn't remember how he had gotten home.

27

"**O**pen up, you son of a bitch!"

The three of them jumped. "Who the fuck is that?" Naomi hissed.

"It's Roberto," they said almost at the same time.

"Open up!" Speedy yelled as he banged on the door. "I know he's in there. I'll beat the shit out of him!"

"Oh, fuck." Naomi grabbed the baggie and ashtray and shoved it under the sofa. "Go away before I call the cops," Naomi shouted back.

"I'll beat the door down."

"Let him in," Marianne said.

Tommy stood up. His stomach was churning. He balled his fists. Speedy had a temper. He'd seen it flare in games. That Gypsy blood. Marianne had it too, but in her it was exciting and wonderful; in him, it was just dangerous.

"I'll kill you!" Speedy shouted as he barrelled past Naomi and rushed at Tommy.

Tommy was stoned and not sure what to do but Marianne stepped in front of Speedy like a matador. "You loco. Stop!" He raised his hand to hit her but she didn't flinch. "Loco!" she shouted again.

"You *puta!*" He shoved her aside and went for Tommy.

"Speedy, stop!" she shouted but he was already tackling Tommy, who was trying to avoid being hit by clamping Speedy's arms. They rolled around, banging into the furniture, bunching up the carpet and knocking over a lamp.

"Fucking stop it!" Naomi screamed. "This is my place and I'm telling you animals to fucking stop it!"

Marianne and Naomi grabbed at them and tried to pull them apart. Marianne had Speedy's collar, while Naomi was on her knees between the boys pushing Tommy away. Reluctantly they got to their feet and stood glaring at each other. Speedy was ready to go at it again.

"Who the fuck do you think you are, barging in like this? The cops?" Naomi screamed at Speedy.

"I'm her brother and I'm protecting my sister."

She was pushing him toward the door. "No, you're not. You're being an asshole."

"It's not your business. This is family."

"Bullshit."

"You fucker!" Speedy spat at Tommy.

"You pig!" Naomi said and slapped him. He stared at her. Though she was much smaller, she didn't seem intimidated.

"Papa's gonna kill you. Mama is going to claw your eyes out."

Marianne stared back at him, saying nothing.

"Why did you do this to my family? You bastard son of a bitch," he shouted at Tommy.

Tommy wiped his face. "I love her."

They all looked at him. He was surprised too.

"Bullshit. You're just saying that so you can screw this *puta*," Speedy shouted.

"Fuck you!" Tommy shouted back.

"You couldn't find one of your own kind to fuck?"

"Out, you pig, or I'll call the cops," Naomi said and picked up the phone.

He hesitated. "Let's go," he yelled at Marianne.

"No!"

He glared at the three of them with murder in his eyes. "We're not finished," he growled and left, slamming the door.

No one said a word. Naomi got the broom and dustpan and swept up pieces of the lamp.

"Shit!" Marianne said, sitting down. She was shaking. "Shit! Shit! Shit!" she repeated over and over again. She began to cry. Naomi went over to the couch and cradled her. Tommy had never seen her cry. He felt angry and helpless.

"They're going to kill me for sure. I'm gonna get kicked out."

"No, they won't. And if they do, you can move in with me," Naomi said, trying to comfort her.

"Are your parents that old-fashioned?" Tommy asked.

"And yours? Are they so modern?" she snapped back at him. He was silent. "No. You're right."

"But because you're a guy it's not such a big deal. You'll just get the usual 'don't get her pregnant' speech. Have fun but don't be serious 'cause she's a shiksa," Marianne said.

"But I mean it," Tommy whispered.

"What?"

"That I love you."

Marianne gathered her stuff. "I better go."

Tommy's parents were in the kitchen waiting for him. He had hardly got in the door when his mother started in on him. "What's the matter with you? Why did you lie to us? Why did you tell us that you were going to be with Speedy and Naomi? Speedy called looking for you. What's happening to you? Who is this Naomi?"

"We're just friends."

"I told you before, a boy and a girl can't be just friends."

"But that's what we are." He paused and took a deep breath. "I like Marianne."

"Speedy's sister?"

"Yes."

"You see? I told you boys and girls can't be friends. And she's not Jewish."

"Tell me something I don't know."

"Don't be a smart alex," his father said and poured himself a glass of soda water. He always drank Eskimo soda water when he was upset. He said the bubbles settled his stomach.

"I'm not being a smart aleck. And it doesn't matter to me if she's not Jewish."

"It matters to me," his mother shouted.

"I know and that's why I didn't tell you."

"You're not serious, are you?"

"I just started seeing her, but I like her a lot."

"Does her family know?"

"No."

"Why not?"

"She didn't tell them for the same reason I didn't tell you."

"See? This is nothing but trouble."

"Not for us."

"You'll see. The first time you have a fight, she'll call you a dirty Jew."

"No, she won't! She's not like that."

"They're all like that. The whole world is. Didn't you see what happened in Israel? Just you wait. Aren't there enough nice Jewish girls in Canada? We didn't come all this way for you to be with a shiksa. I don't want you to see her."

"I want to. I will." He stomped off to his room and slammed the door. He pressed his fingers against his scar. His head was pounding.

2 8

It had been a couple of weeks since Tommy's fight with Speedy. He called Marianne at work every day to see how she was doing.

"The shit hasn't hit the fan yet. I don't know what he's waiting for."

"He's not talking to me," Tommy said.

"Me neither."

"Maybe he's waiting for you to make the first move."

There was silence on the other end.

"I want to see you." Still nothing. "Want to go to Expo on Sunday?"

After a long pause, she spoke. "Yeah," she said, as though she had made up her mind about something.

He felt relieved. "Great. I'll meet you at the Berri métro at ten."

"Yeah! Sounds good," she said with more enthusiasm.

Tommy's parents had bought him an Expo passport as a graduation present. Though he had only completed his second year, for them each year passed was a graduation. No one in the family had ever finished high school. In their eyes, a learned man was a somebody. "It's also something you can take with you if you have to flee," his father often said.

His parents' education stopped with the war. When she talked about it, his mother said, "We went to a different school and got a different kind of education."

Tommy guessed, by his mother's math skills, and her passion for literature, that she was the one who would have done well.

But after the war, a job was more essential than an education. She got one as a bookkeeper even though she had never had any training or experience. She learned quickly and by the end of the year, after her boss was arrested for having been a Nazi sympathizer, she was made head bookkeeper.

In their business here in Canada, she was the one who kept the books, handled the payroll and paid the suppliers. Saturday nights, while Tommy and his father were watching hockey, she would be in the kitchen working on the books and keeping an eye on the simmering soup and roasting meat; the meals for the week.

She was also the handyman. Whenever she had to call a repairman to fix one of the sewing machines, she would watch how he did it. After that, she was able to do the repair herself. Better in my pocket than his, was her motto.

His father was more of a people person. He wasn't interested in the running of the factory. He did the pickups and deliveries, negotiated prices and collected payments. "Always pick up on Mondays," he repeatedly advised Tommy whenever they made a delivery. "Monday people are fresh, so they help you more. You can get the shippers to have the load ready, hold the elevator and help load the van. Of course, it helps that I give those goyims five dollars every week. Always deliver on Thursday with the bill in your hand. And never unload until the cheque is in your hand. This way you have Friday to deposit the money. If you deliver on Friday, they'll tell you that they're busy and come back Monday. By Monday they could be bankrupt. Better in my bank than theirs." And it wasn't only practical advice that he dispensed. "Always be on first-name basis with the bookkeeper. Have a compliment ready for her, even if she's so ugly that she would scare off the Antichrist."

Tommy's father was a great wheeler-dealer. Tommy had often witnessed him haggle for a half hour for a couple of pennies over the price of a jacket. His father's adversaries were pretty good at it too, but his father was better, and he usually got the price his mother told him to get.

His tactics included charm, wit and self-deprecation. He had even used Tommy on occasion. Arms around his son, his father would declare that if he didn't get his price, he wouldn't be able to send his son to college.

"You never know, my wonderful son here might be your lawyer, doctor or accountant someday." He chose the profession just a notch below the other person's child. "Don't you want to feel that you contributed to your family's well-being? You'd be doing a mitzvah for yourself."

His opponents appreciated the struggle for the betterment of their children's lives, so with a sigh, a smile and a shrug they usually agreed to his price.

"Haggling is like fishing." his father always said after one of these encounters. "To catch a fish you gotta give it something. So, I give them a good spiel and make them feel superior. I learned in Mauthausen that winning was surviving. Losing could mean death."

Tommy felt uncomfortable watching his father in action. Tommy knew that he didn't have the same skill or the hunger or the killer instinct his father had. He didn't see the bargaining as life or death. He didn't like the paperwork side of the business either. On the other hand, he did like operating the buttonhole and button machines. But his parents wouldn't allow him to be just a machine operator. They expected him to take over the business. To be the boss. He didn't want to and had already made up his mind to transfer out of Commerce into something else, though he didn't know what. He knew this would be another big hurt in a growing list of hurts.

Tommy spotted Marianne walking towards him. It was always her hair he noticed first, how it glistened and cascaded. It had an undulating motion that hypnotized him. She was wearing a long-sleeved, tie-dyed blouse and her poetry night full-length skirt, the one he had unhooked, unzipped and slipped over her hips. The memory brought a smile to his face.

Maid Marianne, he said to himself and embraced her. When she squeezed him back he felt relieved. When they kissed, he was elated.

She looked him up and down. "Jeans and T-shirt? What happened to the chinos-button-down-shirt-and-tie man?"

"Too uptight. Left him at home," he said.

"Ahh. Cool."

"So, what are you doing here?" she asked.

He picked up on her playfulness. "I'm off to the World's Fair with my girlfriend."

"Ah, and, where is she?" she said looking around.

"She's coming soon."

Marianne burst out laughing. "Oh, is she now?"

"I hope so."

"Well, can I hang out with you till she shows up?"

"*Sí, Señorita.*"

"Won't she be jealous?"

"I hope so. She's wonderfully dangerous when aroused," he said. He reached for her hand as they entered the station.

The escalators took them down six storeys into a massive underground maze. It was bright as day with an arched ceiling and highway-sized walkways that crossed over the gleaming rails. The echo of the crowd and whoosh of trains bouncing off the walls filled the place with endless sound. He felt like an ant among thousands of ants. Though the métro had been completed a couple of months earlier, he had never ridden it. He preferred being above ground.

The sky-blue métro cars were packed. He didn't like crowded trains and wanted to wait for the next one, but Marianne yanked him in. The train started with a jerk, then quickly picked up speed. It sped through a long tunnel that was not only worming itself underground but also under the St. Lawrence River. The air was damp. He felt a tightening in his chest that gave him trouble breathing. Tommy gripped Marianne's hand. He was desperate to get out.

"Ouch," she said and squeezed back.

"Sorry." He eased up but held her hand firmly until the subway rolled into the station.

A *Montreal Welcomes the World* banner greeted the visitors. It was like they had entered another world, the world of tomorrow. An inverted pyramid, a geodesic dome, spirals, cubes, octagonal shapes and a myriad of colours exploded out of the ground. And he was with Marianne.

The long lines for the popular pavilions were trips around the world. People, speaking all sorts of languages, were talking, gesturing and smiling at each other.

"What was that about?" Marianne asked.

"What?"

"The hand crushing."

"Sorry. Nothing really. It's a long story."

"We got time. This lineup is forever."

He was quiet for a moment. He didn't want Marianne to think he was a scaredy-cat. She waited.

"When I was a young kid in Hungary, I used to have dreams about being in underground mazes. I used to love those dreams but at one point, they turned into nightmares of being chased by growling boots with spikey teeth."

"Weird. We'll have to get Dr. Jung to work on that," she said, reaching for his hand. The room darkened.

The 360-degree screen in the Bell Pavilion lit up. The blue sky everywhere made him feel like he was in the air flying. It gave him vertigo and made him dizzy. His knees went weak as he soared through the snow-capped Rockies, swooped low over the wheat-blond fields of the Prairies, over the enormously loud cascading Niagara Falls, over the evergreen forests of Ontario, down the ice of the Montreal Forum, home of the Rocket, and out over the ocean to Newfoundland. When the lights came back on, he turned away from Marianne and took a deep breath. He wanted to make sure that she didn't catch his tenseness. One uptight moment was enough for one date. He didn't want to come off as a total chicken.

"Wow! What a trip. What kind of acid were those filmmakers on? I want some of that," Marianne said once they were outside.

"Yeah," he said halfheartedly.

"Let's go on the monorail."

"This is the future," she said as they snaked above the crowd. She waved her arms like a graceful, colourful, magical bird entering the American geodesic dome while he gripped the handle of the car.

"Dy-na-mite!" she cried out.

"Look!" He pointed to a charred and scorched bell-shaped space capsule.

"Looks so small."

"It's still amazing that a person was in space. To go where no man has gone before."

"Are you one of those *Star Trek* freaks?"

He made the V-fingered Spock salute and smiled.

"So how come you're not crazy about heights?"

He said nothing. They rode in silence.

"Nothing about Viet Nam," she said after they were out.

"Why should there be?"

"They're over there fighting an illegal war."

"This is a place about people coming together, not about wars," he said.

"Oh, yeah. Forgot. Disneyland."

He hooked his arms into hers. "Okay, Comradess, we go to Russia," he said with a Russian accent. "We become Communists. Okay, Comradess?"

"Huh?"

He pointed to the giant hammer-and-sickle sculpture facing the American pavilion from across the artificial river. It fronted a solid rectangular building with a ski-jump-sloped roof. They walked across the bridge. A *Fiftieth Anniversary of Glorious Russian Revolution* sign greeted the visitors.

"Da!" she said.

"Everything is big. Russia is big," he said. "See, Comradess Natasha," Tommy continued in his Russian voice. "America have space capsule, great Russian people have space capsule too."

"*Da*, Comrade Boris Badinov. Imagine what it must have been like. The first man in space."

"I'd be scared shitless," Tommy confessed.

"I don't see you as a person who gets scared. Except in tunnels," she said with a smile. "And at heights."

How did she know that?

"Have you ever flown?" she asked.

"No."

"So, how do you know you'd be scared shitless?"

"I just know."

"So how are you getting to Hungary?" she asked as they strolled through the pavilion. "Gonna swim?"

"No, walk."

"Jesus, eh?" She chuckled.

"Well, he did start out as a nice Jewish boy."

"Are you?"

"But you have to admit there is something unnatural about being thousands of feet up in the sky, in a metal tube. It defies gravity, the natural order of things."

She squeezed his hand hard. "Lots of things do. But imagine being higher than the birds. Flying free, like in the movie." She waved her hands again, and again she was a graceful, colourful, magical bird.

"Now that we've seen the world, let's go for a hot dog," he said.

"*Nein*," she said. "I want a bratwurst. "

"How you feeling?" he asked as they sat on the grass munching Polish sausages.

"Great," she said.

"I don't mean this, I mean..."

"Oh."

"Yeah."

"Well, like I told you, Speedy isn't speaking to me and he hasn't told our parents."

"What's he waiting for?"

"Maybe it's his way of punishing me. Maybe he's waiting till he comes back from Hungary. Speaking of which, my father says that if you guys continue playing the way you're playing, you're going to get creamed."

"Yeah, my father says the same thing. He says they're going to make goulash out of us."

"Maybe you guys should talk."

"Speedy doesn't want to talk. He wants to kill me."

"Maybe we should break up," she said.

He looked at her in disbelief. "Are you ending it?"

"Until you come back from Hungary, I mean."

"No!"

"Okay, then I won't. Don't be scared." She leaned over and gave him a soft kiss.

29

Tommy wanted to skip practice. He was even thinking of quitting. He didn't like confrontations. He didn't mind the physical kind, the shove and push in a game, or the goading, but even there, he would rather avoid them. Though he had to admit that getting Horvath in the nuts and getting the goalie to lose his cool had felt pretty good. Revenge gave him a rush.

Confrontations with family and friends were new to him. The vibes of hate he got from Speedy and his own anger towards him made Tommy anxious. It was more than personal. He both wanted and didn't want to hate him, so he withdrew.

Speedy wasn't in the dressing room when Tommy got to practice. He was both relieved and worried. Speedy was usually one of the first ones in. Everything about Speedy was speedy.

"Where's Speedy?" Schmutz asked, half-dressed.

"How should I know?" Tommy snapped. Why did this boy-girl business have to be so hard? He liked Marianne and she liked him. He had even said he loved her though he had to admit he wasn't completely sure what that was. Everyone was tossing the word around these days, including himself. Peace and love, free love and "Love Is All You Need." He knew he felt great around her even if he couldn't always figure out why. Sometimes it was her scent, sometimes it was what she did, sometimes the way she pushed him. Maybe you weren't supposed to understand. He had read poets who had great difficulty with it and rhapsodized about it. He knew that Marianne made him horny, but she also made him think.

"What's going on between you and Speedy?" Schmutz said.

"Nothing," Tommy said, and finished lacing his cleats. The first practice after their fight was not pretty. Not only did they not talk to each other, but they almost came to blows.

Speedy came in and gave Tommy a hard look, sat on the bench opposite him and began to change. Tommy got up to leave.

"Hey, wait for Speedy!" Schmutz said. It was their ritual to leave the locker room together. Schmutz stared at both of them as Tommy headed for the door. "What's going on?"

Coach Hus was usually first on the field. He'd run a few laps and do his stretches before the boys showed up. Today he was sitting cross-legged with his eyes closed. He looked like Buddha, without the belly. Tommy had never seen him do that before. The boys approached him in silence, not knowing what to make of the scene.

Coach Hus opened his eyes, and told them to sit. "Something is wrong." He said it very quietly. "We haven't been playing well. We're lacking what got us the championship. We have to get it back. Our passes, our coverage, our support for each other and communication is non-existent. We aren't in sync; we aren't playing as one."

Everybody had picked up on the strain between Tommy and Speedy. As a result, everybody was tense. They were making basic mistakes and yelling at each other. When practice finished the coach called out to Schmutz. "I want to talk to you."

"What did I do, Coach?"

"Let's go for a beer," Schmutz said to the two after they dressed and were outside.

"No!" they said almost simultaneously.

"Well, at least you two agree on that. No choice. Coach Hus's orders. I'm not joking. Let's go to Toe's."

Toe's Tavern was famous for cheap beer and for not asking for IDs. It was owned by the legendary coach of the Montreal Canadiens, who sometimes showed up and served the beer. Even a couple of the Habs were known to drop in from time to time. It was where jocks, the unemployed and veterans hung out.

Schmutz wasted no time. As soon as they sat down, he said, "So, what the fuck is up with you two?"

Speedy and Tommy just glared at each other.

"You two had a lovers' quarrel?"

"None of your business," Speedy said.

"Yes it is, 'cause it's affecting the team."

"He doesn't want me to date his sister," Tommy blurted out.

"You got the hots for Marianne?"

Speedy gave Schmutz a dirty look. "Shut your face, Schmutz. Don't talk about my sister like that."

"Yeah, I like her and she likes me."

"So, what's the problem?"

"I'm Jewish and she's not."

"So?"

"So, ask *him.*"

"So?"

"We're Catholics and he's Jewish."

"My mother's Protestant and my father's Catholic. Big fucking deal," Schmutz said and signalled the waiter for three more beers.

"It's not the same."

"Why not?"

"Because."

"Because why?"

"It's also about honour and reputation."

"Whose?"

"The girl's and her family's."

"I respect her," Tommy said. "And I really like her. I wouldn't take advantage of her. Besides, she's old enough to make up her own mind. One thing I know about your sister is that she's got a mind of her own."

"But that's not what's on *your* mind. Is it, Wolfie?"

"Fuck you," Tommy said, balling his hand into fists.

"You don't want to do that," Schmutz said as he meticulously peeled the label off his bottle.

"What?" Tommy asked.

"You don't want to fuck Speedy."

Tommy almost burst out laughing.

"Fuck you," Speedy shouted at Schmutz.

"Shh. Not here, darling," Schmutz said.

Like a dog with a bone, Speedy turned back to Tommy. "If she's got a mind of her own, why doesn't she see that it's stupid?"

"Why is it stupid?"

"Because it's not right. And my parents would go crazy."

"You haven't told them?"

"Are you crazy? My dad would kill both of you."

"I thought they liked me."

"Yeah, but not that way."

"What way?"

"Boyfriend way."

"Who would they like? Schmutz?"

"No, some nice Spanish Catholic boy."

"And when you said that I should fuck my kind of people, who did you mean?"

"Hungarians."

"You sure you didn't mean Jews?"

Speedy averted his eyes, then nodded.

He regarded Speedy not only with anger but curiosity. He wondered if this was how their friendship would end. Was this where an old truth raised its ugly head? Was this how his father felt when his goyim friends watched him being marched off to the cattle cars to be shipped to Mauthausen? His mother was right. But about the wrong Gonzales. Or would she think it too? He was sure she wouldn't.

"What's wrong with Jews?" Tommy asked.

Speedy said nothing for a while. The silence was louder than the loud talk in the tavern.

"Nothing," he said.

Tommy took a long swig. "I told my parents," he said.

Speedy was surprised. "What did they say?"

Tommy took a deep breath. "My mother said that Marianne would call me a dirty Jew the first time we had a fight. They're as afraid, if not more, of me dating a shiksa as your parents are of her dating a Jew-boy."

"What's a *shikass*?" Speedy asked.

"A shiksa. That's a non-Jewish girl, you schmuck," Schmutz said.

"What?" Speedy said.

Tommy laughed. "It's a not-nice name for a non-Jewish girl. Jews don't trust non-Jews. Especially after the last war. Can you blame us?" He paused briefly. "My parents were betrayed by their countrymen and deported to concentration camps just because they were Jews. My mother's mother and younger sister were gassed."

"Holy shit."

Tommy and Speedy eyed each other. The silence became a bridge.

"From what they told me, our family was also persecuted under Franco because we had Gypsy blood. And the other side didn't like us that much either."

"Maybe you guys are related?" Schmutz smiled.

"Well, my mother told me that because she didn't have enough milk I was breastfed by a Gypsy. I don't have Gypsy blood, but I do have Gypsy milk in me. Does that help?"

Speedy gave him a weak smile. Schmutz signalled the waiter. "How about we get more Canadian beer in us?"

30

Slowly the team's chemistry returned. Tommy and Speedy were in sync again, most of the time. Anticipating each other's moves became almost natural again. The spirit of the team picked up. And although Tommy and Speedy didn't hang out after practices, they didn't let that distance interfere with their game. They needed each other to succeed, for the team to succeed, and the team picked up on it. They won their next four games and were in third place. Coach Hustle's yelling was back to his usual pitch. The frustration was gone. Practice now focused on their upcoming games in Hungary.

"We need some sort of advantage over them," Coach Hus told them at the start of practice. "Hustle is one."

"Wolfie told me that they love the Beatles but can't get any of their records. We could bring a few LPs and trade them for goals," Schmutz joked.

"My cousin from Moscow is always asking me for jeans," said Ivan. "Maybe we can bribe them with some."

"My parents send jeans to my cousin too," Tommy said. "I can threaten to cut off his supply unless he lets in a few goals."

"Okay. Enough with the joking," Coach Hus said. "I wish we could find out what kind of system they play."

"Maybe I can," Tommy said.

"How?"

"Let me talk to someone. I'm not promising anything."

"Okay, till then, we hustle and strengthen teamwork." Coach Hustle blew his whistle to start practice.

Tommy showed up at Mr. Papp's store a half hour before closing so there wouldn't be too many customers and Mr. Papp would have time to talk, but not for too long. Mr. Papp liked to talk. He spoke a much more refined Hungarian than Tommy's parents, forcing him to listen more carefully. Mr. Papp was from Budapest and had gone to university. His phrasings were more complex, and sometimes Tommy had trouble following what he said. He didn't mix English and Hungarian. And he spoke softly, forcing people to lean in to hear him.

The bell above the door tinkled as he entered. Mr. Papp was dusting his books before drawing the curtains across the shelves.

"Nice to see you, Tamás. I have your parents' magazines ready." Mr. Papp always called him by his Hungarian name. "One's name is one's heirloom, one should value it. It is one's calling card, it should not be sullied by misuse," he was fond of saying.

"Thank you," Tommy said and paid for the magazines. "I was wondering if you could help me? Well, actually our team."

"How may I help you and your team?"

"Would you know how we could find out something about the Debrecen team? Like, how they play, defensively and offensively? I mean their system, who their star players are and what positions they play. Stuff like that."

"Stuff like that? Tamás, you have to be more careful with the way you use language. Words are precious. People have been celebrated for their brilliant use of them. They're also weapons. People have been imprisoned for their words and many have died because of them."

Uncertain of what he was going on about, Tommy clammed up. He didn't want to say something stupid or something that would set Mr. Papp off on another tangent. He was here for soccer information, not a history or a language lesson.

"Have you read the books I gave you?"

"I've started to but it's slow going because of my poor Hungarian. And I haven't had much time. Too busy with work, practice and games."

"One can never be too busy to read. But yes, I noticed that the team is playing well again. What happened?"

"We hit a rough patch and weren't playing like a team. We seem to be back on track now." Tommy didn't want to get into the whole story.

"My boy," he said taking Tommy's hand in both of his, "in spite of your clichés, I will try to get you some information. By the way, I want to give you this." He went to the record shelf and took down an album.

"Mr. Papp, I can't take this," he said.

"It's my ongoing contribution to your education. You will not always be a soccer player."

"Thank you," he said. It was Gypsy music. More to his father's taste. "I have to go; my parents are expecting me."

"You are a fine young man," Mr. Papp said as he shook his hand. "I will call you when I have the information you and your team seek."

"Thank you." He left quickly. Only a block later did he realize he was going the wrong way.

Tommy took the bus to Naomi's. He was anxious to see Marianne. He hadn't seen her since their day at Expo.

They'd been keeping their relationship low key, not wanting to upset his parents or get Speedy riled up again. Speedy seemed to have grudgingly accepted it. Tommy's parents were aware of their relationship and although he knew they were hurt, there were no shouting matches or ultimatums. He knew it wasn't just about him dating a shiksa. It was about what they had been through. And the family members who had died. Were their deaths for nothing? He felt guilty, but it didn't stop him wanting to be with Marianne. He didn't think it was wrong or a problem. His mother was always going on about girls with loose morals every chance she got. He couldn't convince her that times were different. Women should be equal to men, Naomi was constantly lecturing him. If women are to have equality then they should have it all the way, and that includes control of their bodies. Recently she pinned a bumper sticker on her bedroom door that read *Women equal to men? Why aim so low?*

The argument sounded so much better coming from Naomi. Maybe because she was a woman. His mother didn't believe in women's liberation, even though Tommy thought she was liberated. She ran a business and made most of the business and household decisions but still believed that men and women each had their traditional roles and should behave accordingly. Yet she was the one who took her box of tools and crawled under the sewing machines to repair them.

They had Naomi's apartment to themselves until ten. The anticipation was almost as arousing as when he actually was with her. Just thinking about her got him hard. They'd had sex only twice, but his imagination got him off when she wasn't around. God, girls can really get you horny. Thank God, he said to himself.

He was hardly in the door when he reached for her.

"Slow down." She pushed him away.

"What's wrong?" he asked.

"Nothing, just slow down," she said. "I'm not just a piece of meat to be devoured by a wolf."

Though she smiled, he felt something was off. "How was your day?" he asked.

"A long day of blood sucking."

"Did you know that the guy who played Dracula is Hungarian, Béla Lugosi?"

"No, I didn't. Are you related?"

"Yes," he said and bared his teeth.

She made a cross with her fingers.

"It won't help," he said. "I'm Jewish. Remember?"

"Yes, I do," she said in a serious voice.

They sat on the couch. There were two glasses of wine on the coffee table.

"I see you brought some of their blood home with you."

She smiled but in a nervous way. "I have something to say."

His stomach started to churn.

"You remember what you said during the fight with Speedy?"

"I said a lot of things," he said, trying to figure out what was coming.

"No," she said, wearing a serious expression.

"About loving you?"

"Yeah."

"Yeah. Do you remember what I said?"

He tried but couldn't. "No." He said wondering if he had screwed up again.

"That's because I didn't say anything. I didn't say 'I love you' back. It's been bugging me ever since."

He didn't dare say anything, afraid of what was coming next.

"Well, I think I didn't say anything because I was shocked. It came out of the blue and I thought you said it because you felt that you had to."

"I wasn't thinking, I just said it."

"How did you feel it? What did you feel?"

He tried to remember. He sipped his wine. "There's a Hungarian drink called *pálinka*. It's a kind of schnapps that you drink in one gulp, I don't know what you call it in English."

"A shot."

"What?"

"It's called a shot."

"Oh. Okay. You drink the shot. At first you feel nothing, then it hits you like an explosion that takes your breath away and then your eyes start to water, and then something starts to seep into you, you start to feel a warmth spread all over. The Hungarians say that you become a man when you take your first shot of *pálinka*. That's what I felt."

She stared mutely.

"What's going on?" he asked.

"That's a big thing to say," she said. "And I can't say it."

Here it comes, he thought. She pulled out a joint. She lit up and took a deep drag and passed it over. He took a small toke and sipped some wine to help it go down smoothly.

She leaned in and pretended to be a vampire. "I vant to suck your blaaad." She nipped Tommy's neck.

"Ouch!" he yelped.

"Now you viilll become one of us," she said in her vampire accent.

"Who are the us?"

"We are the unsure and the afraid," she continued in her own voice.

He couldn't imagine her unsure and afraid. "What's going on?"

"I don't know," she said. "I like being with you, but I also like being by myself, free to be me."

"And you can't be free with me?"

"Nobody can be totally free to be themselves in a relationship."

They sat quietly.

"Here, I drink your blood." He toasted her in his best Béla Lugosian.

"And I yours."

He leaned over and with his tongue brushed her moist lips. They tasted of sweet wine and grass. He set down his glass and stood. He reached out to her. She rose to meet him.

"We're here and now and that's enough for me," he lied.

Marianne stroked his face. He liked the feel of her nails on his skin. A hint of her strength, a hint of danger.

Her nail traced the scar behind his ear. "How did you get that?"

"A dog bit me."

"What? Are you serious?" She pushed him back to see if he was kidding. The candlelight in the room made it hard to see.

"Yeah. But it wasn't his fault."

"What do you mean?"

"I was seven. I antagonized him. There were lots of dogs in Békes. Most of them were friendly and were free to roam the streets. Somehow, I got hold of a roll of film and I started to wind it around the tail of one of them. At one point, it got too tight and he leapt backwards and bit my ear."

"Shit, that's funny," Marianne said and started to stroke him again. "And this?" she asked when she touched the scar on his forehead that gave him a brooding look.

"That? I got shot in the head," Tommy said.

"What?"

"That's a story for another time." He said reached out for her.

They were fast asleep when Naomi showed up. "Hey, you lazy lovers," she called. "Up and at 'em." Or were you already up and at 'em?"

They emerged a few minutes later, dishevelled and grinning. Naomi was sitting on the couch, sipping wine and toking. She passed the joint to Marianne.

"What's this?" Naomi asked, turning the album over in her hand.

"Oh. Mr. Papp, the Hungarian bookstore owner, gave it to me. He told me, to use his words, 'your Hungarian education is lacking.' He keeps giving me stuff, like books and records. He thinks I need to know stuff for when I go to Hungary."

"Sándor Lakatos, *Budapest Éjjel*,"Naomi tried but mangled the words. "What's that? Sándor and Budapest is all I can make out of that."

Marianne passed him the joint. He took a toke and held it. Tommy corrected her pronunciation after he exhaled. "A man's name is his calling card; it should be treated with respect."

"What?" Naomi said.

"Another one of his lessons. The title means Budapest Nights."

"Let's give Budapest Nights a Montreal listen then." Naomi tore off the plastic wrapping. "Who's Sándor Lakatos?" she asked, emphasizing the 'sh' of the 's' letters.

"Who knows?"

"So, Mr. Papp is right, you are lacking. Sándor Lakatos, 1924, an educated Gypsy based in Budapest, is a fifth-generation descendant of the Bihari clan and leads one of the finest traditional urban Gypsy orchestras," Naomi read from the back of the album cover. Marianne put the record on. They leaned back and closed their eyes.

The piece began with dramatic violin strokes followed by slow, melancholic lamentation. Tommy's father played this kind of music all the time except it was Yiddish. Tommy had no interest in them. He had preferred the pop songs on the radio. But since smoking grass and listening to Naomi's records, he'd begun to listen a different way. The music on the radio sounded superficial, simple and vapid now.

The music filling the room was heartbreaking. For the first time he understood why his father loved it. It was about loss. And Tommy's parents certainly knew that well. His parents had lost most of their family in the concentration camps and then the life they had pieced together after the war. Maybe it was a kind of balm that soothed the deep pain.

The lamentation became the sound of sparrows. Then a manic rhythm followed. The music alternated between sadness and joy. When it was slow, it made you yearn and when it went manic, it made you want to dance. He opened his eyes and there was Marianne, dancing. One minute she was swaying and the next, doing her fast flamenco moves. He and Naomi watched her weave about the room, swinging her skirt like a matador cape. Tommy rose, raised his index fingers to his head and pretended to be a bull, charging. She sidestepped and swung her dress to let him pass. He charged again and again she let him pass. He charged once more but this time, he grabbed her by the waist and started to do a kind of *csárdás* that he had seen his parents dance at

Bar Mitzvahs. Except he was doing it at breakneck speed. When the music slowed again, he held her close and they hardly moved. Then the music picked up speed and Naomi joined them. They held hands and circled wildly. They were children again.

3 1

"**C**ome by my apartment at seven and I will tell you all that I have learned." Mr. Papp gave Tommy his address.

"I don't want to disturb your evening," Tommy said. "I can come by the store."

"No. The store always has people coming and going and I won't have time to talk. I'll see you tomorrow night."

"I have practice till eight."

"Actually better," Mr. Papp said.

Mr. Papp lived a short distance from his store. Classical music was playing when Tommy entered the small second-floor apartment. Mr. Papp was dressed as formally as he was in his store. But instead of his indigo lab coat, he had on a dark velvet smoking jacket and in place of his bow tie he sported an ascot. His apartment was as meticulously organized and as neatly kept as his store. A floor-to-ceiling bookshelf covered one of the living room walls. Against the other were a dresser-sized stereo cabinet and a record shelf. Everywhere there were paintings of Hussars. One depicted them in colourful traditional costumes on horseback dashing across the plains; another, in a fierce a battle; and another, relaxing in a tavern smoking long-stemmed pipes. Above the record player was a portrait in profile of a man who looked like a Hussar chief. He had shoulder-length hair, an aquiline nose and a distant serious stare.

"It's *his* music on the stereo," said Mr. Papp pointing at the portrait. "Beautiful, isn't it? Liszt's Hungarian Rhapsody number 2."

Tommy listened. It went from slow and simple to fast and toe-tapping, a bit like the Gypsy music he had listened to at Naomi's. Not really knowing much about classical music, he said yes to be polite.

"He captures the soul of our people, melancholy and proud. Tamás, please sit." He pointed to a purplish, corduroy armchair.

Tommy hesitated. It wasn't covered in plastic. "I just came from practice and I'm a bit sweaty. I don't want to mess up your nice chair."

"Would you like to take a shower?"

He was taken aback by the offer. "Thank you, but I didn't bring clean clothes, so I'll wait till I get home," he said.

"All right then. Sit."

Mr. Papp brought out plates of cheese, sliced green peppers, salami and bread. He poured both of them red wine in crystal glasses. Tommy had never been in an adult's house as a guest. He usually went to adults' homes with his parents and was treated like their child. This felt strange. It felt grown up.

"Bull's Blood," Mr. Papp said.

"Huh?" Tommy looked at him in surprise.

"The wine is Hungarian. It is called Bull's Blood."

"Oh."

"Now swirl it gently and sniff it. Like this."

He had seen actors like David Niven swirl and sniff their glasses of wine and say something about bouquet or body but Tommy didn't know what that meant. Mr. Papp watched him swirl and sniff the way a teacher might watch a student answer a question. The wine had a sharp smell.

"Now taste it. Don't take a big gulp, just a little, like this," he said and took a small sip. "Like a sophisticated Natalie Wood." Tommy followed suit. "What do you think?"

Tommy didn't know what to say. He found it a bit acidy. "It's good."

"It's robust. Now eat. You must be hungry after practice." He filled Tommy's plate.

"Yeah. Coach Hus worked us hard."

"From what I hear, and when I watch you boys play, I get the feeling he isn't the most knowledgeable coach. 'Hustle' seems to be his only instruction."

Tommy got defensive. "He coached us to the Canadian University championship."

"Yes, but that's because individually, you boys are very good and luckily you play well together. Until that recent rough patch. I think the team is good in spite of him, not because of him."

Although what Mr. Papp was saying was probably true, Tommy didn't like him putting down his coach. "We're playing well again thanks to him."

"Does he know anything about total soccer?" Mr. Papp asked.

Tommy hesitated. "I don't think so."

"It looks like you don't either. You should study the game, not just play it. Playing is fine but knowing something about the game is as important. It makes you a better player. Did you know that soccer was invented by the Chinese about 5000 BC? It is believed that the game was brought to England by the Romans about 50 BC. And there is record of a game like soccer being played in England around 800 A.D. Supposedly, they used the head of a Viking."

"That's gross! I didn't know that," Tommy said sipping his wine.

"You should," Mr. Papp said firmly.

"Did you find out anything about Debrecen?"

"Yes," Mr. Papp said, leaning close as if revealing a great secret. "They play a style, which your coach should be familiar with, but obviously isn't, called total soccer. It's a style in which any player, except the goalie of course, can take over the role of any other player on a team. It was invented by Rinus Michels, who was the coach of the Netherlands national team."

"What's special about it?"

"Total soccer's success depends on each player being able to quickly switch positions depending on the situation. Players have to be comfortable in multiple positions. It depends on high technical and physical skills."

Tommy listened. As Mr. Papp went on, he had a sinking feeling that they were going to be creamed.

"Hungary, of course, also had a big role creating total soccer in the 1950s. The Communist Party of Hungary, as part of their collectivization plan, gathered all the best players in the league, and put them on one team, Honvéd, that dominated the league. They also became The Mighty Magyars that dominated international soccer. It was because of the best playing together all the time and playing total soccer. Of course, having Puskás made them the best," Mr. Papp said.

"I loved that team, especially Puskás."

"He was special. All of the Debrecen players are good, which is to be expected," Mr. Papp said. "But they do have two stars who will probably play in the first division in a couple of years."

"Who?" Tommy asked, though he knew who one of them might be.

"András Könyves, their left inside, but with total soccer he plays everywhere on the field. He does tend to favour hanging around centre field on the right side. He has an advantage there because of his left foot. The defence tends to forget about it. Also, he's tough."

"And the other is their goalie Gábor Földember with his Grosics-like leaps," Tommy said.

"How do you know this?" Mr. Papp asked, surprised.

Tommy smiled. "He's my cousin. We lived together until my family escaped."

"That is amazing, my boy," Mr. Papp said, placing his hands on Tommy's. They felt warm and soft. "That's definitely worth an article in the Hungarian newspaper."

Tommy looked at his watch. "Well, thanks for your information. I better go now."

"No, you must stay," Mr. Papp said holding onto his hands. "I want to know all about this."

"It's getting late and I have to work tomorrow, and my parents get worried when I stay out late."

"Call them and tell them you won't be too late. I really do need to hear this story."

Tommy's mother answered the phone. He had told his parents that he was going to get some information about the Debrecen team from Mr. Papp but when he told his mother that he was at Mr. Papp's house, she shouted, "Get home right now!"

"I won't be too long," he said.

"No. Now!" she commanded in her no-argument voice.

"I have to go now, Mr. Papp. My mother insists. I have to get up at six."

"Very well. Mothers must be obeyed." He smiled. "But you have to tell me the rest before you go to Hungary so I can write about it." He clasped Tommy's hand with both of his. His eyes had a sadness in them. He seemed lonely.

"I will. I'll come by the store soon. Thanks for all this information and the food and wine. I guess we have a lot of work to do."

"Yes, you do."

3 2

"Shit, I shouldn't have told him about total soccer," Tommy said, throwing his cleat at the dressing room wall.

"Cool it," Speedy said. "We'll get it."

"I don't like this style. I like our style. It works for us."

"Since when are you afraid of trying something new?"

Tommy glared at him. Speedy stared back as hard but with the faintest smile.

"The practices are crazy," Tommy told his father as he slumped down on the TV room couch. "He had us playing unfamiliar positions. Speedy and I were playing fullbacks. We were all over the place. I'm exhausted."

"God not only gave you feet but also brains. Bring them together."

"Go shower and get ready for supper," his mother yelled from the kitchen.

Coach Hus wanted them to be comfortable in different positions. "Get used to being all over the field, feel at home wherever you are; fullbacks up front, forwards in the backfield. Also, think and act like the opposition. Familiarity breeds anticipation. Anticipate," he repeated over and over again. Almost as much as "hustle."

Tommy didn't have strong defensive skills. That required a reactive nature. All his playing had been as a forward. He was used to making the first move. His reactive time was wrong. He missed tackles, was a step late in getting to the ball, and wasn't as quick moving backwards. Even Ivan the Terrible managed to get past him. "Anticipate," Coach Hustle kept yelling at him. Tommy wasn't used to being told that he wasn't playing well. He didn't like it.

He was still grouchy when he left for Naomi's.

"Not late," his mother said.

"Yeah, yeah." He was out the door before she could say another word.

He hadn't seen or spoken to Marianne since last week. He was constantly thinking about her. Even while sitting at the button machine at the factory, repetitively placing buttons in slots, aligning the holes, stepping on the pedal, listening to the explosion of the machine as the needle jab-jabbed the fabric, he wondered if she was thinking of him as she stabbed patients and drew blood.

Marianne called blood the wine of life. He was the one in university, but she was the one with deep insights. Last week, in his modern poetry class, his professor asked him for his interpretation of a line of poetry. Tommy gave it to him but also asked if the poet consciously intended all the symbolism that the critics claimed he did.

"Only two kinds of people ask that question. Idiots and the intelligent," the professor had said, leaving it at that. The class laughed. Tommy blushed and remained silent after that.

Marianne would have blown him away. He smiled thinking how the class would wilt under her bold stare and snappy comebacks. He gazed out the bus window, watching the world come and go. He got off and walked quickly to Naomi's. He was eager to see Marianne. He was always eager to see her.

"So, what have you libbers been up to?" he asked as he passed the joint to Naomi.

"I went to the Prague again. Artie Gold was reading. God, he's good."

Tommy was surprised that she had gone without him. It hadn't occurred to him that she would do that. He felt hurt. Aside from practice, he hadn't been out these days. He couldn't say why but he felt it was wrong of her to do that.

"With who?" he asked. He knew it didn't come out right as soon as he said it.

"With *whom*," she corrected him with a smile. "I called myself up and asked me out. And I said 'yes.'"

Naomi laughed.

"I meant that I would have gone with you," he said.

"I only saw the poster for the reading on the way home from work and decided to go on the spur of the moment. He's good. I spoke to him after."

She sounded like a groupie.

"He invited a bunch of us over to his place. He's got bookcases of poetry. He also has an incredible collection of rocks and bottles. He gave me a beautiful bottle."

"Huh?"

She pointed to an angular-cut clear glass ink bottle on the coffee table.

"He has a fascination with rocks and bottles. His bedroom has all kinds of weird bottles."

"You went into his bedroom?" he almost shouted.

"If you had a bedroom, she might go into yours," Naomi joked.

"Yes, I did. And he did come on to me."

"I'll kill that fucker."

"You sound just like Speedy," Naomi said. She lit a cigarette and sat, back enjoying the show.

"Stay out of this."

"Hey, it's my place. I'm here, I'm free to butt in."

"He came on to every girl there," Marianne said with a laugh.

"And?"

"And I said no thanks, I have a macho boyfriend who'd kill him."

"You told him that?"

"No. I told him I had a man."

"Huh?" Tommy stared at her. Though she was sitting on the couch she seemed miles away.

"Listen, I can take care of myself. I want to be able to take care of myself. I want to come and go as I please. I told my parents that I'm moving in with Naomi."

He didn't know what to say or do. He felt as outnumbered, outflanked and overwhelmed as he had on the field a few hours earlier. "When?" he finally asked.

"I told them last night that I was tired of the long bus rides back and forth. And since I'm going to be taking more dance classes it would make more sense if I lived closer to where I worked. I'm working, I can afford my share of the rent."

"How did they take it?"

"What do you think? My mother went crazy. My father forbade it. Both worried about my honour and the family's honour. It was a full-blown explosion. The kind only we Gitanos are capable of. Our family is good at that. It was pretty bad, everybody screaming and crying. I was scared and was ready to give in."

"So, what happened?"

"Speedy came to my defence."

"What?"

"He told them that if they raised me right, then I would be okay. He told them that they needed to trust me and that times were different now. And after that, when we were alone, he told me that he had spoken with Naomi."

"What?" Tommy looked in disbelief at Naomi.

"Yeah, he came by a week ago. He asked me not to tell anybody. He apologized for his behaviour. We had a long talk about stuff. He's not such a dumb jock. After his parents' big blow-up, he called me and invited me to meet them. More like a chance for his parents to check me out. It was awkward. You would have thought that I was a prospective son-in-law." She laughed and rolled another joint.

"I guess you passed the test."

"I guess I did. So, you better watch yourself or I'll report you."

"Do they know about me, about us?"

"Hey, one thing at a time," Marianne said, taking a deep toke.

3 3

" I want to take a trip with you."

Tommy was surprised. Marianne had never mentioned wanting to go anywhere.

"Where do you want to go?"

"Inner space!"

"What are you talking about?"

"An acid trip."

He turned on his side to look at her. She was staring at the cracks in the ceiling. Her hair cascading down the pillow made Tommy imagine her floating. "Are you crazy? That's heavy shit. Acid can make you permanently crazy. People don't come back from those trips. And it gets you hooked."

When she sat up, the sheet fell, exposing her breasts. She didn't try to cover up. He was amazed how comfortable she was with him. He still put on his underwear under the sheets before getting out of bed.

"It's not true. I spoke with a doctor friend at the hospital and he said that it's a hallucinogenic but not addictive. It doesn't make you crazy. He said that you enter another dimension, another level of consciousness."

He was just getting used to grass, and now, this. She made him crazy. She was always pushing limits. She was always pushing him. It made him angry and scared. It made him love her even more.

"What if something goes wrong?" he asked, stroking her hair. He loved the thickness of it. He grabbed a clump and pulled her towards him.

She kissed him and pushed herself back up. "He told me to call him if something goes wrong."

"You're crazy! And besides, where would we get the stuff?"

"He gave me a couple of hits. It's Owsley Monterey Purple. He tested it and said it was clean."

Again, Tommy felt like an ignoramus next to her, but he knew she wasn't just showing off or trying to make him look stupid. So he asked, "Who's Owsley?"

"Owsley is a chemist in Frisco who makes it. He puts an owl design on his pills. It's his logo. My friend trusts it."

"He took it?"

"Yes."

"And?"

"And he's still sane and a doctor."

Why was she doing this? "When do you want to do it?" he asked, hoping he didn't sound scared.

"Before you leave."

"We're leaving next Friday."

"I know. So how about Sunday?"

"Tomorrow?"

"Yes."

"Is Naomi taking it too?"

"No, she said that she would stay straight, just in case."

"That sounds reassuring."

She laughed and rolled over onto him. "I want it to be just the two of us. It lasts about eight hours, so can you be here for around brunch?"

He felt himself panicking. What if he freaked out and went crazy? His parents would go nuts. He'd be tied up in a straitjacket and taken to the insane asylum. He wouldn't be able to go to Hungary.

"Can't we wait until I come back?"

"I want to do it with you before you leave," she said, sliding her fingers down his chest and under the sheets.

3 4

"I'm going to hang out with some friends today," he told his parents. "I won't see them for a while."

"Are you going to see your girlfriend?"

He was about to lie but decided not to. "Yes."

"Don't get her in trouble," his mother said.

"She's a nice girl even if she isn't Jewish," Tommy said. He hugged her. "I'll be back around ten or eleven, midnight the latest."

Marianne and Naomi were finishing their coffees. Although Tommy was close to their age he always felt they were so much more grown up. Yes, he shaved and was having sex, but when he was with them, he felt like a kid. They were confident. Their actions had an adult feel. They had real jobs, paid rent, shopped, cooked and did their own laundry. Living on their own, they didn't have parents setting rules. They were responsible for themselves. They seemed to have slipped into being grown up naturally, while he still lived at home and his mother still bought his underwear.

"Looks like a beautiful day for a trip," Marianne said.

There she was again, so confident. "You sure about this?" he asked.

"Yeah, I am, but you don't sound it."

"Honestly, I'm not."

"Then don't," Naomi said, lighting up a cigarette.

He wanted to and didn't. He wanted to share her first trip. She wanted him along and that meant a lot to him. But he was still scared. "No, let's do it."

Marianne showed him half a purple pill on her fingertip. She stuck out the tip of her tongue, carefully placed the half tab on it and with a sip of coffee swallowed it. "Here is your half. Open." She put the other half on his tongue and passed him her cup. He felt as if they had just taken vows but instead of exchanging rings, they were sharing LSD. Instead of going on a honeymoon they were going on an acid trip. His stomach churned but he smiled.

"Okay, let's go," Naomi said.

"I thought it took a while for it to start," Tommy said, surprised and worried.

"It does but we thought it would be fun to do it on the mountain," Marianne said.

"I thought we were going to stay here."

"No, I told you I wanted to go on a trip with you." Marianne grabbed his hand and pulled him out the door.

The walk up Guy Street, to the stairs leading to the mountain, took about half an hour. Halfway there, Naomi, who was a heavy smoker, was already breathing audibly. They started up the wooden steps that soon became a winding, meandering gravel path into thickets and among trees that formed a green roof over them. The city disappeared. Only the thrum of cars broke through to remind him where they were. As he listened, the sound of traffic melded with the buzzing of cicadas.

Shafts of light filtered in through the canopy of leaves and branches, giving the path a cathedral look. He remembered the majestic synagogue in Budapest in which they had found shelter when they were escaping. It had a similar kind of light shining through its stained glass dome. Suddenly the word *yarmulke* came to him. That's what he, Gabi, Frog and Carrot called the dome of the synagogue in Hajdúbékes that they used as target for their slingshot contests. Long ago. "A long, long, long time ago," he whispered to himself.

On either side of the path, like children trying to get out of their mothers' shadow, skinny elm, oak and maple treelets were reaching for the light. "I think I'm beginning to trip." He wasn't sure if he said it aloud or if he was just talking to himself.

He looked over his shoulder. Marianne was stroking the trees that she passed. She waved. Her waving blended in with the waving branches and leaves. He continued uphill. His feet felt funny. Funny feet, he thought to himself. Feet aren't funny. When was the last time his feet told him a joke? That was funny. They had a lightness to them and every time he took a step, colours flew from his toes.

"Wait for me," Marianne shouted. She caught up with him and grabbed his hand. His hand melted into hers and he felt a rush of warmth enter him.

"Wow!" he said. She was glowing. She was the light in the forest.

"There is a halo about you," she said.

He felt safe with her. They stared at each other but didn't speak. The chirps of birds, the crunch of gravel, deep breaths taken together and breath-bubbles that prismed the sun awed them into silence. Breath bubbles. Where did that come from? he wondered.

They came to a clearing. Naomi stopped. "Hey, look. There's Beaver Lake," she said, pointing to the little man-made pond.

"Is it in the shape of a beaver?" Marianne asked.

"You know, I've never seen a real live beaver," Tommy said.

"Well, if you haven't seen a real live beaver, then you can't be a real Canadian," Naomi said, lighting up a cigarette. "There are millions in Canada, all kinds, including Spanish beaver. You sure you haven't seen one?"

"I didn't know there were such things as Spanish beavers," Tommy said.

Tommy noticed a wicked smile spread across Naomi's face. "You're such a perv, Noni." Marianne blushed.

He laughed. The laughter became a kite floating against the clear blue sky, tugging at him, pulling him forward.

They reached the lookout. It felt like it had taken forever, it felt like it had taken an instant. The lookout was a huge terrace of a huge chalet that overlooked the huge city. At the edge of it was a semicircular waist-high granite fence. Beyond it, a steep drop.

"Let's go to the chalet," Marianne said. "I've never been inside."

"Granite steps led to a stone hall with massive windows and doors. Tommy felt he was entering another time. Its smooth marble floor had the sheen of an ice rink, big enough for the Habs to play on. He took a couple of hockey strides and pretended to stop in front of the net creating a spray of ice. The spray became light motes rising to the ceiling. He followed them up to the arched wooden rafters from which hung finely wrought iron chandeliers. A medieval hall, Tommy thought to himself—or said aloud.

"I am Sir Wolf, Knight of the Cohens!" Tommy raised his arms.

"And who are the Cohens?" Naomi asked.

"Wench! Hast thou not heard of the great tribe of the Cohens?"

"The only Cohen I know is Leonard Cohen," she laughed.

"He is our Bard. The Cohens are the priests and bold knights of the square matzo. We seek the holy bagel. And that beautiful damsel"—Tommy pointed to Marianne—"in her glorious tie-dyed chemise, is my fair lady. And you, Naomi of the cigarette, are her lady-in-waiting."

"Yes, Sir Wolf." Naomi smiled and curtsied.

The ghosts and the history of the city were painted on the walls. A delicate, goateed white man, wearing a beret, powder-blue cape, lace collar and cuffs, puffy short pants, tights and ballet slippers, one foot delicately extended, stood on a mountaintop, pointing past the lush forest toward a distant river. His thin, sheathed rapier stuck out like a tail. Stoic, half-naked Indians with feathers sticking out of their heads looked on.

He might have been standing right here where I am. Imagine being the first people here, he thought to himself. You *are* imagining it, a voice answered. He turned to see who said it.

Marianne and Naomi were standing beside him, but they were facing away looking at something else. "Oh. It's me talking to me again," he mumbled to himself.

He wandered by other murals of times past, of flags planted, of crosses erected, canoes being loaded with furs, of priests lifting chalices to the trees and the heavens and blessing kneeling people. The last one, of Europeans and Indians at each other's throats, arrows flying, gunpowder bursting and the fort on fire, stopped him. On poles above the smashed gate, staring up to the heavens, were two Indian heads.

"Out of this, mighty Montreal rises," he heard a voice say. It was Naomi.

Marianne was laughing and pointing up at the rafters. "Look. Between the rafters, squirrel gargoyles. Now those'll scare the nuts off invaders."

"Let's get some ice cream," Naomi said. "What kind would Sir Wolf and Lady Marianne like?"

"I want ice cream that doesn't scream," Marianne giggled. She kept her gaze on the squirrels.

"I want… Oh look!" said Tommy, getting distracted by his fingers. "They're dancing!" He watched them wiggle.

"Okay, two vanillas," Naomi decided. She made off for the counter at the far end of the chalet. "Don't you guys move. I mean it."

"Who's dancing?" Marianne asked Tommy.

"What?"

"Who's dancing?"

"I don't know. Who's dancing?"

"I asked you first," she said.

"I don't know. Why don't you?" He leaned over and kissed her. His lips tingled in colours.

Standing still, she slowly lifted and stretched out her arms and spiralled away from him in slow motion. "A lyrical and sensual hurricane," he said to himself. "No, a slowercane," he corrected himself. She was embracing all. All embracing. And all wanted to be embraced by her. He did. Everything was reaching out to her. Standing still, following her spiral and contrail, he felt swept up in her movement. When she reached the far wall, she pushed away from it and spiralled backward, ending up in his arms.

"Far out. Far in," he said kissing her.

"Here is a quiet ice cream for my lady and a dancing fingers ice cream for you, Sir Wolf."

"Thank you," they said, like children thanking their parents.

"Fuck off," Naomi said. "Let's go to the lookout."

Marianne glanced up at the squirrels again. "You guys can't have any of my quiet ice cream." She wagged a finger at them. Holding hands, giggling, they followed Naomi. She pushed open one of the large doors and held it for them. They floated out.

The daylight blinded him. He closed his eyes. Their closing sounded like doors slamming. "Ooh." He winced. He squinted and then opened them wide. Colours were vibrating before him. He focused on the swirl of white. "Mmmm," he sighed and took a slow lick.

"Did you know that ice cream is the Mighty Mother Cow's gift to us?" Marianne said.

"Amen," said Naomi.

"Amoo," said Marianne as they walked to the edge of the lookout.

The city spread out below. His city. He gazed down upon it as a ruler might over his dominion from his parapet.

"Look at those beautiful houses!" He pointed to four-storey greystones, standing on the highest part of the slope. "They are the mansions of lords and ladies."

"And those ugly factories there," Naomi said, pointing to the east of the city, "are the factories of those lords and ladies, ugly monuments to themselves built on stolen land, with the cheap labour of the poor."

"You're sounding more like a communist than a lady-in-waiting." Tommy snapped to attention and saluted. She smiled and gave him the finger.

In the distance, the shimmering St. Lawrence River wound its way. "Look at the beautiful green centipedes tiptoeing across the St. Lawrence," Marianne said, pointing to the bridges.

Ocean-bound tankers floated silently by. He watched one. He was moving it with his eyes. "I forgot that Montreal is an island," he said.

"Montreal is not an island but a mountain," Marianne said, raising her arms as if blessing it.

"Montreal is a mountland," Naomi said.

"No man is an island entire of itself," Tommy said.

"Deep," Naomi said.

"It is," Marianne agreed.

He leaned over. Suddenly he panicked. His knees went weak, his calves felt like water. His heartbeat quickened. He was short of breath. He felt like he was going to jump. He grabbed the railing with one hand.

"Are you okay?" Naomi asked. "Breathe deep and slow." She stroked his arm. He closed his eyes and inhaled. He followed his breath down his throat, to his lungs, large flesh pods hungry, eager, waiting like baby birds, mouths open. A bright pulsating light shone from behind them.

He opened his eyes and slowly moved his head left and right. Everything was brilliant again. "Where is Marianne?" he asked, letting go of the rail.

Naomi looked around. Children were running and shouting. Tourists milled about, admiring the view, taking pictures of the city, of each other, but there was no Marianne.

"Come on." She tugged at his sleeve and as she did, his ice cream flew out of his hand. He watched it arc in slow motion over the edge.

"Oh shit," he said, and a wave of sadness hit him. It reminded him of something but couldn't remember what. "Have a nice cream landing," he called after it.

"Fuck! Come on," she repeated and tugged harder. Her voice had the colour of panic. He felt it. Naomi checked over the ledge as she hurried. She stopped and headed back the other way, dragging Tommy along. "Marianne!" she shouted. "Marianne! Marianne!"

"Marianne!" Tommy chimed in. "What a beautiful name." It moved like a butterfly. "Merry Ann, Marry Ann," he sang.

"This is fucking serious," Naomi shouted at him. When they got to the end of the wall, they spotted her. She was lying on the grass, her arms and legs moving up and down.

"Are you okay?" Naomi shouted.

Tommy knelt on one knee beside her. "Marianne. What are you doing?"

She smiled up at him. "You know," she said, "The universe is our creation. We dream ourselves. And we are all connected. We are reflections of our mind that is creating the universe."

"Yes," Naomi said, sounding relieved. "But what are you doing?"

"Making grass angels."

The walk back was easy. He leaned back. He spread his hands. He was an acrobat walking across a high wire above the world. No vertigo. People passing him on their way up appeared strange. Their faces were distorted, pained, as if they were carrying a huge weight. He felt light. He floated.

The city came back at him with a vengeance. The noise, the hard sidewalks. And though he was in a familiar place, he felt lost. The climb up the stairs to Naomi's seemed longer than the walk to the mountain. He stood in the doorway, reluctant to go in. Naomi took his hand and pulled. He resisted. Marianne grabbed his other hand and pulled. "It's okay," she said. Her voice sounded far away. It took forever to reach him. The living room was large, but he felt confined. He sat on the couch and felt himself sinking into an underground maze.

People are strange when you're a stranger. The words emanated from the corners of the room. He was being chased. He zigzagged but the voice kept chasing him. The maze became a crowded train with people pushing and shoving. His father was carrying him in his arms, trying to get them away from the crowd. Men in leather coats were after them. His mother was falling behind. He reached for her. Marianne was screaming for him to let go of her hair.

Naomi caressed Tommy's fists. They opened and Marianne's hair became a river. The water kept rising. A man with two suitcases was following them. He slipped and fell into the river and drowned. They were standing at the edge of a steep embankment. They sat down and slid. A train was coming. They scrambled to climb up the other side. He was on his father's back flattened against the embankment by the thundering train. They climbed up. A soldier was aiming his rifle at them. He fired.

Tommy's head jerked. An animal leapt. He felt a burning flash streak across his temple. He screamed and grabbed his head. He was sobbing.

Marianne held him and rocked him. She was stroking his hair. He looked at her. She was crying too.

They lay in bed staring at each other. He watched her dissolve into molecules, dancing across the universe. It was cosmic. Scary and beautiful. He reached out to touch her face. It rippled the way a clear still pond ripples at the touch. She reached to touch him; her fingers became mermaids swimming toward him. They changed into spiders. He jumped up and batted them away. She smiled at him sadly and slowly faded away. "Don't go," he said. His voice sounded hoarse, like it was the first time he had spoken in a century. "Don't."

She reached back and their fingers interlaced. He closed his eyes. They drifted, intertwined. He didn't know who was who. One breath, one body, one trip.

Tommy opened his eyes, "Oh God." He took some deep breaths and looked around. It was dark. A light from the street lamp cast shadows of tree branches on the ceiling. He watched them sway. He glanced at Marianne, who was lying beside him.

Slowly, he sat up. "I think I'm down." She slipped over and laid her head in his lap.

He stroked her hair and felt happy and relieved.

"How are you?"

"I'm still buzzed a bit."

He wanted it to be like this forever.

Naomi was lying on the couch when they came out of the bedroom. "I'm exhausted," she said. "You guys back on planet earth yet?"

"Yeah. I wish I could stay but I have to go. I'm already late. They're going to kill me. Again. Can I see you during the week?"

"No. I'm going to sleep at my parents this week. I promised. Speedy is going to have a bunch of adios suppers with family." She grabbed his face and kissed him hard. "See you soon. Have a good trip." She smiled.

The city was vibrating. The darkness glowed. A bus tiptoed by. Everybody was beautiful and melting. Everything had meaning.

His mother opened the door before he could insert the key. "You're late."

She's gotten smaller, he thought. A worried look crossed her face. He wanted to reach out and caress her brow. "Shit. I'm still tripping." He tried to answer in Hungarian but the words weren't there. "We went up to the mountain."

"What? You're Moses now?" his father said.

Tommy started to laugh. "Yes. I got the eleventh commandment."

"Don't be a smart pants," his father said. "Your mother was worried. It's almost midnight."

"I'm nineteen, isn't it time to stop worrying about me?"

"A child, to a parent, is a child no matter how old he is," his father said.

"I'm sorry." He embraced his mother. "You are great parents and I love you."

"Are you okay?" his mother asked. Now she looked even more concerned.

"Yes," he sniffled. I'm becoming a mush, just like my father, he thought to himself. "I'm okay. I'm old enough to be trusted. I wouldn't do bad things. I'm grown up."

"Okay, mister grown up. Come, I'll fix you something."

"It's late."

"Are you hungry?"

"I'm starved."

His mother's chicken soup had never looked so golden and had never tasted so good.

3 5

What a time to get one. Wave after wave of blood beat against his temple. He opened his eyes but the daylight forced them shut again. He yawned to relieve the tightness in his jaw. It helped. He popped a couple of his mother's migraine pills, hoping the codeine would kick in before takeoff. He put a couple of the pills in his shaving kit. His parents were already up, talking quietly.

"We shouldn't have said yes."

"Hannah, he's a big boy, he's a man."

"When he's running the business and has a nice Jewish wife and children, then he's a man."

Tommy walked into the kitchen, rubbing his scar. "I guess I won't be a man for a while." He smiled.

"Hey, elephant ears."

"You have a headache?" his mother asked when she saw him squinting.

"A little."

"Yours are never little. Maybe you shouldn't go."

"Anyu, don't be silly."

"I made cream of wheat, eggs, toast and coffee. Coffee always helps my headache," she said.

"And your pills."

"Is everything packed?" his father asked.

"A week ago," Tommy said.

His parents had bought him two large suitcases. "I'm not moving back there," Tommy protested when he saw them.

"One is to take clothes for your grandfather, Aunt Magda, Emma-mamma and Gabi," his mother said.

"Hannah, do you remember how thrilled we used to be when we got one of Margit's packages?"

"The whole town knew about it."

"You and Emma went through each item, stroking them, patting them, especially the jackets."

"It's where Margit hid the nylons and the money, in the lining of the most tattered jacket, the one that those thieving customs people always passed over. Those rotten lice. They always stole something from the package."

"Why did she hide nylons in jackets?"

"Nylons were valuable, especially ones without seams. They were only available for the wives of Party members. They were worth at least two months' salary. If you could get them. Every woman in town wanted a pair," Hannah said.

"They still do," his father said.

"And the money?"

"American dollars, which were illegal to have, were worth more than gold," his mother said.

"I remember the time she sent two hockey sweaters. You and Gabi were in heaven. They were the Montreal team's jerseys. They even had numbers on them. Both were number nine. You and Gabi wore them all summer even though they were woollen. You boys were the envy of all the other boys. Who knew that one day we would be the ones sending a package. And that you'd be delivering it personally as a Canadian," his father said.

"You're going to make me look like a *homokos*," Tommy joked, watching his mother fill the suitcase with bras and slips.

"You're not one of those!" she snapped.

The first time he heard the word *homokos*, after coming home from Mr. Papp's, Tommy didn't know what it was. *Homok*, he knew, meant sand, so he assumed that *homokos* was a person who had something to do with sand. But Mr. Papp had nothing to do with sand.

"*Homoks* are men who like boys," his mother had explained. "And if you aren't careful, they will turn you into one of them."

Tommy laughed. He had never met a homo, so he wasn't sure what one was like. He and his teammates often joked about them. And now, thinking about how Mr. Papp dressed, talked, how his bookstore seemed to have only male customers, how neat his place was and how soft his hands were… he certainly fit the bill.

Tommy was sure he wasn't a homo—he definitely wasn't interested in kissing or having sex with Speedy or Schmutz—but he wasn't about to tell his parents how he knew.

"No jeans," his mother said when she spotted him putting a pair in his suitcase. "You will wear nice clothes. You will show them our success. Let them drool with envy, those rotten lice!"

"You look beautiful," his father said, when he saw Tommy in his maroon university blazer with the Knights' helmet logo on the pocket, sharply pleated grey pants and polished shoes. "Come here."

His father had on a yarmulke and put one on Tommy. With raised palms he made a canopy over his son, who bowed his head as the blessing was recited.

He was taller than his father. When had that happened? he wondered. Tommy remembered being a small boy sitting on his father's shoulders watching the statue in the town square being pulled down. And at his Bar Mitzvah, he was so small that he had to stand on a step to reach the dais to read his passage.

His father finished, kissed him on both cheeks and embraced him. Tommy mother stood behind his father. She was tight-lipped and stern.

"Always be a mensch. Always do the right thing and come back safety," his father said. He had given up correcting his father about that expression.

"Don't forget to kiss the mezuzah."

Tommy rarely did it, but today he put his fingers to his lips and then to the little metal tube nailed to the doorpost. Just in case, he told himself.

"You have your passport?"

"Oh shit." He ran back to his room to get it.

"He's a man, just like you," his mother said to his father as they pulled out of the driveway and headed for the airport.

He remembered when the passport arrived.

"You got mail," his father shouted as soon as Tommy entered the door.

He never got mail. "Who is it from?"

"It's your passport," his father said holding it aloft like a torch. "It's beautiful, isn't it?"

Tommy ran his hand over the dark blue cover. It was emblazoned in gold with a crown and mythical creatures holding spears with flags of England and France. Tommy opened it and saw himself, serious, and his signature, Tamás Gyorgy Wolfstein, Canadian Citizen. There was also a letter attesting to his Canadian citizenship and the rules about the use and misuse of the passport.

"We will put them in the safety deposit box until you need them," his mother said and took the passport from him.

"This calls for a celebration," his father had said.

They got in the car and went to The Silvery Moon Chinese restaurant in the mall. Over egg rolls, spareribs, pineapple chicken and fried rice, his father recalled how their Hungarian passports were confiscated by the secret police. Tommy remembered bits of it, how the train jerked to a halt, the shouting, the shoving, being held tight by his father and grabbing his mother by her hair.

"They can keep their cursed passports," his mother said as she sipped her tea.

"This passport is more valuable than a hundred of theirs," his father said, raised his bowl and drank.

Tommy burst out laughing.

"This is serious," his father said

"That's a finger bowl, Apu. You're supposed to clean your fingers in it."

3 6

In all the years they'd lived in Montreal they had never been to the airport. They had never gone anywhere by plane. They had come to Canada by boat, and from Halifax to Montreal by train. Once there, they did very little travelling outside the city. "We have wandered enough," his father said when Tommy asked why they didn't go to New York or Florida like their friends. They had travelled outside the province only once. After they had become citizens and bought their first car, his father had insisted that they drive to Ottawa, which he called their New Pest, so they could have their picture taken standing in front of the parliament building and declare that he, Sándor, Hannah and Tommy Wolfstein were Canadians.

Montreal was enough for them. They had come from a village of a couple of thousand and were now living in a city of a million. Békes had one main street, and once you walked it up and down, you had seen everything. "Here, there are enough streets and stores to keep us busy for a lifetime," his mother said.

And now he was about to fly across the ocean to Hungary! His parents were not only afraid of where he was flying to but of him flying at all. Once she agreed to his going, his mother began keeping track of airline crashes. By August, she was up to six. He too was anxious, but he didn't want to show it. The drive to the airport was filled with warnings, advice and his mother's reading of the highway signs to his father. His father, a nervous driver under normal circumstances, was speeding up and braking more than usual, which didn't help Tommy's migraine. It made him queasy. He tried to concentrate on other things. Marianne hadn't called. He hadn't talked to her since their trip. When he asked about her, Speedy said that she had been very quiet all week. Not at all her loudmouth self.

They arrived at the airport three hours before the flight because his parents constantly worried about being late. They were always early for appointments and always the first ones to arrive at parties. You never know what can go wrong, they told him whenever he complained about having to be ready hours in advance.

He was surprised to see the other players and their families already there. Maybe it's an immigrant thing, he thought as he lugged his two suitcases to the check-in counter.

"Check the tags. Make sure your name and address are on them," his mother said.

"Pardon, Miss." His father smiled at the check-in lady. "This is my son, the soccer player. He is the captain and he's going to Hungary. We want to make sure his luggage is also going to Hungary."

Tommy felt like he was a child again. "Apu, I'm sure it is."

"Yes, but is she?"

"Yes, it is," the woman said, smiling.

"Good. Thank you, dear." His father put a five-dollar bill on the counter.

"No, thank you, sir." She pushed it back to him. Tommy stared at his shoes.

"Here you are," she said, handing Tommy's passport back with his ticket and boarding pass.

Tommy went to hang out with the other players. Their group sounded like the United Nations. Parents were talking to their sons in Italian, Greek, Danish, Russian, Hungarian but Tommy didn't hear any Spanish. Where was Speedy?

"Those Spaniards are always late," Schmutz joked. "Always *mañana*."

"There he is. *Fretta! Fretta!*" Luigi shouted.

"*Viasyni.*"

"*Skynde sig!*"

"*Toropit'ya!*"

Tommy added his Hungarian hurry up. "*Sijes!*"

Speedy was waving and smiling. His parents were behind him. When he saw Marianne, Tommy's heart jumped.

"Okay, gather round, boys," Coach Hus shouted. "I want to make sure everyone is here and checked in." After he ticked off the names, he addressed the parents, who stood around beaming. "We will do our best to make Sir George, Canada and you proud."

"We are already proud," Mr. Gonzales shouted. The other parents clapped.

"Okay, it's time to go. Say goodbye to your parents."

Tommy's mother adjusted his tie, held his face in her palms, and brushed his forehead and gently touched his scar. His father held onto him as if for dear life.

Marianne walked over to Tommy, embraced him and kissed him hard. He was shocked. He glanced at Speedy, who was smiling, and at their parents, who weren't. "Have a fun trip," she said and kissed him again. They held each other. She slipped her hand into his jacket pocket. "For you," she said.

37

Tommy was glad to have an aisle seat because he didn't want to see the plane take off. He didn't want to watch land disappear. Schmutz did. Speedy sat in the middle. The demonstration and explanation of emergency procedures by the stewardesses didn't make Tommy feel any better or safer. When the plane began its run and rise, he grabbed the armrest, closed his eyes and breathed deeply. Just like at the lookout. When it banked he grabbed Speedy's hand.

"Relax, amigo." Speedy patted him on the arm. "Marianne told me that you have a fear of heights. She told me to tell you that she's flying with you. She's crazy."

Tommy smiled and relaxed a bit. He let go of Speedy's hand and reached into his pocket to see what she had put there.

"Hey! Since when are you Catholic?" Speedy asked.

"What are you talking about?"

"That's a St. Christopher medal. He's the patron saint of travellers."

"Marianne gave it to me."

"I think she's trying to convert you."

Tommy rubbed the medal between his thumb and forefinger before putting it back in his pocket.

When the pilot announced that they were going to be flying at 33,000 feet, he closed his eyes and planted his head firmly against the headrest. He wondered if he was as high as he'd been on Sunday? No, that trip wasn't about height but depth, at least 33,000 feet deep. He felt that he and Marianne had entered each other's souls, he could feel her flowing through him. That trip had rearranged him. He felt it now. Was it real or was he having an acid flashback, he wondered. He opened his eyes.

This was real, sitting in a metal bird, defying the laws of common sense. He was flying back to his grandfather, Aunt Magda, Emma-mama and his cousin Gabi. He had seen recent pictures of them but they weren't the people he knew. The people he knew were frozen in time. They were an eight-year-old's version of them. He wasn't just going back; he was going back in time.

A sudden drop made him gasp and clutch the armrest.

"Air pocket," shouted Schmutz, who planned to be a pilot. "Isn't it fun?" he said as he clapped his hands together.

"Have a fun trip," he remembered Marianne whispering to him. "Why the hell not?" he asked himself as he reached into his pocket and held onto St. Christopher for dear life.

"Yeah, it's fun," he forced himself to say.

Everyone applauded when the plane touched down. In spite of being told to stay seated till the plane stopped, people were up and getting their bags and coats from the overhead compartments while the plane was taxiing to the terminal. Tommy didn't move. He didn't like crowds and the shoving and pushing that went with it.

"Come on," Schmutz said. "I want to get off. I want to be in Hungary."

Inside the terminal there were soldiers everywhere. Tommy couldn't recall seeing a single soldier in Canada, but here, they were everywhere, rifles slung over shoulders, some cradling machine guns. It made him nervous.

"Everybody line up here," Coach Hus said. "Wolfie, you go first and tell them that we're a team and that only you speak Hungarian."

"Passport! Are you Hungarian?" the soldier asked after seeing his name.

"I was born in Hungary but now I'm a Canadian citizen."

"What is the purpose of the visit?"

He struggled with his Hungarian. "I'm here with a Canadian university soccer team to play." He pointed to the boys behind him. "They don't speak Hungarian, so if you have questions I can stay here and help."

"I'll tell you what you will do," he answered curtly and stamped his passport with a thud. "Stand there."

On the other side of the checkpoint more soldiers and police were strolling in pairs. "This is a country of uniforms, eh? "Speedy noted.

"Sure looks that way," Tommy said as they waited for their suitcases. When everybody finally had theirs, they lugged them over to customs. More uniformed men and women stood ready to inspect.

"You have anything to declare?" one of them asked. She was about his age or a little older.

"Sorry," he said in English.

"What did you say?" she snapped back.

"I don't understand your question," he repeated in Hungarian.

"Did you just say *szar* to me?" she snapped again.

It took him a minute, to remember that *szar* meant "shit" in Hungarian.

"What's so funny?"

"No. No. Sorry means 'sorry' in English," he tried to explain quickly.

She was not amused. She pointed to the suitcases. "Open them up." Tommy fumbled with the buckles. Her eyes glazed over when she saw the bras and slips. He watched her stroke them.

"Why do you have these?" She looked at him strangely.

Tommy was embarrassed. "They are gifts from my mother for my aunts," he said blushing.

"You have a lot of clothes here." She examined the jeans, jackets and shirts. "Are you planning to sell these on the black market?"

He was about to say "sorry" again but caught himself. "I don't know what a black market is," he said.

"Are you planning to sell these illegally?"

"No, no," he tried to assure her. "They are also gifts for the family."

"And what's this?" She picked up the albums.

"They are records," he said, confused.

"Are you trying to be smart?"

"What? No. I'm trying to answer your questions."

"I know what a record is. Don't you know that it is illegal to smuggle in capitalist propaganda?"

He didn't know what she was talking about. "They're records by the Beatles and the Rolling Stones for my cousin."

"That's propaganda," she said. She took them out and placed them behind her.

"Are you bringing in American money?" she asked as she continued to rummage through the suitcases.

"No," he said, almost too quickly.

She studied him for a moment and then waved him on his way.

When he got to the other side, he had a knot in his stomach and hands were clenched.

Two men walked over to him. "I'm Robert Luxton. I'm the cultural attaché from the Canadian Embassy. This is Mr. Nemes. He is your group's interpreter and information officer while the team is in Budapest." They shook hands.

"They took the records I brought for my cousin. She said that it was capitalist propaganda. They're just rock-and-roll records."

"That's capitalist propaganda," said Mr. Nemes, a small wiry man about his father's age.

Tommy was puzzled.

"I will explain later," Mr. Luxton said.

"Welcome to the People's Republic of Hungary," Mr. Nemes addressed the team. "We are very pleased to have you visit our beautiful country. I know that you," he turned to Tommy, "are also the captain. There are reporters waiting outside and they are anxious to ask you questions. I know that you speak Hungarian but I ask you to wait for me to translate the questions and you will answer in English. Then I will translate it into Hungarian."

Before their departure, Tommy and Coach Hus had been called into the Canadian consulate, where they were advised on the proper way to behave. They told Tommy that because he was originally from Hungary, there would be extra attention on him. They informed him not to talk to anyone except those vetted by the information officer.

Tommy had never been interviewed before, except by Mr. Papp, who had interviewed him for the Hungarian paper. But Tommy didn't consider him a real reporter. Here in Hungary there were real photographers and a television crew.

"First we will have a group photograph," Mr. Nemes told them. "Please line up, two rows. The first row on the knees, please, with the captain in the middle. And the comrade coach here beside the end."

Tommy signalled Speedy and Schmutz, Luigi, Derek and Archie to the front. "No," Mr. Nemes said, pointing to Archie, "to the back, please."

"No. Here in the front." Coach Hus spoke quietly but firmly. "He is the assistant captain." He signalled Archie to kneel between Speedy and Tommy.

After the pictures, Mr. Nemes addressed them. "The Hungarian People's Socialist Republic is very pleased to welcome you, the Canadian university soccer champions of Canada, to Hungary. We are very pleased that Canada accepted our invitation, our gift to the Canadian people on their one-hundredth birthday. We hope that your stay will be a pleasant one and that you will see the history, a thousand years old, the beauty of our country, and the hospitality of our people. We look forward to watching you participate in two friendly games against our university champions, first in Debrecen and then in

Budapest. We want to especially welcome you, Wolfstein Tamás, back to your motherland." He faced the cameras and reporters and said that Tommy would now say a few words.

Although he was nervous, he was able to repeat without faltering what the consulate sent him to memorize. "We are very happy and pleased to be here. We would like to thank the people of Hungary for inviting us. We are eager to learn, and to improve our game and skills."

A reporter put up his hand. The way he did it, two fingers up, the rest curled in, reminded Tommy of being back in grade one. If you didn't do it that way you would be struck with a ruler.

"How do you feel being back in your motherland?"

Though he understood, he waited for Mr. Nemes to translate, as instructed. It gave him time to calm his nerves.

"I am very happy to be back in Hungary."

Another reporter raised his hand. "You have a cousin, Gábor Földember, playing for Debrecen. How do you feel about playing against him?"

His responses sounded like time delays. "I am looking forward to meeting my cousin after a long absence. I heard he is very good. We will try our very best."

"Do you think you will win?"

He would have loved to say what Puskás said on being asked that question by a British reporter when they arrived to play England in '53. In his self-assured way Puskás told reporters that they didn't come all this way to lose. But Tommy was just hoping that the Internationals weren't going to get creamed. He looked at his teammates.

"These games are not about winning or losing but doing your best and getting better. It is about sportsmanship. We have a very good team, so we will try our hardest and hope to play well against your best."

Schmutz gave him the thumbs-up.

"Where were you born? Are you going to visit your hometown?"

"I was born in Hajdubékes. It is near Debrecen. Yes, I will visit my relatives there."

"Do you remember any friends from there?"

"I remember one we called Carrot and another who I knew as Frog."

"Tamás says that he remembers," Mr. Nemes translated, "a friend whose nickname was Carrot." The reporters chuckled. "He is looking forward to meeting him and others. Now we will have a few words from the cultural attaché of Canada, Mr. Luxton."

He first addressed the team in English. "We are proud of your achievement and wish you the best of luck. You in your diversity are excellent representatives of the spirit of Canada." He then switched into perfect Hungarian and addressed Mr. Nemes and the reporters. "On behalf of the Canadian government and its people, we want to thank The Hungarian People's Socialist Republic for their kind invitation and this gift on the Centenary anniversary of Canada. Thank you."

"Thank you and that will be all. They had a long flight and we will take them to their hostel." Mr. Nemes said.

"Tomi! Tomi!" A voice called out. A boy about his age but taller was waving and running toward him.

"Gabi!" he shouted back. Though he hadn't really kept in touch, other than through occasional lines his parents made him write in their letters, the brotherly bond that was built over the seven years they lived together suddenly overwhelmed him. They embraced and cried. Cameras flashed.

Mr. Nemes spoke sternly to Gabi. "You will have time to meet when it's time." Gabi stepped back. "Emma-mama says welcome home," Gabi said before turning and making his way through the crowd of reporters. Tommy silently watched him go. He didn't like this growing helpless feeling.

Unlike in Montreal, which was always a tangle of traffic, the two-lane highway from the airport was almost deserted. Back home Tommy's father was always honking at the car ahead to move so he could hurry and make his delivery. "Hurry! Hurry!" was the motto in Montreal. Here there were only a few trucks, buses and the occasional tiny car that looked half the size of his father's Chevy Impala. On either side of the highway large fields of corn and hay spread as far as he could see.

The farmland gave way to a huge, walled-in, barbed-wire compound. "More soldiers," Speedy said, pointing to the ones standing at attention in towers and at gates. Tommy glimpsed tanks and cannons in the compound. He remembered that when he was young one of his favourite things to make was tanks. Gabi taught him how by using a small matchbox and a single match with its red tip sticking out of it. They used to collect matchboxes and have tank battles.

Colourful billboards of muscular men and rosy-cheeked women greeted them on the outskirts of Budapest. Staring proudly into a bright red sun, they praised socialism and urged higher productivity.

"Hey, Hungary has Scouts also!" Derek pointed to the posters of cherubic children in white shirts, blue shorts and red bandanas, waving flags.

"They're called Young Pioneers," Tommy said. "I remember wanting to be one."

"Let me put it to you this way. You can't start indoctrination too early, eh?" Archie chimed in. "It's the way to make socialism work. And in communist countries, you had to join. If your parents didn't want you to join, then they were considered reactionaries and would be watched more than others."

Tommy didn't know if his parents were for it or not. All he remembered was wanting to wear the uniform and march in parades.

"The Nazis did the same thing," Derek said.

A big sign announced Budapest. Uniform grey concrete apartment buildings stood shoulder to shoulder, like soldiers at attention. It didn't resemble the postcards that his parents sometimes received from his relatives.

When they entered the city core, colour returned. Though the buildings were somewhat dilapidated, with their faded colours, missing stucco and cracks, they had a certain shabby elegance.

The bus snaked along the Pest-side road of the Danube that divided Buda and Pest. He had expected it to be much wider. The St. Lawrence was wider at its narrowest point than the Danube at its widest. Buda, on the other side, was hilly. With a statue on the tallest point, it reminded him of the cross on Mount Royal

"Look! A castle!" Kostas shouted.

"This really is the Old World," Schmutz said. "Imagine, kings, queens and knights once lived there. It's like Copenhagen."

The Pest side was crowded with cathedrals, statues and three- to five-storey Baroque-style apartments. Tommy had the feeling that he had entered a vaguely familiar past.

Finally, they arrived at the university dorms on the other side of Budapest. Tommy was exhausted. Unlike Speedy and Schmutz, he hadn't been able to sleep on the eight-hour flight. Every time the plane hit turbulence or veered slightly, he tensed. And when his ears blocked, he panicked about not hearing the engine. Even though the time zone change made it noon in Hungary, he just wanted to sleep.

They gathered in the common room, where Mr. Nemes addressed them. "You will stay here for three days. Then you will take a train to Debrecen and you will play there. And then you will come back in the People's stadium. We will give you tour of the beauty of Budapest after tomorrow. Breakfast in the cafeteria is at seven thirty o'clock, dinner is at twelve o'clock and supper is at eighteen o'clock."

"Where is the soccer field?" Coach Hus asked.

"It is behind the Science building. The university guide will take you."

"Thank you, Mr. Nemes. Now if you don't mind, I would like to speak to the team and the coach about some of the protocols," Mr. Luxton said.

"Certainly. Good day, Mr. Luxton. And goodbye, gentlemen." Mr. Nemes nodded curtly and left.

Mr. Luxton closed the door of the common room and signalled for the boys to sit. "Okay, I just want to give you some basic guidelines about how to behave here. I know that Coach Hus informed you, but I want to make sure there is no misunderstanding. First things first, do not wander off on your own! Not only do most Hungarians not speak English, but you could wander into areas where you are not allowed, and the police can arrest you just like that." He snapped his fingers to emphasize his point. "If someone wants to speak to you or ask you to take a letter to a relative or friend back in Canada, smile, say 'nem,' which means 'no,' and walk away. Always make sure that you have your passport with you. Do not, and I can't stress this enough, travel without it. Always carry it in an inside pocket. Do not give it to anyone except officials and make sure to ask for it back. On campus, you have to give it to the dorm administrator, who will keep it in a safe. I don't want to scare you but be aware that it is most likely that you as individuals and as a team will be watched. It is normal to have foreigners watched. You, Tommy, especially. Does anyone have any questions?"

"Are the rooms bugged?" Schmutz joked.

"Probably."

A silence fell over the boys.

"Why did they take away my albums?" Tommy asked.

Mr. Luxton stood as if he were a professor lecturing a class.

"This may be a bit difficult for you boys who live in a democracy to understand. Here they believe that Western culture is decadent and therefore dangerous. They believe that the West promotes all the wrong values and they want to prevent the promiscuous behavior that rock and roll promotes."

"'I Want to Hold Your Hand' is capitalist propaganda?" Derek asked.

The boys laughed.

"This is a very serious issue for them," Mr. Luxton said firmly.

"Why did they want Archie in the back of the picture?" Luigi wanted to know.

"Because I'm black."

The boys fell silent. "Hungary is a monocultural society," Mr. Luxton said. "They aren't used to diversity. Now, I have to go. Coach Hus knows how to get in touch with me. I'll be at the game. Good luck. Tommy, may I have a word with you in private, please?"

They stepped outside. Mr. Luxton glanced up and down the corridor to make sure it was clear. "Tommy, as I said, you, especially, will be watched, so you have to be extra careful about what you say and do."

Tommy spoke in the same quiet voice as Mr. Luxton. "Can you tell me why Mr. Nemes didn't want me to talk to my cousin? Is it because he's playing for Debrecen?"

"No. Here they want to control everything that happens. Gabi broke that order and Mr. Nemes was worried that someone would see that he didn't have control and report him."

"I thought he was the one watching us."

"Yes, but there is probably someone watching him as well."

38

Needle-like pain was shooting through Tommy's ankle all the way up to his hip. He didn't know how much longer he could stand. He massaged his thigh. The man in the dark suit had light blue eyes. They were other-worldly, cold. There was no compassion in them, even though he was smiling.

"You attempted to rape a Hungarian woman."

Tommy didn't understand. "I'm sorry but I don't know what the word 'rape' means."

"It means that you violated a woman," Chief Barna said. Tommy still didn't understand. "You forcibly had sex with her."

"What? No!" Tommy shouted.

The man in the dark suit glared at him.

"What's this got to do with Szeles?"

"We have proof, a recording of you planning the rape. And witnesses."

"I didn't touch her. I just gave her some money. She invited me to her place. I didn't go."

"You sent your friend to invite her back to your room. He told her that you had nylons that you wanted to give her as a friendly gesture. When she was in your room the two of you attempted to rape her. She screamed; the concierge called the police. When they arrived you attempted to bribe the officers."

"That's not true. I swear. That's not how it happened."

3 9

Speedy was wandering around their room, looking into lamps, behind pictures and under the beds. "What are you doing?" Tommy asked.

Speedy put his finger to his lips and began to hum the theme from *From Russia With Love.*

Tommy smiled. "Speedy, can I ask you a question?"

"Sure," he said as they unpacked.

"Why did Marianne do what she did at the airport?"

"Do what?"

"You know. Kiss me like that."

"Because she likes you, dumbass." Speedy twirled his finger beside his temple. "Because my sister is loca."

Tommy shook his head. "Do you think your parents are mad?"

"Probably. But I think she wanted us out of the way to deal with them. She's crazy, like a fox."

"And you?"

"And me what?"

"What changed your mind about me dating your sister?"

"I was angry at being tricked and lied to by you. You were my friend and you lied to me, all that time you were pretending to know nothing. That pissed me off. I trusted you. I also reacted with the passion of my culture. But I'm also a science guy, which is all about logic. That part of me understood why you lied, and Marianne told me that she asked you to keep it a secret. I kept pushing my emotional side to come up with valid reasons to hate you. I couldn't."

Tommy didn't say anything.

"Also, I didn't like losing."

"I'm glad you don't like losing."

"*Si.*" They shook hands.

The instant his head hit the pillow Speedy was out. Tommy tried to sleep but even though he was exhausted, he couldn't. Maybe it was the time change. Maybe it was because his headache had returned. Or because of a churning in the pit of his stomach that he couldn't calm. Was it caused by his parents' anxiety, flying, his encounter at the airport, seeing the tanks and soldiers? He rubbed his scar to ease the pressure. He thought of Marianne. Breathe, baby, breathe, he heard her say.

He sat cross-legged on the bed, closed his eyes and imagined her lifting her palm up, raising it as if conducting a symphony of air into her lungs, pausing for a moment, then, turning her palm downward, lowering it as if pressing it out. She did this before she performed. Before Tommy knew it, Coach Hus was knocking on his door.

"Wake up, you prima donnas!"

Their practice started slow, to get the kinks out. Slow laps, easy stretches, soft passes to get their accuracy back and easy shots at Derek to warm him up. In the afternoon he pushed them with one-on-one, two-on-one, three-on-ones, total soccer and ended with a spirited pickup game. Tommy felt good. The headache was gone, the churning was gone, and the game was coming back to life.

After supper they gathered around the TV in the lounge to watch themselves. When the images of the team came on, everybody hooted and cheered. Tommy wished his father could see it. How he would love to see his son on Hungarian national TV, playing soccer in Hungary. He remembered summer evenings when he and Gabi worked out with the town team. They would practise moves that the team's coach, he still couldn't remember his name, showed them. Tommy wondered what had become of him. He felt so proud when the coach told him and Gabi that he expected to see them on the youth national team in a few years. In a strange way, his prediction had come true.

"Tomorrow, we're going on a tour of Budapest, so we'll only have morning practice. And there will be photographers and a television crew. So, we'll work on skills, no plays. Derek, your strong side is the right side, so during warm-ups I want you to hold back on your leaps and let in a few soft goals there. Wolfie and Speedy, I don't want you guys taking shots on Derek. Luigi and Schmutz, you guys will warm Derek up. Okay?"

"Coach Hustle's a fox," Speedy said. "I think he really wants to win."

"Don't you?"

"You bet."

"We're going to need every trick in the book and then some."

Coach Hus shut off the TV. "Okay. Bedtime, you prima donnas."

Mr. Nemes showed up with the photographers and TV crew before breakfast. They filmed them eating, getting dressed for practice, running out onto the field and kicking the ball around. They filmed Luigi and Schmutz shooting on net and Derek diving. Tommy and Speedy were heading the ball back and forth.

Speedy smiled. "Coach Hustle ain't so dumb."

"They're curious about us too," Tommy said as he and Speedy tried to keep the ball in the air.

"Maybe they're worried?"

"You think?"

"Tamás, can we have you take some shots on net, please? Mr. Nemes called to him. "Our viewers are interested in the prodigal son. Especially since you are also the team's top scorer."

Tommy was caught off guard. He didn't know what prodigal meant.

"How do you know?"

"Mr. Papp reports for us." He smiled.

Mr. Homokos? he almost joked. "Mr. Papp who owns the bookstore in Montreal?"

"Yes. He writes for the national newspaper about the diaspora."

"Oh. Well, you'll have to ask the coach."

Coach Hus nodded.

"Okay, Lefty," Speedy yelled after him. "Show them what that left foot of yours can do."

Tommy glanced back at Speedy. He smiled and nodded. The other guys gathered to watch. He lobbed a few toward Derek, then to the left and right of him. When he was warmed up, he put power into his shots. Tommy secretly tapped his right or left foot so Derek would know to which side he was going to shoot. He made sure that Derek looked weak on the right side and strong on the left. He also took some right-footed shots that were weaker and less accurate.

Coach Hus blew his whistle. "Okay, boys, cool down and take a shower."

Tommy watched Mr. Nemes, the photographers and cameraman leave, and when they disappeared around the corner, he turned his back to Derek, kicked the ball into the air and, as it came down, he leaped, flattened in mid-air and scissor-kicked the ball into the top left-hand corner. He landed on his back. The boys whooped and circled him. Tommy lay there facing the sky and moved his arms and feet back and forth.

"What the hell are you doing?" Schmutz asked.

"Making grass angels," he said, laughing.

The boys jostled onto the tour bus. The tour guide was an attractive young student from the university. She had no trouble getting their attention.

"Velcome. My name is Anna. I vill be your guide." Her English had a Zsa Zsa Gábor quality. Tommy expected her to call them *dahlings*. The bus started up. "Before I tell you the history of Hungary, I vill tell you the mythologia of Hungary. It is about the Golden Stag. The legend say two brothers, Hunor and Magor, went hunting and saw a Golden Stag. They pursue the animal but it always stay ahead of them all the way to a place called Levidia. There they meet two princess and marry them. Then they make Hungary there. From the brothers' name, as you can hear, we get the names Hungarians and Magyars. Interesting. Yes? The fact? No.

"The Budapest you vill see today is the result of many years of rich history. There have found evidence of people back to second millennium before Christus. First ve have the before Magyar times. The first settlement that is today Budapest vas built by Kelts. The Romans occupied this town in the first century before Christus."

This was as new to Tommy as to the others. "I should have boned up on Hungarian history as Mr. Papp suggested."

"Better late than never, eh?" Speedy elbowed him in the ribs. "I like my history this way." He winked at Anna.

She was flustered for a moment but quickly recovered. "The Hungarian tribes arrive to the Carpathian Basin in 896. Árpád, leader of the Magyars, settled on Csepel island, in the south part of Budapest. In 1000 Hungary's first king is Stephen. He become a Christian and make everybody Christian."

She pointed to the Buda side. "There is Gellért Hill. It is named after Bishop Gellért, killed by barbarians during war against Christianity in 1046. Ve vill pass it over there soon." Anna paused. She scanned the bus. Tommy wasn't sure but he thought that she gave him a quick small smile. He hoped that it was for Speedy.

"The beginning of Buda and Pest begins by French and German settlers who migrates and works along the shores of Buda and Pest in the twelve century. But in 1241 the Mongols come and destroy both cities. Now ve are in Buda and will stop at the Castle Hill which King Béla IV in 1248 lived. You are permitted to take pictures, please."

They got off the bus and walked out to the terrace that overlooked the Danube and the parliament building on the Pest side. The boys ran to the terrace and began clicking their Kodak Instamatics.

"You vant I take picture of team?" Anna asked Tommy.

"Sure." They lined up with Pest in the background.

"Now let's take a picture with you in it." Speedy guided her between him and Tommy. "Schmutz, take a picture of us."

"I am sorry but I am not permitted," she replied. She removed herself from the picture.

The boys wandered around, taking pictures of each other. Anna stood off to the side. When Tommy passed her, she touched his arm. "Hello, captain of team." She smiled and switched to Hungarian. "Do you have any nylons or farmers?" she asked in a low whisper.

"Farmers?" he asked, perplexed.

"Levi Strauss farmers," she said.

"Oh, you mean jeans. Sorry. I only have for me." Tommy had snuck one into his suitcase when his mother wasn't looking.

"Vill you sell them?"

"What are you two talking about?" Speedy asked. He sounded a bit pissed. I'll tell Marianne."

"I'm in room 101," she said, before switching back to English. "Ve must go back on bus now."

When they were all aboard and seated, she began again. "In 1458, the noblemen of Hungary elect Matthias Corvinus as king. He make Buda the most important city in Europe. Then the terrible Turks come to Hungary in 1541. The Turkish occupation last almost 150 years. They built a lot of Turkish baths because Budapest have lots of hot water under the ground. Ve are passing one now. She pointed to a building. It is more than four hundred years old and example of Turkish architecture." She paused while the boys looked out at a long, one-storey building with very small windows and a couple of domed roofs.

"The Austrian Habsburg beat the Turks in 1686 but Buda and Pest are destroyed in the battles. Hungary become part of the Austro Hungarian Empire."

"But Hungary wasn't really an equal partner in this empire," Derek interrupted her.

She faltered. "Yes, you are correct. In 1848 Hungary has a brave revolution against the Habsburgs."

Something stirred in Tommy and he began to recite from memory.

Talpra magyar, hí a haza!
Itt az idő, most vagy soha!
Rabok legyünk vagy szabadok?
Ez a kérdés, válasszatok! –
A magyarok istenére
Esküszünk,
Esküszünk, hogy rabok tovább
Nem leszünk!

She stared at Tommy. He was also surprised.

"You are a real Hungarian," she said in their shared language.

"English, English!" Schmutz yelled out. The rest of the team joined in.

Coach Hus stood up. "Boys! Enough!"

"It is a very famous and important poem for Hungarians, what your captain said." She smiled at him.

Tommy remembered memorizing it in grade one. It was also the poem the people who were placing a noose around a statue in '56 in Békés's town square were reciting. Tommy was sitting on his father's shoulders watching and listening to the people pull and recite until the statue tipped and fell. He remembered the loud cheer as it hit the ground, as its neck snapped, and as the head rolled into the bushes.

Speedy's elbow brought him abruptly back to the present.

"In 1945 Budapest was liberated by the brave soldiers of the Soviet Union. They along with the brave patriots of Hungary, defeat the fascist German invaders. Since then Hungary has been a proud progressive socialist republic."

When the bus came to a final halt, Tommy ran up to his dorm room, grabbed a pair of nylons and ran back to the bus. He pulled Speedy aside. "Here, give this to her but don't let anyone see."

"Okay, everyone fork over twenty forints for Anna for her wonderful tour."

"Thank you, but I am not permitted."

"We insist," Tommy said, and put the money in her hand.

She gave the driver a couple of the twenties. "Thank you," she said and added in a low voice in Hungarian. "This way we are all protected."

"My friend there would like to give you something extra," Tommy said, pointing to Speedy standing by the back of the bus.

4 0

Gabi had called it the Crystal Palace of trains. The last time Tommy had been in the Western Train Station he was holding Gabi's hand, looking up at the stars visible through its glass roof. It had been midnight when they pulled into the station. He'd never been up so late and was excited because he was on an adventure. When they had left Békes, his parents had told him that they were going to Israel. He thought that they had arrived. In the station there were boy and girl soldiers, machine guns slung over their shoulders, strolling, holding hands. They were smiling and speaking Hungarian. Tommy remembered he was happy that they spoke Hungarian in Israel.

Now he was with his teammates waiting for the train to Debrecen to play their first game. He looked up. He couldn't see the sky because of the soot covering the glass panes. And the patrolling soldiers weren't smiling. Today he wasn't feeling the excitement of an eight-year-old on an adventure, but the anxiety of a nineteen-year-old returning to a foreign familiarity. He would never have imagined that he would be returning to Hungary and certainly not as a captain of a soccer team, leading his teammates, the Knights, back to play on the Golden Green.

"How was room 101?" Tommy asked Speedy during a private moment once they had settled into their seats and the other players had settled into theirs.

"Very very hot and pleasant."

"I fell asleep waiting for you. I was beginning to think you defected."

"I was tempted," he said.

"Is she Catholic?"

"Huh?"

"How was one of my kind?"

Speedy smiled. "A fine shikass."

"What are you guys talking about?" Schmutz asked, sitting down next to Speedy.

"Accommodations, guides, loyalties and religion," Speedy said.

"Bullshit," Schmutz said.

Tommy stared out the window as the train departed the station. He saw his reflection staring back. Everything struck him as simultaneously familiar and completely strange. Although he recalled events from his childhood, it felt like it was someone else's. It all felt like so long ago even though it had only been eleven years since he'd last been here. Of course, that was more than half his life. And his mother tongue wasn't his mother tongue anymore. He struggled to understand the words he heard and struggled to speak it. This was his motherland, but it didn't feel or sound like home. Yet here he was.

The land was flat and green with crops, row on row as far as he could see. They were divided by fields of sunflowers. What a strange thing to grow, he thought to himself. Other than sunflower seeds, he didn't know what else they could possibly be good for. Huge heads on such thin stalks. Why didn't they fall over and snap? Incredible.

> *Ah Sun-flower! weary of time,*
> *Who countest the steps of the Sun:*
> *Seeking after that sweet golden clime*
> *Where the traveller's journey is done.*

"Where did you learn that?" Speedy asked.

"We studied it in my Romantic-Victorian Poetry class," Tommy said.

"You're becoming a friggin faggot poet," Schmutz said.

"The teacher dissected it to death. He found more symbols and meanings in that poem than a sunflower has seeds. But you just have to see one to understand it. My grandfather had sunflowers in his garden. I usually spent a week or two in the summer with him in Hajduszabad. He told me that the sunflowers followed the sun. I didn't believe him. So, he made me check them morning, noon and at night. I thought he meant that they actually walked from east to west."

"Did they?" Schmutz asked.

"Schmuck," Speedy said, punching him on the arm.

"We're going to pass my grandfather's town just before we hit Debrecen. My father was in a labour camp there."

"What's a labour camp?" Schmutz asked.

Tommy thought everyone knew what it was but then realized 'everyone' meant Jews. "It's where Hungarian Jewish men were sent when the war broke out. It was part of the army except they weren't allowed to carry guns."

"Why not?"

"Jews were not considered real Hungarians. They weren't trusted with guns. Instead they were given picks, shovels and brooms. They were given all the shitty work: fixing roads, digging ditches, cleaning latrines. And some, according to my father, were sent to the front and used as mine clearers."

"What are mine clearers?" Schmutz asked.

"The ones forced to go clear land mines that the enemy planted before they retreated. They had to go find and explode them before the regular soldiers advanced. Many of them were blown up."

"Shit!"

"Does your grandfather still live there?" Schmutz asked.

"No. He moved in with my aunt in Debrecen. He's pretty old. He was born in the 1890s. Imagine. He was in World War One. He had an armoire with bullet holes in them. I used to stick my fingers in them."

"That's old. My grandfather still lives in the same house he was born in," Schmutz said.

Speedy looked at the passengers looking at them. "Would you recognize him if he got on the train now?"

Tommy looked around. "Probably not. I've seen pictures of him, but I don't think so. He looked old to me then, imagine now. All I remember is that he was very religious. He always wore a yarmulke, prayed a lot and only spoke to me in Yiddish."

"You speak it?"

"No. I understand a few words and expressions but that's it. Do you guys speak your mother tongues fluently?" Tommy asked Luigi and Schmutz. He knew Speedy did.

"Of course," both replied.

Tommy wondered why he didn't. Probably because his parents hated the people who spoke it and drove them from Hungary.

"What about your grandmothers?" Luigi wanted to know. "My father's mother lives with us."

"Both my grandmothers died in concentration camps." He stared out at the moving landscape.

"There it is." Tommy pointed to the train station with the Hajduszabad sign on it. The uniformed stationmaster stood at attention outside the station holding a stick with a red circle on it.

"They do the same thing in Italy," Luigi said

"Spain, too."

"Have you guys been back to your countries?"

"Yeah," Luigi said. "My mother's grandparents live in Vasto, in the south of Italy, on the Adriatic."

"We got stories, too," Kostas said.

"Debrecen next," the conductor called. He hoped Gabi would be there.

They were greeted by a representative of the city holding a bouquet of flowers and two people from the university who also held bouquets of flowers.

"I am Dr. Nagy, the Dean of Physical Culture at the Kossuth Lajos University," he addressed Coach Hus. His English was not as good as Mr. Nemes's but good enough to introduce himself as their host and translator. He then introduced the city's representative, who just nodded and handed the bouquet to the coach.

"I bet he never got so many flowers in his life," Speedy whispered to Tommy. "Maybe they want to date him."

Tommy elbowed Schmutz in the ribs.

"*Köszönöm*," Coach Hus replied, pronouncing the word for thank you perfectly, just as Tommy had taught him.

Everyone applauded. "Please, the Captain?" said Dr. Nagy. Coach Hus signalled to Tommy, who grabbed Speedy and walked with him to the front. "Tommy Wolfstein and Roberto Gonzales," Coach Hus introduced them.

Dr. Nagy introduced the young man standing next to him. "Könyves András, the captain of the Kossuth Lajos university team, the champions of Hungary."

Even in his suit he looked well built, stocky and sturdy. Physically, he resembled Puskás. He probably had a powerful shot too. Derek's going to have his hands full, Tommy thought to himself. Könyves stuck out the bouquet that was tiny in his big paw.

"Careful shaking a Hungarian's hand," Speedy whispered to Tommy.

Tommy smiled. He reached into his jacket pocket and took out a rolled-up Sir George pennant and unfurled it. They had been briefed by the protocol officer at the consulate on these greetings and exchanges. When Tommy, Gabi and his friends used to gather after Sunday afternoon soccer broadcasts to replay the game, Gabi and Frog, who were always the captains, made pretend exchanges the way they were doing now for real. He took the bouquet, offered the pennant and reached out to shake hands. He made sure that he grasped Könyves's hand first so his couldn't be squeezed hard. Könyves smiled and offered the team's pennant to Roberto, who did the same.

"Velcome," the captain said in English.

"*Köszönöm*," Tommy replied. Everyone applauded.

Short speeches were made, and photographs were taken.

"We ask you, Tamás, to say a few words in your mother tongue. Thank you." Tommy hadn't expected this. He assumed the ritual would be the same as in Budapest.

He was nervous, unsure whether he could say something that would sound coherent. "I only went to grade one before we escaped, so I am…," he trailed off. He almost said "sorry" before he remembered the trouble it caused at the airport. "I am, uh, not very good Hungarian. We are very happy to be here in Debrecen. We are waiting to play good games. Thank you."

"Tomikám, Tomikám." A small woman was fiercely elbowing her way past the dignitaries and reporters. "Tomikám, Tomikám," she exclaimed as she reached out and embraced him. She was crying and shaking. She grabbed his arm, pulled his head down to her lips and began kissing him all over his face.

"Aunt Magda, Aunt Magda," Tommy whispered.

41

"Don't talk to anyone."

"I won't," Tommy said as he put the suitcase in the taxi. He assured Coach Hus that he had his passport and that he would be back in the dorm by curfew.

"Where are you from?" the driver asked after Tommy gave him the address.

"Canada," Tommy answered.

"You're a Hajdu."

"How do you know?"

"You have a Hajdu accent."

"I only lived here for seven years."

"It's enough. Do you have American cigarettes?"

"No, I don't smoke."

The driver looked at him through the rear-view mirror. "You live in a country that has all kinds of cigarettes and you don't smoke? What a shame." Tommy shrugged and stared out the window. The taxi wove through narrow cobblestone streets lined by small old houses that reminded him of Old Montreal. It was strange to see streets empty of parked or moving cars. It seemed that people got around mainly by bus, bike or on foot.

The taxi turned onto Széchényi Street, a broad tree-lined street that reminded him of Park Avenue. Park was the first street they had lived on when they arrived in Montreal. It had been one of Montreal's elegant residential streets once, but years of immigration transformed it into a loud and busy commercial street with the babel of Hungarian, Polish, Russian and Yiddish filling its shops and sidewalks. Park was not only a street but also a meeting place where men made deals, mothers pushed baby carriages and old women lugged heavy shopping bags and yelled at latchkey kids like him who chased each other through the crowd. With his parents working from early morning to late evening, he was free to roam and explore his neighbourhood. He loved Park Avenue, its hustle and bustle and sounds and smells.

Széchényi Street was almost deserted, with few people, few shops and hardly any kids about. There was a quiet and sombreness about it.

"Here we are," the driver said.

"How much?" Tommy asked.

"Do you have American money?"

"How much?"

"Five dollars."

Tommy gave it to him. The driver jumped out of the car, grabbed Tommy's suitcase and rushed to the door with it. He handed it to Tommy and pumped his hand with both of his. He danced back to his cab and waved enthusiastically and yelled, "God bless you, Hajdu," and sped off. His parents' warning about using his dollars flashed into his mind. He'd been had. He shrugged and smiled. He rang the bell.

His aunt had, until recently, lived alone. Her husband had died a few years earlier and she had no children. Tommy's grandfather lived with her now. When he asked his mother why his aunt and her husband didn't try to escape with them, she told him that Magda was pregnant in '56. She didn't want to risk the unborn baby. And then it died. Tommy's mother always cried when she told that story. She worshipped her big sister. "She got me through Auschwitz," she had often told him.

A slot in the door slid open and a voice from behind the door asked, "Who do you want?" Tommy was caught off guard. He stepped back to check the number. "Who do you want?" the voice repeated.

"Magda Schwartz."

"There is no Magda Schwartz here," the voice croaked from behind the door.

Then he remembered that Schwartz was her maiden name. "Sorry," he said. "I'm looking for Magda Lukács."

The eye slot closed, a lock turned and the door opened.

A small old woman with a black scarf wrapped around her head eyed him suspiciously. "What do you want with Magda Lukács?"

"She is my aunt."

"Ahh. You're the American?" It was both a statement and a question.

"Canadian," he corrected her.

She looked him up and down. She shrugged her shoulders and turned. Behind the door lay a courtyard with a row of small, attached cottages. In front of each was a neatly kept vegetable plot. He was surprised that people in the city grew food. In Montreal, you just went out the door and were greeted by corner grocery stores and supermarkets, where you could buy not only what you needed but also whatever you wanted. He couldn't understand why some people, like Luigi's and Speedy's parents, would have gardens and make their own wine. Tommy had kidded them about being drunken immigrant farmers.

"Follow me," she said and led the way to a door and knocked. The door opened immediately, as if his aunt had been standing behind it, waiting for the knock. Magda grabbed him and burst into tears. She was so light that he could have easily lifted her. He wondered how this little woman, barely reaching his shoulders, could have been as tough and fearless as his mother had made her out to be. Behind her stood an old man, not much taller, stubbled, with a yarmulke on his head and a collarless shirt buttoned to the throat. He too was teary-eyed.

"Thank you, Mrs. Bogár," his aunt said and slipped a coin into the woman's palm. Mrs. Bogár showed her palm to Tommy as if to teach him how things worked here before she shuffled off. He remembered Gabi's dad cursing concierges, accusing them of being police informants, who collected from both "the mouse and the cat."

As he wrapped his arms around his grandfather, Tommy felt as if he was embracing the past and the present at the same time. When his grandfather kissed him on both cheeks, he felt the stubbles and tears of a frail old man. But then his grandfather firmly shook his hand and raised his calloused palms over Tommy's head to recite the welcome prayer, and the grandfather he remembered reappeared, the one who carried heavy sacks of wheat, who cooked up a mouth-watering vegetable stew out in the fields, whose stories of horses' ears freezing off riveted him, the one from whom he hid in the corn silo after almost running him down with the horse wagon, the one who had a prayer for every action, from waking to going to the bathroom.

Magda took his hand and held it tightly as she led him past a small kitchen, which was dimly lit by a tiny window that had bright red peppers strung across it like a necklace. They entered another small room with drawn curtains. The room, no bigger than his bedroom, was crowded with a sofa, an armchair, a coffee table and the familiar armoire with the bullet holes. In the corner a glass cabinet was filled with porcelain figurines, little shepherd boys playing flutes with little dogs at their side and little girls in folkloric headdresses, blouses and skirts with geese next to them. His parents had the same figurines. Tommy's mother told him that they were valuable, though he couldn't understand why. Maybe because Magda also had them. There were pictures of him with his mother and father at his high school graduation and his Bar Mitzvah picture with a tallit draped around his shoulders and yarmulke on his head.

He sat between his aunt and his grandfather, each gripping one of his hands. He didn't know what to say.

"We're so glad that you are here," Magda said. "Your grandfather stayed up all night praying during your flight."

"And the good Lord answered. We have to have a drink to celebrate," he said, patting Tommy's knee. Magda got up and brought in three glasses and a half-full bottle of clear liquid that had no label.

"Do you know what pálinka is?" he asked Tommy

"A man is not a man until he has drunk *pálinka*," Tommy said, raising his glass.

His grandfather mumbled another prayer.

"Amen and La Chaim," Tommy said when he finished.

"He speaks Yiddish." His grandfather beamed.

"I just know a few words."

"Here, that's a lot." His grandfather and Magda repeated "La Chaim" in unison and drank the *pálinka* in one gulp. Tommy tilted his head and swallowed. He waited for the explosion of fire to shoot through his throat and nostrils. His eyes watered. He pursed his lips.

"Now you're a man, again."

As the warmth spread through his body, Tommy said, "I remember drinking *pálinka* before we left Békes and then before we crossed the border."

"Tell us all about it," his grandfather said. "Hannah didn't write us, so we don't know what happened. We didn't know if you had made it or not for a year. We had visits from the secret police. They kept telling us that they had captured you."

"First we eat," Magda said. She disappeared into the kitchen.

Tommy could smell the familiar food from the living room. Just as he was about to dive into the chicken soup his grandfather put his hand on Tommy's and signalled Magda, who handed Tommy a well-worn fedora. He put it on.

"You look like your grandfather when he was younger," Magda said, beaming.

His grandfather began praying again. Tommy glanced at his aunt and noticed that she wasn't praying and didn't say Amen.

After the meal, Tommy told the story of their time in Budapest in the safe house, watching young kids blow up a tank, staying in the synagogue, the stopping of the train by the secret police, their near arrest, the midnight border crossing, the near capture by a soldier, their sea voyage and their arrival in Montreal.

"Thank God," his grandfather said.

"Rotten lice," Magda spat.

Tommy opened up the suitcase and repeated his mother's instructions about the lining. Magda went through the clothes, separating what was theirs and what was meant for Emma-mama.

"I have to go back now. There is a curfew at the dormitory. We have a practice tomorrow and the game is the day after. And then we have to go to Budapest right away. But I will come back after."

"Wait," his grandfather said and went off to the bedroom. He came back with something wrapped in a handkerchief. "For your Bar Mitzvah."

Tommy was puzzled. His Bar Mitzvah was six years ago.

"We couldn't send it to you," Magda said. "We were afraid it might be stolen by those rotten customs people."

He unfolded the handkerchief. It was a silver cigarette case.

"Open it," she said.

Tommy clicked the catch and it sprung open. It was inscribed to Tommy. *For the Bar Mitzvah of Tamás Wolfstein. Mazel tov.*

"It's beautiful," he said, caressing it. His grandfather took out his handkerchief and dabbed his eyes and blew his nose. Tommy hadn't realized until now how much he missed not having a grandfather all these years.

"Are you and Grandfather coming to the game?" he asked Magda as they stood in the doorway.

"I will. Gabi got me a ticket. But your grandfather isn't well enough."

Tommy stiffened. "What's wrong? Anyu didn't say anything about him being sick."

"She doesn't know. He doesn't want me to tell her. Not yet. I will tell you when you come back next week."

He was about to leave when his grandfather stopped him.

"Tell me one thing." He looked at Tommy in the eyes with a seriousness that comes before words of wisdom. "Tell me. How do they make the airplane and the people so small when it's in the sky?"

For a moment Tommy considered it. "I don't know. A miracle." He embraced him and whispered goodbye.

4 2

C oach Hus blew his whistle and gathered the boys around him. "Okay, boys, last day before Game Day. Let's fool around."

"What do you mean, Coach?" Luigi asked.

"Today's practice is about play. Johan Huizinga, a Dutch historian and cultural theorist, wrote a book called *Homo Ludens*." The boys snickered. "Not that kind," Coach Hus said, shaking his head. "It's Latin, it means 'Playing Man.' Huizinga studied the history and cultural significance of play. He made a distinction between games and play. Games like soccer or hockey, he said, have rules imposed on them: duration, location, as well as conditions under which it is played. Play doesn't. The place, the time and rules are imposed by the players. There is no supervision from the outside. According to him, all creatures, dogs, cats and humans, play. They don't need to be told how, why or when to do it. They just do it. Have fun, boys," he said, and left.

"What the fuck was that?" Ivan asked.

The boys weren't sure what to do. They looked to Tommy and Speedy for guidance. Tommy yelled "Huizinga" as he yanked Speedy's shorts down and took off down the field.

"You loco," Speedy yelled as he tried to pull up his shorts and chase Tommy at the same time. He tripped and went rolling.

Schmutz slipped behind Ivan and got down on all fours. Tito gave Ivan a shove, who went flying ass-backwards. "What the fuck?" he yelled, grabbing Schmutz, and began wrestling with him. Soon they were all chasing each other across the field, kicking balls at each other, pulling down shorts and breaking into groups to see who could keep the ball in the air the longest.

Speedy tackled Tommy and they started laughing. Tommy sat up next to Speedy. "As you said, Coach Hustle is crazy as a fox."

"Did you notice that guy?" Speedy asked.

"Who?"

"That guy standing beside the tree over there?"

Tommy shaded his eyes. "I don't see anyone."

"He's gone now. Maybe he was scout."

"Yeah, or maybe he's a spy," Tommy said jokingly. But as the words left his mouth, he felt a chill.

4 3

Tommy had never been in such a quiet dressing room. It was like being at a funeral. Everybody was in his own world. He laid out his uniform on the bench. Naked, he stood before it as if he were in a trance. He began his ritual: jockstrap, shorts, socks, shin pads, cleats, left then right, and finally his jersey. Number ten. His number since he could say Puskás. Puskás, the captain of the team that beat England, the best in the world, on their home turf, in the game of the century. People said that it could not be done, but they did it. Like Tommy and his parents, Puskás and the team had defected in '56. Puskás had said he would not return until the Russians were gone. He never came back. But now Tommy had.

"We probably won't win this game," Coach Hus said.

Every player looked up. What kind of pep talk is this? Tommy wondered. He stared at the coach.

"But that doesn't matter. What matters is how we play. I want you guys to play like the Canadian university champions that you are. I want you to play like Canadians. You are the Internationals. You and your families came from all over the world to be Canadians. Your parents worked hard to make a better life, to give you a better life. Thank them by doing your best. Make your university, yourselves and Canada proud. I want you to play with pride and heart; hard and like a team. I want you to play and enjoy the game." He clapped his hands and shook hands with every player as they solemnly exited.

Tommy and Speedy led the way into the tunnel beneath the stands. The Debrecen team emerged and lined up beside them.

Their all-white uniforms with a band of blue across the chest made them seem invincible. And Gabi, in black, was like the gatekeeper who allows no one in.

The referee stood before the teams, blew his whistle and led them out onto the field.

A tremendous cheer rose from the crowd. Tommy looked around. The stadium was half full. He felt a kind of vertigo. They had never played in front of such a huge crowd. Thousands of people were yelling and applauding.

The teams lined up on both sides of the referee, facing the dignitaries. In the first row at centre field, Tommy saw his aunt waving. Beside her was another woman, taller and plumper, who was also smiling and waving ecstatically. It was Emma-mama.

The announcer had trouble with the names of the Internationals. Only Tommy's name did he pronounce correctly. Tommy heard a few boos among the polite applause. The cheer and applause for the home team was loud and drawn out. So that's what adulation sounds like, he thought. He closed his eyes and took it in. A charge of electricity shot through him. His heart beat faster. He didn't care that the cheers and applause weren't for him.

The first notes of the Canadian anthem sounded. Strong and declarative. And though it wasn't his native land, it was his home now. Derek began to sing. The others spontaneously put their arms around each other's shoulders and joined him, swaying in unison. It gave him goosebumps. And even though he didn't know all the words, it gave him a sense of pride, and he appreciated his parents' constant declaration of love for Canada.

When the Hungarian national anthem began, Tommy noticed the Debrecen players stiffen. They stood statue-still. Less of an uplifting song than a lament, the anthem was a funeral-sounding dirge with a chorous of words Tommy couldn't make out.

When it was over, Tommy led his teammates towards their opponents. He and Roberto exchanged pennants with Könyves and Gabi. Gabi and Tommy smiled at each other. Their smiles spoke of their shared childhood and the innocence and joy of games played in the dirt yard of their home.

"Have a good game, Grosics."

"You too, Puskás."

Tommy won the toss and elected to start, even though it meant that Derek would be looking into the sun. It would be good to get that first touch of the ball. He looked at each of his teammates as they lined up and nodded. He took a deep breath and tapped the ball to Speedy.

Debrecen swarmed them and before long they were penned in their half. Debrecen was fast, and sharp and accurate with their passes. They played the long ball, the short give and go and made perfect crosses. The Internationals were always one step behind. Coach Hus's ruse about Derek's weak side seemed to be working. And though being in shape helped to keep Debrecen from finishing off their plays and practising total soccer allowed them to bottle up the scoring lanes, Tommy knew it was only a matter of time before Debrecen would score. It happened at the seventeen-minute mark. A cross from the left wing found Könyves inside the sixteen-yard area alone. It took him only a second to turn and shoot to the left corner. Derek dove but it was out of reach. The crowd exploded.

"Shit," Derek said.

The boys came by to encourage him. Schmutz patted him on the rear. "It's okay, man. Lucky goal."

"Let's focus. Let's shit or get in the pot," Ivan yelled to the guys as they headed back to centre field.

Tommy felt as if he had already played a full game. "We have to open up our wings," Speedy said to Tommy as they lined up. "We're playing chase with these guys."

"Luigi, Archie, Schmutz, spread it to the wings," he yelled, passing the ball to Speedy, who laid it out to Luigi on the left half. Speedy took off to the right while Tommy crossed over to the left. Stanislaus was waiting for Luigi's pass and he immediately put it down the line to where Tommy was galloping. It was perfect.

The Debrecen defence shifted and just before their halfback and fullback converged on Tommy, he centred it to Schmutz. who snuck up from his centre-half position and blasted one to the right corner. Gabi leaped and gathered it in. Tommy watched with amazement at how fast and how far he got. He almost applauded.

"That's the way, boys," he heard Coach Hus yell. The chance gave the boys a new life. They were in the game. Although Debrecen still had most of the game, the boys were holding their own. They managed to keep the game around midfield and got a couple shots on nets. They got one more good chance just before the half on a corner. Stanislaus centred a beaut and Tommy out-jumped the guy guarding him. He twisted his head to direct the shot to the left corner. It was heading in when out of nowhere a fist shot out and directed the ball away from danger. God, he's good, Tommy thought, shaking his head in disbelief.

Debrecen took control again and their superior skills began to show. They started to beat the boys on one on one. "Double team. Double team," Coach Hus hollered from the side. Tommy, Speedy and Stanislaus, the three forwards, had to drop back more to support the defence. Derek, inspired by Gabi, was making big saves himself. The crossbar helped out twice.

The whistle blew to end the first half.

"Great. Great!" Coach Hustle patted each of the guys as they walked off the field into the dressing room. He waited for the boys to catch their breath. "You guys were great. You guys are great!" He addressed them as he clapped his hands. "Keep it up. Keep it up. Derek, you're amazing. Archie, good hustle. Ivan, solid, like a Russian tank. Tommy, they're starting to double-team you. That should leave you, Speedy, with some room. Make something happen. You boys are playing great defence. Keep it up."

"He's amazing," Speedy said with admiration.

"Yeah," Tommy said.

"How we gonna score on him?"

Tommy shook his head. "He's got everything, height, speed and range."

Derek leaned over. "Use the sun," he said. "Half the time, I felt blind. If the sun sets the right amount, it should get him directly in the face."

Tommy nodded. "Okay. Boys, shots at sun level," he shouted.

The second half began the same as the first. Debrecen was swarming again but added the one-on-one attack. They spread the game so it was difficult for the Internationals to double team. At the twenty-third minute, a beautiful deke by the right-winger had Tito, the left fullback, turning the wrong way and gave the winger open field. Archie had to cover, which left his guy free for a clear shot that Derek had no chance on.

"Debrecen! Debrecen!" the crowd chanted. The boys, winded, as if the goal had kicked them in the guts, were doubled over. The crowd could see defeat in their heads-down as they marched back to centre field.

As the chanting subsided, Tommy heard Coach Hus yelling. "It ain't over, it ain't over till it's over. It ain't over, it ain't over, till the fat lady sings. Huizinga!"

The boys looked at Coach Hus, who was waving his arms around like some bird trying to take off. "What the fuck?" Ivan shouted. Schmutz laughed and joined Coach Hus. Soon the whole team was chanting "Huizinga," The referee, the Debrecen players and the crowd stared at them, wondering what they were chanting and why they were laughing.

They lined up for the kickoff. Speedy clapped his hands. Okay, here we go. The chant seemed to have lifted the boys' spirit and energy. They kept Debrecen out of their penalty area. Tito, determined not to let the right-winger make that deke again, made a couple of hard but legal tackles on him. Schmutz and Kostas had the captain between them like a hot dog between a bun.

"Wolfie, stay up," Speedy yelled at Tommy. "They got two guys on you, so that's less attack." Tommy nodded, slowed down and hung out around centre field.

"Tired?" one of the Debrecen players kidded him as they watched Debrecen press. Tommy shook his head and smiled.

"You guys are very good," he said, exaggerating his panting. From the corner of his eye, he glimpsed Stanislaus sneaking to the left sideline. Derek laid a lead pass towards him. Tommy jogged lightly in his direction. His two defenders moved as well. Then he took off toward the wing. The two defenders shot after him, which left the middle empty. Speedy and Archie came charging up midfield. Stanislaus lobbed it in and Speedy was in alone. Gabi came out to meet him. Suddenly Speedy passed it to his right and Archie had an open net.

For a minute, the whole stadium was silent. Then, as one and at once, the sound of the crowd's shock and the Internationals' joy erupted. The boys raced to mob Archie.

"Huizinga! Huizinga!" Coach Hustle was yelling and jumping up and down.

The whistle blew. Debrecen won 2-1. Tommy searched for Gabi. They shook hands and embraced. "Good game, Puskás," he said.

"Better game, Grosics," Tommy replied.

The two held onto each other's hands. Tommy was eight again, holding Gabi's hand as they walked past a burning tank.

"Emma-mama and Magda will be waiting for you outside," he said. "I have to go with my team. See you at supper."

"See you at supper," Tommy said, and they embraced again.

Emma spread her arms like a welcoming mother hen to embrace her chick. "Tomikám. Tomikám!" She and Magda were both crying.

"I have to go with the team, but I will be back next week." They smeared him with their tears and lipstick.

The reception dinner was held in the banquet hall of the Golden Stag Hotel. The dignitaries, the mayor, Mr. Luxton and Mr. Nemes, sat at the head table between the two facing tables. Archie, seated next to Tommy, leaned in and whispered, "Look at their faces."

"What?"

"Mr. Nemes is so serious, more than before. Mr. Luxton is grinning, like the Cheshire cat. He seems relieved, probably happy that it hadn't been a blowout. Listen to their speeches," Archie said.

The mayor stood up. Again, he welcomed the boys from Canada, praising their strong effort and their sportsmanship. He congratulated the Debrecen team and expressed the city's pride in their achievement. Mr. Nemes translated, adding in Hungarian that the Party was also proud of their victory and expected that there would be even greater ones ahead. Archie leaned over to Tommy for a translation. Mr. Nemes switched back to English and talked about the achievements of the Party that provided free university to all and equal opportunities to every one of its citizens. He extolled the virtues of the five-year socialist plan that achieved its objectives of raising Hungary from the rubble of the war against fascist elements. There was polite applause.

Archie whispered in his ear. "His speech was a propaganda lecture. And he just gave their team shit for doing so poorly."

"Where the hell did you get that idea?"

Mr. Luxton rose. He thanked the mayor, Dr. Nagy and the people of Debrecen for their warm welcome. He congratulated the Debrecen team on their hard-won victory.

"On behalf of the government and people of Canada, I would like to thank Hungary and its people for this wonderful gift, for this opportunity of our young people, many of whose parents, immigrants, from all over the world, came to Canada seeking opportunities and freedom to pursue their dreams, to see the wonderful progress that Hungary has made. I would like to toast the strong bonds that events and opportunities such as these encounters present to bind the people of Hungary and Canada closer together. And we hope soon to see Hungary's hockey team in Canada so that we may share with you our national sport as you have shared your national sport with us. And as we say, it ain't over till it's over."

The boys hooted and clapped.

"That's *our* propaganda lecture and a dig at their system," Archie commented.

Mr. Nemes nodded and translated a portion of it. Everyone applauded. Tommy looked over at Gabi. He remembered a dream he'd had while his family was in a farmhouse in the woods near the border, waiting for cloud cover before crossing into no man's land. In his dream Gabi was in nets on a muddy field. Tommy was taking shots on him. Each time he kicked the ball towards Gabi, tanks shot it down. He waved. Gabi waved back.

44

Next morning, waiting to board their train back to Budapest, Tommy spotted a kiosk in the station. "Hey, Speedy, watch my stuff. I'll be back in a minute."

He addressed the old lady. "Pardon. Do you sell rock candy?" She stared at him, uncomprehending. "Little pieces, white, crystal."

The old lady smiled. "Ah, yes."

The kiosk was like the one in Békes, where he and Gabi had stopped every day to buy their candy. Even the old lady resembled the one in Békes. They used to call her the turtle lady because she sat in her little kiosk, the size of their outhouse, and only stuck her head out when a customer came by. She made a cone out of a strip of newspaper and showed it to him. He nodded. While he was waiting, he glanced at the newspapers on display. He spotted the *Hungarian People's Sports Daily*, whose headline read "Debrecen Wins!" It had a photo of their game on the front page. Tommy bought a copy.

"Look, guys. We made the front page," he said holding up the paper. The boys rushed him. In his hurry, Schmutz knocked the cone out of his hands.

"Sorry," Schmutz said.

"Hey, asshole, watch what the fuck you're doing!" Tommy yelled. His fists were clenched.

The boys froze. They had never seen or heard Tommy react this way.

"Sorry," Schmutz said again. "I'll buy you another."

"Fuck your sorry," Tommy hissed.

Speedy stepped in. "Cool it, amigo."

Tommy looked at him and then back at Schmutz.

He was shaking inside. "Sorry. Sorry," he repeated, grabbing his suitcase before heading for the train.

"What was that about?" Speedy asked once they settled in.

"Nothing. I don't know."

"Bullshit."

Tommy stared silently out the window. Soon the steady rhythm of the train lulled him to sleep. The sky was dark. Suddenly, shooting stars were flying upward. After reaching their zenith, they paused for a minute before showering down into the dust. A pack of dogs appeared and surrounded the fallen, glistening stars. They licked them up. Tommy took a step toward the stars. He wanted some. The dogs snarled, bared their fangs and coiled to pounce. Tommy reached into his pocket for his knife. It wasn't there.

Somebody was shaking him. "Hey, Wolfie, you okay?" It was Speedy.

Tommy jerked awake, fists, clenched.

"You okay?"

Tommy took a deep breath. "Yeah, yeah, why?"

"You were yelling in Hungarian."

"I was?"

"What's *megolleg*?"

"Huh?"

"You kept repeating *megolleg*."

"I have no idea. At least not the way you're saying it."

"Are you okay?"

"Yeah." He took a deep breath. Still, he felt anxious.

"Okay. In that case, can you translate the article? The guys are curious."

He rubbed his face. "Sure."

They gathered around as he tried to decipher his mother tongue. "The headline says Debrecen Wins. The caption beneath the picture of the first goal says, Captain Könyves András leads by example."

Tommy flipped to the sport section where it was the top story. "Hungary defeats Canada. University soccer champions Debrecen welcomed Canadian university soccer champions with a lesson in soccer. It was not a surprise that Debrecen won. This fine soccer team, with such stalwarts as Könyves András and the excellent goal tending of Földember Gábor, had an easy time defeating the visitors 2-1."

"They beat us, but they had to work their nuts on," Ivan said.

Tommy continued. "It was obvious that Debrecen, in the spirit of friendship, did not go all out against the Canadian team that showed some talent but obviously were not at this elite level. Most of the game was played in Canada's half and they obviously lacked the skills to really make a game of it. It was only toward the end when it was obvious that the game was out of reach that the Debrecen eleven eased up enough to allow our visitors a goal. It was scored by Bellafonte Archie."

The boys cheered and slapped Archie on the back.

"Their top players and co-captains, Wolfstein Tamás and Gonzales Roberto, were easily held in check by the solid defence of Debrecen. Though Wolfstein showed skills, they were not developed to the level to pose a serious threat to his cousin Földember Gábor. They will play their second and final friendly in Budapest at the People's Stadium on Sunday at fourteen o'clock. We look forward to an entertaining game."

"*Cazzo.*" Luigi summed it up with his usual Italian gesture. "It's all bullshit."

"Let them try to get by me again," Tito said. "I'll tackle them into the fucking Danube."

"They're going to come at us like crazy," Coach Hus said as Tommy put down the paper. "This might work in our favour."

"What do you mean, Coach?" Derek asked.

"Let me think on it."

The players drifted back to their seats.

Tommy watched the countryside fly by for a few minutes. Then he went to sit with Schmutz and Kostas.

"Rock candy was my favourite candy when I was a kid. Every day, after school, my cousin and I would buy a coneful at a kiosk, like the one at the station in Debrecen. One day we were there when the school bully arrived with his friends and pushed us aside. The old lady who ran the kiosk told them to wait their turn. After I got mine, the bully smacked me in the head and sent my candies flying. When I bent down to pick them up, he kicked me in the ass and sent me flying. When I got up, he and his gang were laughing at me. The loss of the candy didn't piss me off as much as the feeling of helplessness and humiliation."

Schmutz nodded. "Sorry," Tommy said, extended his hand and returned to his seat.

Archie was lecturing Speedy. "It wasn't meant for you."

"What wasn't meant for Speedy?" Tommy asked as he rejoined them.

"Not Speedy, us. The article wasn't meant for us. It was meant as a public reprimand for the Debrecen team."

"Why, because they only won by one goal?"

"Yes, but more because, for their political system, this wasn't just a friendly game. It was a propaganda match. Their socialist, communist system against capitalism."

"You think anyone cares about a friendly soccer game between a Canadian and Hungarian university team?"

"In Canada? No. But here? Yes," he said. Archie, who never spoke softly when he could preach, was on a roll.

"Hallelujah," shouted Schmutz and some of the other boys who had joined them.

Archie smiled and continued. "You bet, brother. The article was for the Hungarians. Imagine if a Canadian all-star hockey team were to be beaten by a Hungarian team at the Forum. The puck would hit the fan."

"Canada would cream any Hungarian team," Luigi said.

"That's not the point. Your reaction is. Same difference. In propaganda, image is everything. Debrecen may have won but just by our reaction after the game, jumping up and down, tell me, who looked like they had won? They, on the other hand, are probably being told that the score was the same as a loss. Coach is right. They'll be told to show no mercy. Sunday will be a fight for the motherland. They'll be out for blood."

When Tommy and Speedy were alone again Tommy leaned over and quietly said, "*Meg öllek* means I'm gonna kill you."

Dear Marianne

Hope you are doing OK. And that it worked out with your parents. You blew me away with that kiss. Probably your parents too. I miss you. I miss holding you, I miss you making me crazy.

We are busy practising, playing and travelling. I don't know if there is news about us in Mtl. But here, we are in the newspaper, on radio and TV. We lost our 1st game but only by 1 goal. That was pretty good. They're very good. We have one more game in Budapest. I hope we can win this one. I can dream, can't I?

Speedy and I are getting along like old times, I think. Being here is strange. Even though it's my birthplace, I feel like a visitor. Speaking Hungarian feels strange. And people are strange when you're a stranger… the song has new meaning for me.

Being here has brought back memories I had forgotten. Not all good. I've had some bad dreams…bad acid flashbacks? Ha Ha. I'm trying to breathe.

How are the dance classes going? Going to any poetry readings? Say "high" to Naomi. I'll tell you more about everything when I get home. I'll probably be back before this letter gets to you.

I'm going to crash now. Miss you.

Love,
Tommy

4 5

oach Hus called for a meeting, but instead of holding it on the pitch, he found a classroom. He paced as he spoke. "We did good. We showed them that we could play with them. We showed ourselves that we could keep up with them."

"Almost," Tito said, still pissed with himself about the second goal.

"Now let's see if they can play with us."

"What do you mean, Coach?" Ivan asked.

"Well, they certainly have the skills and they can hustle, but I'm wondering if they can play football."

"What are you talking about, Coach?" Kostas asked. "Of course they can. They beat us, didn't they?"

"No, I don't mean soccer, I mean football, Canadian style."

The boys sat in mute silence. They had no idea where the coach was going with this. "You want us to tackle them Canadian football style?" Schmutz joked.

"Did you guys notice what happened on Archie's goal?"

"He scored?" Schmutz said.

"Yeah, but how? Whether you guys knew it or not, we pulled a trap. Wolfie played the decoy. He lured the defence to the left and the middle opened up. Same thing happened when he almost headed one in. So we have to think in terms of traps Canadian football style. We don't have much time to perfect them but if we can pull a couple of basic ones, I think we might surprise them. I think we could work a couple of basketball picks as well."

Coach Hus diagrammed a couple of plays on the blackboard. He kept it simple. Tommy had always thought of Coach Hus as a phys-ed teacher who knew the game from a book. He had joked that he was a star benchwarmer at university. But now, watching him draw Xs and Os, Tommy saw another side of him. His Huizinga practice, his it-ain't-over cheerleading and bringing a Canadian perspective to the game gave Tommy a new respect for him. Mr. Papp was wrong about him. Sitting at old-style wooden desks with inkwells, Tommy and the boys were getting an education. He caught himself sitting up straight with his fingers interlaced. Tommy raised his hand, two fingers pointing to the sky, the way he was taught in grade one. "There's one guy who yells a lot, Coach."

"So? What does he yell about?"

"Their centre half is like a general on the field. He calls plays, which side to load and the like. I could try to do quick translations."

"Ah, our very own fifth columnist," Luigi said.

That afternoon, they walked through the plays that Coach Hustle had diagrammed. If it worked just once or twice, who knew what could happen.

Anna was in the bleachers watching them. She waved. Tommy and Speedy waved back.

Team suppers on the road were usually loud affairs, boys shouting at each other, joking, stealing each other's cutlery, stabbing food from each other's plates. Coach Hus usually had to yell at them to behave, that they were representing their university. Tonight, they ate in near silence. After supper, Luigi, Stanislaus and Ivan didn't engage in one of their loud card games. Tito and Derek weren't arguing about some war. Professor Archie, instead of holding court, was sitting alone reading *Das Kapital,* his favourite book. Even Schmutz in his corner armchair was quiet.

Tommy went outside and sat on the steps. He lifted his eyes up. Clouds drifted by now and then, their shapes shifting. A chilly breeze caressed his face. As he rubbed his scar, it dawned on him that he had come within an inch of not existing. Of not getting to Canada, not meeting Marianne. Of not being part of this team here in Hungary. Was there a purpose to all this? Where were all these crazy thoughts coming from? He tried not to think of anything, but the churning of his stomach wouldn't let him. He rose, stepped into the dark. He gazed up at the starry sky while he took a piss. He shook his head and went in back in.

When Tommy came in, Schmutz began chanting, "spy, spy, spy."

Tommy smiled. "It's what Nemecsek did," he said.

"What? What are you talking about?" Agostino asked.

Tommy settled into an armchair. "Gather round, children, and I will tell you a story."

The boys looked up. No one said a word. "Listen and I will tell you the story of Nemecsek."

"What?" Stanislaus said.

"Not what. Who."

"Okay. Who?" Tito asked.

"This story is about Nemecsek and the deed of the underdog."

"Forget the literary analysis and get on with the story," Archie said, slapping his book shut.

"You're one to talk," Derek said. "You always analyze. Go on, mate."

"Okay, children. Once upon a time, there was a young boy whose name was Nemecsek. He was the smallest, frailest member of the Paul Street boys, a group who had their clubhouse in a lumberyard on Paul Street in Budapest. The lumberyard was their domain. Their enemy was The Red Shirt gang. The Red Shirts wanted to take over their territory. They challenged the Paul Street Boys to do battle for the ownership of the lumberyard."

"A fight. A fight. Good," Ben yelled.

The boys laughed.

"Nemecsek was the lowest-ranked member of the boys."

"Like you," Ivan said, throwing a pillow at Ben.

"Shut up and listen!" Tommy snapped.

The room grew silent. This was the second time the boys had heard Tommy snap like that. Speedy was usually Captain Loud. Tommy was Captain Quiet.

"He was the only private in the group. Every other member had a rank or a title, but not Nemecsek. They were always bossing him around and saying he wasn't big enough, strong enough or brave enough. So, the night before the big battle he sneaks over to the Red Shirts' territory. It was in some sort of a botanical garden. He spies on them to learn their battle plans and to prove himself worthy of membership in the Paul Street gang. The Red Shirts catch him and interrogate him about the Paul Street plans. He refuses to betray his friends. So they dunk him in a pond. He still refuses and they do it again. By the time he gets home he is shivering and catches a very bad cold that makes him feverish and unable to fight with his pals. But he refuses to stay home while his friends are fighting, so he sneaks out and goes to the lumberyard. The battle is going badly for the Paul Street boys. The Red Shirts' leader is about to snatch their flag, which would mean that the battle was over." Tommy rose and walked out of the room.

"Hey! What happened then? You can't leave it like that," Ben shouted after him.

"I'll tell you tomorrow, after the game."

"You're a weird guy, loco in the coco," Speedy said when they were back in their room.

4 6

"Hey, I'm going to check out room 101. Do you have another pair of nylons?"

"No. I don't think you should go."

"Why not? Anna invited me."

"You could get into trouble being out on your own."

"I won't be on my own. It was very okay last time. I will have a lovely Hungarian *chica* to keep me company."

"Don't..."

"I'll be careful, Mamasito. Later, amigo."

Lying in bed, Tommy remembered that the last time he read *The Paul Street Boys* he, Gabi and their parents were in the Dohany Street Synagogue. Tommy wanted to see that synagogue again, to see what it looked like to a nineteen-year-old prodigal son. He drifted off to memories of burnt-out tanks and overturned streetcars.

The door flew open. He jumped awake. It was Speedy with two bulky forms behind him. They shoved Speedy in. Tommy scrambled out of bed.

"Tell him Hungarian girls aren't whores like American girls," one said.

"Who are you?" Tommy said, trying to calm himself.

"We could arrest him. Translate!" the shorter of the two shouted.

Tommy had never seen Speedy so enraged. "What happened?"

"They were waiting inside with her."

There was something familiar in their faces. "Speedy, apologize!" he hissed.

"The bitch set me up," he snarled. "Soon as I got in she yelled rape. I should have…"

Tommy shoved Speedy against the wall. "Look like you're sorry," Tommy growled at him.

He let go of Speedy. "Sirs, please, my friend is very sorry. He understands what he did was wrong and would like to apologize." Tommy went to the night table, took five hundred forints from his wallet and gave it to Speedy. "Shake hands," he told him.

One of the men grabbed Tommy's wallet and took out the rest. He sneered and threw the wallet on the floor. "You say anything to anybody, and we will be back, you pieces of American shit!"

When they were gone, Tommy and Speedy stared at each other in silence.

Speedy kicked the door. "Fuck!"

A shiver shot through Tommy. He squeezed his hands into fists and clenched his jaw. "Rotten lice!"

47

oach Hus wanted the team to get to the stadium early so they could get the feel of the place and get over their nerves. The People's Stadium, Hungary's soccer temple, where Tommy's childhood heroes had performed heroic deeds, could be seen from miles away.

He had never seen a stadium so huge. Not even the Montreal Forum. His father had promised to take him to the People's Stadium when he turned eight. And though he did spend his eighth birthday in Budapest, they weren't there to see Puskás and the rest of the Mighty Magyars vanquish their foes. They were there to escape. Now, eleven years later, he was finally here, not as a fan, but to play on the Golden Green himself. He could hardly believe it.

The groundskeeper led them through the dark corridors that snaked under the stands. He felt like he was in a labyrinth. When they arrived at the dressing room, the groundskeeper opened the door. Tommy was surprised. It was more like a cell than his heros' royal chamber. It was a plain room with worn wooden benches that ran along three walls, peeling paint, rusty hooks and bare bulbs. Jarry Park's dressing room was nicer than this. Still, it felt like a special place. "Speedy. Look." He pointed to a number ten on the wall. He took off his jacket and hung it on the hook below it. "My jacket is hanging on Puskás's hook. I'm sitting in the same dressing room, maybe in the same spot where he sat. I can't wait to tell my father."

He could see tell Speedy was still seething. He placed a hand on his shoulder. "Breathe, amigo. We have a game to play."

"Fucking right," Speedy hissed.

"Something eh? Like sitting in the Habs room where The Rocket put on his jockstrap, eh?" Schmutz said.

"No."

"Why not?"

"When a Canadian kid goes into the Habs' dressing room, he can dream of becoming a Hab, the next Rocket, but I was denied that right."

Coach Hus clapped his hands together. "Okay, boys, Let's go have a look at the field."

Tommy felt small on the huge pitch. He strolled to centre circle, slowly made a full turn, looked at all those empty seats rising to the sky and the nets at both ends, which seemed a million miles away. He lay down on his back, placed his palms on his chest and closed his eyes.

"What are you doing? Grass angels again?" Luigi asked.

"My father told me that the grass of the Golden Green was so soft that you'd want to lie down and sleep on it. He was right." He closed his eyes. He heard 60,000 people call his name. He took a deep breath, as if inhaling its history, its tradition and its glory. This could have been my turf, he thought to himself.

Back in the locker room, Tommy took his time getting dressed. He and Speedy sat side by side and followed their ritual. Today it was even more focused. Both Speedy and he had scores to settle.

"Let's put it into the game," Tommy said.

Speedy nodded. They sat quietly. The room was still but it wasn't the same stillness as in Debrecen. The boys understood they were sharing a special moment, a high they might never experience again.

Speedy stood up. "Okay, Sir Internationals, listen. We've come a long way. We've come from all over the world. We can curse in many languages. We are the Canadian university champions. We have one more game. We're playing in Budapest on the field where Puskás played. Now we're playing on it with our own Puskás. How can we lose?"

"Puskás! Puskás! Puskás!" the boys chanted. Tommy's eyes misted.

"Okay Captain Puskás, lead us out," Schmutz shouted. Tommy stood and circled the room, shaking hands with each of the players, Coach Hus and Ben. He led his teammates through the dark, cleats clicking and echoing, and stopped just where the light entered the tunnel.

The two teams lined up under the stands. Tommy snuck a peek over to Gabi. He wasn't smiling.

A loud cheer greeted the teams. "God, there must be about 5,000 people," said Agostino in awe.

Gabi nodded as they shook hands. Tommy looked him in the eyes. There was a seriousness in them. Then at the last moment, Gabi winked.

Tommy stood at centre field. The ceremonies seemed to go on forever. He felt like he was outside of it all, outside of the world's reach, watching himself. He was in a silence where all chaos was stilled. The only sounds were his heartbeat and his breathing.

The whistle blew and suddenly he was back in the world and everything was happening at a furious pace.

Archie was right. Debrecen was coming at them faster and harder than they had in the last game. But the boys were expecting it. They were ready. And they weren't intimidated.

Coach Hus's preparation focused them. They slowed the game down. "Don't be afraid to play backward. Use Derek. Let him be the quarterback at the beginning," he instructed them before the game. Led by Tommy and Speedy, both of whom were playing with a ferocity that energized the boys, they not only held their ground but pushed Debrecen back.

Debrecen's frustration built as the game wore on. Tommy felt it. Speedy was not only tiring the man covering him but defensively was challenging and tackling his opponents like a vicious beast. The centre half was calling out plays but it had an edge to it. Tommy translated as fast as he could. He didn't try to control the game, just fed Luigi, Schmutz and Archie, who spread the ball to Stanislaus and Kostas on the wings, who were getting shots at Gabi. Nothing dangerous, but it was enough to keep Debrecen off balance.

The game became more of a physical chess match, slow, tactical and mainly taking place midfield. Tommy had the ball. He pivoted to the left to send a short pass to Speedy. All of a sudden, he felt a cleat cut across his left ankle. He buckled. He let out a yell as he collapsed in a heap. He writhed in pain, curled up and grasped his ankle. It felt limp, like it was dangling by a thread. Needles of pain shot through the flesh surrounding the bone. He looked up at the referee. The whistle never came. Debrecen's attack swept in on Derek. A roar exploded in the stadium.

Tommy lay there watching Debrecen mob their captain. Speedy tore off towards the referee.

"Speedy!" Tommy screamed. Schmutz took off after Speedy. Reaching out, he grabbed Speedy by the sweater and yanked him back, just before he reached the referee. Speedy was screaming and cursing the referee in English and Spanish. The referee whipped out a yellow card and flashed it in his face. Schmutz pushed Speedy away.

"Shut the fuck up!" he yelled at Speedy.

Coach Hus and Ben were kneeling next to Tommy. Ben pressed gently on his left ankle.

"Awww shit!" Tommy cried out.

"You okay?" the coach asked. Tommy winced.

"Is it broken?" Ben pressed a bit more firmly. Tommy winced again.

"No, I don't think so, but it's badly bruised. It needs to be taped."

The referee came by. He looked at Tommy. Tommy glared back. He thought of his grade one teacher, Mrs. Gombás, who was supposed to be fair and protect him. In the end she turned on him. The referee signalled Coach Hus to get Tommy off the field and send on a replacement.

"No," Tommy said sharply as he sat up. "Just tape it. Quick."

"I can send you back after."

"No. International rules. Once you're off, you're off."

"You sure?"

"Yeah."

"Okay."

"I'll be back," Tommy said to the referee as Ivan and Luigi helped him limp off. There was polite applause.

Ben unlaced Tommy's left cleat, pulled off his sock and immobilized his ankle. Tommy was biting his lip and staring at the game that had restarted. Debrecen was pushing again but the boys were holding down the fort. Tommy got up and tested his ankle. It hurt like a bitch. But he could walk. He trotted lightly. "Shit," he hissed but kept at it. The throbbing subsided slightly.

"Okay, Coach."

The coach signalled the referee at the next throw-in. There was applause as Tommy limped back onto the field, exaggerating his injury.

"Stay up," Speedy said as he passed him. "It'll force them to keep at least one guy near you, so it'll be even back there."

The half finished with Debrecen leading 1-0.

"What a fucking non-call," Tito shouted and slammed his towel down. "Fuck. He swallowed his whistle."

"What kind of fucking friendly is this?" Stanislaus yelled.

Coach Hus let the boys vent. "How is your ankle?" he asked Tommy.

"Tender, but I'll be okay." He leaned back and watched Ben unlace his cleat again.

"This is gonna hurt." Before Tommy could say anything, Ben ripped off the tape.

"Shit!"

"This will freeze it for a while. I may have to do it once or twice during the game."

The spray was cool on his skin. He stood and hesitantly put weight on it. The boys watched him flex and rotate his ankle. Soon the pain was minimal. "This is great."

"The bruise and the pain are there, you just don't feel it. Be careful," Ben said, taping Tommy's ankle again.

"Okay. Now we know. We have to forget the referee. It's time for Canadian football," the coach said. "Onside kickoff to start. Make them wonder."

Tommy was in the centre circle with Speedy. Kostas, Tito and Luigi lined up on the far right. The Debrecen players looked at the lineup, unsure what was going on. Tommy slipped the ball over to Speedy, who lofted a pass about ten yards, into the cluster of players on the right side. Tito and Kostas criss-crossed like offensive linemen to confuse the defence and to block anyone from getting to Luigi, who sent a sharp pass back to Tommy, who remained at centre. Speedy took off downfield to the opposite wing. Stanislaus followed Speedy, who had picked up Tommy's lead. Speedy dropped the ball back to Stanislaus, who slipped a pass to Archie, who slid it to Schmutz, who blasted a bomb from the sixteen-yard. Gabi leaped and barely managed to push it over the crossbar. The Debrecen players were yelling at each other. Tommy stood next to Gabi as they lined up for the corner.

"How are you?" Gabi asked. Tommy winked. ·

Gabi handled the corner easily and cleared the zone with a strong kick. But the boys were back to defend. Debrecen played a more cautious game now. They slowed it down. The Internationals had momentum, though they rarely got too deep. This gave Tommy a chance to get strength back in his ankle and control the game a little more. Instead of running and putting pressure on his ankle, he fed the halves, who did most of the running. Archie, Luigi and Schmutz were tireless. Gabi was busier than Derek.

There were about ten minutes left in the game. The freezing was wearing off. He stopped by the sideline so Ben could spray it again. "Trap two," Coach Hus yelled. "Trap two."

Tommy dropped the ball back to Schmutz, who dropped it back to Aggie.

Aggie passed it back to Derek, Derek to Ivan, Ivan back to Derek, who made like he was going to kick it upfield but rolled it to Tito. Debrecen players moved into the Internationals' zone, thinking that the Canadians were settling for a respectable 1-0 loss. Debrecen pushed like they needed more.

Archie slipped behind their centre half, who was guarding Speedy. Speedy took off toward Debrecen's net. The centre half guarding him backed up to keep pace with Speedy but was trapped by Archie. Speedy had the ball on Debrecen's sixteen-yard line. Gabi came out to cut down the angle. He remembered what happened the last time and looked for Archie. Tommy had limped to the opposite side. Speedy stopped and arced a pass toward him. Tommy took off and left his defender flatfooted. He remembered practising his header against Gabi and knew that Gabi would try to fist it off his head. They both jumped at the same time. Instead of heading it into Gabi's fists, he arched it over them.

Up in the air, they became one. Tommy remembered how scared he felt when they were ripped apart by the secret police on the train. Here in mid-air, suspended, away from their reach, Tommy felt rejoined.

A groan erupted in the stadium.

Tommy and Gabi came crashing down together. Lying on their backs, they were laughing. The boys came yelling and piling on top of them. Gabi squeezed Tommy's hand and crawled out from under the pileup.

The referee was furiously blowing his whistle. The players unpiled and headed back toward the kickoff circle. The referee continued blowing his whistle and was pointing to the spot beside Gabi.

"Goalie interference," he yelled, awarding a free kick to Debrecen. The boys didn't understand. When Tommy told them, they went berserk. They yelled at the referee in English, Italian, Greek, Portuguese, Polish, Russian. There was even cursing in

Hungarian from the stands. Tommy said nothing. He and Gabi looked at each other.

The referee stood his ground, like a statue pointing toward the Canadian net.

Gabi placed the ball for the free kick. He backed up, took a run at it, stopped, turned and kicked the ball into his own net.

There was a collective gasp from the fans before a deafening silence descended on the stadium.

Gabi's teammates were yelling at him as he stood with his hands on his hips eyeing the referee. The referee hesitated, not sure what to do. Finally, he blew the whistle and pointed to the faceoff circle. The Debrecen coach was yelling at Gabi and signalling him off. He nodded to Tommy and slowly walked off the field. There were loud boos, but Tommy also made out some applause. He started to clap. The rest of the Internationals joined in.

Coach Hus signalled Tommy out of the game. Tommy stared at the coach. He didn't want to leave. "Now!" Coach Hus yelled.

Coach Hus sat next to him. "Do you understand?"

Tommy said nothing. He didn't look at the coach. "You can't be in with your cousin out," he said and patted him on the back. Tommy sat and watched the ball being kicked, passed, headed and caught. It was blur, played in silence until the final whistle blew.

The crowd stood as the two teams lined up at centre field and waved. There was applause but it was sparse and uncertain, as if the fans were waiting for instructions.

The players on both teams faced each other and shook hands. The referee had disappeared. Tommy searched for Gabi. He wasn't there either.

As he shook Tommy's hand, Könyves said under his breath, "Gabi said that he will meet you in Békes. Good game, Puskás," he added.

The freezing was wearing off again. Pain radiated up his leg. He limped off the field, pausing at the lip of the tunnel. He turned and watched the stadium empty.

The boys were whooping and hollering, tossing their jerseys at each other, but Tommy sat motionless. Speedy knelt in front him and began to unlace his cleats. Carefully he rolled down Tommy's socks and slipped off his shin pads. He looked up at Tommy, smiled and ripped off the tape.

"Fuck!"

It felt like a million shards of glass were embedded in his body. Tommy winced and bit his lip. Tears crept from the corners of his eyes. He was laughing.

Mr. Luxton entered the dressing room.

"Quiet down," Coach Hus shouted.

"Boys, you played a wonderful game. I congratulate you all, both on your play and sportsmanship." He smiled at Tommy and Speedy. "You did yourself and Canada proud. Now, I know that you were supposed to be having an official farewell supper with the Debrecen team at the Matyas Pince restaurant tonight but that was cancelled. They will not be joining you. I am sure that you understand."

He glanced at Coach Hus and left. Coach Hus followed him out.

Tommy and Speedy looked at each other without saying anything. Tommy hobbled to the shower. He turned the hot knob full blast and raised his head to meet the jet spray. He cried as the scalding water cleansed him.

Tommy dressed slowly. He was the last to leave. He took one final look around the dressing room. "Apu, we did it! *Szerbusz*," he said, quietly closing the door behind him.

4 8

The Matyas Pince was located a block from the shores of the Danube. "It's world famous," Mr. Papp had told him during one of his Hungarian history lectures. "It was built in 1904. Originally it was a beer house. In 1947, during the first beer festival in Budapest, it served 3,050 litres of beer."

"Maybe we will break that record when we celebrate our victories," Tommy joked.

"Good luck." Mr. Papp smiled.

Tommy wasn't sure if he had been being sarcastic. Probably. Well, they had come close.

Inside the restaurant, sturdy wooden pillars supported high fresco ceilings. From them hung round soccer-ball-sized globes, forever suspended in the air waiting to be headed. The long solid tables and heavy wooden chairs added to the medieval banquet hall feel. He caressed the insignia on his maroon jacket. He was one of the Knights who had gathered here to celebrate their almost victory.

"Not like your uncle's bodega, eh?" Schmutz said to Speedy as they took in the size of the place.

"*Sí*. It sure is bigger."

"But it doesn't have Marianne dancing," Tommy said.

Young waiters, wearing white shirts, black vests and ankle length white aprons stood like an honour guard ready to lead them to one of the long tables. The other, facing them, remained empty.

The waiters brought water and menus and pointed to the back of them, where the offerings and prices were translated into English and U.S. dollars.

"That's smart," Speedy said.

"Let me put it to you this way," Archie said. "They may be communists, but they're not stupid communists. They want our dirty capitalist dollars."

"You and your political analysis. Give it a rest," Schmutz said.

"Everything is political. We are political animals," Archie shot back.

"I'm not a political animal, I'm a hungry animal," Schmutz said, looking over the menu.

"Would he have done it if you weren't his cousin?" Speedy asked.

"I've been thinking about that, too. Would you?"

"Honestly, I don't know. Maybe in a friendly, but in a final for the championship, I'm not sure."

"I wouldn't have," Schmutz said. "A game is for winning."

"But he did the right thing," Tommy said.

"He did a brave, honourable thing. He went against the system and the ruling class. Therefore, he did the wrong thing," Archie chimed in.

"What ruling class are you talking about? This is communism," Derek said from across the table. "Communism is about the dictatorship of the proletariat."

"Even they must have a ruling class," Archie countered. "The ref represents the overseer for the ruling class and so what the ref did was right. Your cousin did the wrong thing. In dictatorships, even in the proletariat kind, his actions can have serious consequences."

"What do you mean by serious?" Tommy asked.

Archie leaned over. "If you had done what he did back home, you might have been called stupid by those who believe winning is the only thing that matters." He looked at Schmutz. "Or you might be praised for doing the honourable thing. Here doing the right thing, especially so publicly, is the wrong thing; it might encourage others to do so as well. That's dangerous to the system. So, they have to nip it in the bud. This will probably affect him for the rest of his life."

"Enough with that politics. Here comes the vino," Schmutz shouted as the waiters appeared with bottles of wine.

Speedy picked up one of the bottles. "What's Bika Vér?"

Tommy laughed.

"What's so funny?"

"It's perfect for you, Speedy. It's Bull's Blood."

Coach Hus stood up and clinked his knife on his wineglass. The room quieted down. "I'm proud of you guys," he began before choking up and stopping mid-thought. "*Salut!*" he said quietly. He took a sip and sat down.

Surprising himself, Tommy stood up. "On behalf of the team, I would like to thank Coach Hus for his dedication, for bringing out the best in us. He's not only a great coach but also a great teacher. He reminded us that play is an essential part of the game. He taught us to use our individual strengths to play together and make us a championship team. And doing the right thing is the most important thing. To Coach Hus. Thank you."

"To Coach Hus," the boys toasted.

"I want to say one last thing. Even though they're not here, I want to toast the players of the University of Debrecen." Tommy raised his glass and pointed to the empty table. The boys rose and did the same.

Tommy hadn't realized how hungry he was until the heaping plate of beef goulash with gnocchi arrived and he took that first mouthful. Like his father, he closed his eyes to savour it, the Wolfstein way.

It was Mr. Papp who had suggested, or rather had insisted, that Tommy order the goulash once he found out where the team was going to have its last meal. He had somehow gotten hold of the team's agenda from a connection in the Hungarian consulate.

"You must. It is our national dish and the chef at Matyas Pince is its master. His seasoning of caraway and thyme is delicate, and the tenderness of the beef is unmatched. I have it every time I am in Budapest." Tommy couldn't get enough of it.

Gypsy musicians wearing vests embroidered with elaborate flower designs took to the stage. Three men with slicked-down brilliant black hair and immaculately trimmed mustaches bowed to them.

Tommy poked Speedy. "Hungarian Gitanos."

Wistful notes rose from the violin. Like sparrows from branches, one after another they took flight to sing their songs to a beloved far away. Marianne would have loved this; she would have gotten up and danced to the music. He wondered what she was up to. Was she missing him? He hoped so, but knowing her, he wasn't sure. He hoped she wasn't hanging out with that bastard poet.

"Is all your Gypsy music so depressing?" Schmutz asked after the second lament.

"You're an ignorant Danish meatball," Speedy shouted back. "They're *cante jondos*."

Derek laughed. "What's that? Spanish bullshit?"

Fuelled by their performance and Bull's Blood, the Sir Internationals' trash talk began. Ivan called Stanislaus Sir Limp Sausage, who called Kostas Sir Screw Kebob, who called Luigi Sir Thin Linguini, who called Archie Sir Soft Bananas. On it went, a toast after each name until everyone had been knighted. Even Coach Hus got dubbed Sir Huizinga Burger.

Tommy, Sir Goulash Puskás, signalled for the violinist to come over. He handed him a hundred-forint bill and asked him to play the "Internationale." The Gypsy looked at him as though he was crazy. He wasn't. He was slightly drunk and ridiculously happy and sad. It was the team's last night in Hungary.

4 9

The boys and their bags crowded the dorm lounge as they waited for the bus to take them to the airport. Tommy was making the rounds, shaking hands with each of the guys.

"I can't find anything in this crazy-language paper," Schmutz said, waving the *Hungarian People's Sports Daily*. "Can you?" He shoved it at Tommy.

Tommy leafed through. Honvéd, his old favourite team, was near the bottom of the standings. He wished he could see them play but they were out of town. Maybe it was just as well. It was better to hold on to the glory team of old. The good old days, he thought.

"Here it is." Tommy pointed to a small column at the back of the paper. "It says that a friendly game was played between us and Debrecen. Both teams displayed the spirit of friendship. The game ended in a 1-1 tie."

"That's it?" Agostino asked.

"That sucks," Schmutz said.

"Shit, the game would be front-page news in *The Gazette*." Derek said. "Your cousin's action would be national news."

"Let me put it to you guys this way. It *is* national news here, that's why it's hidden like that," Archie said.

Tommy hoped Gabi was okay.

"Bus time, boys," announced Coach Hus.

Tommy clasped Speedy. They nodded to each other. "Say hi to Marianne."

"Will do and thanks. By the way, how does the story end?"

"What story?"

"The story you started the other night."

"I'll tell you when I get back."

"Loco in the coco," he said and punched Tommy on the arm. "Okay, amigo. See you soon."

Coach Hus took Tommy aside. "Enjoy yourself, and take care of that ankle." Lowering his voice, he said, "Be careful."

"Yeah, I will. Thanks, Coach."

Tommy watched the bus turn the corner and disappear. He asked the concierge to call him a taxi. The concierge waited with him. Tommy didn't tip him. He was probably a stoolie. Let the cops pay him. He wasn't going to be a paying mouse.

The taxi wove through the streets of Pest. Tommy didn't know his way around but felt that he was being taken for a ride. "Where are we?" he asked when the taxi stopped at a light.

"Dohany Street."

Tommy looked around. "I'll get out here."

"This isn't the train station."

"I know."

He opened the door before the light changed, grabbed his suitcase and paid. Dohany Street Synagogue was still impressive. He recognized the onion domes, the huge Ten Commandment tablets on top and the massive door that had opened when his father had said his Jewish name. He had a couple of hours before the train to Békes.

Inside, the towering ceilings and stained glass windows overwhelmed him. He strolled past the pews, remembering his last time here. He had turned eight in the synagogue. They had gone there for shelter after they fled the safe house where he had seen indoor plumbing for the first time, where he had been woken by the rumbling sound of a Russian tank and had seen the tank blown up by kids younger than he was now, where the explosions shattered windows and where he got a face full of glass slivers.

Tommy limped over to the Garden of Remembrance. Emma-mama had called the willows in the courtyard the Family

Trees and the stones beneath them the fallen leaves. He hadn't understood then that this was the cemetery of the Jews killed by the Hungarian Fascists during the war.

His ankle throbbing, he gingerly hobbled up to the museum on the second floor. Gabi and he had run up there eleven years ago, hoping to see knights' armours, shields and swords, but found only silver goblets, censors and breastplates for the Torah. In a corner, in a dark room, which Tommy had hoped was a dungeon, was a drum skin made from a desecrated Torah and dresses sewn from prayer shawls. He was surprised to see them still on display along with the same photographs of dead Jews piled in a heap. This isn't a museum, he thought to himself. This is a Wailing Wall. He remembered being sad and crying back then but not knowing why. This time he knew but didn't cry. Instead he was angry. The exhibit hadn't changed in eleven years. He had.

5 0

Gabi was waiting for him at the Hajdubékes station. Their embrace was fierce, as if a precious piece of their childhood had been returned. As if what began in mid-air on the Golden Green was now complete. "Welcome back," Gabi said, as he picked up Tommy's suitcases. He set off in a hurry to get him home. Tommy lagged behind. "Sorry." Gabi slowed down. "I forgot. Is it still bad?"

"It's tender and weak. I can't put my full weight on it yet, but it'll be okay."

"That was a cheap shot. That prick should have been red carded. Our coach should have been carded too."

"Never mind that. How are *you*?" Tommy wanted to know but didn't want to push Gabi on the subject. He didn't know how far he could go. Archie had suggested caution. Gabi didn't seem worried, but he could have been putting up a front.

"The referee should be hanged by his balls. If he had any," Gabi said.

Gabi sounded like his dad. Dezsö-papa had always spoken his mind, even if it got him into trouble. And it often did, according to Tommy's parents. Dezsö was always being reprimanded or demoted. He ended up drinking too much and dying too young, his father once told him. Since Gabi seemed open to talking, he decided to ask, "Are you in trouble?"

"Some."

"What kind?"

"Well, I'm off the team. And I have to attend some special classes."

"What kind of classes?"

"Where they correct your thinking."

"What?"

"I'll explain later. Don't say anything to my mother."

"Doesn't she know?"

"Not about the classes."

They walked along Market Street. In spite of the changes and the fact that he'd been only seven years old the last time he was here, the place felt familiar. Tommy stopped at the town square. He looked up at the statue. The last time he'd seen it, it was being pulled down by a mob.

"Wasn't it a statue of a soldier that was there?"

"Yeah, it was a Russian soldier."

"Who's that?"

"That's Lajos Kossuth."

"Who's he? Isn't your university called that?"

Gabi set down the suitcase. "Kossuth is the father of Hungarian democracy and freedom. Too bad we don't have live ones like him anymore. Now, men like him only exist in stone. It's safer." Gabi turned and pointed to a store across from the statue. "Do you remember that?" They walked toward it.

"Apu's hardware store." Tommy's father had been the manager of The People's Hardware. Often, he ran in there to get a few pennies to buy his candy. "What happened to Gyuri?" Tommy asked.

"You remember him?"

"After Puskás, Gyuri was my hero. He was the star of the Békés soccer team. Then he informed on Apu to the police."

"Yeah, the pig. Your father recruited him, got him a cushy job at the hardware store, even gave him money now and then, and then he went and betrayed him. My dad told me that your dad was fired for having too much inventory!"

"Apu never tires of cursing him. I still don't understand how having too much stock is a crime. What happened to him?"

"He made it up to Division II. Played a couple of seasons for Debrecen but drank too much and ended up in jail."

"Apu will be happy to hear that."

"There used to be a candy kiosk there." He pointed to where a fountain now stood spouting water through fish mouths.

"You remember a lot," Gabi said.

"I don't remember her name."

"Mrs. Tátrás. She died about three years ago."

"So where do you get your rock candy now?"

"I get my candy from some very sweet ladies," Gabi smiled.

For a minute, Tommy didn't get it. Then he guffawed.

"There's our old school. Remember that?"

"Yeah. Is Mrs. Gombás still teaching there? And Small Potato?"

"Mrs. Gombás got transferred after the Russians restored order. Some say she got sent to a re-education class. She never came back to Békes."

"Anyu will be glad to hear that."

"And Small Potato is now the principal. Too bad it's vacation time. He's away. We could've paid him a visit."

As they were standing in the schoolyard in front of the soccer pitch, a policeman approached. "So, the traitors have returned?" he said.

Tommy was taken aback. The officer was about their age. His hard, round, piggish face looked like it had been in a few fights.

Gabi said nothing.

"How much did this Judas give you to sell out your motherland?"

"What do you want, Szeles?" Gabi said.

Tommy tensed.

"*Officer* Szeles," the policeman replied. He eyed Tommy. "Your passport."

"Why?" Tommy asked.

"Because a police officer is asking for it. Your passport," he commanded.

Tommy clenched his fist. He felt a familiar anger rising in him. Gabi patted his arm as if to say, leave it be. Tommy took a deep breath and handed it over. Szeles examined the cover.

"So, Canada is where you are hiding now," he said. "Where is that?"

"In Canada," Tommy said.

Szeles gave him a stern look. Gabi smiled. Szeles flipped through the pages. "You can get it back from the police station when you leave."

"No. I would like it back now."

"What did you say?"

"I am a Canadian citizen and I would like to have my passport back now."

"You are now in the People's Socialist Republic of Hungary and you obey its officers and its laws. Do you want to be arrested?"

"No, but I would like my passport back, please," he said firmly.

"We will go with you to the station now," Gabi said, "and talk to Police Chief Barna, if you want."

"Dirty traitors," he muttered, dropping the passport on the ground.

Tommy bent to retrieve it. Gabi reached over and squeezed his hand to stop him. He stared at Szeles. Szeles turned and walked away.

Gabi bent down to pick up the passport. Tommy wanted to lash out but didn't. That made him angrier.

"How did he become a policeman?" Tommy asked.

"He can intimidate people. Rotten louse," Gabi said, and spat. Tommy did too. They walked the rest of the way in silence.

"Well, here we are," Gabi announced, pointing to a small house. It looked ancient. Large cracks like veins spread across its pale blue walls and chunks of stucco were missing. The door was askew. Gabi had to lean hard against it to push it open. Tommy reached out to touch the doorpost. The hollow was still there but not the mezuzah. He rubbed it lightly and stepped over the threshold.

"We're here!" Gabi called out.

"Tomikám! Tomikám!" Emma squealed as she came running out from the kitchen. She grabbed him and celebrated the miracle of his return with a shower of tears and a bouquet of loud kisses. She took a step back but held onto his wrists tightly. "Oh my. Oh my," she repeated between sobs of joy. Her hands slid over his face, stroking his lips, cheeks, and forehead.

"Oh, my little Tomikám."

Lunch was served on the verandah, at the same table that he had played the blind game with his father in the mornings. Sitting on the table in his pyjamas, Tommy would cry out, "I can't see! I can't see."

"Why? Oh, why?" his father would ask with great worry as he brought him his morning cup of hot milk.

"Because my eyes are shut," Tommy would shout, then open his eyes wide and grab the mug from his father, who would slap his palms to his beaming face and exclaim, "A miracle! A miracle!"

He looked out into the dirt yard, busy with the chickens strutting, clucking and pecking. "I'd forgotten about them," Tommy said. The playground of his first seven years was so much smaller than he remembered.

"Do you remember how I tried to stop you from sucking your thumb?" Gabi asked.

"I'd forgotten that I even did that."

"Oh, you were a great thumb sucker. A real loud sucker. Your parents were worried that you'd be doing it in school. They tried to shame you by saying that it was something only babies did, tried to bribe you with rock candy, and slapped your thumb out of your mouth whenever they caught you sucking it. Nothing worked. Then I came up with the brilliant idea of putting chicken shit on your thumb. You yelled and screamed and went running to your mother and she said 'good' and told me I should put chicken shit on your thumb anytime I saw you sucking your thumb. And it worked."

"It sure did," Tommy said, sticking his thumb in his mouth. He made loud slurping sounds.

"Watch out, because I can easily get some more!" He pointed to the chicken coop. It was still there, kitty corner to the outhouse.

"You still use that?" Tommy asked, pointing to the outhouse.

"Yup. And still no running water. But the good old well is still there. And we do have electricity."

How could so little have changed? Tommy wondered. Change was what Montreal was all about. Every day a store was opening or closing, a new song was number one, a new fashion was coming into fashion. Change was the only constant. But not here. I guess that's why it's called the Old World, Tommy thought to himself. "Anyu and Apu told me to get all the news. So, tell me."

"Well, we're doing well. I'm a year away from graduating. I'll probably work in Debrecen, so I won't be far from Anyu."

"But still far enough for me be alone," Emma said her eyes misting.

Tommy and Gabi waited in silence.

"Aside from us, the only other Jews left in Békes are the Sterns," Emma continued.

"How is Rabbi Stern?"

"So-so. He's not all there." Gabi pointed at his temple. "After he was beaten and stuffed into a chicken coop by those thugs, he was never the same."

"His wife takes care of him, but she isn't well either," said Emma-mama.

"You remember their son, Yossie?"

"Yeah, he was the smartest kid in school, but he always got picked on because of his *payos* and yarmulke."

"He's up in Budapest studying medicine."

"That's great!"

"Once, when he was visiting, he told me that he wanted to come back and practise medicine in Békes."

"Why?"

"He said he wanted those who hurt him and his family to come see him and call him Doctor Sir. He wanted to tell them to drop their pants, bend over and jab them with needles. And then, have them thank him."

Tommy laughed but understood the depth of Yossie's desire for revenge. "Who else is still around?" he asked.

"You remember Carrot?"

"Yeah."

"He's in the army. I told his mother that you were coming. He's supposed to be home on leave this weekend, so he might join us on Saturday night."

"And Frog?"

Gabi didn't answer.

"I'd like to see him."

He lowered his voice "I don't think it's a good idea."

"Why?"

"He's changed a lot."

"How?"

"Many ways. And it's caused him problems."

"You know, when I was asked by reporters in Budapest if I was going to visit old friends, I mentioned Frog. But the translator left his name out. And after I asked the Canadian Consul why, he hinted that Frog may be a person who's in trouble with the government and advised me against connecting with him."

"Yes, that's him."

"What kind of trouble is he in?"

"All kinds, or he was. It seems to be resolved, but it's still not the best thing to be seen with him."

"What happened?"

"It's a long story and I don't know all of it."

When Gabi saw Emma returning with coffee and *pogácsa*, he put his finger to his lips.

"Enough of the news from Békes," Emma said as she served. "Tell us what happened after we were taken off the train?"

"Didn't Mr. Darvas or the Baroness tell you?"

"Tell me what?" Emma almost shouted. "They escaped with you!"

"No. They turned back at the border."

"They didn't come back here. What happened?" Emma asked.

"Anyu and Apu didn't write to you or Magda for a year because they thought that the mail would be opened and figured it would be dangerous for you. And they thought that Mr. Darvas or the Baroness would tell you."

"Oh, it was being opened for sure!" Emma said. "The first letter we received was resealed in such a way as to let us know that they were watching us."

"It's one of their scare tactics. Those pigs still do it and make it obvious."

"Gabi." Emma lowered her voice and shot him a stern look.

"Yes, you pigs!" Gabi shouted at the wall.

Tommy had to smile. Gabi's father also used to shout at the walls when he talked about the secret police. It was one of his ways of fighting Big Brother. Tommy read *1984* in high school and remembered his teacher talking about it as a dark satire of Communism. Gabi had probably never heard of the book. It seemed to Tommy that they were living it.

"What happened to you?" Tommy asked.

Emma sipped her coffee and stared off into the distance. "After Dezsö punched the secret police guy in the face, chaos broke out in the car," she said. "Everybody was pushing, shoving, falling, yelling, crying. Dezsö got beaten up badly. They broke his nose and arm. We didn't see you or your parents. You disappeared. What happened?"

"Apu did some fancy footwork pretending to be a policeman. Remember the leather coat he was so proud of?"

Emma nodded. "Dezsö called it Sanyi's AVO coat because it's what the secret policemen liked to wear."

"Somehow Apu was able to blend in with them in the chaos. And when Anyu and I were being ordered off, he shoved us into the train bathroom and locked the door. We rode all the way to Sopron in there. It stank worse than that outhouse."

Gabi laughed.

"Aunt Magda told me that Dezsö-papa got two years."

"Yes. And I got six months."

Gabi sneered. "That meant hard labour and beatings. They call that re-education."

Tommy now understood why Gabi didn't want her to know about his coming re-education.

"Magda, God bless her, took Gabi. Dezsö came back a broken man. He went silent and moody and began drinking heavily. He always liked to drink but it got out of control. One day he didn't come home. They found him in a ditch outside of town."

Emma began to cry. Gabi held her and let her cry. He glanced over her shoulder at Tommy.

"Dad used to tell me silence gives them power," Gabi said.

"But, what happened to you?" Emma asked as she dried her eyes. She blew her nose.

"Oh. Well, our guide, you remember him, took us to his mother's house near the border. We waited for dark and then he took us to the edge of the forest and told us to walk until we got to a shallow part of the river and cross it. We found the river but not the shallow part. We still managed to cross it but Mr. Darvas almost drowned. You remember, he was carrying these two big suitcases attached by a cord around his neck. He slipped and fell, and the cord wound around his neck. Anyu and Apu saved him. His wife, the Baroness, got so scared that she refused to cross. They turned back."

"Why did they call her the Baroness?" Gabi asked.

"Hannah named her that. Péter Darvas was a member of the Party. That made them big shots. She liked to make people know that she was special."

"What happened next?" Gabi asked, as rapt as a child listening to an adventure story.

"When we got to the train tracks we had to cross, the embankments were so steep that we had to slide down. Just as we got to the bottom, we heard a train coming. There weren't supposed to be any."

Emma clasped her hands. "Oh, my God."

"We started scrambling back up, but didn't make it all the way. We had to flatten ourselves against the slope. I remember

I was pushed into the embankment by the force. And the noise. That scared me more than anything else." Tommy paused.

"And then?" Gabi urged.

"And then we made it up the other side. But just as we were getting up, a soldier yelled at us to stop."

Emma clapped her hand over her mouth.

"We were standing there. Apu offered the soldier the bottle of *pálinka*. According to Apu, the soldier was already drunk. I guess he had taken a number of bribes already. As the soldier came toward Apu to take the bottle, he tripped and fell and his rifle went off."

"Thank God no one was shot."

"Actually, I was."

"What?" Emma shouted.

"Yes, but the bullet just grazed me across the temple." He showed them the scar.

"Oh, God." She reached over to stroke his temple.

"Then what happened?"

"Apu carried me. Anyu told me that she was crazy with fear. She said that she kept putting her hand over my nose to make sure that I was breathing. She said that they were so panicked that they got lost, walked in circles in the sucking mud of no man's land until somehow they managed to get to the Austrian village on the other side."

"Oh, my God! Oh, my God! What an adventure!"

"Yeah, it sure was," Tommy said.

Loud clanging filled the air. Tommy glanced across the fence. "They're still here?"

"Oh. Yes. Every morning at seven, the music begins."

"Joska, Dragon Mouth and Fire?"

"Un hunh."

"And Attila?"

"He died a few years ago. He was quite old. But they got a new one. They can't wait to see you."

"Sure, but hang on a minute. I have to get something Apu gave me to give them."

As they made their way across to the blacksmiths' yard, a German shepherd charged toward them. "Attila, stop!" Gabi commanded.

"I thought you said he died."

"He did. They named this one Attila too."

It seemed that nothing had changed. Except the yard was smaller. It was still filled with wagons and wheelbarrows waiting to be fixed. The three-sided barn with its huge hearth was still smoky, warm and inviting. And the three figures hammering away in leather aprons still reminded him of powerful giants.

Gabi yelled out to them and the hammering stopped. Tommy remembered them as makers of fire that melted iron. They were sorcerers who had made Gabi and him magical swords that transformed them into brave Hajdus who fought nobly against the terrible Turks. They had made Tommy and Gabi invincible.

Though Joska, the chief blacksmith, now had grey hair, he still looked like he could strike the red-white hot iron with a force that would send sparks exploding into the air. Dragon Mouth still had his fierce black eyes that glowed like the fiery hearth he tended. When he saw Tommy, he opened his mouth in a wide smile. Most of his teeth were gone, which made him even fiercer looking. And there was Fire, his face sooty, glistening with sweat and his ear-to-ear grin, just as Tommy remembered.

Tommy reached out to shake hands with Joska. Joska pulled him in and like a bear, squeezed so hard that Tommy almost cried out in pain. "Little Tomi," Joska shouted as he pounded him hard on his back. Tommy gasped. The smell of the fire-infused leather apron filled his nostrils. He felt protected.

He and Gabi had spent many mornings having breakfasts with the blacksmiths, playing in the yard with Attila, patting the horses' necks and stroking their manes while Joska shod them. The last time he had seen the blacksmiths was on a dark night. The three of them and old Attila were defending Tommy and Gabi's families from the mob outside their home.

Tommy extended a gift-wrapped box to Joska. "From Apu and Anyu."

"What a fancy box," Dragon Mouth said when Joska passed it to him.

Fire undid the ribbon with a woman's delicateness. He passed it over to Dragon Mouth, who ran his rough fingers tenderly over the shiny silky red ribbon and carefully rolled it up.

"Just tear it."

They looked at Tommy as if he were crazy.

"I don't want to tear the paper, it's so beautiful," Fire said.

"We don't have paper like that here," Gabi explained.

Tommy nodded and reached for his Swiss Army knife. He took the box from Fire, felt for the Scotch-taped part and with the tip, delicately sliced it. He gently removed the box and gave the paper to Gabi, who folded it neatly and gave it to Joska.

"My wife will love it," he said.

"My father told me to tell you that he hopes you will like what's inside." He returned the box to Joska.

Joska held the blue box of Crown Royal whisky as if he were holding King Stephen's crown. He opened it, careful not to damage it, and reached inside. He lifted the velvet-bagged bottle out of the box. The gold drawstring and the dark royal velvet with stitched lettering drew ahhs and ohhs from the blacksmiths.

"My God," Joska said. "This *is* for a king."

"What do the words say?" Gabi asked.

"Crown Royal," Tommy translated and laughed. He pulled the drawstrings apart and took out the bottle. "Scotch for three fine kings," he added and handed the bottle to Joska who stroked the bottle the way a man might caress a woman.

Joska's eyes shone as he smiled at Tommy. "This calls for a toast." Joska shouted. Gabi ran back to the house and returned with five shot glasses. Joska poured each a glass. They sniffed it.

"To your Godly health and return," Joska said.

"To your Godly health and return." They saluted Tommy.

"To honourable men," Tommy replied.

The five men lifted their glasses and saluted each other. In unison they downed the whisky, smacked their lips and sighed.

Crossing back to their yard, Tommy and Gabi stopped at the gate and watched Emma among her roses. To his seven-year-old sense of time she was forever bending over them, stroking their petals and inhaling their fragrance. Now in her flower-patterned dress, she seemed to have become one with them.

"Remember how she'd come after us with her broom whenever we kicked the ball into the bushes?"

"Yeah. And chasing us down the street with the same broom, sweeping us to *Chaider* when we would rather have been playing soccer?"

"I even remember her dancing with it when she swept the verandah."

"Yeah, she wanted to be a dancer. She told me she used to sneak off to the dance master's classes until she got caught by her father."

"Why didn't your grandfather let her be a dancer?"

"Her father was very religious and thought that being a professional dancer was the same as being a prostitute. And then the war came along."

And then the war came along. So many of his parents' generation's dreams ended with that phrase. So many of them had died because of that simple fact.

Emma waved. She arranged the cut roses in a vase on the verandah and disappeared into to the kitchen.

Emma-mama had done most of the cooking when he was a kid. The delicious smells wafting from the kitchen was a rich part of his childhood. "You know, Gabi, I didn't know how much I missed you and Emma-mama until now."

Gabi put his arm around Tommy and squeezed hard.

"They're the best in the world," Tommy said as he dunked the golden-crusted *pogácsa* in his after-lunch coffee.

Emma beamed and went to fetch more. "The last time I made it for you was when we set out to escape." She got choked up and closed her eyes.

"Apu sent a joke for you. I'm not as good a joke teller as he is, especially in Hungarian, but I'll try."

His butchering of it made Emma laugh. "Apu also told me to tell you to not pee yourself." Emma ran off to the kitchen holding her sides.

"It's good to see her happy like this," Gabi said. "She doesn't do it much nowadays."

"Why not?"

"She's lonely. She really misses your mother and especially your father. Since Apu died, she's even lonelier 'cause she has no one to be angry at. She feels abandoned. And me leaving next year and you being here makes it worse."

"Why was she angry at him?"

"I'll tell you later," he said as Emma returned with another plate of steaming *pogácsa*.

"Can we go down to the Békes soccer field?"

"Sure, we'll go after supper. That's when they practise."

"Okay."

"How about the synagogue? Apu gave me something for Rabbi Stern."

"If you're going, take some soup." Emma went into the kitchen to fill a pot.

"What happened after you and your parents came back?" Tommy asked as they walked toward the synagogue.

"I was still too young to know the consequences of their escape attempt. They didn't say anything to me about it. After serving their sentences, Apu was given the shitty job of cleaning out the stalls at the collective farm. He didn't mind that; he was a farmer at heart and for him that was no punishment. But they assigned him to the collective farm that once belonged to his family, until the Party nationalized it. They wanted to rub his nose in that, and he was angry about it. He drank more and more and took up with another woman. He abandoned us."

Listening to Gabi, Tommy felt uneasy. He was having an adult conversation. It was as if the roles between child and parent had been changed. There was a maturity to Gabi that Tommy didn't feel he had.

For a while they walked in silence. Tommy noticed that people were staring at them.

Tommy wasn't used to being stared at. Everybody in Békes knew Gabi. He was a local hero, at least until the last game. Now he was the plague. People avoided him. But they were curious about Tommy, so they had to acknowledge Gabi. Tommy was an exotic animal. He was the stranger from Békes.

"We kept to ourselves. Carrot and Frog were the only ones I played with," Gabi said, as he stared back, forcing people to avert their eyes. They still called me names at recess but after a couple of fights, they stopped. I had a few fights with Szeles. My punches had a lot of anger in them. Did you know that Szeles's father was one of the leaders of the mob that attacked our house?"

"No, I didn't." Tommy wasn't sure if he remembered it or it was his parents' recollection of that evening. They had all sat in the kitchen, his father and Dezső-papa armed with hammers, his mother clutching a kitchen knife and Emma-mama holding her broom. They waited. Though Tommy and Gabi didn't really understand what was going on, they knew it was serious. They ran to the kitchen stove and from behind it drew out their swords and stood beside their parents.

"Anyu told me," Gabi said, "that after the uprising was subdued, most of the people pretended that nothing happened. But since my sin, it seems okay again to show their hate. It's almost like they feel they have to. Until they accept that something did happen, nothing will change." He paused. "You know, it felt good kicking that ball into my net."

The synagogue was damaged beyond repair. The outside walls, leaning precariously, were riddled with bullet holes. The door had been ripped off and all the windows smashed. The inside reeked. Mould and rot gave it a sickly-sweet smell. The pews were overturned and chopped up. Most of the roof was gone. Only the spiderwebbed frames of the stained glass dome that Tommy, Gabi, Frog and Carrot had used for slingshot contests remained. The bright sun shone down on the desolation. Their footsteps set off scattering noises.

"Rats," Gabi said.

Gabi knocked on the door of a small building next to the synagogue. A slot in the door slid open and a pair of frightened eyes peered out. "Mrs. Stern, I brought Tomi Wolfstein, Sandor's son from Canada. He came to see the rabbi. And my mother sent some soup."

A tired-looking woman in a tatty sweater and black shawl opened the door.

The windows were shuttered. It took Tommy's eyes a minute to adjust to the darkness. The mustiness made him sneeze.

He heard a man's voice. "*Tsu gezunt.*"

Tommy squinted at the lump in the armchair. As he approached, he could make out a small man with a yarmulke on his nearly bald head, a bushy salt-and-pepper beard and a shawl like his wife's draped over his shoulders. Although the man was no older than Tommy's father, he looked ancient.

"Shalom Aleichem, Rabbi Stern. I have returned," Tommy said in Yiddish, as his father taught him.

The rabbi's eyes came alive at those words. He stood. "Aleichem Shalom!" He began rattling away at him in Yiddish.

"I'm sorry, but I don't speak Yiddish," Tommy apologized.

"So, what was that?" Rabbi Stern asked.

"Just a phrase my father taught me."

The rabbi shook his head. "You would think in a free country like America, you would be happy to learn Yiddish."

Tommy expected a slap to the back of his head, the way the rabbi used to hit them when they didn't know the alphabet or how to pronounce a word or couldn't remember a Biblical name or a prayer or when they weren't paying attention. Slaps to the back of the head were more frequently handed out than praise. It was more the rule than the exception.

Again, the obvious struck Tommy. Everything was much smaller than he remembered, even Rabbi Stern. Though Tommy was a head taller, he was still intimidated by the little man before him wrapped in a shawl.

The rabbi's wife pointed to the bench. "Sit, sit."

It was the same bench where he had once sat reciting the alphabet, the names of prophets and the lineage of the Jews. Anxiously, he had eyed the rabbi, at the head of the table, waiting for him to nod off so he could sneak out to play soccer.

"How are you?" Tommy asked awkwardly.

"God knows, and that's enough."

Tommy reached into his shopping bag and presented him with a carton of cigarettes. "Anyu and Apu said smoke in good health. They also wanted to give you this." He handed over an envelope which Rabbi Stern slipped into his pocket unopened.

"May God bless them," he said.

"They also sent this." Tommy handed him a small box that contained a mezuzah.

The rabbi's eyes widened with joy when he opened the box. He gazed upward, past the ceiling toward the heavens. "What a great gift from God. And a blessing on his deliverer," the Rabbi exclaimed.

"Oh, my God. It's beautiful," his wife declared, watching him stroke the silver mezuzah, tracing every contour of it. He smiled as if he had just been brought back to life.

"Do you want me to put it up, Rabbi?" Gabi asked.

"There are nails with it," Tommy said.

"God is generous," the rabbi's wife said. "I'll get the hammer."

"And two yarmulkes," said Rabbi Stern.

Gabi took the hammer. "No," Rabbi Stern said. "Zev Yankov Ben Shmiel Yisroel drives in the first nail."

Tommy was surprised that the Rabbi remembered his Jewish name. He was being given a special honour, like being called up to recite from the Torah. He walked over to the doorpost and tried to slip it into the existing empty space.

"No," the rabbi said. "Leave that hole as a reminder of what happened. Put it next to it to show its miraculous return."

Tommy tapped in the top nail and handed the hammer to the rabbi, who gave it to Gabi.

"Now you," Rabbi Stern said.

After Gabi hammered in the bottom nail, the rabbi reached up and stroked it. "Now repeat after me. Blessed are You, Lord our God, King of the Universe, who has sanctified us with His commandments and commanded us to affix a Mezuzah."

Rabbi Stern raised two fingers to his lips and touched the mezuzah. He signalled for the boys to do the same. Tommy reached out and touched it with his kissed fingertips. Gabi hesitated.

"His father's son," Rabbi Stern said.

Gabi nodded then followed suit.

Mrs. Stern appeared with a bottle of *pálinka* and three glasses. The rabbi poured and recited a prayer. "La Chaim," Tommy said as they drank it down.

"You and your family have done a great mitzvah," Mrs. Stern said to Tommy as the boys were leaving. In the gloom behind her Tommy watched the rabbi disappear, back into his armchair. A wave of guilt passed through Tommy.

"I'm sorry," he said under his breath as they left.

Tommy pointed to a small, dilapidated box overgrown with weeds. "Is that the chicken coop they stuffed him in?" Gabi nodded. The way Tommy's father described the scene when he and Dezsö-papa came upon it after the mob night was funny. But now, imagining that bearded little man, a rabbi, a survivor, a human being, in that confined coop, face pressed against the chicken wire, made his stomach churn. How could anyone pretend that nothing had happened? he wondered. He lifted his camera to take a picture but stopped himself. "Bastards," he muttered under his breath.

"What?" Gabi asked.

"Nothing."

They walked in silence for a while, Tommy lost in his thoughts about what happened.

"What's the story about Frog?" he asked after a while. "Why are you saying we shouldn't go see him?"

"As I told you, it's a long story."

When they got back, Emma was in the kitchen preparing supper. Tommy and Gabi sat on the verandah, watching the summer afternoon turn into a perfect cool summer evening. He was glad to be sitting. His ankle throbbed from all the walking. He was afraid to take his shoe off for fear of never getting it back on. He was glad Ben had left him the spray.

Emma brought out steaming chicken soup. "Your father liked it to burn the roof of his mouth."

"He still does."

"What is life like in Canada?" Emma asked as she sat and watched him eat.

"Fine. Anyu and Apu work really hard, from early morning to late at night, but they are happy. Apu was homesick for the first couple of years. He kept a suitcase under the bed. Anyu told him if he wanted to go, then he should, but without her and me. Oh, I'll be right back." He came back with an envelope. "Here are some pictures they sent for you."

Tommy spread out pictures of his Bar Mitzvah, of his parents in their factory, of Margit in front of her restaurant with her name on the sign and one of his father beaming next to his Chevy Impala. Emma and Gabi were transfixed.

"I heard that you can go wherever and whenever you want," Gabi said.

"Sure. Why not?"

"Have you ever met Indians?" Gabi asked, still studying the pictures.

"Wait till I come back," Emma said. She gathered the soup plates and brought out a plateful of salami, peppers and boiled eggs. "Go on."

"Once," Tommy said. "There is an Indian reservation…." He didn't know the Hungarian word for it. He searched and tried different word. "Like a ghetto."

"Canada has ghettos?" she asked, horrified.

"No, it's not like the ones the Jews were in," he reassured her. "It's a special place for Indians. They want to live there. There is one not far from Montreal. I went once on a school outing. The Indians get all dressed up in their costumes and dance for tourists."

"Are they allowed out of the ghetto?"

"Sure. I think so," he said, though he had never seen one in Montreal.

"And Eskimos? Have you seen any?" Gabi asked.

"No. They live far away in the North."

"Is it always cold there?"

"Yes." He tried to remember what he had learned about them in school. There were some stories about Indians but nothing much about Eskimos.

"They live in snow houses. And there's no sun half the year."

"No sun? How can they live like that? Do they sleep for six months?" Emma asked.

Tommy laughed. "I don't think so. I don't know much about them."

"I know places where there is no sun at all," Gabi said.

"Gabi!" Emma hissed. "I heard that Canada is a big country." She said it more as a question than a fact.

"Yeah, it's very big. I think it's bigger than Russia, but we haven't travelled that much. We've been to Ottawa, the capital city of Canada. I think it takes about two weeks to go from the east coast to the west coast."

"That's big. Here you can go anywhere in a day, when the trains work," Gabi joked. After a pause he added, "and if you have the right papers."

"Is Montreal big and beautiful?" Emma asked.

He hadn't thought much about the city until he tripped with Marianne and Naomi on the mountain. From the lookout he'd seen a beautiful vista of greenery sloping down, meeting high-rises of glass, concrete and steel and ending where the St Lawrence River began. "Montreal is the largest city in Canada. It's an island and it has a mountain in the middle of it. And the Man and His World Fair is amazing."

"Are there a lot of people in Canada?"

"Yeah, about 20 million. People from all over the world live there and you know what? They get along. My team is made up of all nationalities, but the majority in Quebec, that's one of the ten provinces, is French."

"You speak French?" Gabi asked.

"My French isn't so good. The French live on the east side of town, while the English live on the west side. They usually don't have much to do with each other. The English call the French frogs and the French call the English squareheads."

Gabi frowned. "Why?"

"I really don't know. I learned in my history class that Quebec was first owned by the French but then got taken over by the English. The French are Catholics and the English are Protestants and most of the immigrant kids go to English school. We usually end up on the English side because most business is done in English. If you want a good job, it's easier if you speak English. Also, you have to be Catholic to go to French school. The English schools are Protestant, but they accept Jews. Most of the French speak English. Most English don't speak French."

"Boy, what a goulash. Thank God for Communism," Gabi said. "Here everybody speaks Hungarian. We're supposed to learn Russian, but nobody does. 'Da' and 'Nyet' are more than enough."

"Are there many Jews in Montreal?" Emma asked.

"Yeah, there are about a dozen synagogues and a couple of Jewish schools. And I got kicked out of one of them. I didn't have Emma-mama chasing me with a broom," Tommy said with a grin. Emma leaned over and pinched his cheek.

"Isn't that something?" Emma went back to the pictures. "They left with the clothes on their backs and now they make them in their own factory. They are their own bosses; they have their own house and their own car. They are important people. It's wonderful what is possible when you have freedom." She rose and pinched his cheek again. "And their beautiful son is here with us."

"And does this beautiful son have a beautiful girlfriend to comb?" Gabi asked.

Tommy didn't understand. "To comb?"

"Gabi!" Emma slapped Gabi playfully upside the head.

Tommy blushed. "Yes, I have a girlfriend."

"You have a picture of her?"

"No." Not having a picture of Marianne surprised him. How could he not have asked for one? "We just started to see each other. She's Spanish, she works in a hospital and she's a flamenco dancer."

"Oh, I wanted to be a dancer," Emma said. "She must be beautiful. What is she like?"

"Yeah," he smiled. "I think she is beautiful. She is very free; nobody can tell her what to do."

"Is she Jewish?"

"No. Anyu and Apu would like me to have a Jewish girlfriend, but…"

"Here it's almost impossible, but I don't really care," Gabi said.

"But there it's possible," Emma said.

"Anyu and Apu like her, but they're afraid. They say that people who aren't the same religion can't get along. Especially a Jew and a non-Jew because as Apu says you can't…" Tommy searched for the Hungarian word. He knew the Yiddish but not the Hungarian. "…you know," he said, making a scissor gesture, "not cut off your prick."

"What?" Gabi stared at him.

Emma snorted and began to laugh uncontrollably. "He means uncircumsize," she said between gasps.

"That's a big difference," Gabi said.

"That's what Apu and Anyu say also." Tommy joined in their laughter.

"But they're right," Emma said, serious again. "You should never forget what we went through for just being different."

Though it seemed stupid, and he wanted to deny it, Tommy had to admit that the emphasis on differences was everywhere. He had seen and experienced its consequences, even in Canada.

"What are you studying? What do you want to be?"

"I'm in the Commerce program but I don't really know what I want to do. Anyu and Apu want me to take over the business. But I don't think I'm cut out for that. And there's no future in soccer. I should have become a hockey player. Maybe after school, I'll travel for a year or two."

"You can just do that? Are you a hippie?" Gabi asked.

"Peace and Love. What's wrong with that? Better than War and Hate," Tommy said.

"You're so naïve," Gabi said.

Tommy shrugged his shoulders and flashed a V sign. They smiled at each other.

There was knock at the door. "Who disturbs the peace?" Gabi called out as he went to the door. "Coach Varga," Gabi announced, returning with a small but well-built man.

Yes. That's his name, Tommy remembered. He stood up quickly but as he did, his left ankle buckled. Coach Varga reached out and caught him.

"Be careful," he said.

"Sit down, Zoli. I'll make you a coffee."

"Thank you, but no, Emma. I have to go to practice. I just wanted to see Tomi before I did."

"We were planning to go and see you," Gabi said.

"So, I saved you a trip."

"I wanted to see the field we trained on and see the Békes team practise," Tommy said as he rubbed his ankle.

"Not as good as in your dad's days. He knew how to get the best guys. He had a nose for good players."

"Well, we'll walk out with you."

Coach Varga hesitated and averted his eyes from Gabi. "Maybe it would be better if you didn't."

Tommy glanced at Gabi, who remained silent.

"I saw you play. You're very good. I wish your parents had stayed. You and Gabi would make a dynamic duo on the under-twenty team. And your team was surprisingly good, but I wasn't so surprised after seeing the team practice. Your coach works you hard but also lets you play and have fun. That's good coaching."

"When did you see us practise?"

"In Debrecen."

"It was you who was watching us?"

Coach Varga nodded.

"Why didn't you come over?"

"I wasn't allowed until after the games."

"I don't understand."

"And now?" Gabi asked. Tommy felt the chill in Gabi's voice.

Coach Varga shifted from foot to foot. "Not really."

"Why?"

"Mainly because of what you did."

"What do you think of what I did?"

"It was stupid." He paused. "But right."

Gabi's lips were pursed in a tight smile.

"Tommy, I want to give you something for your father." He handed Tommy a small photo of a soccer team.

Tommy didn't know what to make of the picture. "Is that the '56 Békes team?" he asked.

"Oh, my God!" Emma cried out.

"What?" Tommy and Gabi asked.

Emma was silent as she studied the photo. "That's Sanyi, your father," Emma said pointing to the player in the second row. It's the labour camp soccer team. Where did you get this?" Emma asked.

"As the town archivist I was collecting material from the years between 1935 and 1945. Way back I asked Sanyi if he knew or had anything from that period. You know Sanyi, he was the best at getting things that no one else could. He got me some very interesting material about the Jewish community in Békes and he gave me this. You left before I could return it and I forgot all about it until I heard that you were coming."

"Thank you." Tommy couldn't take his eyes off the picture. "He'll be very happy to have this."

"I'm glad that I could return it to him. I should go now. Give him my greetings."

"I certainly will." Tommy shook his hand.

"We were planning to go to the cemetery. It's on the way. Is it okay if we walk with you till there?" Gabi asked.

To Tommy it sounded more like a challenge than a question. The silence was uncomfortable.

"I'd enjoy the company," Coach Varga said, like a man who had made a decision about something important. "I hope the streets are not too crowded," he joked.

Gabi nodded.

"Maybe Tommy could tell me something about his coach's methods. Our team sure could use some new ideas."

Hardly anyone was out as they walked toward the station. "Let's take the side streets so Tommy can see how the town has changed and get a look at some of the old places," Gabi suggested.

As they meandered, Coach Varga reminisced and asked questions while Gabi pointed out various old landmarks. Whenever they stopped in front of one, Tommy caught Gabi and Coach Varga glancing back. There was a man strolling casually at a distance behind them.

"Here we are." Coach Varga turned to Gabi. "Keep up the good work, and maybe one day, we'll see you play for Honvéd." He put his hand on Tommy's shoulder. "And give your father my best." When he was gone Tommy and Gabi turned onto a deeply rutted dirt road. The man behind them had disappeared.

"What's going on?" Tommy asked.

Gabi signalled to keep walking. "The usual, except more obviously."

It wasn't usual for Tommy. Occasionally he felt paranoid walking the streets of Montreal after smoking a joint and sometimes he felt that cops were watching him. Some of Naomi's friends were convinced their phones were bugged. It was almost a badge of honour. But this felt different, more real and dangerous.

At the gate of the cemetery, Gabi knelt and retrieved a key from under a flat rock. Although a chain-link fence enclosed the cemetery, it looked ready to fall over with the slightest push. It was overgrown with weeds. Gravestones stuck out of the earth like crooked decayed teeth about to fall out. Most of the eroded inscriptions were impossible to read.

"This is Apu's," Gabi said. Tommy picked up three pebbles and placed them on top of Dezsö-papa's headstone.

"Why'd you do that?" Gabi asked.

Tommy was surprised that Gabi didn't know. "It's to show that you were here to pay your respects."

"Why three?"

"One from Apu, one from Anyu and one from me." He reached into his back pocket, pulled out a little booklet and recited Kaddish.

"I thought you didn't speak or read Yiddish," Gabi said.

"I don't. This is Hebrew and Apu made me practise before I came. It also has a phonetic version."

"I appreciate the gesture, but he didn't believe."

"Why not?"

"Because, like many Jews, he couldn't believe in a God that let the Holocaust happen. Or, as he said, 'sat on his hands with his thumb up his ass.'"

"That sounds like your father." Tommy smiled. "And you?" he asked as he wandered about the cemetery trying to read the names and dates on the headstones.

"I'm a man of facts and figures. I believe what I can test and verify. There has to be a reason for everything. And you?" Gabi asked.

"I don't know. I also can't accept a God that let the Holocaust happen. But Anyu and Apu believe. Though I have heard Anyu question God, wanting to know what sin her fourteen-year-old sister could have committed to deserve to be gassed. I've asked them a few times how they can believe after all that. My father always says that we aren't God so we can't know. They don't like to talk about it, so I don't push it. I don't think I believe, but for them I do this."

"There!" Gabi pointed to a shiny large black marble stone in the far corner. It was the only new one in the cemetery. Tommy's parents had had it shipped from Canada.

Tommy's grandmother wasn't actually buried there. She died in Auschwitz. Beneath the blessing and a split-fingered V sign of the Cohen, their names, Miklos Wolfstein and Rosie Stulberger. And beneath their names, the family history: children Sándor and Margit, daughter-in-law Hannah, and grandchild Tamás, were engraved and painted in brilliant gold. "So everyone will see and never forget," his mother had said.

Tommy stared at his roots. He put three pebbles on their glistening marble headstone, wished them peace, and recited Kaddish again.

"I don't know anything about my grandfather. All I know about my father's father is that he died in 1925 and was a hot-tempered man who died because he bit a cow."

Gabi gave Tommy a quizzical look, thinking he had misunderstood. "What?"

"Apparently, the cow bit him first. Apu said that one of his cows bit him and he got so angry that he bit the cow back. Soon after he got some kind of disease and died."

Tommy and Gabi laughed hysterically as they left the cemetery.

It was getting dark, but the streetlights hadn't come on yet. Even though there were lights on in the houses they passed, there was a ghostly feel to the village. Tommy felt as if he were somewhere between day and night, between safety and danger.

"Want an ice cream?" Gabi asked.

"Sure."

"Here's the Nylon. It's got great ice cream."

Tommy glanced at the sign. The People's Diner. His mother had worked there. "Why is it called the Nylon?"

"Because," Gabi said, pointing to the lit neon sign, "when it opened, it was the only place in the county that had a nylon sign. It was a big deal then. So, people called it The Nylon."

It took Tommy a few moments to understand the neon, nylon word confusion.

"What kind of ice cream do you want?"

"Cherry," he said. He felt like a kid again.

"The Nylon is like a socialist Dobos," Gabi said, while they waited.

"Huh?"

"It's my description of its architectural space. Here, this small space with an open window onto the street, is the ice cream parlour. You could think of it as the icing. The next layer, behind it, is the dining room. The body, the layers, the people and tables. And at the back, a closed-off area, that's the bar. We'll go there tomorrow night."

"What part of the Dobos is the bar?"

"The bottom. Where the darkness is."

Tommy didn't get it. He took a lick. "Mmm. It's delicious." The ice cream brought back memories of the mountain, Marianne and the acid trip. What a different, faraway world this place is, he thought.

"It's about time you got back," Emma said when they walked in the door. "Do you want to eat anything?"

"No, thanks. I'm really tired," Tommy said.

"I've made up your bed."

It was his parents' bed. Once upon a time, he had slept there, squeezed between them, feeling warm and protected. Now it was Gabi's.

"I fart in my sleep," Gabi said.

"I probably do, too," Tommy snickered.

"Remember where the outhouse is?" Gabi asked.

"Oh, God."

"You can piss over there." Gabi pointed to the tree by the well.

"Thanks."

"I'm going to read for a bit," Gabi said and walked to the kitchen.

As he lay in bed, Tommy looked at the picture Coach Varga had given him. His much-younger father was wiry, and sported a Charlie Chaplin moustache. Judging from his expression, he had no idea he was about to be shipped off to a concentration camp. Ignorant of the looming horror, he found joy and escape in a soccer game.

5 1

"Think about it," the man in the dark suit said. "You're in a lot of trouble. You may never get out of here unless you cooperate."

"But I have been. I've been telling you the truth."

"Not really."

"Yes! I have!"

"You attempted to smuggle in capitalist propaganda. You brought in clothing to sell on the black market and traded in forbidden currency. These are subversive acts against the Socialist Republic of Hungary."

"What are you talking about?" Tommy shouted.

"And of course, there are the criminal acts you committed against the people of Hungary."

The man in the dark suit lit a cigarette and said nothing. He let the silence speak.

"What do you want?" Tommy asked him.

"For you to do your duty for your motherland."

"How?"

"That's not important. There are many ways that one can serve. The important thing is to want to serve. And benefit everyone." His tone had changed. He wasn't shouting and snapping.

"What do you mean?"

"A true Hungarian can serve his motherland even in Canada. You would be helping your family, cousin, aunts, grandfather and, of course, your parents."

Tommy didn't know what to think. He felt weak. He wanted to sleep so he could wake from this nightmare.

"Think about it."

5 2

Tommy was in a damp, dark, dirt basement sitting on a wooden crate. His bicycle was upside down. He was rubbing the chain, link by link, with axle grease. When he finished, he turned the pedal very slowly, wiping off the excess. The chain glistened in the dark. He turned the pedal faster and faster. Suddenly an iron bar was jammed between the rear wheel spokes. His wrist twisted. He cried out. A hand holding a switchblade flashed in the dark. It jabbed the tire and disappeared. It flashed again and again, stabbing the tire. Tommy grabbed the wrist, but his greasy hands could not get a firm grip. The knife-wielding hand slipped out and as it did, the knife sliced his palm.

Tommy bolted upright up and cried out. He was drenched in a sweat.

Gabi grabbed him. "Are you okay?"

Breathing rapidly, he stared into the darkness.

"Are you okay?" Gabi repeated.

He took a couple of deep breaths. "Yeah. Yeah. I had a bad dream. It's okay." He stared at his palms. They felt clammy. "I'm going for a piss."

Tommy walked out to the yard in his bare feet. His heart was pumping rapidly. The damp ground soaked the soles of his feet. It calmed him.

He returned to the verandah, sat on the steps and listened to the silence of Hajdubékes. There were no city sounds: no cars, trucks or trains keeping the night awake. No one was out and about. Not even a barking dog or mewling cat. It sounded so unfamiliar to his Montreal ears. It was under a similar peaceful night sky he had heard loud footsteps along the cobblestone street marching toward his house, chanting "kill the Commies" and "kill the Jews." The mob had stopped outside of his house. János, the blacksmith shouted, "This is Sándor Wolfstein's house." Tommy, Gabi and their parents ran to the window. The three blacksmiths were out in front, facing the mob. "No one is going in! No one is going to touch them!" He remembered old Attila barking.

Tommy stood, took a deep breath and under a starlit Hajdubékes night, slowly, faultlessly, recited the poem "Lullaby" by Attila Josef he had memorized eleven years ago.

53

A strange sound startled Tommy awake. For a minute he didn't know what it was or where he was. He sat up, trying to orient himself. He was in Békes. A rooster was crowing.

"Good morning," he said as he walked into the kitchen.

"Good morning," Emma replied. Her back was to him and she was preparing breakfast. Water was boiling on the wood stove. "You boys go sit; I'll bring you breakfast."

"Are you okay?" Gabi asked.

Emma brought out the plate of sliced peppers, cheese, salami, boiled eggs and fresh *pogácsa*. It had been a long time since he had had this kind of breakfast. Breakfast in Canada was a fast affair. He was now a Canadian cereal-toast-and-coffee guy.

"Gabi told me you had a bad dream. What was it about?"

"I can't remember. It was bits and pieces of being lost in the dark," he said, not wanting to worry them.

"Maybe being in Békes has brought back some old memories," Emma said and made a spitting sound. His mother and his aunt made the same sounds when they cursed.

Tommy nodded and bit into a hot, golden-crusted *pogácsa*. He leaned in to smell the fresh roses in the vase and then looked to the bushes. "Your roses have really grown. Let's take a picture. Anyu will love to see them," Tommy said and hobbled off to get his camera.

Standing next to Emma in front of the bush, he put his arms around her.

"Now, me and Gabi in front of the outhouse."

"No," Emma said, "don't be silly."

"Why not?" Gabi said. "Roses and shit."

"Gabi!" Emma scolded.

The boys put their arms around each other's shoulders and smiled. Tommy took a picture of the vegetable garden, the well and the chicken coop.

After breakfast, while Emma washed dishes and Gabi stacked wood next to the stove and swept the verandah, Tommy wrote some postcards.

Dear Marianne,

I miss you. I'm in my hometown. But I'm not. Some of the buildings have friendly memories waving from their windows, some have fists. I know it's corny but it's true. I've been having strange dreams. I have so much to tell you, but this postcard is too small. So I'll just say I love you and see you soon.

Dear Anyu and Apu,

Everything is going well. I am spending time with Gabi and Emma-mama. Things are great. I met the blacksmiths, Rabbi Stern and Coach Varga. They say hello. I will tell you more when I get home.
Love.

Dear Aunt Margit,

I am eating some wonderful Hungarian food but it's not as good as yours. I will tell you more when I get home.
Love.

Tommy laid down the pen. "I'm going to mail some postcards. Where can I get stamps?"

"At the post office. Do you want me to come with you?"

"No. It's okay. I'm a big boy," he joked. I also want to walk around town and take some pictures."

"Be back by lunch," Emma called after him.

Gabi walked him to the gate. "Don't get lost."

"If I do, I'll ask the guy who was following us for directions."

Gabi put his hand on Tommy's shoulder. "They're not joking. You don't know how serious they are. Be careful."

Tommy nodded. "I'll be back soon."

Lowering his voice, Gabi asked, "Do you still want to visit Frog this afternoon?"

"Yes."

As he strolled, Tommy took pictures of fat geese waddling along the streets, young boys and girls filling buckets at the corner pump, a horse-drawn wagon filled with burlap bags of grain and huge stork nests nestled on chimneys. He photographed scenes that were from another time and another world, scenes that would have been the everyday had his family not left.

The church, the tallest structure in town, was on the left side of the square. He craned his neck to see the small windows below the belfry and the clock. He'd been up there once with his father when it was his father's turn for fire-watch duty. His father showed him the world from there: Hajdudobos, the nearest village six kilometres away, the Hajdubékes Golden Green, the collective farm that had once belonged to Gabi's family, and the cemetery where his grandfather was buried. Though he had been so much higher and seen so much more since that time, at this moment he still believed that the church lookout was the tallest place in the world. He tried the door but it was locked. Maybe it was for the best. He took a picture of it instead. When he aimed the camera at Kossuth's statue in the middle of the square, he peered around to see if there were any men in fedoras. There were but they were staring, it seemed, more out of curiosity than surveillance.

He took a picture of what used to be his father's hardware store and was now a bookstore. It felt strange entering the place after so many years. He was the only customer. The four clerks, all young women about Marianne's age, were wearing identical indigo lab coats just like Mr. Papp's. One was sitting at the cash, smoking as she flipped through a magazine. The others were dusting books in a way that would have made Mr. Papp fire them immediately.

He was surprised to find books by Tolstoy, Dostoyevsky, Dickens, Shakespeare, Balzac, Hugo, Zola and Petőfi, his mother's favourite poet. Békes didn't strike him as a cultured place. There were also books by Marx, Engels and Mao Tse Tung as well as children's books; *Ali Baba and The Forty Thieves*, books about Huszars, Hajdus, Young Pioneers, and, of course, *The Paul Street Boys*. And laid out in the glass display cases, like artifacts from another century, were nibbed pens, ink bottles, blotting papers and wooden pencil cases. They were from a time that now belonged in his memory museum. One memory was the night before his first day of school, his mother at the kitchen table, wrapping his notebooks in brown butcher's paper, gluing labels with his name inscribed on them in her beautiful handwriting.

He bought a copy of Petőfi's poems for his mother, a key chain with a soccer ball dangling from it for his father and, for Marianne, a notebook that had the printed and cursive alphabet at the top of each alternating page.

"You're Földember Gabi's cousin from America," the girl at the cash said.

"Yes. From Canada."

She leaned in close as she took the money. "Do you have any nylons?"

Tommy looked around at the girls, who were all watching him intently. "No," he said almost sharply. "Can you tell me where the post office is?"

The cashier glanced at the others and shook her head. They returned to their dusting. "Over there," she muttered under breath. She pointed to City Hall across the square, picked up her cigarette and went back to her magazine.

Although it was only two stories high, the cavernous building was still as foreboding as a giant's palace. He hesitated before reaching for the large brass handles. The last time he had been there his parents were applying for a visa to leave the country. It was here that he'd seen his father stand up to a man who'd called him a traitor. It was here he heard the words *concentration camp* for the first time.

The ceiling was still high, the counter with the wickets was still long and in spite of the lineup, it was as quiet as a principal's waiting room. He still felt small in it.

"Three stamps for postcards to Canada, please."

A woman with a stern face handed him a piece of paper with a number on it and told him to wait until his number was called.

"But all I want are three stamps."

"Your number will be called," she said curtly. She wasn't used to people talking back to her. She signalled for the next person. Tommy went to sit with the others on the hard bench that ran along the wall.

"Making people wait is a way to control you," his father had once told him. He was talking about his time in Mauthausen. "It's a way to make you feel powerless." Maybe it was why his parents were upset whenever he was late.

Tommy watched the old grandfather clock pendulum swing back and forth.

"Wolfstein Tamás."

He almost jumped. A police officer was standing beside him.

"Wolfstein Tamás," he said again.

Tommy stood. "Yes?" he answered nervously.

"Come with me."

"Why?"

The police officer gently but firmly prodded him. Everyone stopped what they were doing and watched. Tommy rose and followed him. The officer's shoes clicked across the granite floor. They paused in front of another wicket.

"Give him your ticket," the officer said to Tommy. "Tell him what you want."

The man behind the wicket reached into his drawer and gave him three stamps. "Three forints," he said.

"Now come this way," the officer said. He pointed at a door that said Chief of Police.

"Sit here." He pointed to a bench and left.

A few minutes later, a man in a suit and tie came out from the office. He had a smoothly shaven face and a neatly trimmed moustache. He extended his hand to Tommy. "Little Tamás," he said.

Noticing Tommy's confusion, he smiled. "Of course, you don't remember me. Barna László. I was a good friend of your father's. My wife worked with your mother at the Nylon. Your dad and I often went to soccer games together. I remember you and Gabi standing beside us, jumping up and down during the games." He motioned Tommy into his office.

Tommy's heartbeat slowed down to almost normal. His stomach settled.

"Sit. How are your father and mother?"

"They're very well. Thank you."

"I am glad to hear that. I was worried when your mother's Identification Book was sent to me. I was asked to investigate your family's disappearance."

Tommy wasn't sure what to say.

"How are you liking your visit in your hometown?"

"It's nice to see my aunt and cousin."

"I'm sorry I didn't get to see you play, but I heard that your games went well and that you and Gabi played really well."

Tommy studied Chief Barna, not sure if he was being sarcastic.

"I've read about your exploits," the chief continued. Feri writes highly of you in the paper."

"Who?"

"Papp Ferenc."

Tommy was surprised. "You know him?"

"We went to university together. We keep in touch. Too bad you aren't playing for your motherland."

"Yes," he said. He wanted to add that it wasn't his fault but thought better of it. "Yes, I always dreamed of playing for Hungary like Puskás."

"I've been told that you haven't registered yet."

The sudden change of topic made Tommy anxious again. "I was planning to after I bought the stamps," he lied.

The chief nodded. "How long are you staying?"

"I'm leaving the day after tomorrow."

"Does your father ever think of coming back?"

"I've never asked him." He had often heard his father declare his love for Canada, calling it the greatest country in the world. He'd also heard his mother use her favourite curse when talking about Hungary. "I don't think so."

"What about you?"

He was taken aback by the question. It had never occurred to him. "I could never leave them. And I'm a Canadian now," he added.

"You are right. A child should always be there for his parents. But you would be very welcome here, I guarantee it." The chief studied him in silence. Then he stood, shook Tommy's hand and led him out of the office. "Give my best to your mother and father. Your father and I were good friends. I miss him. Here is my address if he wants to write to me." He slipped him a piece of paper.

Tommy was walking toward the wicket to register, reading the card, when he got bumped and dropped it. He was about to apologize when a gruff voice asked, "Do Jews still eat dirt?"

He looked up. Szeles had an ugly smile on his face. He saluted and walked on.

Tommy felt lightheaded. Outside, he stopped. Without thinking, he walked toward the man in a fedora sitting on a bench facing City Hall. He sat down next to him. The man stood up and walked away. Tommy watched people come and go as if nothing had happened.

Tommy stopped in front of the schoolyard. He saw his seven-year-old self there, after being kicked out by Mrs. Gombás. Szeles and his gang were standing around the bike rack smiling. Tommy eyed each of them. They turned their gazes toward his bike, the beautiful bike his father had brought for him from

Budapest, on which he became a brave Hajdu riding to fight the terrible Turks. Its tires were slashed. The bright red enamel on the crossbar had been scraped away, the chain was off and coated with dirt and its Superla logo was missing. "You stupid animal!" he had screamed, charging. He took Szeles by surprise. They fell to the ground. Tommy fought to stay on top. He punched Szeles as hard as he could. Blood spurted from Szeles's nose. Tommy hit him repeatedly.

"I won't cry. I won't cry!" he shouted.

Szeles threw him off and rolled over onto him, pinning Tommy's arms with his legs. Szeles's blood dripped onto Tommy's face as Szeles hit him and spat on him.

"Jews! Jews! Dirty Jews! Jews eat dirt," he taunted, stuffing a handful of dirt down Tommy's throat. Tommy twisted his head but Szeles had him by the hair. "Jews eat dirt. Dirty Jews eat dirt!" Szeles was howling.

"What took you so long?" a worried Emma asked. She was sitting on the verandah darning socks. His mother used to darn socks in their early days in Canada, but he hadn't seen her do it in years. She just threw them out now. It was one of the luxuries she allowed herself. He himself was Canadian in the sense that he lost pens, crumpled up half-used sheets of paper and left half-eaten sandwiches at restaurants without thinking twice about them. Emma rose, gathered the socks, put the darning egg and needle carefully back into her basket and placed it on a shelf.

Tommy sat down next to Gabi, who was reading the *Hungarian People's Sports Daily*. "I wandered around and took pictures," he told Emma. He glanced at the paper. "Any big sports news?"

"Nothing since we played you guys," Gabi joked.

"So, where did you go on your secret journey?" Gabi asked while Emma set the table.

"I went to mail the postcards. God, the bureaucracy required to buy stamps." He put his foot up on the bench, glad to get the weight off his ankle.

"It keeps everyone employed," Gabi replied. He neatly folded his paper and put it down.

"Oh, and while at the post office, I met Police Chief Barna. He said he was a friend of Apu's."

"He was. What did he want?" Gabi asked checking to see where Emma was.

"Just wanted me to give him his greetings." He decided not to tell him about bumping into Szeles. Gabi had enough to worry about.

"Carrot dropped by. I told him we'll meet him at the Nylon tonight."

"Good. And Frog?"

"You still want to see him?"

This was the third time Gabi had tried to dissuade him. "Yes."

"Okay. After lunch. But don't say anything to my mother."

Tommy nodded.

Emma called them to eat.

Cold cherry soup always evoked summer for Tommy. It was the ice cream of soups. He loved soaking fresh rye bread in its rich pink liquid and squeezing it out in his mouth. "You get the flavour twice."

"You sound like Sanyi," Emma said.

"Yes, he taught it to me," Tommy said during his second helping.

"What are you going to do this afternoon?" Emma asked.

"We're just going for a walk. Tomi wants to take more pictures."

"Don't be too long."

A light breeze under a blue sky accompanied them to the *putri*. He remembered the way. He had been there often to go frog catching with the best frog catcher in the world. His friend had the patience, the stillness and the quickness that Tommy didn't. He couldn't remember a time when Frog's gunnysack wasn't full after a hunt. His mother used to boil them to make medicine and potions. She also fried their legs, which tasted like chicken.

"Why do you think Chief Barna really wanted to talk to me?"

"Because he was your father's friend."

"That's it, you think?"

"In this country, nothing is simple. What did he say?" Gabi asked. "If all he wanted to do was to tell you to say hello to your parents, he would have come by our house. But since he took you into his office, he wanted to remind your dad that he was a policeman and has power. You know the trouble your dad got into before you escaped?"

"Yeah."

"Did you know that Chief Barna covered it up?"

"No. Really?""

"He got him out of the jam. So maybe he wanted you to tell your dad that he felt that your father owed him. Or maybe that he could still cause problems for him."

"How? We're in Canada."

"Yes, but *we* aren't. Your Aunt Magda and grandfather aren't."

"What does he expect?"

"Maybe he thinks that your father should send him something in the packages you send us."

"Like what?"

"American dollars."

"And what about him saying I'd be welcomed back?" Tommy asked.

"I'm not sure. Maybe he was asking you to work for them."

"What? Be a spy?" Tommy almost shouted.

"He talked to me before you came and suggested that I keep him informed about what we talked about."

"What? You're joking." He eyed Gabi, trying to figure out who he really was. "Why? What could I say or do?"

"You could try to convince me to be a spy for Canada."

"What? I'm a university student and a jock. What would I know about spying? Are you serious?"

"Here everything is serious. Especially after what I did."

Tommy was silent for a minute. "I didn't want to say anything in front of Emma, but I saw the guy who was following us the other day again today."

"Not surprising. I would be more surprised if they weren't following you. I wouldn't be surprised if Chief Barna isn't also being watched. Here everybody is watching everybody. And everybody knows it."

"So, what do you do?"

"Live a watched life."

"Can we sit for a minute?" Tommy asked.

"Sure." They sat by the edge of a ditch that ran along the road.

Tommy rubbed his ankle. "What kind of trouble was Frog in?"

"As I told you, I don't know all of it. He doesn't talk about it much. Maybe he'll tell you."

"What do you know?"

"We were good friends in Békes, and both of us went to the same university, but we drifted apart there. It's a big university. We went into different disciplines, and made new friends, though I heard that he didn't really have any. Also, I got really involved in soccer, and as you know when you get on a team, your teammates become your friends, your world."

"Yup."

"I didn't have any contact with him, though I heard he got into trouble because of his big mouth."

"How?"

"Because he did so well in high school, The Party wanted to make him the shining example of socialist success. They've wanted to integrate the Gypsies into Hungarian society for a long time. He was the educated, civilized symbol of what could be. He was a rising poet who could show his people the way."

A poet showing the way? Hah. Artie Gold was a poet, but he didn't show anybody the way. Except maybe some girls into his bedroom, the bastard. "Then what happened?"

"I don't know everything, but I heard he started questioning his professors."

"He got kicked out for *that?*"

"And for his poetry, which I don't know much about."

Tommy couldn't even imagine the government in Canada hassling a poet for what he wrote. "What happened after that?"

"We better get going."

They got up. No one seemed to be following them. "I lost track of Frog after that. He disappeared. The next thing I heard was that he was conscripted."

Tommy didn't believe Gabi was telling him everything.

"There's the *putri.*" Gabi pointed to a field dotted with mud-and-straw-stubbled brick shanties. Wisps of smoke curled up through zigzag chimneys of tin. Paneless windows too small to let in light stared back at him. Doors hung precariously from loose hinges. The shanties were on the verge of collapse. Skinny hens pecked at the dirt. An old mare was tethered to a broken-down wagon. Small boys were chasing each other, wrestling, duelling with sticks. Their shouts and laughter filled the air. Young girls in rags were singing and dancing, while women with babies were gathered around the well, chattering loudly and drawing water. Men, squatting between the shanties, smoked, drank and played cards. Tommy felt as though he had stepped into another world.

When the children spotted Gabi and Tommy, they ran toward them with outstretched palms.

"Don't give them any money or we'll never get out of here," Gabi warned. By the time they reached Frog's house, Tommy was sure that half the *putri* was following them.

Gabi knocked on the doorpost. "Ancsa?"

"Oh, my little Gabi, enter," a voice called out.

"I brought your other son, Hannah Wolfstein's Tomi."

"Oh, my little Tomi!" A gnarled hand grabbed his and pulled him in. The smell of pipe tobacco embraced him. "Oh, my little Tomi," she kept repeating as she stroked, pressed and caressed his face. She pulled it close to hers and planted wet kisses all over his cheeks.

He was a child again.

"Oh, the summer horses brought you. Come, sit. May they be blessed forever, and may the evil eye keep away."

Her face glistened. Tommy knew she was about his mother's age but, like Rabbi Stern, she looked much older. Deep wrinkles creased her face, though her hair, still black as the night, had a sheen that reminded him of Marianne's. Her coal-dark eyes sparkled, and her smile revealed teeth of gold. This was the woman whose breasts had suckled him, whose hands had bathed him and whose stories had enchanted him.

"My mother sends her best wishes and this gift." He presented her the plastic bag.

She held it up as if it were a holy object. "How smooth it is, as if the sun had polished it," she said, stroking it. She reached in and drew out a bright yellow polka-dotted cardigan. It was an old one his mother no longer wore.

"May Sara–la-Kali bless her," Frog's mother cried out. She held up the cardigan for the crowd that had gathered inside to see. The women clapped their hands and praised the gift. "The sun will always shine on me," she said, holding it to her chest. She caressed and sniffed it.

"And this is from me," Tommy said, handing her a packet of pipe tobacco that Gabi had suggested he buy for her.

She stuck her nose into the pouch and inhaled deeply. Taking her pipe from her apron pocket, she stuffed it, tamped it and lit it up. "Ahh such fine smoke," she sighed after a couple of puffs.

"And how's your sweet blessed mother?"

"She's fine, in good health."

"That is good. The spirits have been kind to her."

"Yes." He was trying to remember if Ancsa had always talked like this. "And how have the spirits been to you?" he asked, before he realized that he was speaking her way.

"They have been fair and foul. They come and go. But today, now that you and Gabi and Frog are together again, they are fair."

"Dear little mother, where is Frog?" Gabi asked.

"He is here and there," she said. "Here, he is in the woods, there, he is in his head."

"We will go and see him there," Gabi said.

She smothered both of them again with loud kisses. "You are milk brothers," she said to Tommy. Goose bumps rose along the nape of his neck.

"Come on," Gabi said.

"Where are we going?"

"To see Frog."

The crowd parted to let them through.

"How do you know where he is? She didn't say."

"She told us he was in the forest."

"A forest is a big place."

"Not here. Come on."

What a difference it was from the bare dirt, treeless yards and collapsing shacks. The woods were rich with colour: leaves, flowers and in little clearings, carpets like the magic carpets of his childhood stories.

Gabi pointed to a fork on the left. "I think it's there."

"How do you know?"

Frog was sitting cross-legged, with a notebook on his lap. The first thing Tommy noticed about him was how his taut, smoky-coloured face blended with the colours around him. He seemed to be part of this place. The girl was the second. She was reclining on the carpet, her head resting on her palm, sleeping.

"Hey, Frog," Gabi called out.

Frog raised his eyes from his notebook. "I am no longer Frog. I am Broshkoy."

"What?"

"I am my language. I am my words. I am Broshkoy. It means frog in my mother tongue."

His words hung in the air. Tommy recalled Mr. Papp's words about names.

"Mishto avilian amende. Taves baxtalo ando amaro. Sit," he said and patted the carpet. He gently shook the girl's ankle. "Rosie, we have visitors." The gentle tinkling of her ankle bracelet bells mingled with the chirps of the birds. She had wild uncombed shoulder-length hair and a puggish nose. Like Ancsa and Frog, she had coal-black eyes.

Rosie sat up, brushed her long hair out of her eyes and glared at Tommy. She seemed to be looking into him, not at him. He turned away and reached into his shopping bag and took out a bottle of wine and his Swiss Army knife. He passed the open bottle to Frog. He found it weird calling him Broshkoy. To him he was still Frog, the skinny, shoeless kid he had shared a childhood with. Frog took a small swig and passed it to Gabi, who passed the bottle to Rosie, who in turn passed it to Tommy.

"He's much younger than you," she said to Frog.

"No, we're the same age," Tommy said.

"But you're much younger," she said, ending the conversation.

Tommy wondered what she meant.

"I am glad that you came."

"Me too. How have you been?"

"I have been well and not well and well again," Frog said.

Tommy wasn't sure how to respond to that. He waited. After what seemed like a long silence he said, "Gabi told me that you write poetry."

"I did, then I didn't and now I do."

There was awkwardness to the conversation that wasn't just because of language, years and distance. Frog seemed to be pushing him toward something, but Tommy didn't know what. "Gabi told me that after being expelled you disappeared."

"No. I did not disappear. I wandered. I travelled to *putris* listening to wonderful stories, beautiful songs, and I learned my history. I learned the beauty and the horrors of our diaspora, of our difference. And you know one of the things I discovered was how much like the Jews we are. Maybe we are the lost tribe."

Tommy smiled. "How are we the same?"

"Well, we are both considered Christ killers."

"How are you Christ killers? I thought we were the only ones who had that privilege."

"Once upon a time, a long, long, time ago, we were the Athingani, iron mongers. We were the blacksmiths who forged the nails that were driven into Christ's hands. And thus, we were set on the road of suffering. So the story goes. Once upon a time, we were untouchables, child killers who needed the blood of young children for our black arts. So the story goes."

"Sure sounds familiar," Tommy said

"And we also were victims of the Holocaust. We weren't six million but during the war 25,000 of us were deported to Transnistrian concentration camp. Half of us died there. About 30,000 of us were deported to other death camps. Only two to three thousand of us came back. Often the Hungarian gendarmes and German soldiers did not bother to send us anywhere but lined us up outside our homes and shot us. About 600,000 of us were killed. Who cares?"

"Does anyone?" Tommy asked.

"I do."

"So, you wrote poems about that and it got you into trouble," Gabi said.

"How could I not? Writing poems, if they're real, will get you into trouble eventually. Real poems don't know borders, don't follow collective orders, and don't have five-year plans. Often you yourself don't know what's going on. They are like us Romas, unpredictable, wanderers. We sing, cry, curse, spit, dance and are. We lie to tell the truth. We are trouble." He stared at Gabi. "Being a poet is not a career choice. You, you decided to be an engineer, so you followed a prescribed plan to become one. I didn't decide to be a poet. I started writing not really knowing that I was writing poems. I liked the sound of words; I liked the way I could arrange them and how they created ways of seeing. Each poem made me want to write more. I learned that if the poem is strong and true, they make the reader pay attention. Maybe it began with Mrs. Gombás. Do you remember we had to memorize and recite a poem in grade one?"

"Yes."

"I still remember that I had a lot of trouble memorizing it. You helped me and in the end, I was the only one who didn't make a mistake. Aside from the pride of not making a mistake, I enjoyed how it took me away from the real and took me to the real real. And seeing how Mrs. Gombás belittled my mother because she shouted out her joy—called her uncivilized—made me feel helpless and angry. And so began my descent into that world."

"What world?"

"The world of trouble. You also knew your poem by heart, better than me, but you weren't allowed to recite. You got kicked out. Maybe seeing that also set me on the road."

"And because of that…?" Tommy asked.

"Yes. I got conscripted."

"I don't understand."

"Hungarians say that there are only three kinds of Hungarians: those who have been in prison, those who are in prison and those who will be in prison. Eventually they get everybody. This is especially true for artists. The army was my prison."

"Why the army?"

"Because they could break me, body and spirit, under the guise of trying to make me fit to defend my country. Imagine how desperate Hungary must be to need a myopic who is 158.5 centimetres and 49.9 kilos." He shook his head. "They could humiliate me, degrade me and have my fellow soldiers do their dirty work by having them turn on me. I resisted as long as I could and when I couldn't anymore, I slit my wrists."

Tommy, shocked, turned to Gabi.

"I didn't know if he wanted you to know that, so I didn't say anything."

Broshkoy-Frog spoke with detachment, as if recalling facts, as if the story was someone else's from another time.

"I tried to kill myself because I didn't want them to kill me. Because I didn't want them to be in charge of my death as they were in charge of my life. I failed. The army didn't. After they emptied me, they didn't have anything to worry about, and they let me go." He glanced at Rosie.

"And I would have ended up like Smith, but this woman saved me."

"Who is Smith?" Gabi asked.

"Tomi knows," Frog said.

"I'm sorry but I don't know a Smith," Tommy said

"*1984*," Frog said.

"Oh." Tomi was surprised that Frog knew of Orwell's book. He nodded. "How did Rosie save you?"

"She tried to kill me."

"What?" Tommy and Gabi exclaimed almost simultaneously.

"All I'll tell you is that as she had her fingers around my throat and as she was choking me, she kept asking, "better dead than alive?"

"And?" Tomi asked.

"I'm here, aren't I?"

Tommy now understood why Rosie had said that he was younger than Frog. Even though Tommy had had experiences, even though he had been shot, it was nothing compared to Broshkoy's hell. Tommy was too young to have had important choices to make. Compared to Broshkoy, he was still in diapers. Broshkoy spoke with a sureness that came from knowing what he needed to do.

"You don't have a choice about being born. You don't have choice to whom you are born. Or the world you are born into. You are a victim of those circumstances. But what is optional is the way you live in it. Victim or victor?"

Tommy sensed that he was speaking not only about himself but about his people.

"I have learned that those of us who are fortunate enough or cursed enough to see and think must try. Otherwise we will be choked to death." He turned to Rosie, who was still glaring at Tommy.

Tommy tried to take it all in.

"Therefore, I write." He took a swig. "What is your life like?" Broshkoy asked.

"I hadn't really thought about it. I guess it's good."

"It can't really be that good if you haven't thought about it. Have you read Socrates?"

"No."

"You should," Broshkoy said in a way that made Tommy uncomfortable. After a long silence he added, "I have a task for you. I want you to take my poems to Canada and get them translated and published." It wasn't a request.

"I don't understand."

"It's important for my people."

"Do you know somebody who can translate them?" Tommy asked.

"You," he said.

"My Hungarian is not good enough."

"Make it good enough," Broshkoy said calmly, as if what he had told Tommy to do was as simple as getting a glass of water.

Tommy turned to Gabi for guidance as he had often done when they were kids. Gabi was the older one, the one who made the decisions. But Gabi was pokerfaced. It's crazy, Tommy thought to himself. What a stupid thing to get into trouble for. "What difference can a poem make?" Tommy asked Broshkoy.

"A world of difference," Broshkoy said quietly.

Tommy thought for a moment. He thought of Marianne. He nodded.

"He's not so young now," Rosie said, and scrambled up the oak tree under which their carpet lay. She came down with an old briefcase that she gave to Broshkoy. He took out a sheaf of papers and handed it to Tommy. There was a handwritten essay and about two dozen poems. Tommy scanned the first one but couldn't really understand it. He folded the papers and slipped them in his jacket's inside pocket.

"We should be going," Gabi said. "Don't forget, we're meeting Carrot tonight at the Nylon. Be there."

His skinny, bug-eyed childhood friend made Tommy consider his own purpose in this world. He'd been letting life move him along. He had that luxury. Broshkoy and Gabi didn't. There was a weight they carried that he didn't. It was in their talk; in the way they considered every word. It was in the way they carried themselves, always attuned to their surroundings. As Gabi said, here you lived a watched life. But Tommy sensed something else as well. The weight also seemed to have made their life more meaningful. It made them appreciate the value of it, how it meant nothing and everything. And as they walked back silently to Békes, into a setting sun, Tommy changed his mind. His life was easy, which didn't necessarily make it good. It made it simpler. Although since he met Marianne, it had certainly become more intense and complicated. Maybe that was what being grown up was all about.

He was already having second thoughts about smuggling out Broshkoy's manuscript. How could he have made such a stupid promise? He remembered Mr. Luxton's warnings about taking letters out of the country. What did Tommy really know of what went on in this country? What would happen to him if he got caught? He wasn't in Canada. Whom could he trust here? Even Gabi admitted that he had been asked to spy on him. Who knew if he wasn't doing it now? Was he being set up? He could throw the papers away once he left Békes. Aside from people like that woman-stealing poet in Montreal, who would care about a Hungarian Gypsy poet's poem? Maybe Marianne?

As they approached the house, they could hear music wafting from the kitchen. Gabi put a finger to his lips and signalled Tommy to follow him quietly. Emma was humming while she cut up potatoes and plopped them in the pot. Stirring, she swayed her hips to the rhythm.

"We're back," Gabi announced.

Emma jumped and clasped her chest. "Are you insane?" she shouted and swatted him with the spoon. Gabi was laughing.

"Get out of here! Scaring your poor mother to death." Emma turned to Tommy. "Are you hungry?"

"Not yet. I'm pooped. My ankle is still sore. I'm going to take a nap, okay?"

"Go ahead."

"Do you want me to wake you up?" Gabi asked.

"If I'm not up in an hour."

"Okay," Gabi mimicked Tommy.

Tommy stood for a moment on the verandah, looking out over his childhood playground, and wondered what would have become of him if his family had not left. Would he be a hot soccer prospect, would he be a good Hungarian? Would he be a troublemaker? He sighed and reached up to the shelf and took Emma's sewing basket into his room.

He laid his blazer on his lap and carefully slipped his knife's blade tip through the thread in the middle of the lining. He picked at it the way his mother did and opened the seam about six inches. He slipped in Broshkoy's manuscript. Patting it flat, he lifted the jacket. The papers settled in a bunch at the bottom, making the back lumpy He laid the jacket down again, reshuffled the papers and sewed the lining on either side of the papers to the back of the jacket, making a pocket for them. With his back to the mirror, he twisted his neck to see if he could detect any major bulges. It looked passable. But he knew his mother would have made him do it again. So, he did. When he was finished, he hung up the jacket and crawled into bed.

The darkness of his sleep became a land of mud in which he was being chased by shadows. He tried to run, but the mud was sucking him down. The darkness began to spin. He felt as if he were in a whirlpool, spinning out of control as he was being sucked down. In circles, in circles, in circles he went. There was a light he could never get to. He stretched out his hand but there was no hand to hold onto. In circles, in circles he spun.

Gabi's knock stopped the spinning. Tommy sat up and held his head between his palms. He took a couple of deep breaths and rubbed his temple. He hoped that it wasn't a migraine coming on.

It was his last night in Békes and Emma had prepared her delicious chicken paprika. And for dessert, of course, *pogácsa*.

"I vaguely remember that in one of the books Anyu read to me, there was a boy setting off to fight the giant or ogre and his mother put *pogácsa* in his knapsack. Is it true? Or am I just imagining it?"

"I don't remember a story like that," Gabi said, "but I know it's a Hungarian tradition. Every time a child graduates, the mother gives him a little bag of *pogácsa*."

Tommy put his lips to it as if he were kissing Marianne for the first time, letting its heat warm his lips. He took a small bite and closed his eyes.

"So like your father," Emma said, smiling. "How I miss him."

"We should go. I told Carrot that we would meet him around nineteen thirty."

5 4

The Nylon bar reeked of cigarettes and beer. It was crowded, mainly with young men, shouting, laughing and drinking away the week's work.

He felt self-conscious in his tailored team jacket and slim tie. The locals' were ill-fitting and shabby, and the ties were wide and sloppily knotted. I'm looking with my mother's eyes, he thought to himself.

A muscled young red-headed man in a sharply pressed army uniform was waving at them from a table near the bar. The Carrot Tommy remembered was a skinny kid in patched shorts who was one of the regulars he played soccer with after school. His father was the train stationmaster and the official scorekeeper for the Békes soccer team. Carrot, along with Broshkoy, was the only one who continued to play with Tommy and Gabi after Tommy was kicked out of school.

They shook hands formally. Tommy removed his jacket, put it on the back of his chair, loosened his tie and ordered a round. They reminisced about the good old days.

Tommy put down his glass. "Do you still think we killed Christ?" he asked.

"What?" Carrot asked, puzzled.

"I remember once being called a Christ killer. I didn't know what the kid was talking about. I asked Gabi because he was older, and I thought he knew everything," Tommy smiled as he looked at Gabi. "He said that you had told him that the Jews killed Christ and that's why they're hated so much. I was wondering if you still think that?"

Carrot lifted his glass of beer and sipped.

"You remember strange things," Gabi said, trying to break the tension.

"The visit with Broshkoy made that memory jump into my head."

"I honestly don't remember saying that, but I've heard my father say it, so I might have."

"Do you still think so?"

He paused. "I don't really know. I haven't read the Bible and I don't go to church, so I really don't know. And I don't really care."

Tommy smiled.

"What's funny?" Gabi asked.

"There's a waiter in Montreal whose name is Jesus. In case you still believed it, I just wanted to let you know that he is alive and well."

For a moment, Carrot and Gabi said nothing, then they all burst out laughing.

"Frog's here," Carrot said, waving to him. He was carrying a package and pushing his way through the crowd. Even though he was small and skinny, he parted the bodies with authority. Tommy hoped that the package was not another thing Broshkoy wanted him to smuggle out of Hungary.

"We haven't all been together since 1956. Eleven years," Carrot said.

Broshkoy toasted the group. "To eleven lost years. May tonight bring them back. To your health."

"To your health," they responded.

"I brought you something," Broshkoy said to Tommy. He handed him the package wrapped in newspaper and tied with a string.

"Thank you," he said.

"How can you thank me if you haven't seen what I am giving you?"

It felt a bit heavy. Tommy nervously untied the string, gave it to Gabi and unwrapped the paper. It was a beautiful shawl. Tommy didn't understand why he would give him a shawl.

Broshkoy had to shout to make himself heard. "Open it."

Something was rolled up inside. Tommy couldn't believe it. It was his sword! The one the blacksmiths had made for him all those years ago. He ran his fingers over the dragon head handle, down the shiny blade to the sharp tip.

"Thank you," he shouted, holding it in salute.

"So, the dirty traitors are here," growled a voice. Tommy turned and saw a drunk-eyed Szeles standing behind him.

"You're drunk. Go back to your buddies," Gabi said.

"Fuck you, traitor Jew. You betrayed your motherland for your fucking Jew cousin. This place is only for true Hungarians," he said, slurring his words.

"Shut your ignorant mouth," Broshkoy snapped.

"Dirty Gypsies don't talk like that to a Hungarian. The fucking Jew and the fucking Gypsy." He shoved Tommy hard, sending him and beer glasses flying. Then he grabbed Broshkoy and threw him down onto the floor.

"You horse's prick," Carrot shouted and punched Szeles, who spun and fell toward Tommy and Broshkoy. Szeles landed between the two, face down. A loud, piercing scream filled Tommy's ears.

Time stopped.

When the police arrived, the crowd that had formed around Tommy and Broshkoy parted. Chief Barna knelt over the body. Bile was mixed with the blood on Szeles's chest. Chief Barna sniffed and wrinkled his nose. "What happened here?" he asked.

"Tommy threw up on him," Carrot said.

"Good God," the chief said, noticing the bloody sword lying beside him. "Whose is that?"

"It's mine," Tommy and Broshkoy answered at once.

"It can't belong to both of you," he said sternly.

"It was Tomi's when he was a kid," Gabi said. "Frog has had it since Tomi left. He was giving it back to him."

Tommy stared at his hands.

"All four of you are coming with me." Chief Barna nodded to the policeman to escort them to the station. He ordered the other officer to collect statements and stay with the body.

Tommy and Broshkoy sat between Gabi and Carrot. A policeman stood next to them to make sure that nobody talked. Tommy's mouth tasted vile; his stomach churned.

After what seemed forever, they had taken Carrot, Gabi and Broshkoy into the office. Police Chief Barna emerged and signalled to the guard. The officer prodded Tommy, who was rubbing at the dried blood on his palm, a brownish stain fading into his skin, leaving just its outline. He stood and followed the guard.

"Tamás, come in," the chief said.

The officer prodded him again.

"I've had enough of him. Get him out of here," the man in the suit said to Chief Barna.

Tommy, too numb with fatigue to feel relieved, turned to leave.

"Where do you think you're going?" the man in the dark suit shouted.

Tommy faced Chief Barna.

"You are under arrest," the Chief said.

"What?" Tommy yelled. A rush of adrenalin woke him.

Two officers escorted him downstairs into the basement of City Hall, where there were four metal doors. The guard opened the first, pushed him in and shut it behind him. The slam of metal on metal made him jump. He spun around and faced the door. His heart raced but he was unable to move. He felt short of breath. He didn't know what to do. He listened. Breathe, he heard himself say. A dim overhead light bulb made shadows of the corners. The walls glistened. He took tentative steps, reached out and touched one. He jerked his hand back and rubbed the slime on his pants. His foot struck something metallic. He recoiled and looked down. A bucket was sticking out from beneath the cot. He sat.

Even though the mattress was damp and stank of piss, he was glad to be sitting. The light went out. He panicked. He clenched his hands, ready to ward off any attack. He wanted to run but there was nowhere to go. The walls and the darkness closed in on him.

5 5

He was scared. This wasn't real. He wanted his parents. But they weren't here. They were in another world and couldn't help him. They didn't even know that he was in jail. His mother had warned him. He was on his own now. There was Gabi and Emma-mama and Aunt Magda and his grandfather, but what could they do? They were Hungarians. They had no power. He panicked and started to shake. He sat down and grabbed the edge of the cot. He squeezed hard and tried to take deep breaths. He rubbed his face and forehead. He felt his scar. A migraine was coming on. He rubbed deeper and harder as wave after wave of blood flooded the base of his neck and moved up over his brain, tightening his scalp, crashing against his temple and pressing at the back of his eyes, wanting out. He passed out.

The bare bulb exploded with light. Tommy jumped up from the cot. He was still in the same cell with the same frightening shadows as yesterday. He was in one of his nightmare mazes with no way out. But this one was for real. The heavy metal door looked impenetrable. His head was still pounding.

The door opened. The guard came in and motioned him out.

Tommy could barely get the words out. "Where are we going?"

"No talking," the guard said and pointed down the corridor.

For a moment he thought that there was mirror at the end of the hall, but it was Broshkoy walking toward him followed by a guard. He had a large purplish welt on his cheek. He nodded. The guard pointed to the right. They came to an open space with a wide plank along the wall. It had four holes. Broshkoy was at one end, Tommy was at the other.

"Go," his guard said. At first Tommy wasn't sure what he meant. He saw Broshkoy drop his pants and sit. Tommy averted his eyes. The guard nudged him. "Go," he said again.

He shook his head. Tommy glanced at Broshkoy, who was wiping himself.

The guard pointed back toward his cell. There was a tray with a bowl of greyish gruel, a spoon and a piece of rye bread on his bed. Sitting on the cot, he tried to make sense of all this. He had no idea what to do. This isn't real, he said to himself, as he spooned the lukewarm gruel into his mouth.

5 6

Tommy listened. He heard a movement. Then nothing. Then he heard something again. He had no idea what time it was. The light had gone off twice since he'd last seen Broshkoy. He had to shit. He pulled the rusted bucket out from under the cot. It stank worse than the outhouse. He kicked it back under the cot with his foot. His ankle still hurt.

The door opened. The guard stood at the door. Nobody spoke. A man in a blue overall picked up the tray. "Thank you," Tommy said. "Get back!" the guard snapped and slammed the door. Tommy stood there, numb. Then the light went out. The world outside was gone. He was in darkness again.

Something scuttled across his shoes. He stiffened. He swung his foot toward it. "Fuck you! Fuck you! Fuck you, motherfucker!" he swore as he kicked wildly at the dank air. He was playing blind soccer. He was kicking the man in the dark suit, the referee, the player who slashed his ankle, Mrs. Gombás, the drunk soldier, the men who stuffed the rabbi in the chicken coop and Szeles, father and son. He felt the depth of his parents' hatred for this place. He thought about them and what they had gone through. He felt his parents' fierceness. Anticipate, he told himself. He closed his eyes and listened. He kicked. A high-pitched screech pierced the silence followed by absolute silence.

Fear and anger were his cellmates. The light turning on had become as scary as it being shut off. He sat on the cot with his head in his hands. The migraine persisted. Victim or victor? he heard the voice in his head ask.

He was taken to the latrine several more times. But he never saw Broshkoy. "Go," the guard ordered each time. Each time he couldn't but this time he dropped his pants and sat. Tommy was shaking. From somewhere in his belly, a low growl emanated, a primal mass of anger clenched tight. The howling rose. He imagined the man in the dark suit beneath him. "Shit or get in the pot," Tommy shouted. He laughed and let go.

Back in his cell he sat, relieved. He heard scurrying. He got up and listened. You afraid of a little mouse? the voice in his head asked. What did he do to you? He comes and goes. He's free, let him be. Tommy sat down and stared into the darkness.

5 7

"It's in the dark cell that the interrogations begin," he remembered Broshkoy saying when he'd told Tommy about his experience after the suicide attempt. "That's how your world is taken from you, in pure, total darkness. You have to create light," he had said.

You, Tamás Wolfstein, he heard his voice say, are a child of survivors, of parents who risked their lives for freedom. You are the son of heroes, not mice. You, Wolfie, are Captain Puskás of champions, a knight of the warrior Cohen tribe, Sir Wolf of the square matzo. He smiled and the darkness withdrew into the corners of his cell.

He did push-ups. He walked miles. He shouted Beware. He thought about Marianne, her dancing, their lovemaking, their trip, stepping outside the gravity of reality. Flying, free. He lay down on the floor. Dirt angels! he shouted as he moved his legs and arms up and down.

He didn't know how long he had been locked up. If he counted by the number of interrogations, then it was a week, if by the light turning on and off, then at least a month, and if by what filled his mind, then it was years.

5 8

He was led upstairs again. The bright light hurt his eyes. Each interrogation began the same way. The man in the dark suit made him stand and wait while he lit a cigarette and opened his file folder. He read and smoked.

"Who had the knife?" he asked every time. "Did you?"

"I told you, I don't know."

"You will go to jail for murder."

Breathe, Tommy repeated to himself.

"Well?"

Tommy stared at his shirt cuff caked with dirt, slime and dried blood. He felt a strange lightness. "What about Broshkoy?"

"That's not your business."

"He's my friend."

"He turned on you. He said you had the knife."

"Tell us he did it. We'll take your word over his," Chief Barna said.

Tommy took a few more deep breaths. Be a man, he told himself. He went over in his mind what had happened. He was shoved by a drunk Szeles, who sent him and Broshkoy flying. He remembered that when he started to get up Szeles was falling toward them. He heard a hiss, like a ball deflating. He heard a scream in his ear. He felt warm liquid seeping into his hand, then Broshkoy's hand wrapped itself around his and tugged. Tommy stiffened and then his hand jerked. He heard a grunt, and then, nothing. He closed his eyes.

When he opened them he was surrounded by a circle of faces. He turned to his right where Szeles, with his eyes wide open, lay staring at him. Carrot and Gabi turned Szeles over. As they did, blood seeped out of him and like a spill of wine, it spread over the front of his shirt.

Gabi and Carrot reached down and pulled Tommy and Broshkoy up. They stared at each other and then down at Szeles. The sword lay glistening in a pool of blood next to Szeles. People were pushing and shoving to get a closer look. Tommy was outside of himself watching everything happening fast and slow at the same time and spinning. His stomach churned. Before he had time to turn away, Tommy threw up on Szeles. Gabi grabbed Tommy as he buckled and was about to faint. "Tomi. Tomi!" Gabi had shouted, shaking him.

Real time returned.

"Well?"

Victim or victor, he said to himself. He ran through all possible scenarios. If he said that he was the last one holding the sword, he would be convicted. If he told them Broshkoy was holding it, then Broshkoy would be convicted. That would make him, Tamás Wolfstein, a traitor.

"I don't know who was holding the sword."

"Witnesses said that you were," the man said.

Tommy took a deep breath. "Then I guess I was."

"You're confessing?"

"To holding the sword?"

"To killing Officer Szeles."

"No."

The man in the suit stepped in front him. They were almost nose to nose. Tommy was about to take a step back but stopped himself.

"You desert your motherland, you come back and you kill a Hungarian police officer and you think you can get away with it because you're from America? You are a spoiled capitalist kid. You are a traitor," the man in the suit shouted.

Tommy balled his hands into fists "I'm not a traitor. Hungary betrayed me. We were forced out by our countrymen who didn't want us, who didn't think we belonged."

The man in the black suit punched him in the gut. Tommy gasped and doubled over. He unclenched his fists. Slowly, he straightened up and faced the man.

"You are right," he said softly, controlling his breath. "This not my home. Thank God."

"Get out!" the man in the dark suit shouted.

Tommy didn't move. He waited to be taken back to his cell.

"I said get out!" the man in the dark suit shouted again.

Tommy said nothing. He stood and waited..

"You are free to go," Chief Barna said. "Your Gypsy friend confessed that he took the knife from you and killed Officer Szeles."

Was it another trick? Were they waiting for him to contradict him? Why did Broshkoy want to take the blame? Hadn't he spent enough time in prison? He tried to see the moves behind the moves. He couldn't. If it was true, was Broshkoy being noble? It suddenly dawned on him that Broshkoy wasn't being noble. He was protecting his poems. He was doing the stupid and the right thing.

"Szeles fell on the knife."

"Get out before I arrest you for rape and murder," the man shouted. Tommy took a tentative step toward the door.

"Tamás," Chief Barna called out. He stopped. So, they were playing with him. He turned back to face him.

"Here is your jacket and passport. We have to keep the sword. I'll give it to Gabi after we're finished with it."

Tommy unclenched his jaw and fists. He stared at his sword. It had killed a man. He didn't want it anymore. "Throw it back in the well."

Slowly he put on his jacket and put the passport in his pocket. Chief Barna put his hand on his back. His hand rested on the poems. Tommy stiffened.

"Give your father my best," the chief said.

Tommy nodded.

5 9

As soon as Gabi saw Tommy, he grabbed and hugged him hard. Mr. Luxton, with a tight smile on his face, stood behind Gabi.

They were led outside through a side door. The sky was bright. Tommy closed his eyes. A breeze brushed his face. They walked in silence.

"What about Broshkoy?" Tommy asked as they turned onto their street.

"I don't know. I tried to find out, but they wouldn't tell me anything."

"They said he confessed."

"They can't charge him with murder, but they'll find something," Mr. Luxton said.

"We have to do something."

"There isn't much we can do. It's an internal matter," Mr. Luxton said. "However, Frog does have some security and connections because of his writing."

"His name is Broshkoy," Tommy corrected him coldly. "From what he told me, they didn't do much to protect him last time."

"Maybe you can do something once you're back in Canada," Gabi said.

"No, he can't." Mr. Luxton said firmly. "It's an internal matter."

"Do my parents know?"

"Of course. They are very worried. They wanted to come, but we told them not to. I told them that you were being released today. We will call them from the embassy and you can talk to them."

Emma and Magda were waiting outside the house gate. When they saw him, they ran towards him. They grabbed him by the arms and pulled him fiercely towards them. "Oh God. Oh God," they sobbed, covering his face in teary kisses.

They wouldn't let go, pulling him toward the safety of the house. Once in the yard, Mr. Luxton ordered Tommy to pack. "We're leaving right now. You're flying out tonight."

"No," Emma said. "You eat first."

Mr. Luxton was equally adamant. "We have to leave now. Go pack. I'm afraid we don't have much time. I'm here to make sure that you catch your plane. If not, then we will have all sorts of problems. So, now!" Tommy understood the urgency but didn't move.

"I need to wash," he said. Tommy walked toward the well and began to undress. Gabi hauled up a bucket of water. He took off his blood-caked shirt and was about to throw it on the ground but stopped. He folded it neatly and put it on the bench next to the well. He did the same with the rest of his clothes. It felt great to be naked. He didn't care if they watched. He closed his eyes and stood still. Gabi poured the bucket over his head. The shock of the cold water made him gasp. It was refreshing. He washed himself back to life.

Tommy took his clothes inside and got dressed. Emma had a bag of *pogácsa* in her hand. She began to sob and buried her head in his chest. He whispered in her ear. "A man desperately wants to marry off his ugly daughter. His friend says I know a man who might be interested. The man comes over and looks at the girl. He says I would like to see her naked. The father says no. The man says okay, then no marriage. The father sighs and says okay. He tells his daughter to undress. The man looks her over, and then he says NO. The father is furious; he asks why not? The man looks at the daughter and says, her ears are too big."

Emma chortled.

"Don't pee in your pants," Tommy said. He reached out and grabbed Gabi. They embraced.

"*Szerbusz*, Grosics."

"*Szerbusz*, Puskás."

"I'm not Puskás. I'm Tamás."

Mr. Luxton's car had a Canadian flag on its aerial. Tommy stroked it as he got in.

He waved. Emma and Magda were gripping Gabi's arm. Békés disappeared behind him.

"How did you know I was in trouble?" he asked after a long silence.

"There aren't that many Canadians in Hungary at any one time. We usually know where our citizens are. You, we knew from the start."

"But how did you know I was in trouble?"

"Your cousin called the embassy, but we already knew. It's not only Hungarians who have men with fedoras."

Tommy watched the passing scenery, the villages, the countryside, the people. You go back, he thought, but you know you can't. He had read it somewhere. You can stand on a corner and watch yourself, a kid in knee pants, with all his adventures ahead of him, with all the joys to be celebrated, all the scrapes to be cried over. You can watch yourself touch familiar corners but gut-know that you can't go back. He had discovered again and again that he didn't want to. But, he thought, staring out at the blur of scenery, maybe the path forward begins with a journey back.

"Tommy!" Mr. Luxton woke him from his reverie. "We ask you not to speak of what happened in Békés to anyone except your parents. They already agreed."

"How can the people in Canada not know?"

"The government here controls the news. But if the news got out, it would be a problem for your relatives here."

Tommy suspected as much. He said nothing.

"Dictatorships don't like this kind of news to be public for a whole slew of reasons I won't go into. I'm pretty sure you can figure it out for yourself. They would not be happy and…." He didn't finish his sentence.

Tommy was silent for a while. He knew that Mr. Luxton was right. But he needed to do something. He tried to think like his father, who always told him when you're bargaining, think of how this works for them and then how can you make it work for you.

"You know, we didn't rape the girl. It was a setup. And it wasn't us who started the fight. That drunk did. And during the interrogation, they hinted that I could help myself if I cooperated in certain ways. They reminded me I was a son of Hungary. And you know how even with the best intentions, news gets out. You know that the newspapers will want to interview me. Mr. Papp will want to write about my exploits."

Anger flashed in Mr. Luxton's eyes.

"If you could make it so that Gabi doesn't have to go to re-education camp, I would really appreciate it." Tommy didn't tell him that he had something else planned to help Broshkoy, even though he wasn't at all certain whether his plan would work.

Mr. Luxton smiled politely. "We'll see what we can do."

The phone call with his parents was emotional. His father cried and his mother cursed. He tried to reassure them that all was okay and that he would see them in a few hours.

When they pulled into the diplomatic parking area at the airport, Mr. Luxton escorted him to the airline counter and flashed some papers. Tommy asked for a window seat. He and Mr. Luxton shook hands. "You fellows did Canada proud," he said and then he was gone.

"Do you have anything to declare?" the customs officer asked.

"No."

"Are you taking any cultural or heritage material out of the country?"

"No. Just myself."

The plane roared. He clenched the armrests. He grunted and let go. He reached into his pocket and rubbed the cigarette case. He forced himself to look out the window. The plane rose and soon the land below him receded until it was an amorphous blob. The plane tore through the clouds. Hungary disappeared. He pushed against his seat. The poems pushed back.

As soon as the seat belt light went off, he went to the bathroom, took out his knife and unstitched his jacket's lining. He carefully took out the sheaves of paper and returned to his seat. He began the difficult task of reading.

J'ACCUSE!

I speak to you as an equal, something you don't expect or accept. I speak to you man to man, something you can't or don't want to face. I speak to you as neighbour, countryman, and comrade. I speak to you this way because you need to be spoken to like this. I don't ask for your permission to do this.

We will always be unlike you. Our sunbaked faces are the maps of where we are from, where we are and where we are going. We will always be your freedom that you are afraid to take back from your overlord.

I have lived in your shadow. I have lived as your game to be hunted, as your slave, as your servant. I live in your putris and mud shacks, half-naked, fully hungry. I live drunk, puking and pissing in your cities, on your streets, in your alleys. I live begging on your streets, in markets, reading your palms, telling your fortunes. I am ignorant because you need me to be ignorant, because you would deny me the power to think for myself. Because when I do, I will ask questions you don't want to hear. Questions you don't want to answer.

My questions question your authority and your legitimacy. They question your knowledge and wisdom. My questions ask you to question yourself. My questions ask you to look in the mirror.

I have looked in the mirror and see beneath my rags a history rich in knowledge, cunning, skills, traditions, songs and stories. I see behind our beaten brows and tired eyes, pride, joy, laughter, life. I see in the begging child's palms innocence. I see in our women's tears strength, beauty and wisdom.

We weren't born beggars, drunks and thieves. By your swords, laws, and lies, you have made us these things.

We are nomadic. We value what we can carry: our stories, our words, our ways, our songs and truths. We own what we need. We are what you used to be before you gave up that life to become what you are today. We are people who have made you better. We value our freedom. You mistake that for irresponsibility, for being uncivilized.

Our word is a spit and a handshake. That spit is our spirit, our bond. For us the land is not to measure, fence, claim, or to chop each other up for. The land is to travel on, to rest upon, to dream on, to feed off, to play upon, to be buried in.

What have we stolen from you in comparison to what you have stolen from us?

What have you given us compared to what we have given you? What have we done to you compared to what you have done to us?

Look in the mirror!

60

Tommy put the manuscript on his lap, leaned back and closed his eyes. He massaged his brow.

They all had their hands up—his father, his mother, him. His father was edging away from him. Tommy didn't want his father to leave him. He called out after him. The border guard turned and stumbled. There was a flash and a deafening sound. A fiery streak burned across his forehead. A panther leapt on the soldier's back. It roared and raised its front paw. Its claws gleamed in the moonlight. "Hannah!" his father screamed. She turned toward him. There was a slash. She shouted, "Never again!"

Tommy was falling. The sudden air pocket woke him. He was sweating; his jaw and hands were clenched. He took a deep breath. "Let go," he whispered. "Let go."

But, how could he? He had gone back to play a game he loved on the Golden Green of his dreams and discovered that the beautiful game was neither beautiful nor a game. The Golden Green turned out to be a battlefield. He had gone back to his birthplace and found and lost parts of himself. He had become a man, by taking a life. He joined Broshkoy in an act of death and freedom. They were milk brothers before. Now they were blood brothers. How do you let go of that? You don't. But, maybe by doing the stupid and the right thing you become the change you want to see in yourself and the world. Maybe you can let go and hold on.

He stared ahead and waited for something. He wasn't sure what. Then it came to him.

I am my mother's child. I am my father's son. I am…

"We are over Newfoundland and will be landing in Montreal in about three hours the captain announced.

Tamás looked out the window. What a big country, he mused. My country. My home. I know nothing of it. I'd like to see it all. Maybe one day he and Marianne would drive across it from sea to sea, to see what they could see. He closed his eyes. He was in freefall. He smiled.

GLOSSARY

Sp.=Spanish
R.=Romani
Fr.=French
I.=Italian
Rs.=Russian
G.=Greek
He.=Hebrew
H.=Hungarian
Y.=Yiddish

Adio   G. Goodbye.

Ándale   Sp. Hurry up.

Athingani   R. The name came to be associated
                                with the Romani people.

Attila Josef   Hungarian poet.

Budapest Honvéd   Hungarian soccer team.

Calvert   Fr. Variation on "Calvary."
                                A Québécois curse.

Cante jondos.   Sp. The deepest, most serious forms
                                of flamenco music.

Cazzo   I. (curse) dick.

Chicas hermosas   Sp. Beautiful girls.

Ciboire	Fr. The ciborium cup. A Québécois curse.
Cimbalom	H. A large Hungarian dulcimer.
Csárdás	Hungarian folk dance.
Da	Rs. Yes.
Dobos	H. Hungarian cake.
Efcharisto	G. Thank you.
Fillér	H. Small coins (10 fillér=1 forint).
Forint	H. Small coins.
Gnocchi	I. A potato-based dumpling.
Goyim	Y. Derogatory term for non-Jewish males.
Grosics	Hungarian goalie considered the best in his time.
Habs	Fr. Abbreviation for "habitants" nickname for Montreal Canadiens hockey club.
Hajrá Magyar	H. A cheer. "Go Hungarians."
Hostie	Fr. The host taken at communion. A Québécois curse.
Hui	Rs. Curse meaning "dick."
Kala	G. Fine. Response to greeting.
La Chaim	Y. A toast to life.
Matzo	He. Passover flat bread.
Mauthausen	A concentration camp.
Mazel tov	Y. Congratulations
Meg öllek	H. Kill him.
Meshuganah	Y. Crazy.

Mishto avilian amende	R. Welcome among us.
Nyet	Rs. No.
Öld meg öket	H: Kill them.
Pálinka	H. Brandy.
Payos	He. Sidelocks worn by Jewish Orthodox males.
Petőfi, Sándor	Hungarian poet.
Pogácsa	H. scone.
Puskás	Hungarian soccer player.
Puta	Sp. Whore.
Putri	R. Hovel, Gypsy camp.
Sara-la-Kali	R. Patron saint of Romani people.
Seder	He. Passover ritual.
Shalom Aleichem	He. Greeting.
Shiksa	Y. Derogatory term for non-Jewish female.
Shmata	Y. Rags—used as a term for clothing factory.
Spiel	Y. A story, typically one intended as a means of persuasion.
Szerbusz	H. Familiar greeting both as hello and goodbye.
Tabernak	F. Tabernacle. A Québécois curse.
Tallit	He. A fringed garment, traditionally worn as a prayer shawl by religious Jews.

Taves baxtalo ando amaro	R. Welcome to our country.
Tefillin	He. A set of small black leather boxes containing scrolls inscribed with verses from the Torah.
Torah	The first five books of the twenty-four books of the Hebrew Bible.
Tsikanis	G. Hello. How are you?
Tsu Gezunt	Y. To your health.
Yeshiva	He. A Jewish institution of higher learning that focuses on the study of traditional religious texts.

ABOUT THE AUTHOR

The son of Holocaust survivors, Endre Farkas was born in Hajdunánás, Hungary. He escaped with his parents during the 1956 Hungarian Uprising and settled in Montreal. A poet, playwright and novelist, Farkas has published nine books of poetry — including *Murders in the Welcome Café, Romantic at Heart & Other Faults, How To,* and *Quotidian Fever, New and Selected Poems,* as well as one novel, *Never, Again.* He has also had two plays produced — *Haunted House,* which is based on the life and work of the poet A.M. Klein, and *Surviving Wor(l)ds,* an adaptation of his book of poems *Surviving Words.* He collaborated with poet Carolyn Marie Souaid on the video poem *Blood is Blood,* which won first prize at The Berlin International Poetry Film Festival in 2012. Farkas has given readings throughout Canada, USA, Europe and Latin America. He is also the two-time regional winner of the CBC Poetry Face-Off competition. His poems have been translated into French, Spanish, Hungarian, Italian, Slovenian and Turkish.

Eco-Audit
Printing this book using Rolland Enviro 100 Book
instead of virgin fibres paper saved the following resources:

Trees	Energy	Water	Air Emissions
6	10 GJ	2,000 L	377 kg